DELL

Greystel River
Vanadahl Manor
Greenwark District
ttinger Street
Highbridge
Ruthar Manor
Crown District
Wrenith District
The Dark Horse
Dridon Street
Anthir Headquarters
The Traveler's Road
Westmire District
The Drowned Crow
Enchant Shop
Rathsborne Street
Ari's Workshop
Adair Manor
The Houndswood
Ruthar
Vanadahl

NDERLAIN

Our Deadly Designs

ALSO BY KALYN JOSEPHSON

The Storm Crow
The Crow Rider

Ravenfall
Hollowthorn
Witchwood
Ravenguard

This Dark Descent

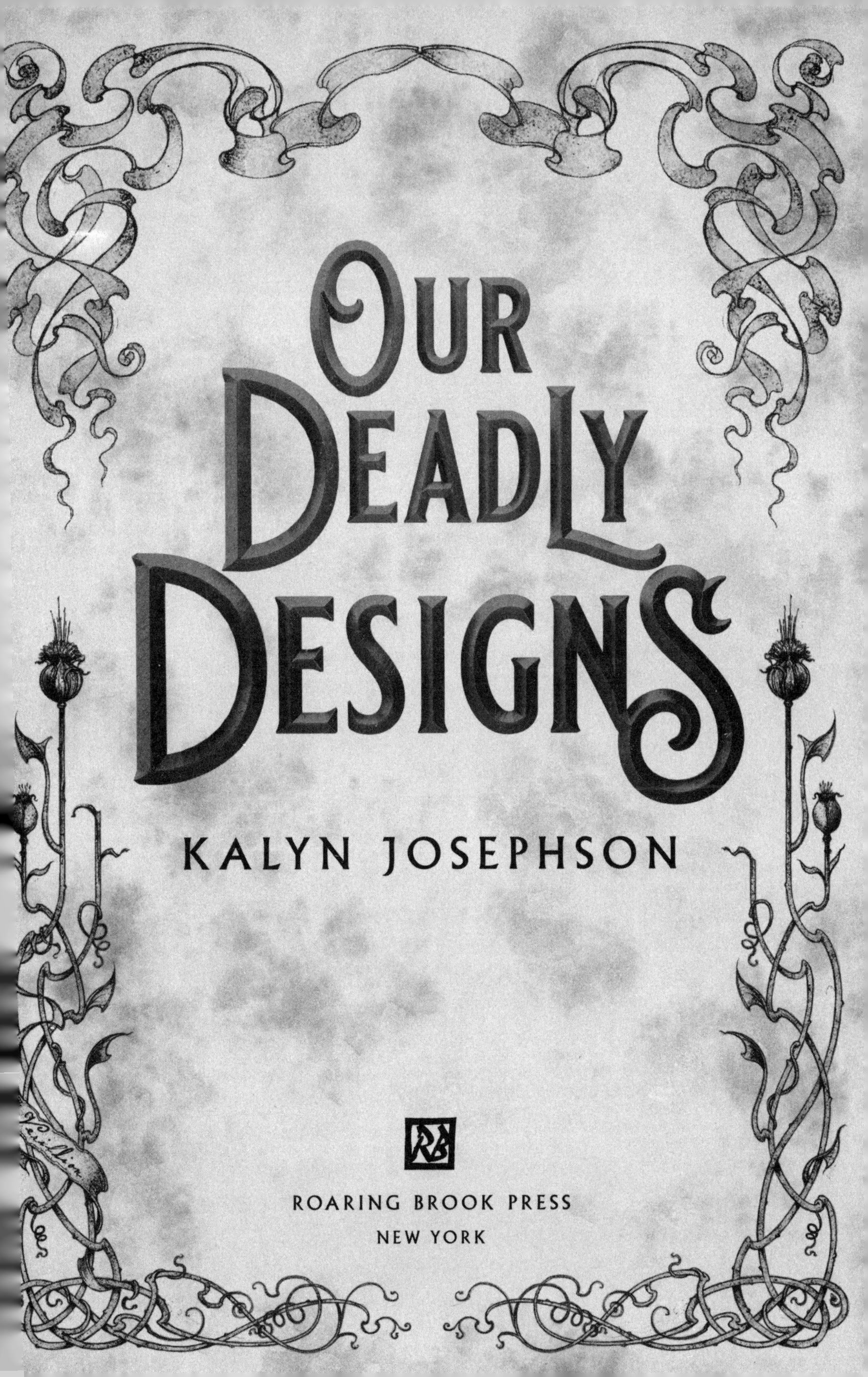

Our Deadly Designs

KALYN JOSEPHSON

ROARING BROOK PRESS
NEW YORK

Published by Roaring Brook Press
Roaring Brook Press is a division of
Holtzbrinck Publishing Holdings Limited Partnership
120 Broadway, New York, NY 10271 • fiercereads.com

Our books may be purchased in bulk for promotional, educational, or business use. Please contact your local bookseller or the Macmillan Corporate and Premium Sales Department at (800) 221-7945 ext. 5442 or by email at MacmillanSpecialMarkets@macmillan.com.

Library of Congress Cataloging-in-Publication Data is available.

First edition, 2024
Book design by Samira Iravani
Printed in the United States of America

ISBN 978-1-250-81238-4 (hardcover)
1 3 5 7 9 10 8 6 4 2

To Rowan, for reading all my terrible first drafts

LAST TIME, IN *THIS DARK DESCENT . . .*

ALL MIKIRA RUSEL wants is to breed enchanted horses, keep her family safe, and, one day, compete in a real race. But with an unofficial embargo on the Rusels' enchanted horse business courtesy of Rezek Kelbra, heir to the city of Veradell's richest house, sales are dwindling. When Rezek discovers Mikira's father is an unlicensed enchanter, a capital crime in the land of Enderlain, he offers her a deal: If she can win the Illinir—a series of four vicious enchanted races—on an uncharmed horse, he'll pardon her father. If she loses, their fabled horses become his, and her father remains trapped in Rezek's employ.

Without the funds to enter, Mikira secures sponsorship from Damien Adair, a furtive house lord with a vendetta against Rezek. Damien promises her an undetectable enchanted horse made by Arielle Kadar, an unlicensed enchanter practicing illegal Kinnish magic that enables her to create golems in place of enchanted animals. In exchange, he agrees to get Ari an official enchant license.

After an incident with her magic left her grandfather dead, Ari fled to Veradell, where she uses her Kinnish spellbook to create golems, instilling them with physical, behavioral, energy, and ethereal charms using the four gemstones and magic found in verillion plants. But as she works on the golem horse for Mikira, her magic becomes more unwieldy, a presence inside her growing that she dismisses as exhaustion. Meanwhile, Mikira trains for the race with the help of Reid Haldane, Damien's best friend, medical expert, and all-around pain in the ass. Her time spent with them slowly breaks down her walls, giving way to friendship.

As an attraction grows between Damien and Ari, so does the presence in her mind, and she seeks Damien's help. He suspects her spellbook is a Racari, a book of magic from the four Harbingers, the gods of the Kinnish religion. They were taken by the Heretics, enchanters who caused the Cataclysm, a magical eruption that destroyed the kingdom of Kinahara. Together, Ari and Damien discover bloodstones, which enable magical bonds. Realizing that a Heretic bonded to the Racari last, they suspect its soul remains and is influencing Ari through her magic.

As their connection grows, Damien reveals that he's in the midst of an ascension battle with his siblings, Loic and Shira. Whoever can deal the greatest blow to a rival house will become head of House Adair, and Damien has a bet with Rezek: If Mikira wins, Damien gets the Illinir rights, but if she loses, he turns over all of House Adair's racing assets.

Meanwhile, Mikira fights her way through the Illinir's dangers with the help of her long-lost childhood friend, Talyana, who claims Damien is a murderer. Mikira won't turn on her new partner without proof—but when a body washes up on her property clutching Damien's house ring, she's not sure whom to trust.

Racked with indecision, Mikira risks telling Talyana about the ring—only to discover that she's a sergeant investigating Damien, and she wants the ring as evidence. As Damien is arrested, Rezek kidnaps Ari, torturing her for answers about how Mikira is winning the races. Ari holds out until she's rescued by Reid, who knows about Mikira's admission to Talyana, and takes the ring from her.

With tensions running high, the final race arrives, and it takes all of them working together for Mikira to win. With her victory, Damien secures the rights to the Illinir and submits them for his family's Ascension. Shira all but forfeits the competition, while Loic makes a desperate attempt to win by killing Rezek's father. But their father names Damien heir, and Loic is arrested.

Broken and humiliated, Rezek retreats into seclusion, unbeknownst to Mikira, who attends the final Illinir ball in hopes of cornering him to free her father. There, Talyana introduces her to Princess Eshlin, revealing they're part of a growing rebellion that wants Mikira to join. And when Damien discovers that Mikira is the one who caused his arrest and excommunicates her, Mikira agrees to hear out the rebels.

As the ball ends, Damien uses the royal boon granted to the Illinir winner to replace House Kelbra with House Adair as a greater house. But Ari isn't fully present to witness it, as her body is no longer under her control. She finds herself taken to an alcove with another Racari, where Rezek Kelbra awaits, his eyes bright white, and there she realizes the Heretic she thought was bonded to the Racari is actually possessing her—and there's one controlling Rezek too.

ANTHIR

The city guard. Arrests and prosecutes criminals.

ROYAL FAMILY

THE VAULT

The bureaucratic branch of the government responsible for documentation, records, and application of the law to individual cases by berators.

THE FOUR GREATER HOUSES

The most powerful houses. Responsible for overseeing kingdom-level duties enacted by the Council of Lords.

THE COUNCIL OF LORDS

Consists of the heads of the four greater houses and either the ruling king or queen at the time. Creates and passes new laws, oversees military, handles kingdom-level responsibilities.

THE EIGHT LESSER HOUSES

ZALAIRE

THIELAN

Oversees implementation of laws, handles city and district-level responsibilities.

THE ROYAL FAMILY

RANIER LINE
ZUERLIN LINE

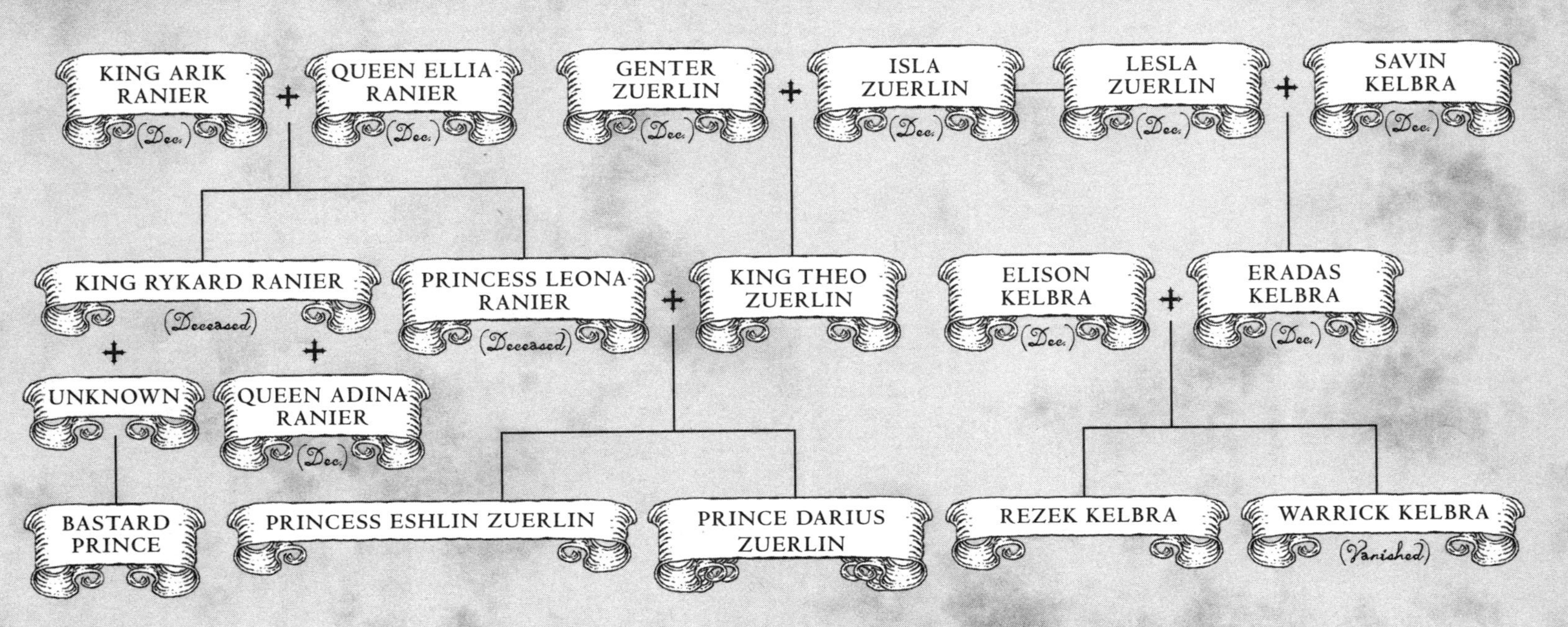
KING ARIK RANIER
(Dec.)
+
QUEEN ELLIA RANIER
(Dec.)
GENTER ZUERLIN
(Dec.)
+
ISLA ZUERLIN
(Dec.)
LESLA ZUERLIN
(Dec.)
+
SAVIN KELBRA
(Dec.)
KING RYKARD RANIER
(Deceased)
PRINCESS LEONA RANIER
(Deceased)
+
KING THEO ZUERLIN
ELISON KELBRA
(Dec.)
+
ERADAS KELBRA
(Dec.)
+
UNKNOWN
+
QUEEN ADINA RANIER
(Dec.)
BASTARD PRINCE
PRINCESS ESHLIN ZUERLIN
PRINCE DARIUS ZUERLIN
REZEK KELBRA
WARRICK KELBRA
(Vanished)

✦ PART 1 ✦

In the end, the Heretics destroyed everything the Harbingers had built.
Lyzairin's schools crumbled to ruin;

Rach's observatory was left to rot.

The wisdom Skylis imparted was lost to time,

and Aslir's once vibrant hope . . . withered.

Humanity was lost.

CHAPTER 1

ARIELLE

ARIELLE DIDN'T FEEL like a monster.

The floor-length mirror before her told one story—a girl wrapped in a dress of midnight velvet, Aslir's silver fang gathered in the hollow of her throat and the weight of a noble house behind her—but her eyes told another. When she gazed into them, she saw fear, and she hated herself for it.

She pressed her fingertips into the skin of her arm, her belly, her throat, seeking some sign of the creature that lurked underneath, but whatever the Heretic inside her was, spirit or beast or phantom, there was no line between where she ended and it began.

I won't let you make me afraid, she told the Heretic. It had been quiet following her encounter with Rezek Kelbra at the closing Illinir ball. Ever since Ari had realized that the century-old enchanter's spirit wasn't possessing her Saba's spellbook, but *her*. It'd been a week since that night, and the secret of Rezek's offer weighed on her more each day.

I can give you answers, he'd promised, his eyes the white of fresh snow from the magic coursing through him. But she knew better than to trust Rezek, and Damien would never forgive her for accepting the help of his greatest enemy. So she'd run.

Still, it gnawed at her that the knowledge she sought was just out of reach.

"Arielle?" Damien's voice slid over her like a warm cloak, and she let herself be enveloped by it, by him as he appeared behind her in the mirror, his arms enfolding her in a steady embrace. His bedroom was a shadowed alcove at his back, the curtains drawn against the approaching dusk, but the enchanted lights illuminated the newfound heaviness in his gray eyes.

His lips brushed her cheek. "You look formidable."

She did. Her hair had been woven into a braided crown, loose curls spiraling around her face. Kohl encircled her eyes, making the brown bright and deep. She wore a black dress embroidered in white and silver thread, the mirror image of his charcoal waistcoat and black satin-lined jacket. His hair was neatly styled, not a strand out of place to betray the turmoil beneath his steely exterior.

Ari turned inside the circle of his arms, her hands sliding past the Lonlarra revolvers holstered at his ribs before her fingers locked in the small of his back. "I only wish it were for another purpose."

Damien let out a quiet breath. He'd barely spoken of his father's death since the news arrived only days after his Ascension to the head of House Adair. Galan Adair had passed quietly in his sleep with the knowledge his family's future was secure, and Damien had spent every night since in his chair by the fire with a glass of whiskey, staring out into the dark.

He tucked a curl behind her ear with careful fingers. "I'm just glad you're here with me," he said at last. "The wolves will be circling."

"It's your father's funeral. Would they really be so crass?"

"Of course. They expect to find me at my weakest, and they'd never let an opportunity like that pass."

Ari's fingers tightened into knots. Damien ought to be mourning his father, not playing Enderlain's twisted games. But by winning the Illinir, he'd been granted a royal boon, requesting that the Adairs be made one of the four great houses in place of the Kelbras. Tonight's funeral and subsequent wake would be his first test as head of House Adair. There would be those seeking his alliance, and those plotting his downfall, all of them eager for a piece of him.

Together, Ari and Damien would face them all, and begin forging the new House Adair.

Ari placed a kiss against Damien's lips. It was soft and tender, but she felt him stir. Felt his fingers curl against her hips and the heat building in her core. His presence centered her like nothing else, the way he looked at her as if the world fell away.

"This," said a disgruntled voice from the doorway, "is getting to become a habit."

Damien's lips turned to a faint smile against hers as he pulled away. Reid stood with his arms folded, the disheveled counterpoint to Damien's polished exterior. His black hair resembled a crow's nest, his shirt untucked without vest or jacket, and his sleeves rolled up to bare the twisting lines of his tattoos.

Without Mikira around, he'd given up all pretense of making an effort. Ari wished he wouldn't. Seeing him like this only reminded her of her friend's absence all the more, and she already felt it like a missing limb. They hadn't seen Mikira since the closing ball, when Damien had learned she'd kept something from him. Evidence that tied him to a crime. Evidence that could have ruined him.

Yet another thing they hadn't spoken about, but Ari knew now was not the time.

"Everything's ready," Reid said. "They're waiting on you to begin."

Ari laced her fingers with Damien's, his grip tightening in return. He needed her, and Ari would be right there by his side. Reid trailed behind them as they stepped into the rapidly cooling night, tracing the manor's open-aired corridor before emerging into the outer grounds.

Long fingers of lavender beckoned them toward a small crowd seated before a platform, where Damien's sister, Shira, waited for them in a suit of dark navy. There was something starkly unsettling about seeing her there without all her knives, her usually braided hair gathered into a neat bun at the nape of her neck.

Like her brother, Shira hid her grief behind a practiced mask.

The city of Veradell's elite occupied their chairs like an opposing army, a sea of flowing gowns and gemstone-lined jackets turning hungry eyes toward them. The attention reminded Ari so much of her Saba's funeral that she nearly faltered. Memories of the Sage's recitation of prayers, of tearing her clothes in grief and her sister's piercing cries, came surging back to her.

Everyone had stared then too.

Struck by the urge to disappear beneath their assessing gazes, she burned the verillion she'd consumed on reflex. The warmth of the plant's magic spiraled through her in a familiar buzz. She'd used it sparingly the last few days, suspecting that it made her connection with the Heretic stronger. But she could not relinquish her power entirely, unable to deny how reassuring it felt each time she had it back.

She charmed herself for calm using the ruby ring on her finger, now nestled beside the emerald one Damien had given her. She would let the enchantment settle her, then release it.

Damien squeezed her arm, and she looked up into his questioning gaze. For so much of her life, she had been taught not to draw attention to herself, to remain hidden. Entering a battleground of Veradell's elite flew in the face of that, and he wanted to ensure she was ready.

Ari thought of Mikira, who had walked among these wolves and dared them to bite her, and lifted her chin.

She would not be afraid.

ARI STOOD AS the ceremony concluded, the crowd trailing Reid back toward the house, where the wake would be held in the main courtyard. She'd never witnessed a Celairen funeral, where the casket was open for all to see, Galan's pale body dressed in a suit of silver and black. It felt disrespectful to stare at him, and she kept her eyes averted.

Damien and Shira descended the stage, joining Ari in the front row as the pallbearers lifted the casket.

"We don't follow them?" Ari asked.

Shira shook her head. "Our father was very clear that he didn't want his actual burial made a spectacle. I'll handle his interment while Damien attends our guests."

It felt like such a sudden conclusion to a process Ari knew was endless. Grief was not a quick thing. She and her sister had sat in mourning with their parents for seven days after their Saba's funeral, receiving neighbors and friends in their home, and that was only the beginning. But Damien had told her death was not so solemn in Celair, a kingdom that had learned to live alongside it beneath Enderlain's endless conquest.

Tonight would be as much a celebration of their father's life as a mourning of its loss.

"Will you be returning to the party?" Damien asked Shira with a practiced disinterest.

Her mouth curved in an indication that she recognized it too. "No, little brother. I'll let you have your night." She looked for a moment as if she might hug him, but refrained, laying a hand instead on Ari's shoulder. "Don't let him glower at anyone too intently."

"I make no promises," Ari replied, enjoying the way Damien's jaw clenched.

Shira departed after the pallbearers, and Ari hooked her arm through Damien's, escorting him toward the house. "Are you ready?" she asked as they entered the inner corridor.

Damien straightened the cuffs of his jacket. "Let's go."

The arched corridor opened into a spacious courtyard bedecked in silver and white, the melody of an enchanted piano rising on the air. A massive white lion statue towered above the crowd in honor of Aslir, now House Adair's patron Harbinger. Even the signet ring on Damien's right hand had been born anew, made of diamonds shaped in a lion's fang.

They descended into the milling crowd, greeting people as they passed. The head of the Anthir, Inspector Elrihan, shook Damien's hand, offering his condolences. Others stopped them with a kind word or a wistful memory of Galan, and Damien accepted them all graciously, though Ari knew they weren't what he sought.

He had already identified a list of important guests, and it was those that he spent extra time with, forging connections he might later need. Everyone here wanted something of him, and he of them, and through the course of the night they would lay the groundwork for House Adair's future, just as Galan would have wanted. All the while she kept her verillion simmering, telling herself just one moment more, and then she would stop.

The night slid by in a stream of conversation and glasses of champagne, short dances and stolen bites of food. As the sun set and the enchanted lights cast a lazy glow over the courtyard, a familiar pain settled at the base of Ari's skull. The headaches were a constant companion, and she was well used to forcing her way through them, but they still spoiled her evenings.

"Excuse me," she murmured to Damien, and broke from their circle for the open-aired corridor at the edge of the crowd. Spotting Reid by the refreshment table, she joined him, taking deep breaths of cool night air.

He gave her a quick once-over as she arrived. "Had enough yet?"

She pressed a hand to her temple. "Do you have any of that tea?"

He withdrew a flask from his pocket, and she nearly rolled her eyes. "You know, that's not what these are for," she muttered as he handed it to her. The tea was lukewarm, but relief swept through her at the taste of chamomile on her tongue.

"One day," he began drily, "one of you is just going to say thank you."

Her lips quirked. "Thank you."

Predictably, that only made him scowl harder. Her smile slipped as the full impact of his words settled: *one of you.* Her and Damien, yes, but she could tell from the forced slouch of his shoulders and the way he wouldn't look her in the eye that it was Mikira on his mind.

Ari handed him back the flask, then squeezed his arm. "We'll find a way to fix this, Reid. I promise."

"What part of Damien being an expert at holding grudges slipped by you?" he asked bitterly. "He wouldn't know forgiveness if it bit him in the ass."

He was right. Damien had hardly listened to her protestations before excommunicating Mikira, and she was tired of pretending her friend's loss didn't affect her, of tucking it away like some shameful secret. The thought stoked her frustration, the humming in her mind rising.

I can feel your fury, little lion, came a quiet whisper in her mind. *Unleash it.*

Ari startled at the Heretic's voice, at how smoothly it slid into her thoughts. It felt fuller than before, more tangible, as though she could reach out a hand and—Ari squeezed her eyes shut, silencing the notion, but she couldn't block out the unease that eddied in her chest.

Where have you been? she demanded, certain the creature's absence was not without reason.

I despise gatherings like this, the Heretic replied as if it hadn't heard her. *Everyone here is a counterfeit and a liar.*

Ari gritted her teeth at its evasiveness. She'd all but given up on convincing the Heretic to share anything about itself. Its silence the last few days had made it easier for her to pretend everything was okay, but her frustration at its cryptic messages only redoubled now.

And what are you? she snapped.

The Heretic's answer settled into her mind like a drop of poison.

Retribution.

"Ari?" Reid asked uncertainly, but she barely heard him. A low humming reverberated in her ears, the feeling reminiscent of the one she detected along the link she shared with her golems. It suffused her senses, cocooned her, became her—

Something bumped her from behind. Ari whirled, knocking a tray of glasses to the ground and sending a startled server flying into a nearby pillar. Without realizing it, she'd accessed the emerald gemstone in her other ring, binding a strength enchantment. The information reached her like the buzz of a gnat, too inconsequential to truly register.

The server gaped at her, fear making him inert. Ari stared at him unblinkingly.

"Arielle?" Damien's hand on her arm drew her back to the present, to the look in his eye that told her he missed nothing. Except he still thought the Heretic bound to her Saba's spellbook, merely a voice in her head reaching down the bond that linked them.

He didn't know the truth.

So much had happened so quickly since the ball that she'd yet to find the right time to tell him, and with everything demanding his attention, she didn't want to burden him further.

"Arielle?" Damien's mask had cracked, concern spilling out. "What's wrong?"

"It's nothing." Ari tore free of him, the crowd's eyes following her down the corridor. Some distant part of her knew this anger was not truly hers, not all of it, but it suffused her like a heady perfume.

Damien followed, slowing at her side behind another pillar. "I know it isn't nothing."

Guilt cut through her growing wooziness, but she could barely think through the thrumming in her mind. "So what if it isn't?" she snapped. "What if I told you that I'm furious at you for what you've done to Mikira and that you're being unreasonable?"

A line of tension descended through Damien like a steel rod. "I've told you before," he replied in a too-even tone. "Mikira and I are done."

"She's our friend," Ari countered.

"She ceased to be that the moment she betrayed me."

Reid joined them, his anguished look switching between them. "Can we just—"

Ari cut across him, her simmering frustration finally boiling over. "She didn't betray anything. It was a misunderstanding, and you refuse to see that!"

"People are listening," Reid said more forcefully.

Ari knew now was not the time to be addressing this, but she was more upset than she'd realized, and with every passing second that fury swelled. It coiled about her heart, squeezing until it was all she knew.

"Arielle?" Damien reached for her. She seized his hand, bending it backward hard enough to make him drop to his knees with a hiss. For an instant, she stared at him without recognition, trying to place his face, why the flash of pain in his expression worried her. Then she came back to herself like a lock snapping into place.

She ripped her hand away, falling to her knees alongside him. "I'm so sorry. I—I don't know what happened."

"Your eyes." He clutched his injured wrist. "They went white again."

"No." Her fingers brushed her cheek. Her verillion—she'd nearly burned through her entire store without realizing it, racking up hours of using her magic.

Get out of my head, she hissed at the Heretic.

A beat of silence, and then the voice rumbled back, *It is* our *head now.*

Ari pressed a hand to her mouth, her stomach threatening to upend. Because as surely as the Heretic could read her emotions, Ari could sense the truth in the spirit's words. Day by day, their connection had grown, fueled by the magic she could not relinquish. It had become a part of her, as deeply woven as blood or bone. She couldn't just stop, and this wouldn't be the last time she lost control, the last time the Heretic stole her body from her.

"I'm sorry," she said again as she pulled Damien to his feet. "I'll fix this. I promise. I—"

"Lady Kadar?" A servant stood in the doorway to Damien's suite. "I apologize for interrupting, but this girl was adamant that she speak to you."

"Who—" Ari cut off, the air evaporating from her lungs as someone stepped into the hall. Someone she'd thought she'd never see again.

Her sister was here.

CHAPTER 2

ARIELLE

RIVKAH?" ARI BREATHED in disbelief.

Her sister's brown eyes, always a shade lighter than her own, were wide with alarm. Dirt stained her thinning clothes, her dark curls gathered in a messy side braid and her olive skin tanned from the sun.

Ari reached out a hand, her fingers hovering over her sister's cheek in fear that they would pass straight through. But then Rivkah was in her arms and there was no denying her realness. She'd gotten taller, her head nearly striking Ari's chin, but she was still thin and bony and smelled of the rugelach she consumed like air.

"You're alive." Rivkah's voice broke, and the sound of it nearly shattered Ari.

It had been nearly a year since she'd left Rivkah behind, terrified of her own power and racked with guilt over their Saba's death. A year since she'd seen her sister's face or heard her raucous laughter.

A thousand questions rose at once, but Ari gave herself another moment to simply hold her sister before she had to face them. By the time they pulled away, both their faces were wet with tears.

Damien took in the scene with sharp understanding. "We'll give you some privacy." He gestured at Reid, who followed him, though not without shooting Rivkah a suspicious look.

Ari ushered her sister into the suite, her heart overflowing with excitement. She gestured at the chaise. "Please, sit. I can get you tea or whiskey. Or—no, you're only fifteen. Though maybe today—" She cut off, struck by the question she should have asked the moment she set eyes on her sister.

With an exhale, she dropped onto the chaise. "How are you here?"

"I meant to ask you the same thing." Rivkah set her bag down and joined her. "I've been looking for you for weeks."

Ari's eyes widened. "You've been what? But Mother and Father—Riv, they must be worried sick."

Her expression darkened. "That didn't stop you from leaving."

"That was different." Ari's gaze dropped to her sister's collarbone, where a thin scar peeked out from beneath her shirt. It was one of many from that first golem. "I had to go. You know that."

Rivkah shook her head. "No, you didn't. You wanted to. You wanted to leave for years before that, and you just used what happened as an excuse."

"I was a danger to you all."

"You were my sister!" Rivkah shot to her feet. "You were scared and lost and didn't even give us a chance to figure things out. You *left* me."

Ari flinched at the raw pain in her sister's voice. She didn't have the words to explain the terror that had rooted inside her that day, how it had crept through every bit of her until it'd become her. Her entire life, her parents had cautioned her to be quiet, to be careful, and only now did she know why.

It was not her family that people had feared; it was her. Because somewhere along the line, she had found her Saba's spellbook, and the Heretic's soul had been bound to hers, and she must have done things, used magic she couldn't control or that no one recognized. Had she hurt someone, or had they only feared the attention she would draw?

A Kinnish enchanter would only bring them pain.

"You're right," she said. "I wanted to go long before that. There wasn't a place for me in Aversheen. But I didn't want to leave you, Riv. Never you."

Rivkah deflated back onto the chaise. Ari wanted to wrap her arms around her until what was broken between them was whole again, but she didn't know if that would ever be possible, no matter how strongly she wished it.

It was Rivkah who drew Ari out of her shell. Who forced her headlong into adventure when she pranked the baker's boys outside the temple or snuck backstage at performances in the town edah. Losing Rivkah had been like losing the spark that kept her alive, and she'd fallen into a version of living that barely classified as survival.

Until the day Damien walked through her door.

"I'm here now, though," Rivkah said softly, knocking her shoulder with Ari's.

"Yes," Ari whispered. "You are."

They talked after that. Talked in a way Ari hadn't talked with anyone in months. About the challah cart Ari desperately missed back home, about how vast Veradell was, full of secrets Rivkah wanted to uncover. About everything except the magic that drove her away. Except golems, except their Saba, except the year of time between them.

Eventually the door cracked open, and Damien and Reid entered, the latter bearing a platter of bite-sized cakes and pies. The noise of the party was gone.

"It's over?" she asked.

"I thought it best considering the circumstances." Damien secured a glass of Adair whiskey from the drink cart before taking his customary chair by the fire, sinking into it with an uncharacteristic exhaustion. If it were anyone other than Rivkah here, she would have asked them to leave, certain that what he needed now was quiet. But he knew how important Rivkah was to her, and so he only sipped his drink.

Reid glowered at her and Rivkah. "You're in my seat."

Rivkah pointed at the empty chair beside Damien. "Oh, look, another one."

Reid's scowl deepened, and he dropped the platter of desserts unceremoniously onto the stacks of books that served as a table. Rivkah took one, and then a second, and then a third. Not everything had changed, it seemed; her sister never could resist sweets.

Ari forced down a smile. "Rivkah, meet Reid Haldane and Damien Adair."

Damien lifted his glass in greeting, but Reid only snatched up a piece of cake and stomped over to the other chair, collapsing into it. Just then, the chaise cushion shifted, and a moment later a little black shape wriggled out from the cushion crevice.

The tiny cat had one brief moment to descend into a deep stretch before Rivkah seized him with a shriek. "He's adorable!" She hoisted him above her head, her fingers sticky with chocolate cake.

Reid nearly choked on his food. "He's not a toy!"

Widget's legs flailed uselessly in the air, and Ari quickly drew the golem cat from her sister's arms. "I see your way with animals hasn't improved," she remarked, rising to deposit Widget in Reid's lap, where the cat promptly climbed up his shirt. Reid secured him there with one arm, glaring at Rivkah with twice his usual intensity.

Rivkah gave her a bashful grin, and the familiarity of the whole scene made Ari's heart clench. She'd missed this, missed Rivkah with a need so fierce she'd buried it, knowing it would consume her. But now that her sister was here, it'd come clawing back.

Rivkah surveyed the opulent suite as Ari rejoined her, skimming over Damien's exposed revolvers with open-faced suspicion. "So is this where you've been this whole time?" she asked. "With . . . them?"

Ari's hand closed around her Saba's necklace, and in that moment, everything that had happened the last few months welled up inside her. Atara and the Illinir, her exploration into magic with Damien, the Heretics,

Mikira—she wanted to tell Rivkah all of it, like she had once told her everything.

So that you can hurt her again? whispered the voice. *Oh, little lion. Haven't you done enough?*

Ari squeezed the necklace tighter, as if she could crush the spirit's presence. Its ebb and flow was unsettling enough, but what worried her the most, what threatened to send her reeling, was how closely it understood her. The creature did not seem able to read her mind, but it could feel her emotions, and it teased them apart with the ease of a scalpel through flesh and twined them with its own.

And it was right.

For everything that had changed, one thing had stayed the same—Ari's magic was dangerous, and her sister wasn't safe around her.

"Ari?" Rivkah asked uncertainly.

"You should go, Riv," Ari said, strengthening her resolve when her sister frowned. "It's not—*I'm* not safe right now."

"Because of your magic?"

Ari stilled, and Damien set his glass on the side table, leaning toward her. "What do you know of it?"

Rivkah eyed him with an unreadable look, but it was Ari she spoke to. "After you left, Mother and Father told me the truth about your spellbook. That it's one of the four Racari and that you were bound to it somehow. I thought if I could find out more about it, find other people like you, they might be able to help you."

Other people like you. Ari's mind flashed instantly to Rezek, to his offer of answers.

"I've been working in the record room at a temple in town." Rivkah's enthusiasm bubbled out with her words. "They're letting me dig through the archives, and I got to thinking: for you to have that spellbook, someone must have gotten it out of Kinahara after the Cataclysm. Maybe they went back to the Harbingers, and we could find one—"

Ari laughed. "Find a Harbinger?"

"They're real, Ari," Rivkah challenged, folding her arms in an all too familiar pout. "But if they don't have them, then we just have to find out who does. If I can find—"

"No." Ari cut across her, standing. "You can't get involved in this. It's too dangerous."

Rivkah's excitement withered, and in that moment, Ari was struck by how much her sister had grown. She was only fifteen, and yet she'd come to find Ari, traveling alone through hostile land and arriving with what she thought was a solution.

"I can assure you that we're doing everything we can to help Arielle with her magic," Damien added, earning another harrowing look from Rivkah. "We have things under control."

"Funny," Reid muttered, slumping down in his chair. "It didn't look like that when she was breaking your—"

He cut off at Damien's cool-eyed stare, and Ari stepped into the silence. "I'm just trying to protect you, Riv. That's all I've ever done."

Rivkah rose, seizing Ari's hands. "You don't have to anymore, and you don't have to remain here either. I can help you."

Ari realized then what the looks her sister had been giving Damien meant: she thought he was keeping her here somehow, that he was the reason Ari hadn't come back. She didn't realize it was Ari's choice.

"I know someone who will help us," Rivkah pressed. "She'll give us a safe place to stay while we make plans to go home."

Ari made a sound of disbelief. Go *home*? Once, that had been all she wanted. To learn to control her magic, to make sure what happened with her Saba never did again in hopes that she could return to Aversheen, to Rivkah. But after everything she'd done, after Kyvin and Rezek, how could she ever go home?

"Rivkah." A familiar edge had crept into Damien's voice. "How did you find Arielle?"

Rivkah's annoyance flared, and she reminded Ari of Mikira in that moment, her emotions plain to read. "I went temple to temple asking after her." Her attention swung back to Ari. "You used to spend so long staring at the one in Aversheen I thought you might go to one here. At the last one, some woman with too many knives said she knew where to find you."

Reid groaned, and Damien's jaw shifted. Ari didn't need to ask anything more than that. Shira really did seem to be everywhere.

"What?" Rivkah looked among them all.

"It's late," Damien replied, rising to his feet. "Will you be staying here?"

"I have a room at the Drowned Crow," she replied tightly, and any doubt Ari had of Shira's involvement evaporated. The inn was run by Vix, a close friend of the eldest Adair. "You can come with me, Ari."

Ari shuddered, and she curled her fingers tight about Rivkah's. "I can't. Not yet."

"Then let me help you," Rivkah pressed, but Ari was already shaking her head.

"I'm going to fix everything," she promised her. "For now, I just need you to stay safe. Please, Rivkah, go home."

Rivkah's hopeful expression crumpled, and she let her hands fall to her side. She shifted back a step, and that small distance between them cut Ari to the core. "Whatever you say, achot."

Ari flinched at the Kinnish word for "sister," wielded like a weapon, but didn't waver. She only watched as Rivkah gathered up her bag and made her way toward the door, every inch of her coiled tight. She paused at the top of the landing, narrowed eyes finding Damien once more.

"Take care of her," she commanded as if she were not speaking to the head of a greater noble house, but Damien only nodded.

Then she looked to Ari and said in Kinnish, "I love you."

Everything inside Ari seized at the words. She wanted to scream that she didn't deserve love. That Rivkah shouldn't have come all this way, for there was a monster wearing Ari's skin, a Dybbuk with a false face. But she would find a way to change that. To make herself worthy of her sister's love and forgiveness. To seize hold of her magic and rip it free of the Heretic's hands.

What had happened to that power she'd found in Damien's manor? That strength? It belonged to her, and she would no sooner let the Heretic take it from her than those men who'd broken into her home.

Only once the suite door shut did Ari whisper, "I love you too."

The silence that swallowed her in Rivkah's wake made it difficult to breathe. She forced herself to sit lest she collapse, her entire body cold as ice.

You made the right choice, the voice consoled her. *She will only come to harm.*

Ari shivered, her gaze falling on her Saba's spellbook where it sat on Damien's desk. Made of dark leather banded in pearlescent bone, the Racari had a single olive stone shot through with red pressed into the center—the bloodstone that bound it to her a century after it had belonged to the Heretic inside her. Damien had been translating it from old Kinnish for her, but he hadn't touched it since before the closing ball, consumed by his new responsibilities as the head of House Adair.

He must have sensed where her mind was going, because he settled on the chaise beside her, encircling her hands with his. "We'll find a solution," he said. "I promise."

"About that," Reid cut in, Widget now securely curled up in his arms. "I have an idea."

CHAPTER 3

DAMIEN

IT ALWAYS BEGAN the same, in a hallway thick with the scent of blood.

Damien knew even before he arrived in the foyer what he would find, and yet he still prayed he was wrong. Still bargained with every god he'd never believed in as his body carried him unwillingly onward.

He saw her slippered feet first, legs twisted across each other like a discarded doll. Then the embroidered hem of her nightgown, the silk deceptively white. It was not until he emerged fully into the moonlight cascading in from the upper windows that the truth was laid bare.

A knife protruded from his mother's chest, her gown stained scarlet to the waist. Her dark hair lay matted about her head in a crude halo, her once-watchful eyes caught in an endless stare.

She was dead, and it was his fault.

A pale hand reached out from the darkness, long fingers curling about the hilt of the blade. It came free with the sound of tearing flesh, and the owner stepped carelessly over his mother's corpse.

The moonlight caught in Rezek's copper hair, on the blade he'd used to murder Damien's mother. He wiped the flat of it along his diamond-lined jacket, the metal scraping against the stones in a breaking cry.

"You should probably join her," his once-friend said, and started toward him.

Suddenly Damien was a child again, his steps too short to outrun Rezek's long strides. Even if he could run, he didn't want to. Because Rezek was right—he should join her. For failing to save her, for letting Rezek win, for every mistake he'd made in the years since.

The knife transformed in Rezek's hand, becoming a Lonlarra revolver. He pressed the barrel to Damien's forehead, the metal searingly cold.

He mouthed a single word. "Bang."

Damien jerked upright with a gasp, his chest constricting with every breath. For one wild moment his hands went to his head, seeking the bullet wound. But of course it wasn't there, because it had only been a nightmare, as it always was.

They'd plagued him for months after his mother's death, each one twisting his memories into fresh and different horrors. Rezek killing his mother, killing him, killing Loic and Shira, each one more lifelike than the last. Never mind that Damien hadn't actually seen Rezek murder his mother. That dark memory belonged to Loic; Damien had only found her bleeding out, the life fleeing from her once-vibrant eyes.

And now his father was gone as well.

A fresh wave of grief nearly pinned Damien back to the bed, but morning sunlight was creeping in around the curtains, and he knew sleep was lost to him. He was lucky he hadn't woken Arielle, who lay beside him in a crescent, her full lips parting with each quiet breath. He focused on that for a moment, on her life, her warmth.

She was the only thing that kept him from spiraling out of control.

As quietly as he could, Damien slid free and went to get ready, his shoulder aching from the nearly healed wound of Hyle's bullet. Arielle was still asleep when he emerged and slipped silently from the bedroom, closing the door behind him.

Reid sat at his desk, an unnecessarily large cup of tea in one hand and a pencil in the other. Widget lounged across his shoulders, snoring softly as Reid's hand danced across his sketchbook, adding shading to the bow of someone's lips.

"That hardly looks like research," Damien said by way of greeting, dropping his jacket across the back of his armchair.

Reid practically leapt from his seat, sending tea flooding across his sketchbook and Widget five feet into the air. The golem cat landed back on his shoulders with a dexterity beyond that of even his species and promptly dismounted, likely to find a bed that didn't move.

"What are you doing awake?" Reid demanded, swiftly gathering his sketches. The fervor with which he collected them didn't escape Damien, and he had no doubt whose face he'd see if he unfurled one.

"I wanted to prepare for the day." He made toward the drink cart to pour himself a cup of tea. "I have my first council meeting soon."

He'd never told Reid about the nightmares, not when they'd hounded him after his mother's death or in the years since. They weren't the only ones he had. Sometimes they were dreams of his family on the street, his father having lost his job in the Kelbra verillion fields. Sometimes they were his mother growing ill as his father begged Eradas Kelbra to save her. He wasn't even alive when his father's feud with Eradas began, and yet his mind conjured stories as if to torture him with them.

They are only reminders, he told himself. *Of what I work to change.*

Nearly every last one of his family's tragedies could be traced to Veradell's corrupt systems, and now Damien was at the head of it, a member of the Council of Lords.

A system he meant to dismantle starting today.

"Right." Reid vanished into his room, and Damien crossed to the desk, sliding out a sketch from the folder. Mikira's face stared up at him, her loosely braided hair caught in an invisible wind. A small noise of alarm echoed from Reid's doorway, where he stood clutching a towel. Color flushed his cheeks as he marched forward, shoving the sketch back into the folder before mopping up the tea.

He didn't say anything, and Damien didn't ask. Mikira's betrayal skirted too close to the unruly well of emotions churning in his gut. He'd trusted her, like he'd once trusted Rezek, and she'd handed evidence against him to the Anthir. She was the reason Talyana had arrested him, the reason he hadn't been there when Rezek's men took Arielle.

He remembered every moment of pacing that Anthir cell, unable to go to her, unable to do *anything*. It was a helplessness he hadn't felt since the day he found his mother bleeding out in their foyer. A paralysis he'd fought every day never to experience again, and Reid and Arielle wanted him to forgive her?

Even he didn't have that level of mastery over his emotions.

Reid wiped up the last of the tea. "I haven't started researching because my subject is still asleep," he said, no doubt hoping to shift Damien's thoughts. Yet he couldn't quite let go of the sketch, of the question it brought to mind. Could Reid betray him too?

"I'll need some of Ari's blood if I'm going to start looking for a solution."

Damien adjusted one sleeve, then the other, focusing on the minute movements that centered him. He had to focus on this, on helping Arielle.

It was a brilliant idea that Reid had suggested last night, theorizing that if her magic was tied to her blackouts and loss of control, then they ought to begin by finding the source of her magic. There was something that made enchanters different from ordinary humans, that enabled them to consume magic from verillion without rotting from the inside out, and Reid's theory was that it was a cell.

"Cells produce enzymes," he'd explained. "Enzymes break things down. Maybe there's a cell in enchanters that breaks down magic, enabling them to consume it, or somehow protects them."

He only had to find it.

Damien downed the rest of his tea, the burn of it scalding away the dregs of his dream. When he looked up from retrieving his jacket, Reid was staring at him. "What?"

Reid gritted his teeth, and Damien all but watched him readjust what he'd been about to say. Instead he asked, "Have you changed your mind about your death mission?"

Damien sighed. "It's not a death mission, Reid. It's an opening move."

"Of death."

"The other council members need to know that I have the power to enforce my interests, and targeting the draft tax and exemption fee is an easy win." He set the teacup on the desk and shrugged his jacket on. "There's no point in playing coy. They know where I stand. Deferring to them isn't going to get them on my side. They already hate me for taking Rezek's place."

Reid dropped back into his chair, clasping a new cup of tea close. "Just be careful."

Damien snorted softly. "Always."

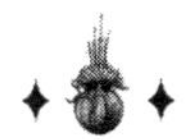

DAMIEN FLICKED HIS mother's pocket watch open and shut, open and shut as he walked through the castle hallway. His footsteps echoed in the cavernous corridor, every inch of it lined with ornately framed portraits and delicate landscape paintings, including several he recognized by Kinnish painters, which had been stolen during Enderlain's invasion of Kinahara. Of course, the Enderlish history texts told a much different story.

A story that he wanted to change.

His mother had been a scholar, a historian, and she'd shared her love of those things with him, though for her they had always been inseparably tied to her Kinnish beliefs. In history, she saw the opportunity to learn from past mistakes, to improve upon them.

To repair the world, she would tell him, nestled in a patch of long grass by the creek that ran through their estate. *It is one of the most important tasks Aslir trusted us with.*

Damien put no stock in the Harbingers, whose absence was as good as complacence in his mind, but he did believe in the ability to change things through sheer will alone. To repair what had been broken, as he'd promised himself he would the day he'd found his mother dying. But that required the right tools and a willingness to act. The latter he'd always possessed, but it was the former that he sought now.

Two guards framed the ruby-lined doorway of the council chamber ahead, each with an enchanted wolfhound charmed to sense danger. One of the guards' gazes flickered to Damien's ribs, where the black-and-silver handle of one revolver was visible. Only days ago, they would have taken his weapons, but now they only bowed their heads and opened the double doors.

Such was the respect afforded to a high lord.

Was this what life had been like for Rezek all these years? Doors opened for him; heads bowed everywhere he looked. Was this what he'd killed Damien's mother for, shattering their friendship and securing his place as heir of House Kelbra? That betrayal had become a part of Damien, like rot in the roots of a tree. So much of who he was grew from that polluted source, and no matter how he'd tried to cut it away across the years, it'd only sunk deeper.

With his family's Ascension, his father had given him the chance to take the monster Rezek had made of him and turn it on his old friend, to have the revenge he'd sought for years, and Damien had not wasted it. He'd become head of House Adair, made his family a greater house, and now he would use that power to make a difference in Enderlain.

A difference that began with this meeting.

Damien entered the chamber of the Council of Lords. Sparsely furnished, with only a large circular oak table and a well-stocked drink cart, the room was one of the humblest he'd seen in the castle. The same could not be said for the woman seated across from him. Her dark hair fell in waves across her shoulders, her verdant eyes locking on him like vises.

"Princess Eshlin," he greeted with a small bow.

Her lips quirked in a smile. "High Lord Adair."

The chamber was otherwise empty save for a golden-skinned woman with an arching brow and shoulder-length black hair poised to take notes in the corner. Niora, the royal berator. She witnessed each council meeting and reported decisions to be documented in the Vault.

It was one of the many things his father had taught him: always know everyone in the room when conducting business. Unknown faces meant unknown intentions, and the less one knew, the less they could control.

"The others appear to be late," he remarked.

Eshlin shrugged. "Or perhaps we're early."

Damien slid his pocket watch back into his vest pocket with a frown. He hated being late. Careful timing could mean the difference between a plan that succeeded and one that shattered into pieces, but he was not surprised to find that these people operated as if the world turned on their order. In a way, it did.

"Congratulations on your Ascension," the princess said as he took one of the cushioned chairs opposite her. "Yours and your house's."

"Thank you," he replied, settling into the back-and-forth he'd come to expect from her. He knew her brother, Prince Darius, far better than her, but their few encounters had taught him that they shared a similar mindset. Every word she spoke had a purpose, and he paid them the same mind he would a well-aimed blade.

"How do you find being head of House Adair?" she pressed.

"Busy." He'd had little time to himself the last few days, his world a flurry of paperwork, meetings, and handling the fallout from Loic's arrest. Then his father had passed, and his life had been consumed by the funeral.

Eshlin folded her hands atop the table. "I was sorry to hear of your father's passing, and so soon after your brother's troubles."

Damien kept his hands beneath the table, where the princess could not see them tighten into fists. He hated the ease with which people referenced Loic's arrest. But it had been highly public, filling the newspapers for days.

Adair Arrested
Adair Murders Kelbra

The headlines were seared into his mind, alongside the sight of his brother holding Eradas Kelbra's severed head. Loic had killed him as his Ascension submission, while Damien had presented the rights to the Illinir, taken from House Kelbra. If Reid hadn't arrived with the Anthir when he did, he honestly didn't know who his father would have chosen. But in the end, Damien had become heir, and Loic had been escorted to a prison cell to await trial.

Damien's eyes flitted across the table. "Speaking of, shouldn't yours be here?"

"My father is too sick to attend," Eshlin replied, and Damien caught sight of something shifting about her shoulders. An enchanted dress? "Darius and I are meant to come in his place, but as you can see, only one of us knows how to tell time."

It was a glib remark, but Damien saw it for what it was: a reminder of who to watch out for. Darius had never been the political sort, most of his support coming from the nobility who propped up his family for their own gain. He'd have no interest in running the kingdom, likely content to wait for his father to initiate the Rite of Ascension, which would decide the next king or queen. But Eshlin recognized an opportunity to consolidate power, same as he.

The Council of Lords was the heart of the kingdom, drafting legislation for everything from taxes to the registry, kingdom-wide decisions that the lesser houses enacted throughout the city. The four heads of the greater houses together with the ruling monarch could influence almost every corner of Enderlish life, and now Damien was a part of it.

"Found the place, did you?" asked a sneering voice over his shoulder. "I'm surprised the dogs didn't attack you at the door. They are trained to sense threats, aren't they?"

A tall, fair-skinned man with a ruby-encrusted waistcoat strode into the room, a glass of whiskey in hand. In his midthirties, with a thick black beard and a thin mouth, High Lord Vanadahl had the bearing of a vole, if a vole's hands and ears were laden with rubies the size of their eyes.

Mark every detail, his father's voice reminded him. *You never know which will become valuable later.*

"I wasn't aware you found me threatening, High Lord Vanadahl," Damien intoned.

The man's lips curled at the twist of his words. "Not you, boy. It's your foolish ideals I don't care for."

"That's hardly a proper greeting for our newest colleague, Royce." Niekla Dramara swept into the room wearing a dress of deepest sapphire, a silver serpent eating its own tail etched around the bodice. With white skin, auburn hair drawn up in a tight bun, and brown eyes so dark the pupils were lost, she was the most severe woman Damien had ever seen.

"There's nothing proper about this, Niekla." Royce snorted dismissively as they both took their seats. "Removing Rezek at the whim of a child?"

"At the whim of a king," Eshlin said softly, and the color rose in Royce's pale skin.

"Of course, Your Highness." He ignored the smug look Niekla was giving, leaning back to ensure Niora hadn't included that remark in the official minutes. The king might only be able to demote a greater house in favor of elevating a new one once every five years, but it was still unwise to invoke his ire. Not when any legislation Royce might propose required a majority vote, one of which belonged to the king.

Or rather, Eshlin now.

The door had nearly swung shut when someone caught it. A broad-shouldered man with light brown skin and a tranquil bearing entered, bowing his head.

"I apologize for my tardiness, Your Highness," Cassian Ruthar said.

"Not to worry, Cassian." Eshlin reclined in her chair. "We were all just getting acquainted."

Damien surveyed Cassian. He was the only one in this room whose ideals remotely aligned with Damien's own. Royce had practically been Rezek's lapdog, all too happy for his gemstone mining business to flourish beneath the demands of the Eternal War, and Niekla was known to be capricious. House Ruthar, on the other hand, frequently voted in favor of measures against the war, and that was one of Damien's ultimate targets.

Such was the game he now had to play. The delicate art of balancing his true disposition with the one he had to present here would test every skill his father had taught him. These were the people who poisoned Enderlain, who upheld the system of violence and fear that had seen his father trapped beneath the Kelbras' poor working conditions, his family nearly put on the street when his mother was ill. That had led to a young boy holding his mother's body as it grew cold.

Damien would take their power from them and make it his. He would strip away all that they had granted themselves, chip at the foundation of Enderlain's oppression, and plot a new course for its future, ensuring that what happened to his family would never happen to another.

He would change everything.

CHAPTER 4

MIKIRA

IF HORSES COULD speak, Atara would be screaming at her right now.

Having recognized the rosebush-lined path they were heading up, she hadn't stopped nickering, snorting, and all-around complaining for the last five minutes, despite Mikira's repeated attempts to assure her that they were not riding toward their deaths. Then again, Atara was charmed to sense danger, so perhaps the horse knew better than she did.

"I don't want to go to Rezek's either," she told the mare, whose ebony ears flicked backward to listen. "But I'm not leaving my father in his hands a second longer."

The Illinir had been over for a week now, and Mikira had spent every day attempting to make contact with Rezek to retrieve her father. But with the loss of his own and his house's disgrace, Rezek had retreated into seclusion and turned away all visitors, and Damien had abandoned her to handle this herself.

A warm breeze caught the roses, carrying the sickly sweet scent to her nose. The smell was an all-too-potent reminder of the last time she was here, when Rezek had convinced Prince Darius to let his jockey ride her brother's beloved horse, Iri, in the Illinir, and she'd discovered Talyana's true identity as an Anthir sergeant.

That was the night everything had begun to fall apart. The rest, Mikira had done herself.

The gates of Kelbra Manor had been pinned open like two giant white wings, granting them entrance to a circular drive. The guards that had foiled her last few visits were absent, and she dismounted with a growing unease.

The whole manor felt too quiet.

Head on a swivel, she pounded her fist against the front door. When only silence followed, she knocked again, then a third time. She was about ready to tell Atara to break it down when it swung open.

"Miss Rusel."

A shiver dropped down her spine at Rezek's low rasp. He lounged inside the doorframe, the posture uncharacteristically indolent. His presence had always reminded her of a freshly sharpened blade, every inch of him prepared to cut.

Mikira summoned all her strength, refusing to be the same terrified girl she'd always been before him. She was the youngest winner of the Illinir in history, daughter of the illustrious Keirian Rusel and head of the foremost enchanted horse ranch in all of Enderlain—Rezek couldn't touch her now.

"I've come for my father," she said.

Rezek's cold blue eyes swept across the grounds, then back to her. "Alone? My, my, trouble in paradise?"

Her hands curled into fists, and it was enough of a reaction to make Rezek smile. He pushed off the doorframe with a wave of his ring-laden hand. "I can't say I'm surprised. Damien never was very good at sharing the spotlight."

That wasn't why he'd turned his back on her. He'd seen her revelation of his missing house ring as a betrayal, even though she hadn't known that Talyana was an Anthir sergeant. She hadn't spoken to him in days, or Ari and Reid. The silence made her heart ache, but what would she say? That she was sorry? Was that even true? After everything Damien had done, she wasn't sure that she wanted to reconcile. At least, not with him. But Ari and Reid . . .

She stopped herself from going any deeper.

"Where's my father?" she demanded.

Rezek regarded her coolly, before beckoning at something deeper in the house. A man hurried forward, his dark auburn hair threaded through with gray and his white skin a sickly pale yellow. But his eyes, every bit as green as her brother's had once been, were clear and bright.

"Father!" Mikira flung herself into his arms. He caught her, enveloping her in a hug she wished could last forever.

"Kira, I'm so glad you're okay," he whispered.

Mikira held back the tears that burned her eyes. "Are *you* okay?" she asked, knowing that he never could be, but he nodded nonetheless and held her tight until Rezek's impatient cough broke them apart.

"Our deal is done," he said. "Your debts to my family have been erased, and your father is freed." His eyes flitted to Atara, who watched in utter stillness, prepared to intervene should Rezek threaten them. But there was something immeasurably heavy about Rezek's bearing now that softened his usually menacing demeanor.

"Take that beast and get off my property," he ordered, and slammed the door.

Mikira led her father down the steps, all too aware of the changes his months here had wrought. He moved like a skittish colt, as if he were still navigating a treacherous terrain that could bare teeth at any moment. She'd felt the same way around Rezek, always waiting for him to twist the knife deeper.

But her father was here. He was alive.

"She's gorgeous." Her father ran a hand along Atara's neck. She bobbed her head at him, always quick to warm to anyone who complimented her. Mikira helped him mount, and then swung up in front of him. He wrapped his arms about her, and she felt then how thin they were, his exhaustion palpable.

"Your shoulder," he said softly as he noticed the bandage near her collarbone. The stitches would be removed in a couple days, and the worst of the pain had subsided, but it still felt stiff and achy. It was one of many injuries she'd sustained during the Illinir, the others scabbed over or already fading bruises.

"It's nothing," she assured him, though she longed to tell him all about it. For once, she wished she could share a little of the burden without worrying he would break.

They made their way back down the drive and along the Traveler's Road. It wasn't a long ride to the Rusel Ranch, but long enough for Mikira to feel every inch of the expanding silence. Things had been strained between them before, the loss of her mother and brother nearly too much for their family to bear, and now there were a thousand unspoken things between them.

She had won the Illinir, Enderlain's foremost enchanted horse race, but she'd lost Iri, the horse that had been her last connection to her brother. She'd secured the coin that came with her victory, but control of it belonged to Damien, who was dispersing it to her in installments as a means of ensuring she kept his secrets. Her father was safe and coming home at last, but there were parts of him that might never return, just as parts of her would never be the same.

Atara's ears pricked suddenly, and then Mikira caught the sound too: someone's frantic shouts. The noise was coming from the ranch ahead of them, and her instinct to ride toward it was tempered only by the realization of whose house it was: Noah Harlan, the boy who had been Mikira's childhood friend before she turned down his advances.

Reid was the only one she'd ever told about that, how pathetic it'd made her feel.

"Kira?" her father asked when she slowed Atara.

"Hold on," she said, and he secured his grip a moment before she sent Atara into an outright gallop. They veered around an Anthir coach and into the wide front drive.

Noah was on his knees at the base of the stairs, one Anthir constable locking his wrists in irons while the other held back Noah's mother. Her pale face was flushed with tears, but Noah's dark eyes were hard as he met Mikira's gaze. He looked so small kneeling there, making her wonder how he could have ever loomed so large in her life.

"Mrs. Harlan," Mikira called as she dismounted. "What's happening?"

The constable arresting Noah raised a hand to ward her back. "This has nothing to do with you."

"He's been conscripted!" Mrs. Harlan wailed, her hands tangling in her skirts. Mikira could just see the small shapes of Noah's younger siblings gathered at her back, and for a moment all she could think of was Nelda and Ailene crowding behind her.

"Failed to report for duty, you mean," the constable nearest her sneered. "Should be thrown into the cells with the other criminals, if you ask me."

Noah turned and spat at him. The one closest to him backhanded him hard enough to leave a mark before hoisting him to his feet. He swayed dizzily.

"Kira," her father warned, but she ignored him. She hadn't seen Noah since they were children, and as much as she resented the way he'd treated her, she also knew how his family depended on him with their father gone.

Mikira stepped into the constable's path. "I'll pay the exemption fee."

The surprise that flooded the constable's face was nothing compared to Noah's. He gawked at Mikira like a fish snared on the line, and a small part of her couldn't help the thrum of satisfaction that arose. But she kept it tamped down and withdrew a small pouch of coin from her pocket, part of Damien's first deposit of her winnings.

"This should cover it," she said.

The constable looked over his shoulder at his partner, whose eyes narrowed. "It's too late for that. The crime's been committed, and I—"

"You can take my coin," Mikira said. "Or I can take this matter to High Lord Adair."

The constable's mouth snapped shut, and the nearest one eyed her anew, then balked. "Miss Rusel," he said swiftly. "We didn't recognize you. Paying the fee now is fine, of course." He hastily unlocked Noah's irons, and Mikira tried not to cringe at invoking Damien's name. It might have helped, but to the public, he was still her sponsor, her friend, and she wasn't sure how she felt about that.

The irons came off, and Noah lurched immediately for his mother, who enveloped him in her arms. Mikira shoved the coin pouch into the constable's chest, then remounted Atara with her father, whose face she couldn't read. She didn't spare Noah another glance before sending Atara at a trot back down the path, every beat of the horse's hooves mirroring the slowly fading pound of adrenaline through her veins.

Her sisters were waiting for them on the front porch when they rode up the gravel drive, outfitted in new day dresses she'd bought them with her winnings. Nelda was threading pieces of grass together into a crown, Ailene drawing a rendition of Wolf, her golem dog, on her leg cast. The scruffy white creature was curled up beside her with his head in her lap, a sore reminder of Ari every time Mikira saw it.

Nelda leapt from the stairs with a cry as they rode up, Ailene taking longer to follow on her crutch. Wolf barked, dancing around Atara's hooves as Mikira dismounted, then aided her father, who was practically swallowed up by Ailene's and Nelda's frantic hugs. Atara shifted behind them, keeping her father upright as he laughed and pulled them both close at once.

For a moment, Mikira just breathed, content to let this moment play out forever. What remained of her family was whole once more, or at least as close as they'd ever get after what they'd been through.

"I've made lunch!" Nelda tugged at their father's hand.

"I'll be inside in a moment," he replied. "Why don't the two of you set the table? I need to speak with your sister."

Nelda seized Ailene's hand in place of his, helping her back to the house as Wolf trotted alongside them. Mikira watched them go, somehow knowing that she didn't want to hear what her father had to say.

She led Atara over to her pasture, letting the golem horse graze while she removed her tack and brushed her down with what had once been Iri's brushes, Iri's grass. Memories of him still threaded through everything she did, and there was a part of her that looked at Atara and wished for another horse, a stallion with a single white star on his forehead who she knew down to his bones.

But Iri was gone.

Atara had killed him to protect her, and like so much of Mikira's life now, she could not separate the good from the bad. She could only accept everything, or none of it at all. Except that did nothing to dispel the nightmares that permeated her sleep, the keening cry of a dying horse and blood so thick it coated her hands like mud. She wouldn't race again for a very long time.

Perhaps she never would again.

Her father surveyed the ranch, taking in the few improvements Mikira had already made: the repaired and freshly painted pasture fences, the rust-free water troughs, and the new barn door with RUSEL RANCH in bright gold script across it.

Their family name meant something again, and it felt good to see it so proudly displayed.

"We have new horses coming in from Fenden," she said as she worked. They would be nothing in comparison to the Rusel enchants they'd lost, but they would make for a good starting point in rebuilding their fabled lines. "Soon, the ranch will look just like it used to before . . ."

She trailed off. Before her mother slowly poisoned herself to death with verillion. Before Lochlyn was conscripted into the Eternal War as a result of her foolishness. Before Rezek's iron grip on the ranch had nearly sent them into ruin and she'd been forced to risk her life in that bloodbath of a race and Iri—she sheared through the thought, forcing it away.

The Illinir already haunted her in her sleep; she would not let it have the daylight too.

"It looks amazing, Kira," her father said gently. "I'm so proud of what you've accomplished. Not just with the Illinir, but here, at home. Your sisters are lucky to have you."

Mikira paused with her fingers buried in Atara's sweaty fur, a curry comb clutched in one hand. Those were the words she'd always wanted her father to say, the acknowledgment she'd needed when he buried himself in his verillion research night after night, seeking a new discovery that would put the Rusel name on the map again.

She couldn't help feeling they were too little, too late.

The sound of hoofbeats echoed up the gravel path, and a brown-skinned girl with a long braid of dark hair flying behind her rode up the drive on a pale horse, a grin already breaking across her beautiful face. She reined her horse in short of them.

"Mr. Rusel," Talyana greeted with a tip of her head. "It's been a while."

Her father blinked curiously at Talyana, who he hadn't seen since she was a child. Her parents had shipped her off to a military academy after Rezek injured her, and Mikira hadn't seen her for years until recently.

"Talyana Haraver," Mikira reminded him.

"Of course," he said with a warm smile. "It's good to see you."

"And you." Talyana bowed her head. "If you don't mind, I need to borrow your daughter."

Her father hesitated, no doubt thinking of what he'd meant to share with Mikira. Whatever it was, though, it seemed he didn't want to do it in front of company.

Instead, he folded his thin arms and said, "I expect her home before dark."

The grin Talyana flashed him was nothing short of mischievous, and between the two of them Mikira felt her face heating, even as a part of her balked at her father's concern. Real or not, it felt forced, like so much of the last hour, and she had to swallow the urge to tell him that if she could win the Illinir, she could handle herself among some rebels.

Except he didn't know that was where she was going.

Neither did her sisters, who would only worry. But she was doing this for them, for a better future for them all. She wouldn't risk her family by incriminating them with knowledge of her activities.

As her father made his way back to the house, Mikira opened Atara's pasture gate, intending to let her rest since she'd already been out for one ride to town.

"Bring her," Talyana said. "It'll be good for people to see the two of you together."

Mikira paused with a frown. "What do you mean?"

Talyana gestured between them. "Come on, Kira. The two of you are practically a symbol of resistance after what you accomplished. Together, you're a legend."

A legend.

The words swelled inside her in a way she didn't expect, and Atara bobbed her head vigorously in agreement. She never had been shy about praise, and lately, neither had Mikira.

Talyana turned her horse about. "Come on. We've got a meeting to get to."

CHAPTER 5

DAMIEN

DAMIEN WATCHED AS the council agenda unfolded, letting the conversation ebb and flow around him to get a feel for its players. The majority of it followed discussions for potential legislation, or summaries of the aftermath of laws already passed, but it was the people he paid the most attention to.

Cassian was the easiest to read, his votes tending to favor humanitarian efforts. Royce was a close second, clearly seeking to increase profit at every turn. Niekla was more difficult, sometimes refusing to even give her opinion. She was careful, approaching each decision with a businesswoman's acumen.

But it was Eshlin who surprised him the most.

He'd known the princess was in support of the Eternal War, having served briefly herself, but she was ruthless in her decision-making, refusing to give ground that did not somehow benefit the crown. He'd always thought her more approachable than her brother, but she handed down decisions with a general's deportment.

"I think that covers today's agenda," she said as they neared the hour mark.

"Actually," Damien interceded before the others could respond, "I have a proposal."

Royce's disbelieving gaze cut toward him. No doubt he'd been expecting Damien to sit quietly and let the grown-ups talk, but he had not worked so hard to get here not to use his newfound power.

"Yes?" Eshlin prompted warily.

Damien held her gaze. "I propose that we eliminate the draft tax and exemption fee."

"What?" Royce demanded over the sound of Niekla's sharp breath. Cassian regarded him with narrowed eyes, and Eshlin only bared her teeth in a smile.

The draft tax was paid by those whose names entered the conscription lottery for the Eternal War, but who weren't selected, and the exemption fee could be paid to keep one's name from the lottery altogether. They were the twin pillars that propped up the war effort, and Damien intended to knock them down.

Royce bit out a derisive laugh. "Why would we ever pass such a proposal?"

It was a fair question. All the coin went straight to the war fund, which had once been the responsibility of House Kelbra. In turn, the Kelbras had paid themselves and the other great houses a stipend, effectively turning it into a resource pool for their own use. Now, however, that fund was Damien's responsibility, and he had other plans for it.

"I went through House Kelbra's books," he explained. "It appears these payments were made to you as loans, which I now hold. You can either pass this proposal, and only repay me two-thirds the amounts, or you cannot, and I will demand the entirety with interest."

Something shifted in Eshlin's expression. Had she wanted his proposal to fail? It made sense considering her support of the war, but from what he'd observed, she seemed to be avoiding anything that aligned her too closely with Royce, who looked ready to throttle Damien.

"How dare you undermine our country's interests," Royce ground out, his lip curling. "Then again, perhaps that's exactly what we should have expected."

Damien tilted his head. "Meaning?"

Royce scoffed. "Your parents, of course. One Kinnish, the other Celairen. You don't have a drop of Enderlish blood in you, do you?"

A silence fell in the wake of Royce's words. He'd lived in Enderlain his entire life, and yet with every rung up the ladder his family rose, those same whispers followed them. Followed him. He didn't hide his identity the way Loic did, but neither was it as prominent as Shira's. As a result, he'd deflected his fair share of veiled statements and vicious implications, but never so directly. Even the others seemed surprised by Royce's bluntness.

"I see," Damien said quietly. "I'm the foreigner come to steal what's yours, is that it?"

Royce shrugged as if to say he couldn't be blamed for what was true, and Damien swallowed down the vitriol rising in his gut. "And what about what you have stolen, Royce? When you take from your own people, what does that make you?"

A flush colored Royce's pale skin, but Damien didn't relent. "Perhaps you don't really care that I'm Kinnish, or Celairen, only that I'm threatening your power." He gestured with one splayed hand. "I'll have what's owed to me either way. Cast your votes."

Royce slammed his fist atop the table. "You don't know the game you're playing, boy."

"I think he knows it better than you." Cassian's voice cut easily through the rising tension, a notable appreciation in his dark eyes. "I vote yes."

"As do I, naturally." Damien still held Royce's gaze.

Eshlin folded her arms. "I vote against it. The war is in a precarious state; we shouldn't risk turmoil."

As reasonable as it sounded, Damien couldn't quiet the feeling that there was more to her decision. That left only Niekla, whose vote would decide everything. She tapped her fingers against the table's edge, the gemstone flecks on her neatly manicured nails catching the sunlight.

His proposal was meant to accomplish several things, first and foremost the abolishment of a practice that preyed on the poor and desperate, but it was also a means of learning more about all of them. Cassian had agreed easily, despite having accepted the funds to begin with, which suggested to Damien a guilty conscience. Royce had refused out of pride and bigotry alone, even though he'd likely end up owing more in repayment than he'd lose from the fund.

And Niekla—she thought carefully through it, the way he imagined she would a game of chess.

Every detail, Father, he thought.

"I vote in favor of the proposal," Niekla said at last, ignoring Royce's red-faced protests.

Eshlin's grimace was subtle. "Then it passes."

Two down, Damien thought with a sense of satisfaction. Bit by bit, he would take away all the things they used to make themselves powerful, to prey on those beneath them. *I will fix it all, Mother.*

A knock sounded at the door, and it swung open to reveal a bowing servant. "I apologize for the interruption, but King Theo has requested everyone's presence in the throne room," she said. "Immediately."

DAMIEN AND THE other council members hovered outside the closed throne room doors, where Eshlin had entered to join her father and brother. Royce and Niekla descended into inaudible whispers, while Cassian stood with his arms folded, deep in thought.

Whatever this was, they hadn't expected it either.

Several minutes passed before the door opened. Prince Darius, Princess Eshlin, and King Theo stood upon the dais in quiet conversation with two people clutching briefcases. One was Niora, but the other wore the crisp white robes of the berators of the Vault, the source of all paperwork and truth in Enderlain. He had a small diamond pin on his chest that denoted him as the liaison between the Vault and royal family.

The prince's ice-blue eyes narrowed on Damien as he entered. Apparently he hadn't been forgiven for removing Darius's favored cousin from his seat of power. So much for all the favor Damien had curried with the man over the course of the Illinir.

The doors swung shut behind them, leaving the nine of them alone without even a guard or servant. Anticipation trickled down Damien's neck, and he glanced at Eshlin, whose easy bearing had tightened into something ready to pounce.

So, it's time, he thought grimly.

King Theo settled into his throne, a gemstone-lined monstrosity that nearly consumed his thinning body. The rest of the room was equally garish, the high ceilings lit with enchanted glass windows and walls crowded by gilded paintings and gemstone figurines. Damien wondered how much of this had been paid for with the people's money, and how much had simply been taken.

"Thank you for coming," the king said hoarsely. Eshlin and Darius stood on either side of him, the two berators descending to join the house leaders. From the looks Royce and Niekla were exchanging, he suspected they'd figured out what was coming too.

"My health has taken a turn for the worst in recent days, and I can no longer put off the inevitable," the king said. "Therefore I am initiating the royal Rite of Ascension."

Eshlin's clasped hands tightened, and a sharp smile cut across Darius's face. It was so much like Rezek's that Damien wanted to ruin it. He hadn't seen his old friend since the last race of the Illinir, and news of him had been quiet, but this was exactly the sort of thing that might draw him back into the fray.

"However"—the king's voice took on an edge—"I am amending the usual rules that limit the Ascension to only my children and opening it to all those with royal blood."

Darius's head jerked toward his father. "You can't do that."

"He most certainly can," Eshlin returned more calmly, though even her voice was strained. It might be tradition for the Rite of Ascension to only be open to one's children, but the rules were ultimately up to the one initiating it.

And for some reason, King Theo didn't want his children to win.

Ignoring Darius's outburst, King Theo continued, "The task I set is this: whoever locates and retrieves the bastard prince will inherit the throne."

So it was true, then. The last Ranier king had left behind an illegitimate heir, a child King Theo had spent his entire rule claiming didn't exist. If the boy had, he would have inherited the throne after his father, King Rykard, with no siblings to challenge for the Ascension. Instead, Rykard's sister, Leona, had Ascended and married Theo.

Which made the Ranier prince the only threat to Zuerlin rule.

Damien's gaze cut to Darius. Perhaps there was a way to use his crumbling favor with the prince after all.

King Theo waved his hand. "You are dismissed."

Eshlin remained behind, whispering furiously to her father, while the other council members led the way out. Royce's and Niekla's heads were bent together, no doubt conspiring how to turn this in their favor. The Zuerlins had plenty of distant cousins they could place on the throne as puppets, but the true race would be between Eshlin and Darius.

Damien waited until the prince broke from the pack, then followed him, purposefully making his footfalls loud enough to hear. Darius drew up, leveling an irritated frown over his shoulder.

"Adair," he intoned. "To what do I owe the displeasure?"

Damien inclined his head in more of a bow than the prince deserved, but if this were to work, he would need the prince to think him contrite. "Your Highness. I'd like to offer you my services in the Ascension."

Surprise flitted across Darius's face, but it quickly turned to interest. "Rezek has told me about your extensive network, and your skill at uncovering truths, and seeing as he won't reply to any of my messages . . ." His eyes narrowed. "Why would you want to help me?"

Damien straightened. "It's the least I can do after what happened."

"Yes, out of the kindness of your heart," the prince sneered. "Tell me truly."

Damien forced a look of hesitation onto his face, but when Darius made to go, he said quickly, "I recognize an opportunity when I see one." The prince paused, turning back to him, and Damien continued, "There's no end to the benefit of having the ear of a king."

Satisfaction blossomed across Darius's face. It was like playing out the lines to a script; make the prince think he was hiding something, then grudgingly reveal his truth. Darius would never look any deeper, because Damien had given him exactly what he expected: another man seeking power.

"Very well," the prince agreed. "Starting now, you work for me."

CHAPTER 6

MIKIRA

MIKIRA FELT AS though she were seeing Veradell through new eyes. For so long, the city had felt like a hostile place to her, near claustrophobic with its tightly pressed stone buildings and busy streets. But where Iri's danger charm had put him constantly on edge, Atara marched along the cobblestones as if she owned them—and people *moved* for her.

Mikira had barely been to town since the closing Illinir ball, but it was clear from the moment they hit Ashfield Street that she'd never pass through it unacknowledged again.

It felt like everyone knew her name.

Men tipped their caps to her as she passed, and children raced alongside Atara's long strides, giggling with laughter when she flicked her tail at them. Others called out, greeting her as if they were friends or else trying to entice her into their shops, and while she hated feeling as though she owed Damien anything, she couldn't deny how much her comfort with this kind of attention had grown, thanks to him.

But behind the cheer and curiosity, the real Veradell still persisted.

There was a line around the corner at the draft office, full of gaunt-faced men wringing their hats and women knotting their fists into their skirts. Like Noah, their names would have been recently drawn from the lottery, their lives forfeit to the Eternal War in Celair.

She couldn't help imagining her brother in a line just like it after Rezek's men dragged him away. She saw his face in each of theirs. How many would make it back? How many of their families would get somber-faced soldiers on their doorstep, full of empty apologies?

These were the people they were fighting for, and yet Mikira couldn't help wondering what they truly wanted. Would they support the rebels' cause to unseat the monarchy, or curse them for inviting more trouble? She knew the feeling of wanting to curl up around everything you had and hold fast, to let the blows keep raining down no matter how much they hurt, because that at least was certain. Known. But if they didn't fight, nothing would ever change.

And Mikira wanted it to change.

Talyana led them along a maze of deserted side streets until they reached one that had been blocked off, warning of a chemical spill. A man sat on a crate smoking, and he nodded to them as they passed. Mikira caught the glint of a revolver tucked in his jacket.

The road narrowed, then ended in a brick wall. "Tal?" Mikira asked uncertainly when she didn't slow.

Talyana flashed a grin—and rode straight through the wall. Mikira gaped before her mind caught up to her eyes; it was an illusion enchantment. As if sensing the spell, Atara surged forward. Mikira couldn't help bracing, but they only passed through open air.

"The underground tunnels?" Mikira surveyed the stone passageway. It was one of many under the city, left over from Enderlain's once burgeoning gemstone mining industry, when the tunnels had been used to transport miners and gemstones beneath the city so as not to clog up the main streets.

"We just call it the tunnels," Talyana replied from where she waited ahead. "They're isolated, abandoned, and easy to defend. What better place for a rebel hideout?"

Mikira let Atara follow after them. "Somewhere with windows would be nice." She was no stranger to the passages, having participated in her friend Jenest's illegal underground races countless times when she needed coin, but after her last visit during the Illinir, stepping inside felt like revisiting the harrowing darkness of the final race.

Her fingers brushed one knife hilt for reassurance, and the blade vibrated comfortingly in its sheath. She still hadn't gotten used to the enchantment that enabled them to carry out her will, but thankfully their magic only came alight when she touched them, or else they'd be leaping to her aid at all hours.

Ancient enchanted lights cast a dim glow across the damp earth as they followed the winding tunnels deeper underground. Recruitment posters peeled from the walls, Aslir's visage demanding Enderlish loyalty and service for the ongoing war. Mikira tore them loose as they went, revealing messages from arriving refugees and fleeing conscripts scrawled underneath.

Some days, she let herself imagine there was a message from Lochlyn down here somewhere. That the soldiers who came to their door had been wrong, and rather than perish in the war, her brother had escaped through the tunnels in the dark of night. Others, she simply lay in bed in the morning and tried to remember the fading details of his face.

A noise echoed from ahead, and Mikira had a knife drawn before she saw the mouse scurrying past.

"It looked absolutely ferocious," Talyana said drily.

Mikira didn't laugh. "This isn't a game, Tal. If anyone sees me . . ." She left the thought unfinished. Without Damien's protection, she'd be lucky if she only ended up in a cell. All the work she'd put into rebuilding the Rusel name would be forfeit and she'd put her family in more danger than ever before.

Talyana sighed. "I know, Kira. I'm sorry. But I promise you these tunnels are secure. We patrol them regularly, and if anyone stumbles too close, the whole area is full of warnings of a chemical spill. Beyond that, we have guards, and beyond that, several defensive enchantments."

A soft whistle cut through the air, and Talyana replied in a two-beat note. A figure emerged around the corner ahead, armed with a Sherakin rifle. Guns were difficult to obtain in Enderlain, what with the stringent import restrictions and high taxes, which meant the rebels likely had only a few.

Mikira blinked as the figure's face resolved into familiarity. They were short and wiry, with brown skin and the kind of presence that cut through a crowd.

"Jenest!" she exclaimed.

Dressed in off-white fatigues with her dark hair braided down her back, Jenest was a far cry from the eccentric race runner Mikira remembered. She frowned suspiciously up at Mikira, who realized belatedly that she'd always worn a mask during the underground races. Then Jenest's expression shifted, and an easy grin broke across her face.

"I know that voice," she said. "Come to win all my coin again, Nightflyer?"

Mikira was still trying to process the fact that the race runner she'd known for the last year was actually a rebel. "But then—the races. Why risk them?"

"Funding." Jenest rubbed her thumb against two fingers. "An operation of this size takes a lot of money. Not to mention the underground racing sort make for a good recruiting pool." She gave Mikira a pointed look before nodding over her shoulder. "Come on. The princess is waiting." She laid a hand on the nearest wall and a golden light filled the corridor crosswise like a partition, then dissolved.

"Combination of an energy charm for movement and an ethereal one for illusions," Talyana explained to Mikira's mystified look. "If someone the enchantment doesn't recognize crosses while it's active, it notifies us and traps them in an illusion until we can get here."

Jenest reinstated the enchantments after they crossed, then led them deeper into the tunnels. They passed two guard posts before the tunnel ended at a set of reinforced metal doors.

"This is the old mining headquarters." Jenest touched the padlock on the door, and it clicked open. "The lock's enchanted to only let certain people through. Our enchanter will have to add you to it."

"How many enchanters are working with the rebellion?" Mikira asked her.

Talyana's eyes darkened. "Only one."

"She and Tal don't get along," Jenest added, earning a look of annoyance from Talyana that Jenest only grinned at.

"We get along," Talyana replied tersely. "Along to a cliff edge, or into the sea. Really any impromptu grave will do."

"Who—" Mikira's question was cut off as the door swung open with a screech, revealing an expansive cavern the size of several racetracks over again. People in cream-colored fatigues bustled about, organizing and relocating crates of supplies or running laps in a cordoned-off training area. A line had formed along a table handing out pillows and blankets, and children chased each other among the tumult.

Although Talyana had explained that the rebellion took in people off the streets and the families of those exposed as rebels, the extent of the operation still astounded her. It brought the reality of what she was doing crashing down around her, triggering the old urge to up and flee. She'd spent years trying to disentangle herself from Veradell's machinations, and now she was thrusting herself straight into the warpath.

Warm fingers curled about her own, and she met Talyana's steady gaze. "You can do this," she said, squeezing gently. "I'm right here."

Mikira wasn't sure what to say. The two of them hadn't had much time together since the closing ball, and she didn't know quite where they stood. After all, Talyana had lied to and manipulated her, but she had also helped Mikira win the Illinir. Without her, Mikira wouldn't have survived, let alone been able to keep Atara's secret.

Then there was the way Mikira's skin came alight when Talyana touched her. It at once thrilled and unnerved her, sending her heart into a skittering whirlwind before it lodged firmly in her throat. Physical touch had never held an attraction to her, and still didn't, but the more time she spent with Talyana, the more she craved the closeness simple gestures like this brought.

I can't do this alone, she thought. She needed at least one person on her side, and beyond that, she *wanted* things to be okay between them. After everything she'd been through, Mikira didn't want to lose Talyana too.

By now, people had begun to take notice of them, whispers curling through the air like verillion smoke. Talyana drew back, letting everyone's attention fall squarely on Mikira and Atara. Once, she would have shrunk beneath it. Now, she embraced it with her head high.

This, she could do.

"That's Mikira Rusel," said one voice.

"Atara's even more beautiful up close."

"It's true! There aren't gold flecks in her eyes."

Word had spread that she'd won the Illinir on an unenchanted horse, a feat that only added to her reputation. Part of her recoiled at the lie, but the truth would expose Ari, and she had to admit a part of her liked the way people gazed at them like the Harbingers returned.

"My, aren't you the celebrity?" asked a new voice.

Mikira spun, coming face-to-face with Shira Adair. She wore her usual dark attire, an array of blades strapped across her lithe body in plain view. Somehow, Mikira was entirely unsurprised to see her. She knew little of Damien's sister, except that she had a tendency to appear in unexpected places with the air of someone who'd been waiting for a very long time.

"Talyana," Mikira said stiffly. "What is she doing here?"

"Rebelling, naturally," Shira replied first. Atara pushed forward, and Shira caught the mare's muzzle in her hands. "It's good to see you too."

"I don't understand why you're here," Mikira pressed, trying not to feel betrayed at Atara's friendliness with the woman. "You're a noble, and of a *greater* house now. Why would you want to change anything?"

Shira gazed into Atara's eyes as she replied, "We all have our reasons."

"Some just mutter about them more obscurely than others." Talyana folded her arms. Shira ignored her, and Mikira realized that she must be the enchanter Jenest had mentioned. Clearly Mikira wasn't the only one who distrusted her presence here.

Jenest patted Talyana's shoulder comfortingly. "Cliffs and seas, my friend, cliffs and seas."

Somehow Mikira got the feeling that Shira knew exactly what Jenest was referencing, though she didn't react, just turned on her heel. "Come on, Eshlin's address is about to begin."

Mikira exchanged looks with Jenest, who shrugged. "Best get used to it. She's Eshlin's second-in-command."

To have balanced life as an Adair with that of the rebels couldn't have been easy, especially with a brother like Damien, who prided himself on always being a step ahead. Everything Shira did fell under the public eye, and discovery meant death.

Just as it would for Mikira.

But if they succeeded, if they could truly bring down the house system and enact change, then perhaps her family could finally live in peace, and no one would ever have to suffer as they did beneath someone like Rezek again.

Eyes followed her and Atara as they joined a growing crowd, and Mikira winked at a little girl who peered up at them in awe. As the idle chatter mounted, Talyana shifted nervously at her side. "She's late," she muttered. "She's never late."

"I'm sure it's nothing," Mikira reassured her, but Talyana toyed with the end of her braid as if she could pick answers apart from inside it.

Just as Talyana's fidgeting had reached a fever pitch, a cheer rose throughout the crowd. A tall woman emerged from a nearby office, her harried expression instantly melting away. Her long black hair fell in two braids down her back, her thick body easily filling out the military fatigues she wore.

Even in full uniform, Princess Eshlin had a grace to her that Mikira longed to emulate. She clasped hands with people as she passed, leaning in to speak briefly with them before shifting to the next. The princess she knew was clever and sure, but here she was a beacon of warmth and welcome, drawing the people in with a palpable magnetism.

"Something's wrong," Talyana muttered, and Mikira instinctively shifted closer to her.

Jenest handed Eshlin a charmed loudspeaker as the princess approached the front of the stage, where Mikira could just make out the outline of the camouflaged golem snake she carried about her shoulders.

"Welcome, my friends!" Eshlin called in a richly timbred voice. A cheer went up, and the princess waited until it settled to continue. "We are closer now to our goal than ever before, and we owe every inch of progress we've made to each other. Without every single one of you, this organization would not be what it has become today."

Mikira watched the crowd as Eshlin spoke. Her words clearly affected them, several people shouldering each other in acknowledgment or crooking smiles. They believed every word she said, but Mikira wasn't so sure. There was a part of her that still felt as though this was all an impossible task, one that could see them all dead. That part of her wanted to leap onto Atara's back and flee, never looking back.

But there was another part of her, one that had been ground into the dirt over and over again, forced to fight for her life and the lives of her family, that demanded she stay.

As if sensing her thoughts, Atara nudged her with her nose. Mikira laid a hand against her shoulder, standing tall.

"This kingdom's leadership has failed it." Eshlin's voice resounded through the cavern. "Time and time again, it has put itself ahead of its people. It has used you as fodder for a war you didn't want, has measured your lives in terms of profit you'll never see a drop of." Her voice had an edge now, one that was coursing through the crowd in a current of assenting murmurs.

Mikira felt it too. The years of pent-up rage. The fear. The desolation. She'd lost her brother to the Eternal War at the whim of a capricious lord. Watched her mother poison herself with illegal verillion fed into the underbelly by sellers capitalizing on wartime prices. Watched her family's enchant business dwindle into nothing, crushed beneath an uncaring boot.

"I've been there when they bartered away your livelihoods." Eshlin's voice rose higher. "I've seen how easily they cast aside your lives. My family is every bit as guilty as the noble houses, every bit as unworthy of leading, which is why I've made it my goal to facilitate the transfer of leadership from the noble houses to the people. To you."

A hand slid into hers, Talyana's fingers curling tight. This time, Mikira felt only the surety in Talyana's touch, the strength. Atara dropped her head over Mikira's shoulder, her ears pitched forward to capture Eshlin's final words.

The princess lifted her head to survey the crowd. "The time has come to take back your power."

THE CROWD DISPERSED with the end of the Eshlin's speech, a new energy buzzing through them. Even Mikira was surprised by how deeply the princess's words resonated. Eshlin might be royalty, but she'd made her intentions clear: she would help them dismantle the house system and the monarchy, putting the power in the hands of the people.

Together they would forge a new Enderlain.

Mikira wanted to believe that more than anything, but years of being burned by nobles had taught her otherwise.

"You look like you swallowed a lemon." Talyana raised an eyebrow at her.

"It's just . . . well, how much do you trust Eshlin?" Mikira asked. "She served in the Eternal War, after all. She's still one of them."

Talyana gave her a knowing look. "She volunteered to fight against her father's wishes. Told him that if Enderlain's people had to serve, then so did she."

"Oh." That, Mikira hadn't known, though it didn't erase her uncertainty.

"Don't take my word for it." Talyana nudged Mikira's hip with her own. "You can form your opinion."

Mikira followed her to where Shira was waiting for them in the doorway of the room Eshlin had emerged from earlier. A woman stood beside her clutching a bucket of green apples that Atara immediately went for, while Mikira and Talyana followed Shira inside.

Eshlin sat behind a simple wooden desk with a map of Veradell spread across it. The tension from before her speech had come swarming back, and she tapped the desk impatiently until Shira perched against the windowsill beside her, arms folded.

"Close the door, please," Eshlin instructed, and Talyana obeyed.

Mikira shifted with a growing sense of unease. "What's going on?"

Eshlin folded her hands in her lap. "My father has initiated the Royal Ascension."

Mikira and Talyana exchanged surprised looks. Despite the king's failing health, no one had expected the Ascension to come so soon.

"What does it mean?" Mikira asked.

"It means we may be able to accomplish our goals nonviolently." Eshlin rose, approaching a drink cart to pour tea as she explained, "The rebellion's plan has been fairly simple thus far: our overall goal is to dismantle the hereditary house system and replace it with elected leadership by district. To do that, we need to nullify the current house heads either through cooperation or coercion and occupy the throne, all of which requires funding and weapons we don't yet have."

"But if you can win the Ascension, then you'll already have the throne," Mikira finished for her, and Eshlin nodded. They would still have to deal with the heads of houses, but Eshlin's power as queen would put an army at her command. She might be able to sway the Council of Lords without bloodshed, which, though Mikira was loath to admit, might just be possible with Damien seated in place of Rezek.

Except, would Eshlin still want to do that if she became queen? Ousting her father and turning down the throne herself were two very different things.

"I understand your hesitation."

Mikira jerked free of her thoughts to find the princess studying her intently, but she refused to wilt beneath her stare as Eshlin continued, "I would be suspicious of me too if I were you. But I promise you, I have no interest in the throne."

"Why?" Mikira recognized the directness of the question, if only because Talyana's eyes widened in her direction, but she needed to know. Eshlin had asked her to be the face of their rebellion, to risk the safety she'd fought so hard to obtain, and she wanted to know why.

Shira's lips curled wryly, but the princess seemed unfazed. "It's a fair question, but I fear my answer is less than impressive: I'm selfish."

Mikira blinked at her, numbly accepting the cup of tea Eshlin handed her. "My uncle was murdered, my mother died of a broken heart, and I'm fairly sure that someone, perhaps even my brother, is poisoning my father." Eshlin held another cup out to Talyana, who made a face as if the princess had offered her something vile.

Keeping the cup, Eshlin resettled in her chair. "I've served in a war that I abhorred, played every kind of political game you can imagine, and spent my entire life looking over my shoulder—a feeling I suspect that you're familiar with."

The princess's dismay only deepened as she said, "I'm tired, Mikira. Tired of watching my family tear itself apart, tired of playing this endless game. I want it to end."

There was a chasm in the princess's eyes that called to Mikira, a feeling of exhaustion that reached too deep to ever exorcise fully. She couldn't have been older than her midtwenties, and yet in that moment, the princess seemed ancient.

In it, Mikira found that she believed her.

"What do you want us to do?" she asked.

CHAPTER 7

MIKIRA

THE VAULT WAS larger than Mikira had realized.

A circular building with a domed top, it was visible from almost anywhere in the Wrenith District, banded by rings of windows at each level and built entirely of stark white stone. It reminded her of a larger version of the Sendian churches scattered throughout town. The white-robed berators rushing in and out even had the supplicating hands of Sendia sewn into their breast pockets, an ode to the religious power that had once dominated Enderlain.

They'd boarded Atara and Talyana's horse a few blocks away to avoid notice. Mikira wore a hood over her distinctive red hair, and the two of them slipped unheeded inside the Vault. It felt even larger inside. The ceiling soared a sky away, the inside ringed with open corridors like the rib cage of a beast. Enchanted lifts carried people floor to floor, and novice berators directed people about from a circular desk in the center.

Somewhere in here, they hoped to find information about the Ranier prince.

"Mikira?" called a startled voice.

Her body responded on its own, turning instinctively toward something familiar and welcome a second before the truth struck home.

Reid gawked at her, a bundle of microscope blueprints haphazardly clutched to his chest. He looked every bit the whirlwind she remembered, his dark clothes nearly as disarrayed as his raven-black hair, the sleeves of his shirt pushed up to expose the lines of his tattoos. His too-bright eyes widened in alarm, as if a chance encounter might spell disaster for them both.

Talyana shifted none too subtly in front of her. "You had better not be following us, Haldane."

In a flash, Reid's surprise melted into a familiar scowl that made Mikira's heart ache. "Yes, because I have nothing better to do. I'm pretty sure stalking people is your party trick, *Sergeant*."

"And yours would be what, glowering at people until they punch you in the face?" Talyana edged forward a little more. "Because I'm happy to oblige."

"Enough," Mikira hissed, seizing hold of herself at last. Whereas thoughts of Ari had slipped in the last few days, Mikira had all but shut those of Reid out. Seeing him here now felt like peering through a window into a shop full of things she could never have. Despite the distance between them, Ari didn't feel lost to her—Reid might as well be an ocean away with how loyal he was to Damien.

"If the two of you are done bickering," she said, "I want to talk to a berator about my family's signet ring." The cover story came easily, though it left Mikira off-kilter. Putting on a show like this for Reid didn't feel right.

It felt even worse when his scowl gave way to narrow-eyed curiosity. "Are you commissioning a new one? I could draw—"

"Nope!" Talyana hooked her arm with Mikira's. "I think *you've* done enough."

Before Mikira could protest, Talyana dragged her deeper into the cavernous room. She felt the intensity of Reid's gaze with every step, and it took all of her restraint not to look back.

She hadn't realized how much she missed him.

Talyana only released her once they reached the directory at the back of the room. Rows of cubbyholes with alphabetical lettering filled one wall, each containing a list of locations where related files were stored, from birth certificates to marriage contracts to racing bets.

Mercifully, Talyana said nothing more about the encounter, but Mikira felt her silence all the same as they jotted down locations from under Ranier, royal family, and birth certificates. By the time they squeezed into an enchanted lift with a pair of berators, she felt ready to burst.

"Just say it already," she demanded as they emerged onto the fourth floor.

Talyana continued into the nearest row of shelves. "I don't have anything to say. You know what I think of him."

She did. It was the same thing Talyana thought of anyone tied to Damien, but worse, because she blamed Reid for telling Damien that Mikira had his signet ring. What Mikira didn't know for sure was what *she* thought.

Silence returned as they dug through record books and files, old contracts and copied letters, things Mikira hadn't even realized that the Vault kept. The place was half-archive, half-museum, maintaining unimportant documents for their sheer existence. Talyana found it fascinating, but she'd always been easily swept away by other people's lives. As children, she'd gotten lost in the stories Mikira's father used to tell them of far-off places, swearing that she'd one day see them.

Mikira had always loved that about her, how big she dreamed, when she herself had never been able to see further ahead than the next day.

The final location they'd written down took them along a narrow hall and into a small room whose enchanted lights struggled to turn on. Mikira thought she glimpsed someone, but as the light steadied, there was no one there.

They split the files they found, taking them to a table by the window to read. Before long Mikira's eyes ached from squinting, and her stomach was rumbling, making it hard to focus. It didn't help that half her mind was still on the run-in with Reid, or that Talyana's feet kept entangling with her own under the desk.

Mikira dropped her head into her hands with a groan. "There's nothing here. Why would there be? Filing a birth certificate for the prince with the Vault would be like a giant arrow pointing straight at him. There's no way his existence could be kept a secret all this time if information like that was just sitting around in here."

Talyana leaned back in her chair, rubbing her eyes. "You're right, but we have to keep looking. The king must have filed something, unless all those rumors just came from the people who witnessed the birth."

Mikira's head jerked up as an idea struck. "Maybe he did." She leapt to her feet, Talyana following as Mikira retraced their steps to the birth records section. But rather than stop there, she continued to the room next door.

"Death certificates?" Talyana asked as they entered a spacious room with a long central table, rows of filing cabinets reaching all the way to the ceiling with a ladder leaning in the corner. "But the whole point is that he isn't dead."

Mikira pulled the ladder over to the center. "King Rykard wanted it to be like he never existed, but people talk. The rumors had to come from somewhere, which means someone knew about the affair and likely even the pregnancy, even if it was only the people who witnessed the birth. So what's the next best thing to never existing?"

A wry grin split across Talyana's face. "Being dead."

The cabinets were labeled by year, the certificates organized by month inside. Mikira pulled free handfuls from around the time of the prince's birth, handing them down to Talyana until they had them all. They spread them out along the table, searching swiftly through until—

"Got it." Mikira slid a piece of paper out for Talyana to see. "Torren Ranier, born and died on the same day."

Talyana took the document. "He must not have filed his birth certificate because he didn't want easy confirmation of the prince's existence out there. But if someone who knew he was born dug deeper, the death certificate would throw them off the scent."

"Isn't there usually a copy of the birth certificate bound with it?" Mikira asked.

Talyana flipped the paper over and pointed to a spot that appeared as if it'd once been glued. "It looks like someone tore something off here. Maybe it was stolen?"

"Let me see it." Mikira took the paper, trying to make out the sigils of the house rings at the bottom. "Aside from the royal symbol, there are two other signets here. If this really is a fake and Prince Torren is alive, they might know what happened."

"Let's check the signet ring archives for who they belong to." Talyana kept the death certificate as they traced their way down to the second floor.

As they exited the lift, a bleary-eyed berator stepped into their path. "I'm sorry, but I must ask you to leave. The Vault is closing early today."

"We just need to check one more thing," Talyana said. "We'll be quick."

But the berator spread her arms, blocking their path. "You can return when we reopen in the morning. Please don't make me call security."

"We won't," Mikira cut in before Talyana could press. She hesitated—they didn't want anyone to know they were there, but they needed this information quickly. As long as the berator didn't know why they'd come, it should be safe.

She lowered her hood, watching the berator's eyes widen with recognition.

"Miss Rusel," she said with a tone Mikira knew well by now. She'd been hoping for it.

"It's nice to meet you." Mikira held out her hand, drawing on countless hours at Illinir balls convincing people she was a societal darling. Except where those people expected acknowledgment, the berator looked shocked to receive it, and shook Mikira's hand with openmouthed wonder.

Talyana eyed Mikira as she flashed her best stage grin. "We're sorry to be a pain, but we only need a couple minutes. I'd really appreciate it."

The berator hesitated, then visibly relented. "Oh, all right. Five minutes. But be quick, please! And, Miss Rusel?"

Mikira paused halfway past the berator, turning back to find a proffered pen and paper and a slight flush to the woman's cheeks. "If you wouldn't mind?"

"Not at all." Mikira signed the paper and handed it back.

"You are getting way too comfortable with that," Talyana said as Mikira rejoined her.

"Or you're jealous," she countered.

Talyana's gaze snapped to her, an unexpected heat behind it that made Mikira falter. "Oh, when I'm jealous, you'll know."

Fighting a flush, Mikira followed Talyana into the file room. Someone had left a gas lamp on the table, and Mikira studied the certificate under the improved lighting. One sigil was too smudged to decipher more than the point of a star, but the other was letter-based, with a large *D* in the center surrounded by jagged lines like waves.

She tucked the certificate into her pocket and started leafing through the *D*s. Every signet had an enlarged drawing of its symbol, along with a picture of the actual ring, and it didn't take long for Mikira to reach the end of the cabinet and sigh.

"It's not here."

"Kira." The tautness in Talyana's voice had Mikira drawing a knife before she'd even finished standing.

"I wouldn't," said a low voice, and Mikira stilled. A Skylis-masked figure hovered behind Talyana, a blade held to her throat. Mikira's mind flashed back to the last room, when she'd sworn she'd seen someone, and she cursed herself for not trusting her eyes.

The man beckoned with an empty hand. "The certificate."

"Don't—" Talyana cut off as the knife bit into her skin, a bead of blood tracing the column of her throat.

"If you hurt her, I'll kill you," Mikira snarled. The man only gestured again.

Slowly, Mikira pulled the folded certificate from her pocket. But rather than hand it to him, she tossed it onto the table beside them. If he wanted it that badly, he'd have to release Talyana to get it.

The man shoved Talyana toward her and darted for the table. Mikira caught Talyana with one arm and commanded her knife to fly after the attacker with the other. It soared through the air of its own accord and struck him—handle first.

Mikira cursed as the man seized a chair, flinging it at them and forcing them to duck. By the time they regained their feet, he'd vanished. Mikira charged after him. He wouldn't be able to leave with the document; the Vault's antitheft charms would ensure it. Which meant he had to stay in the building until he could copy the information over—she jerked to a halt.

Sitting in the middle of the corridor, nothing more than a pile of smoking ash, were the remains of the death certificate.

CHAPTER 8

ARIELLE

ARI SHIFTED IN her chair, unable to get comfortable. Rivkah's parting look of despair had haunted her into the night, and she'd woken up feeling even more exhausted than when she'd gone to sleep, something that was becoming more and more frequent. She originally thought the culprit might be Damien, who she sat up with when his nightmares woke her, but he hadn't disturbed her at all last night, and she'd still felt like a lead weight all afternoon.

Her thoughts moved like mud as she tried to focus on the book splayed in her lap. With Damien at his first council meeting and Reid hovering over a microscope inspecting her blood, she'd decided to try to learn more about the Heretic inside her. But so little documentation remained after the Burning, when the Sendian Church incinerated nearly all of Enderlain's records on magic after the Cataclysm a century ago. Even the one she had was a secondhand account, and she'd reread the same page twice now in her delirium.

The thrum of magic preceded the Heretic's surprisingly gentle voice: *Perhaps you should rest.*

Sure, right after you tell me what you want, Ari countered.

She expected the silence that followed, but it still grated on her. As much as she tried to control it, she couldn't deny the steadily growing pit of fear coiled inside her chest. Her body was not her own, her magic more unwieldy than ever, and she couldn't shake the feeling that whatever the spirit wanted from her, it would not end well.

What were you and your friends trying to accomplish? Ari pressed. All she knew was that the four of them had been pushing the boundaries of magic when they caused the Cataclysm, destroying much of Kinahara and leaving the rest uninhabitable, but what had their goal been?

A beat of silence followed before the Heretic said, *They were not my friends.*

"Ow, Widget!" The sound of claws in cloth followed Reid's hiss of pain, and the tiny cat appeared a moment later on his shoulder, where he promptly curled up.

Sighing, Ari closed her book and retrieved a cup of chamomile tea from the drink cart, setting it on the desk beside Reid's empty one. "Any progress?"

Reid held Widget in place with one hand while he leaned forward to peer into his microscope. "Yes, I discovered a heretofore-unknown cell after only hours of study, and rather than tell you, I thought it'd be fun to stay craned over a microscope for the rest of the day."

"Reid." Ari didn't mean for her desperation to escape, but it simmered so close to the surface she felt in danger of coming apart.

He lifted his head a fraction, enough for her to catch the solemnity in his gaze. "I'll figure it out, Ari. I promise."

Ari nodded, forcing a slow breath. She had to believe that, had to trust that Rezek was not her only hope of ever seeing her sister again, of ever feeling safe. It was one of the reasons she hadn't reached out to Mikira either. The girl had been through enough as it was; Ari didn't want to put her in more danger.

The suite door clicked open, and Damien entered, sweeping raindrops from his dark hair. His olive skin was flushed from the heat of the carriage, and he took one look at Ari's evident distress and made straight for her. Her body moved of its own accord, already seeking the comfort of his arms the moment he descended the steps.

He enveloped her, the warmth of him eating away at the chill of her thoughts. His sheer presence was enough to steady her, his voice a gentle rumble as he asked, "What do you need?"

"Just this." She gave herself another moment just to breathe before she pulled away. "I'm all right."

Damien's attention remained squarely on her, his concern palpable, so she made a point of showing him she meant it. She retrieved a cup of tea and settled comfortably on the chaise. Only then did he seem satisfied, his gaze shifting to a stack of papers on the desk.

He frowned as he picked them up. "Reid, did you go through these?"

Reid didn't look up from the microscope. "I straightened them."

A muscle flexed in Damien's jaw, and he tossed the papers back onto the desk with unexpected vehemence before retreating to the fire. Reid's eyes met Ari's with an unspoken question. Had Damien left those out on purpose to see if anyone moved them?

He'd been even more careful than usual the last couple weeks, tightening security around the manor and refreshing the defensive enchantments on the family coaches. She knew Hyle's decision to work for Loic had gotten under his skin nearly as much as the situation with Mikira, but she was starting to think she'd underestimated the impact.

Reid's gaze tracked Damien to the fire. "How did the council meeting go?"

"The draft tax and exemption fee have been eliminated," Damien replied as if he hadn't just made one of the most momentous changes Enderlain had seen in a decade. "The news should be out within the hour."

There was a glint in his eye that had Ari leaning over her knees toward him. "And?"

The corner of his lips curved. "The king has initiated the Royal Ascension. Whoever of royal blood finds the Ranier prince first takes the throne. I've offered to help Darius."

She didn't need Damien to elaborate to know where his mind had gone: if he put Darius on the throne, the prince would be in his debt, and Damien would have a direct line to an easily influenced king. Still, Reid looked momentarily expectant, as though he thought Damien would continue, and Ari found she did too. Not because his plan didn't seem like enough, but because of the look in his eye. One she doubted he was even aware of, or else he would have cut it away.

Damien knew her in a way no one else did, understood her, and she him, and that was why she knew that he had not told them everything.

ARI FOLDED UP her newspaper, the jarring of the enchanted coach threatening to make her ill. The news of the council's decision had been in every paper within the hour, each one giving credit for the sweeping tax changes to House Adair, and she wondered how many of them Damien had prepped in advance should he succeed.

He sat with his head on his fist, his elbow propped against the seam of the carriage window. It bordered so drastically on irreverent that she could only surmise he was deep in thought, but she liked the way it softened his edges. It made her want to trace the lines of him.

The city flashed by in rows of crooked brick buildings and brief glimpses of the Greystel River as they crossed Roughshaw Bridge into what had once been Kelbra territory. The district belonged to one of the two lesser houses that now fell under House Adair's jurisdiction.

Houses Zalaire and Thielan handled the day-to-day responsibilities of their districts, but they did the bare minimum, investing as little as possible back into the streets of their people. Damien intended to change that by redirecting the draft tax and exemption fee funds into the community, but that was not the purpose for this trip.

They were on the hunt.

It was the sort of thing Reid usually did with Damien, but with the boy focused entirely on his search for the enchanter cell, Ari had volunteered to come. Though she knew Damien had plenty of others at his disposal, he'd been working with them less and less the last few days.

The enchanted coach came to a halt in Canburrow Square, and they emerged from the carriage to the sweet scent of caramel. A confectioner's shop had its door open nearby, a line stretching outside of excited children and lovers arm in arm. Shoppers peered curiously into wide display windows, and a violinist tuned their instrument by the central fountain.

Damien proffered a folded paper to her. "This is who we're looking for."

She unfurled it to find a photograph of a young woman with short black hair and an angular face, Aslir's fang looped around her neck alongside a crescent moon charm with a Kenzeni symbol of strength that Ari recognized. On the back someone had drawn a family crest: the same fang against a circular backdrop, the name Arkizien written beneath.

"Not long before the Illinir, one of my spies picked up chatter that the king had begun quietly searching for the Ranier prince," he explained as she handed back the paper. "Hyle found a birth certificate he suspected belonged to the prince in the Vault, signed by two families: Arkizien and Dalart. An Elidon Dalart served as a royal guard at that time, but Hyle couldn't find any sign of him."

"So you want to find an Arkizien instead," she surmised.

"The *only* Arkizien." He tucked the paper back into his pocket. "The rest of her family is dead. My informants say she's a retired army medic who runs a clinic here."

Ari slid her arm through his, pulling tight. "See?" she teased at his sudden openness. "That wasn't so difficult, was it?"

Damien's gaze cut to her with an unexpected intensity. She stilled, feeling as though he was on the verge of saying something important—then his expression softened, and he trailed the tips of his fingers along the edge of her face as if reminding himself that she was truly there.

"Nothing is, with you," he said.

Ari kissed his cheek. "Let's start on the far side."

They picked their way through the Illinir decorations still littering the square. Strings of lapis lazuli scales strung together in emulation of Lyzairin's serpentine body hung over doorways, the cobblestones littered with crimson Skylis feathers that crackled underfoot. A Rach mask perched on the fountain's edge, emerald ribbons ensnared on its arching horns, and above it all towered Aslir, the once pure white of his leonine body stained with soot from the factories.

It felt wrong to see the Harbingers used so carelessly, then cast aside to wilt beneath Enderlain's autumn rain. Kinnism forbade the creation of idols like these, but the Enderlish treated them like baubles, just another thing to be chewed up and spat out by this city's greed.

They found the medical center tucked away in a corner. A line of hunched gray shapes extended out the door, people with missing limbs and stretches of burnt skin. Many wore threadbare military fatigues, veterans discarded after their usefulness ran out; others were barely Rivkah's age or younger, children huddled together without a parent to guide them.

This kingdom's avarice knows no bounds, rumbled the Heretic. *It will consume even itself.*

There was something in the spirit's voice that disquieted Ari, an undercurrent of anger, not of injustice, but of disgust.

They are not responsible for this, Ari countered, but the Heretic only hummed.

The center had seen better days, and though the inside was clean, the enchanted lights were in dire need of refreshment and half the windows were boarded up. People shifted out of Damien's way as he approached the harried-looking receptionist at the front. "I'm looking for Zivaya Arkizien."

"Do you have an appoint—" The woman cut off as she lifted her head. "Apologies, High Lord Adair. I'll get her now." She disappeared into the back, returning alongside a golden-skinned woman in a white coat with a slight limp. She had the bearing of a soldier, and her dark eyes evaluated them swiftly before she indicated for them to follow her out the side door.

"Peace be upon you," Ari said in Kinnish as the door clicked shut behind them.

Zivaya's posture softened. "And unto you, peace."

"We apologize for interrupting your day, Dr. Arkizien," Damien continued in Kinnish. "I'd just like to ask you a few questions, and we'll be out of your way."

The doctor inclined her head. "Very well."

"Someone in your family witnessed a birth," Damien began, and the shift in Zivaya's expression told them everything they needed to know. Her easy air turned wary once more, and Ari instinctively burned verillion, threading an enchantment for strength.

"You have the wrong person." Zivaya edged toward the door. "If you'll excuse me—"

"I don't expect information for free," Damien said, and the doctor stilled. "What you're doing here is vital to this community, but you're clearly understaffed, and your facility is one health inspector's visit away from being shut down."

Zivaya's hands curled into fists. "Is that a threat?"

"It's an observation," Ari cut in. Damien didn't need her help making bargains, but he did have a way of making every offer sound like it had teeth. "One we'd like to change, in exchange for answers."

The doctor's hesitation only intensified—then the fight drained from her like a snuffed candle. "You're looking for the Ranier prince." She said it like a curse. "My mother is the one you want, though you won't find her. She grew paranoid that someone would come looking for her after the prince's birth, and the stress ate away at her. She took her own life."

Damien inclined his head. "May her memory be a blessing."

Zivaya closed her eyes, releasing a quiet breath. "I do know someone who can help you, but in exchange, I ask that you fully restore my clinic."

"Done," Damien replied.

"His name is Elidon Dalart," Zivaya said. "But he goes by Elidon Shaw now."

Ari tuned out the sound of their voices, her attention captured by something she couldn't explain. It was a feeling that crept down her spine and pooled in her gut. A familiar humming rose in the back of her mind, making her think at first that she'd only sensed the Heretic awakening, except—there, the scrape of boots on stone.

She flared her verillion just as the voice cried, *Above!*

Ari knocked a flying blade from the air. It sliced her palm, but the verillion healed her nearly instantly. Then ropes appeared along the walls, two figures descending into the alley behind them, their faces obscured by blue-and-white scaled Lyzairin masks.

"Assassins," she breathed as Damien drew a revolver.

"Don't move," said a voice behind them. They spun to find a third assailant holding a gun to Zivaya's head. "We just want the little lord. There's no need for the two of you to die too."

"Did Royce send you?" Damien's revolver rested at his side, his finger on the trigger.

The gun wielder shrugged. "That hardly matters."

A flicker of movement caught Ari's attention. Zivaya was tapping her fingers against her leg in a steady rhythm. Ari had heard of a code soldiers used to communicate, and she had no hope of reading it, but the message was clear from the look in Zivaya's eyes: *Be ready.*

"You can have him." Ari held up her hands, injecting a tremor into her voice. "Please, just let us go."

"Wise choice." The moment the gun wielder lifted the barrel toward Damien, Zivaya moved. She dropped into a crouch, sweeping her leg through the assassin's ankles. The gun went off, but Ari had stepped between him and Damien. The bullet caught Ari in the side, and then Damien's arm was reaching over her shoulder. He fired once, and the assassin stilled.

The bullet clattered to the ground, forced from Ari's side by the healing tissue as a thrumming burst free in her mind. Then she was moving, but not of her own accord. It was like that moment at the closing ball; her mind was still present, but her body was not her own.

She descended upon the two other attackers, her fist breaking the ribs of one, her elbow cracking the skull of another. Her magic roared more fiercely, and distantly she felt the Heretic's laughter, as palpable as the sudden bloodlust curling through her.

"Stop!" she shrieked, but it felt like screaming underwater, like no matter how hard she tried, no one would ever hear her. Then her vision darkened.

She came back to herself with her arm pressed to Damien's throat.

She had him pinned against the wall, his windpipe impossibly delicate beneath her forearm. His fingers pried at her, but her strength enchantment was too strong. Too powerful—for him, for this city, for this kingdom that had stolen so much from her.

A piece of her recognized that she was killing him, that whoever deserved this unending well of anger inside of her, it was not him. She loved him, she—

Ari gasped, ripping control back from the Heretic. Damien sucked in a ragged breath, only just keeping his footing, his pupils blown wide enough to overtake the gray.

"Your eyes changed again," he rasped. "I couldn't bring you back."

"I'm sorry," she whispered. Then, more desperately, "I'm so sorry."

Around her, the assassins were dead, their bodies broken in ways she didn't remember doing. She looked to the blood on her hands, a sight that no longer fazed her, and remembered another night, another death. Her Saba's pained cries, her sister's fearful screams. Bone breaking. Blood, hot and sticky and suffocating.

Why are you doing this to me? she demanded.

Who is to say what is I, and what is you? replied the Heretic.

Ari shook her head, backing into the alley wall as if she might escape the voice threading through her veins. *You want to hurt them—the Enderlish. And you're using me to do it.*

She felt the Heretic's satisfaction like a thrum deep in her belly. *I am* helping *you to do it. Don't you see, little lion? You wanted trust—I give you strength. This is what true power looks like.*

A shiver rattled Ari's spine and Damien pulled her close. She clung to him, to the knowledge that she could have killed him, and tried to remember how to breathe.

"You have my thanks for your help here," Damien said over her shoulder to the doctor. "I'll see my end of the bargain held." Then he was ushering Ari out of the alley and into their waiting coach, which carried them swiftly away.

Ari wrapped her arms about herself, the silence of the cab quickly growing full of unspoken questions. In it, Damien flicked his mother's pocket watch open and shut with a fervor she'd never seen. It snapped shut a final time, and his hand closed in a fist over it. "Why didn't you tell me you were still blacking out?"

"I thought I had it handled." At least well enough to wait for Reid to find the enchanter cell. She hadn't been blacking out, hadn't been waking up in unexpected places.

Damien leaned toward her, the motion jarring her back to the present. "Arielle," he said. "You're losing control."

"And there could be nothing worse as far as you're concerned," she muttered, even as her stomach clenched in agreement. The feeling of his throat pinned beneath her forearm was seared into her memory to the point of nausea.

He withdrew slowly, a new understanding forming in his expression. "Are you angry with me?"

She didn't know how to explain the overwhelming knot of emotion forming in her chest. The pain, the guilt—the fear. She needed air.

She seized the door handle. "I need to walk."

Flinging open the coach door, she descended onto the cobblestone street in a frantic rush. Damien frowned down at her from his seat, his knuckles gone white from where they clutched the pocket watch. "It isn't safe for you to be alone right now."

"Those assassins were after you, not me." She lifted her ring-laden hand. "And I can take care of myself. I'll see you back at the manor."

She knew that she was being unfair, that he was only worried for her well-being, but this conversation strayed too close to the truth. Right now, she needed space to think, to decide her next move, so she turned on her heel, heading north along Tea Street toward Ettinger.

The truth was she hadn't told Damien that the blackouts were still happening because doing so meant telling him about Rezek too. It meant explaining that she'd lost control of her body to the Heretic in the midst of the closing ball and come face-to-face with the only person who could truly help her.

A person Damien would never accept.

He had been betrayed by the people closest to him again and again. Rezek, Mikira, Hyle, Reid—she couldn't be another name on that list. He wouldn't survive it. *They* wouldn't survive it, and she would not lose him.

But she could not keep putting him in danger either.

What if next time she didn't regain control in time? What if it was Rivkah's or Mikira's throat beneath her arm? After everything she'd done to learn to use her power, she would not let it take someone she loved from her again.

If that meant accepting Rezek's help, then so be it.

CHAPTER 9

Damien

DAMIEN SAT VERY still.

It felt like if he moved, he'd never stop. He'd tear through the coach door and anyone who stood on the other side if only so that he could *do* something. Anything other than sit here as Arielle walked away, terrified and angry, and all the same emotions spiking through him.

He'd missed something vital. She'd been angry with him in a way he'd never seen before, and he didn't think it was just about what he'd said. Still, he wished he'd said it differently. That he'd only told her that he was worried about her. He knew what her power meant to her, but he also knew that it couldn't be separated from the Heretic.

Every time she used it, that thing's connection to her grew stronger, and he was supposed to be *helping* her with it. Instead, he'd pushed her away. But she'd lied to him. Kept things from him so that he thought she was all right when in truth—in truth, he didn't know what was happening to her. He'd turned to every book, every journal he owned, and nothing said a word about the blackouts. If ever that knowledge had existed, it turned to ash in the Burning.

His fist slammed into the coach door.

It was the only thing he allowed himself, that one burst of anger at the ineffectiveness searing through him. Then he locked it away. Losing himself to emotion would fix nothing, and he had to trust that Reid's investigation into the enchanter cell would bear fruit.

In the meantime, he had a prince to find.

IT WAS WELL outside the morning visiting hours when Damien arrived at the Anthir headquarters, but they let him in anyway. He followed a constable to the end of the cells, where she opened another door, granting Damien entrance to a private room with a single cell. He stepped inside, waiting until she'd left before approaching the hunkered shape in the corner.

Loic didn't greet him, offering him the same interest he showed the amenities Damien had secured for him. The blanket lay balled up in the far corner. The books Loic had reduced to a pile of scattered pages. He'd even gone so far as to refuse to wash, his beard beginning to grow out and his hair dusting the edges of his vision.

Something insidious inside Damien rumbled with satisfaction at the sight. Growing up, everyone had liked Loic. He was charming, handsome, and loud, whereas Damien had always been quiet and contemplative. He'd worked hard to earn the respect of those around him and found a deeper level of connection with them than his brother's shallow camaraderie, but it didn't stop people from flocking to Loic like sheep.

A part of him had always been jealous of that, the same part that saw his brother locked in a cell and thought it no less than he deserved. He gave himself one moment to revel in that selfishness, and then he sealed it away. No matter what had happened between them, Loic was still his brother, still an Adair.

"I thought I told you not to visit again." Loic tapped one finger against the gray stone floor of the cell. "You never did listen to me."

He had. Once. When Loic's respect had meant something to him. Then his brother had witnessed Rezek murder their mother and done nothing to stop it, and that desire had died right along with her.

"Your advice was rarely worth taking," Damien replied with a quiet bitterness. "It only ever served you."

That wasn't entirely true, but it felt good to say. There'd been a time when Loic had looked out for his siblings. When Damien and Shira had been worth fighting for. But with each passing day, he became more like the Enderlish elite he'd once despised, and now Damien hardly recognized him.

Loic chuckled darkly, tilting his head back against the stone. "Why are you here, Dara?" His Kinnish name was its own weapon in Loic's hands, a reminder that his brother never went by his.

"I brought you something." Damien pulled his father's signet ring from his pocket and tossed it between the bars. Loic caught it, brow knotting as he turned it over in his hands. Damien half expected for him to send it flying back—their father had chosen Damien as heir after all, and Loic hadn't even requested furlough to attend his funeral—but Loic just stared at it.

Damien gave him a moment before he asked, "Are you familiar with an Elidon Shaw?" He might never have approved of the company his brother kept, but there was no denying Loic was well-connected among the nobility and their compatriots.

Loic snorted, pocketing the ring. "Of course. The real reason for your visit at last."

"If you don't know—"

"Elidon Shaw is a recluse known for throwing parties he never attends," Loic snapped, always quick to rise to bait. "If I'm not mistaken, Eridice is fast approaching."

"In three days," Damien confirmed. A yearly holiday that celebrated the Goddess Sendia's mercy, Erice was an excuse people used for lavish parties. If Shaw was already known for his events, he'd likely be hosting one.

Damien had only to secure an invitation.

He started to leave, but his brother's voice floated over his shoulder. "Will you go yourself, now that Hyle's gone?"

Damien stilled despite himself. He could practically feel Loic's satisfaction as he turned slowly back around.

"Though I hear he isn't the only one who abandoned you," Loic said lightly, as if he hadn't been the one to turn Damien's foremost spy against him. "There's that little Rusel girl too. How long before your enchanter deserts you too?"

The question hooked sharp talons under his skin, and he thought again of Arielle's arm at his throat, the secrets that she'd kept. What else wasn't she telling him?

Loic made a low tsking noise. "Or perhaps she already has. What a pity. You do have a hard time holding on to people, don't you?"

He knew what Loic was doing, knew that he was trying to carve out some vestige of control, and yet Damien couldn't block out his words. The list of betrayals was beginning to feel endless, as if everyone's name would inevitably be inscribed there. Even Reid had lied to him, keeping the truth of Mikira's possession of his signet ring from him.

He knew better than to fire back at Loic directly, so he sought something he knew would vex him just as deeply.

"I had my first council meeting." He watched Loic's face harden with jealousy. Loic never had been able to control his emotions like his siblings, and Damien knew how much his success would rile him. "My influence with them is tenuous for now, but I'm working to steady it."

Loic snorted derisively. "Then you have what you always wanted: more power than anyone else around you. How does it feel to be a god, little brother?"

Damien gritted his teeth. "This has nothing to do with power. It's about changing the way things are. It's about *fixing* them."

"So you keep telling yourself, and anyone who will listen." Loic tilted his head to the side. "You always were a good liar."

"It's not a lie." He *didn't* lie, and his brother knew that, just like he knew what words would slip beneath Damien's skin.

Loic pressed a hand to the wall behind him, guiding himself to his feet. He looked a little unsteady when he stood, and Damien wondered if he'd been eating the extra rations he'd been paying for. Judging by the state of everything else Damien had tried to give him, likely not.

"Do you truly believe that you've made it?" Loic stepped toward him. "That those fools in their gemstone jackets and gilded halls care anything for your opinion? Cassian's the only decent one among them."

"I know who I'm dealing with, Loic," Damien replied. He knew how Royce and Niekla looked at him, how they accused him of wanting to take power as if they weren't doing the very same. At least he wanted to make a difference with it, while they hoarded it for themselves.

Loic halted just behind the bars, his fingers threading about the metal. "Everything you are is nothing but a threat to them, Dara. It's bad enough that you want to do things differently; how would it look if the one to change Enderlain was not one of them, but the son of two immigrants? Of countries Enderlain was meant to have crushed? At best you'll humiliate them; at worst you're everything they fear come to take revenge."

It was nothing Damien didn't already know, yet it still rankled him. Where Shira had thrown herself into their Kinnish heritage and Loic had rejected it, he'd toed the line of his identity for years, unable to fully embrace it for fear of what it would mean, yet nonetheless tied to it.

All it took was a single word of Kinnish, one whisper of his other name, and the people he'd spent years establishing relationships with suddenly saw him as something foreign and unknown.

Something dangerous.

Being Celairen wasn't much better. The city was full of refugees fleeing the Eternal War that the Enderlish saw as competition for jobs, or drains on resources, never as the consequence of their government's choices. Did they whisper the same of him since he'd ascended to the council? Was he only a thief in their eyes?

Loic pressed his face to the bars. "If you continue on this path, they'll destroy you."

To anyone else, it might have sounded as if Loic cared. As if he were trying to protect his little brother from a terrible fate. But Loic had not seen him as a brother for a very, very long time. Not since their mother's death, which Loic had blamed him for from the beginning.

No, he didn't care. He just wanted Damien to be afraid.

"I can handle them just fine," Damien replied, though the memory of that afternoon's attack sat heavy in the back of his mind. He was certain Royce or Niekla had sent the assassins, spurred by his tax proposal, but that wasn't what concerned him. He wanted to know how they'd found him.

He wanted to know if there was a spy in his midst.

One corner of Loic's mouth curved in a mocking smile. "I've been running in these people's circles for years; you'll never be anything but the boy who stole from them."

Damien leaned close as he whispered, "I'll take that over being their lapdog."

Loic seized his wrist. He tried to pull free, but his brother had always been stronger than him, and Loic dragged him to the bars. "If you think I'm going to allow Father's decision to stand for a second, think again, little brother. I will get out of here, and when I do, I will take everything from you."

Damien searched his brother's gaze, looking for something familiar, but all that stared back was an empty void desperate to consume. He'd intended to find a way to free Loic, to start over in the name of family, but the brother he knew had been gone for a long time. He simply hadn't let himself see it.

"No," Damien said softly. "You'll rot in here until you die."

He ripped his arm free.

"Goodbye, Loic."

Damien swept from the cell, ignoring the insults Loic hurled after him, and slammed the door shut behind him. The silence felt like a physical presence after the tension of their conversation, and in it his mind whirled like a gear seeking purchase. His fingers sought his mother's pocket watch, and he resisted the urge to flip it open and shut.

He would prove Loic wrong. He'd do whatever he had to.

He would save Enderlain from itself, even if he first had to tear it down brick by brick.

CHAPTER 10

MIKIRA

MIKIRA'S EXHAUSTION SETTLED over her like a shroud as she finished brushing down Atara and trudged toward the house. After trying and failing to find their attacker from the Vault, she'd parted ways with Talyana, who'd returned to the rebel headquarters to report in. She suspected the man had been working for someone else looking for the prince, likely Prince Darius or a council member, but that was all the information they had.

"Kira!" Nelda called from the study doorway as Mikira entered. She had a wooden spoon clutched in her hand, her apron dusted with flour. "You're just in time for dinner."

"I'm not hungry," Mikira said tiredly, already moving toward the stairs. Nelda's face crumpled into her mothering scowl, and she cut off Mikira's retreat.

"You've missed dinner three days in a row now." Nelda gestured at her with the spoon.

Mikira leaned back to avoid it. "I'm exhausted, Nelda."

"And you don't have time for us anymore." Nelda folded her arms. "I get it."

"That's not true. I—" She pressed a hand to her forehead, forcing a breath. Everything she was doing—revitalizing the ranch, working with the rebels—was for them. But Nelda didn't know half the strain she was under. To her, it just looked as if Mikira didn't care.

"Okay," she said. "Let's have dinner."

Nelda released a squeal of excitement, all but dragging her into the kitchen. Ailene and their father were already seated at the small table, upon which sat a roasted chicken with carrots and potatoes and a fresh loaf of bread.

This was the other reason Mikira wanted to avoid family meals—her father.

He looked surprised to see her, but let the moment pass as Ailene continued rattling off a list of historical facts about the gemstone mining industry that she'd learned in school and Nelda fussed over whether the vegetables had too much salt. Mikira ate hers in silence, trying to focus on her sisters rather than the litany of problems resounding in her brain.

Suddenly the food was gone, and Nelda and Ailene were washing the dishes, and it was just her and her father at the table.

"Kira," he said softly. "I still need to speak with you."

A list of ready-made excuses rose to her lips, but the look in her father's eyes stopped her. It was the same one he'd had the day he marched into Rezek's coach, straight-backed and clear-eyed. She nodded and followed him to his study, closing the door behind them as he picked up a little black notebook from the desk. It was the journal he'd left for her to read with his notes about bloodstones and her knives.

"Did you read this?" he asked.

She folded her arms. "I did."

"Then you know about the knives?"

"I do." Her eyes flitted to the blades at her hips, their bloodstone-set hilts glinting in the sunlight. Her knowledge of enchanting was limited to what Ari had taught her and the complex game of inheritance that came with breeding enchants, but even she knew that there were only four gemstones capable of binding enchantments.

Yet here were her knives, charmed by a fifth.

She'd spent some time experimenting with them since the Illinir, giving them different commands: *fly straight, hit that tree, cut this apple in half*. At first, the knives had responded half-heartedly, and she'd learned that the enchantment performed best when she truly focused her intent. Half wanting something made for poor results. Still, she struggled to control them, and after today's failure, she intended to spend more time training with them.

"Rezek knows about the bloodstones too," her father said grimly. "He's running some sort of experiment in the cells beneath his manor. I don't know the details, only that it's why he's been seeking unlicensed enchanters like me, to do work for him off the books."

Mikira wanted nothing more to do with Rezek. She wanted to clamp her hands over her ears and say it was not her responsibility, not her job to witness Rezek's atrocities and put an end to them. But she'd learned by now that if she did nothing, neither would anything change.

She faced her father, who held out a small vial of clear liquid. "I stole some of what he was working on, but to be frank, I'm not sure who to report something like this to."

Mikira took the vial from him, pocketing it. "I know someone who can help."

Shira might have an idea of where to start, though the person she'd really thought of was Reid. Her heart gave a hollow pang at the impossibility, her mind conjuring the way he'd looked at her at the Vault, as if it pained him.

Her father hesitated before he asked quietly, "A rebel someone?"

She stilled. The sudden urge to tell him everything nearly overwhelmed her, to beg him to take this responsibility from her, to fix it like he was meant to. But she'd learned long ago not to rely on other people to rescue her. If she wanted something done, she had to do it herself.

"You're not the only one with connections." Her father moved toward her. "I've heard rumors that you and High Lord Adair are at odds, so if it's not him you're going to, then—"

"It doesn't matter," she cut across him. "I'll handle it."

Her father stopped short, one hand curling atop the other against his stomach. "It matters to me, Kira. I'm worried about you. The rebellion is dangerous. You—"

"No." Mikira bit the word out with all the control she could muster. "You don't get to do this. You don't get to worry about me *now*."

He recoiled. "I've always worried about you."

She let out a bitter laugh. "Then where were you when I was riding illegal races to put food on the table? Where were you when I went door to door looking for a single soul in this city willing to buy our horses? Where were you—" Her voice pitched low. "Where were you when they took Lochlyn?"

A stark sort of pain twisted her father's expression, and he let his hand fall to his side. She knew it wasn't fair, that her father couldn't have stopped those men from taking Lochlyn, but he hadn't done *anything*.

"I know I haven't always been there to protect you the way I should have," he began, and she swallowed back a scornful sound. "But I'm here now, and what you're doing, Kira—it's going to put all of us in danger. Haven't we been through enough? This isn't your fight. Come home and let the people who are equipped to handle this do their jobs. Please."

But Mikira was already shaking her head. "Don't you get it? That's how they win. When people like us decide to sit back and let someone else handle it. But that's what you've always done, isn't it?"

Her father flinched. "I just don't want you to get hurt. I don't want your sisters to lose someone else."

"I'm doing this *for* them. For you, and everyone like us in Enderlain who has had to bow and scrape and grind themselves into dust just to survive!" Mikira's voice trembled. "You had your chance to care. Don't try to be my father now."

The words seemed to take something from him, his shoulders falling. She at once wished she could take back what she'd said and was glad she'd finally given voice to the vortex inside her. She loved her father, and she knew that he wasn't the enemy, but she couldn't help wishing that he'd been a little stronger . . . so that she didn't have to be.

He pressed his palms against his eyes, forcing a deep breath, and when he spoke, his voice was steadier than she'd ever heard it. "I'm taking the girls away from Veradell. It isn't safe here."

His eyes found hers, and Mikira steeled herself against the words she knew were coming. "Come with us, Kira. It isn't too late to make another choice."

She expected it to stoke her anger, to want to turn him away without hesitation, but she wanted so badly to say yes. To leave Enderlain to the rebels, to Damien, to the wolves to fight over until only scraps remained. She wanted open fields and the wind in her hair. She wanted the sound of horses against the backdrop of her sisters' laughter.

She wanted peace and safety, the likes of which she'd never known.

But she couldn't have those things so long as Enderlain remained the same. So long as people like Lochlyn kept dying in the Eternal War. She couldn't turn her back on something she knew she could change.

"I can't." The words were all she could manage.

The disappointment in her father's gaze nearly broke her. Then he was before her, his long arms wrapping securely around her, and she pressed her face into his chest, into the familiar scent of old books and fresh hay, and bit her tongue hard enough to bleed because she would not, *could not* fall apart now.

"I'll fix this," she said into the knit of his sweater. "I promise."

"I love you." He kissed the crown of her head. "I'll tell the girls."

Mikira remained where she was as he left. She held on to the feeling of her father's arms around her, on to the knowledge that what she did, she did for them, and everyone like them.

She held on to it and prayed it would be enough.

CHAPTER 11

ARIELLE

ARI WALKED UNTIL the fire in her veins calmed, her feet carrying her along the familiar path of Ettinger Street. High-end dress shops and stores full of ancient antiques lined the cobblestones beside confectioners with sweets priced at a day's wages and pubs with towering glass windows revealing polished oak bars and rich leather chairs.

She was dressed nicely enough to blend in with those milling along the streets, yet eyes still followed her as she went. Reflexively, she tucked her Saba's necklace beneath her collar, walking a little quicker.

As the shops began to dwindle and the path turned from stone to packed earth, the scent of roses filled the evening air. Kelbra Manor sat just on the edge of the city proper, surrounded by acres of verillion. The long-stemmed plants swayed in the evening breeze, their golden light soft as a candle's glow. The gates were open, the drive deserted.

Ari felt like a gathering storm as she stopped at the edge of the gate. She'd reconsidered her decision enough times that the arguments had taken on a life of their own, flying back and forth inside her mind in rapid fire.

Rezek was the only one that could help her.

Damien would never forgive her.

She could have *killed* him.

It was that which had finally driven her here, the feeling of Damien's throat beneath her arm. After everything she'd done, everything she'd learned in order to control her magic so that she would never hurt someone like she had her Saba again, she would not go back to where she'd begun—terrified of her own power.

She started up the drive, the cloying scent of roses suffocating her senses.

The Heretic's presence surged into her mind with a hum. *You shouldn't be here,* it warned. *Leave before it's too late.*

You do not command me, Ari thought back, and ignored the twinge of fear in her chest that told her otherwise. But that was why she was here; she was losing control, and she couldn't wait for Reid to fix it. If Rezek had answers, then she had to at least ask.

An idea occurred to her then, and she slowed at the base of the manor stairs. *If you don't want me here, then stop me,* she said. When the Heretic didn't immediately reply, Ari pressed, *You can't, can you? You used up all your strength earlier. Even you have your limits.*

Ari felt the Heretic's presence retreat, and she climbed the steps and knocked before her doubt could stop her. A few moments later, the door cracked open.

Rezek Kelbra stared at her, and she at him.

She'd half expected him to be out hunting the Ranier prince too, but with his house's fall, he seemed to have lost all interest in posturing. Gone were his diamond-studded waistcoat and jacket, replaced by a loosely buttoned shirt. Gone was the neat style to his bun of copper hair, now scattered across his shoulders. Gone was the sharp, sleek predator she remembered, replaced by someone hollow-eyed and sickly pale.

There was something undeniably forlorn about him now, a bitter exhaustion years in the making.

"Are you going to invite me in?" She forced the words out through gritted teeth.

He moved aside, and she brushed past him, trying not to feel as though she'd just stepped into the jaws of a beast. She was standing face-to-face with a man she despised, thinking about all the ways she might take him apart should this be a trap. In turn, Rezek regarded her with the sharp, ice-blue gaze of a wolf about to pounce. Unlike Damien, his injuries from the final race had healed thanks to verillion, the rake of her golem hawk's claws gone from his eye.

Ari surveyed the manor. What had once been a vibrant and richly furnished foyer had clearly been neglected. The floor hadn't been cleaned since before the ball, the high ceilings gathering cobwebs. Several enchanted lights had gone out, leaving holes of darkness like watchful eyes, and the furniture appeared as though someone had taken a baton to it.

"Have you seen enough?" Rezek asked with a forced lightness. There was something about the way he spoke that made it seem as if his words always carried an underlying threat. In response, Ari burned verillion. It filled her with an instant buzzing warmth, a reminder that should she need it, she could bind a strength enchantment fast enough to defend herself.

"What happened here?" she asked, though she thought she knew. Only days ago, Rezek had lost everything to House Adair. His family's right to run the decadal Illinir. The Kelbras' place as one of the four great noble houses. His father, murdered by Damien's brother. There was only so much one could take before they spiraled apart, as destructive as any storm.

Rezek's gaze flicked over her as if seeking something beneath her skin, and she repressed a shiver. "I think you know something of losing yourself," he replied tightly, his eyes dropping to the bloodied spot at her side. "It appears someone's been using you as target practice."

"It's not the first time." That honor belonged to him.

The Rezek she knew would have offered her a caustic smile and an even more biting response, but this one hardly seemed to have the energy.

"If we're comparing wounds," he said tiredly, "I distinctly remember your golem hawk trying to claw my face off."

"You tried to kill my boyfriend."

At that, Rezek actually *flinched.* She stared at him in open astonishment before he swept past her. "Well, now that we've each attempted to kill the other at least once, why don't you tell me why you're here."

She followed him. "You offered me answers."

"I suppose I did." He led her through hallways she expected to be full of servants but found vacant and disarrayed. They veered through a set of doors with enchanted glass panels, each with a flutter of falling white feathers reflective of the Kelbras' lost crest of Aslir.

A large sitting room spread before her, wrapped in wall-to-wall bookcases. A spiral staircase in one corner led to an open second-floor hallway with more books, and a third floor above that. It was a library more extensive than she'd ever seen, more than even Damien's, and she longed to explore every shelf.

Rezek went straight for a drink cart, and the similarity of the motion to Damien's left her off-kilter. But where Damien was controlled and purposeful in everything he did, Rezek poured and consumed his drink as if he relished the way it set him on fire from the inside.

Ari lingered in the doorway, not quite willing to abandon her escape route. "Your eyes—they were white, like mine when the Heretic takes control, and that book . . . was it—"

"A Racari." Rezek poured himself another drink. "Just like the one you have, and like mine." His eyes flitted to a great oak desk centered on the far wall. Upon it sat a dark leather tome, similar to the spellbook she'd taken from her Saba's workroom. A feeling like an invisible string tugging at her chest drew her toward it, but she resisted.

"Then you're possessed by a Heretic too." She felt a strange sense of relief at the words.

A friend of yours? she asked the voice, but there was no answer. She'd have expected the Heretic to jump at the chance to speak to one of its old collaborators, who it likely hadn't encountered in a century, but it was quiet. Was it only weakened from seizing control of her, or was there something more?

Rezek's lips curved in a hollow imitation of a smile. "Possession, is that what you're calling it? Interesting. I long ago stopped thinking of myself and Selvin as separate."

"You know its *name*?" she asked.

"I know more than *his* name," Rezek replied in a tone that made her wonder if he saw that knowledge as a gift or a curse. "How much do you know of the Racari?"

Nowhere near as much as she wanted to, but telling Rezek that felt like giving him leverage. He took her silence as a cue and continued, "The Racari are all different, containing spellwork, history, and philosophy pertaining to different Harbingers. The one in the castle once belonged to Lyzairin, mine to Rach, and, I suspect, yours to Aslir."

The idea that her spellbook had once belonged to the Bright Star, the foremost god of the Kinnish religion and the most powerful creature to ever walk this earth, was not something Ari's mind felt equipped to process.

They're real, Ari, echoed Rivkah's voice.

She latched on to a much easier topic. "Why do you think that?"

"The horse," he said through gritted teeth, a flash of the vicious creature she knew lurked beneath. "Atara. She's a golem, isn't she?"

Ari's face remained impassive. This was the knowledge they'd sought to keep from Rezek for months. Damien had kept his promise to her for creating Atara, issuing her a retroactive enchant license once House Adair became a greater house. Just like that, she'd been made legitimate—except even he could not legalize the practice of Kinnish magic.

"Don't make me ask again," Rezek warned, and in his voice she heard the man who had terrorized Mikira's family for years. The layers of exhaustion that surrounded him and the state of his manor had lulled her into a false sense of security, but he was still Rezek Kelbra, cousin of the royal family and once–high lord.

"I can't prove it, and I can't undo my deal with Damien," he continued bitterly. "There's no point in lying to me now."

"How did you know?" She was already threading the verillion through the emerald ring, prepared to cast a strength charm.

"I didn't, at first." He set down his empty glass. "It wasn't until the final race, when Loic tried to kill me, and your eyes went white. Kinnish magic is all but extinct, the ways of creating golems long lost, but I knew the original source still existed: Aslir's Racari. If you had a Racari, it made sense it would be his, and that you would have learned to create golems from it."

Kinnish magic was nearly gone because Enderlain had tried to eradicate it. First when they invaded Kinahara before the Cataclysm, and then every day since, when Ari's people were forced to flee into the lands of their conquerors to survive. Their magic was illegal, though the divide between it and Enderlish magic was found mainly in their application: Ari crafted golems, beings made of clay, while Enderlish enchanters charmed objects and living animals.

Ari's mind hovered over the binding spell. "And how do you intend to use this information?" He could turn it over to the Anthir and have her arrested or hold it over her to use against her.

Rezek made a soft tsking noise. "You've been spending too much time with Damien. *I* don't want to use it. What I want is your help."

She recoiled in surprise. "My *help*?"

Rezek started toward the spiral staircase in the room's center. Reluctantly, Ari abandoned her spot in the doorway to follow. "I presume you know more of the Heretics than you do the Racari?" he asked.

"I know what everyone does," she replied. "They sought to expand their abilities, and in their pursuit of power, they lost control of their magic. The eruption nearly destroyed Kinahara."

Rezek paused at the second-floor landing. "Congratulations, you've read a textbook." He ignored her glower. "What the books don't tell you is that when they died, their souls were captured in the Racari they were bound to. When we bonded to those Racari with our blood, it created a link with our magic, enabling them to enter our bodies. Your Heretic has been feeding on your power ever since, growing stronger each time you use it."

Damien had theorized as much, but it felt different receiving confirmation that the strength she'd come to rely on was now being turned against her. It made her want to scrape her veins raw, scrub her skin down to bone until she could separate herself from the creature inside.

Rezek continued up the staircase to the third floor. "That's about as much as we know about the bond. It's one of many things about magic we've been seeking to better understand."

"We," she repeated softly. She had never thought of herself and the voice as "we" before. How long exactly had Rezek been possessed?

They exited the staircase on the third-floor landing, and Ari drew to a halt. "I still don't understand what you get out of all of this. What exactly are you asking of me?"

Rezek peered over his shoulder at her. "Simple. We want access to your Racari."

It felt as though he'd just asked for her deepest, mostly closely guarded secret. The sudden protectiveness of the book surprised her, seeing as she'd once tried to drown the thing, and part of her still blamed it for what she'd done to her Saba. But neither did she like the idea of handing it over to Rezek.

"In exchange," Rezek added, "I help you with your little *possession* problem."

He started forward again, Ari reluctantly following. She knew there was more to his demand, but Rezek was her best chance of learning to control the Heretic before she did something she couldn't take back.

Rezek pushed open an arched doorway between two bookcases, and they entered a circular room that was half workshop, half library. Books filled the walls, the room occupied by several long tables with equipment she didn't know the purpose of, but that she was fairly sure Reid would have a conniption over.

Bowls of the four gemstones lined one, but there were also bloodstones, the fifth enchanting stone she and Damien had discovered only weeks ago, capable of creating bonds like the one that linked the Racari to her. And beside those, a dark, shiny stone she didn't recognize, and another, iridescent one she thought might be opal.

"There are more gemstones," she breathed.

"Four," Rezek confirmed. "They're called the Godstones, a part of the power the Heretics were pursuing before the Cataclysm. Knowledge of them was destroyed in the Burning."

All that remained was of the four basic stones: emeralds for physical enchantments, rubies for emotion, sapphire for energy charms, and diamond for ethereal. Decades of magical history were lost in the Burning, driving knowledge of enchanting back to a rudimentary level and erasing all but whispers of the Heretics and the Racari they possessed.

All because of these stones.

All because of you, Ari thought to the voice, but its stubborn silence remained. She found it strange the spirit didn't want to reach out to Rezek's, or that his hadn't asked after hers. Perhaps the Heretic hadn't been lying when it said they weren't friends, but in the very least she'd have expected it to protest Ari's decision again.

Rezek drifted into the room. "This library contains all of the surviving enchanting texts I could find from before the Burning and those created since." He held out a hand, in which rested a single seed. "I could show you things about magic you've never even dreamed of."

The seed cracked apart, transforming into an elegant red rose. He offered it to her, and she took it just to confirm it was real, and not some illusion enchantment. But its waxy stem was solid between her fingers, the soft floral scent unmistakable, and she felt the stirrings of a familiar feeling in her chest.

"In exchange for access to my Racari," she said doubtfully. "What do you want with it?"

He shook his head. "I told you, too much time with Damien. Selvin and I wish only to understand the extent of our magic and what led to the Cataclysm. To embrace our power instead of hide it. I got the impression that was something that would appeal to you."

It did, more than she wanted to admit, because though she believed Rezek, she was certain that there was more he wasn't telling her. But she didn't know how long it would take Reid to succeed, if he ever would. She knew only that her power had caused her Saba's death. It had cleaved her from her family, from Rivkah, whose terror on that night still haunted Ari. It had led her to do things she'd never imagined herself capable of, and it had very nearly taken Damien's life.

Rezek was the only one who had any hope of helping her gain control.

She had no choice.

"Okay," she said at last, and prayed it was not a mistake. "But you get access to my Racari only after you've helped me."

Rezek inclined his head just as a door opened in the library below, and a voice called, "Lord Kelbra? It's nearly time."

So the entire staff isn't gone after all, she thought as Rezek led her out. Her gaze lingered on the Godstones as he shut and locked the workshop door.

"Join me tomorrow afternoon," he said as they descended the steps. "We'll discuss options."

Ari turned the rose between her fingers as she emerged from the Kelbra estate, her mind awash with too many thoughts. If someone had told her only days ago that she might consider willingly calling on Rezek Kelbra, she'd have checked them for a fever. She wasn't a fool; she knew he was after her Racari for more than academic purposes, and that the prospect of learning about the Godstones was just bait he'd dangled before her, another lure to draw her in.

Between that and the temptation of his knowledge about the Heretic, he'd played his cards well. These things he'd shared with her—they were power, a promise of answers to questions she hadn't even realized she wanted to ask, and she wasn't sure she could resist.

Her curiosity always had been a dangerous thing.

✦ PART 2 ✦

Some say the Harbingers still live among humanity,
others that they returned to the world to come.
Some believe they simply disappeared,
reverted to the magic that birthed them.

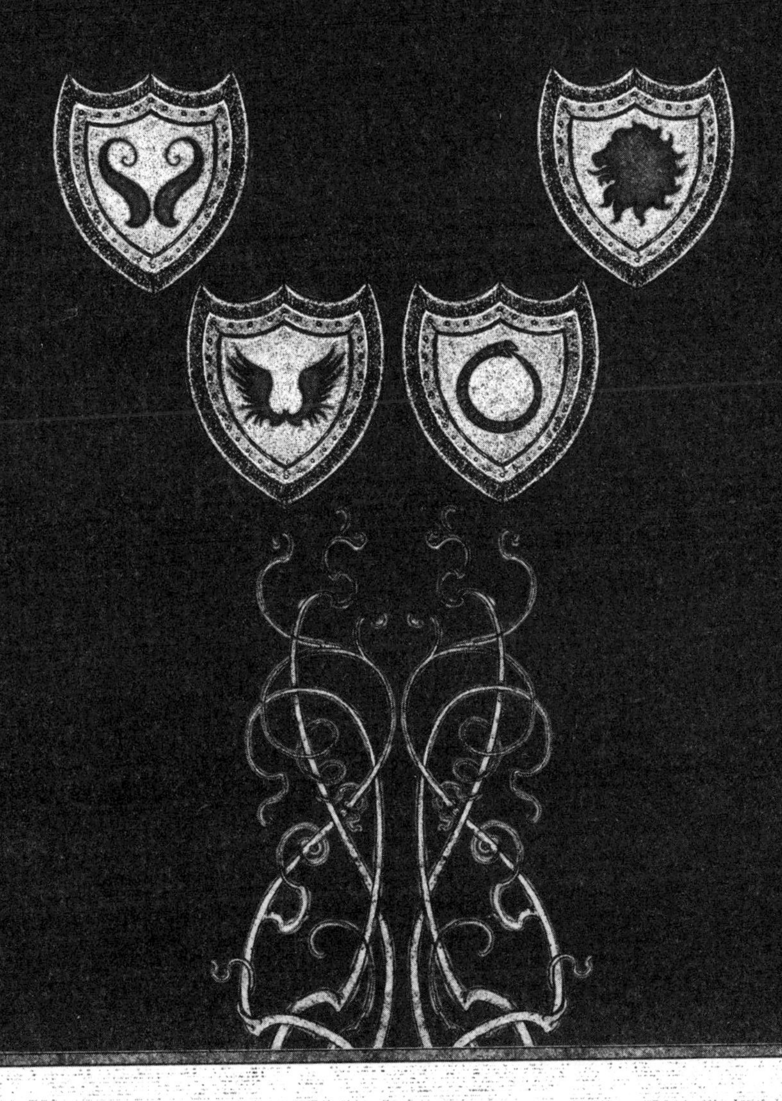

CHAPTER 12

ARIELLE

ARI DREAMED OF an open-aired castle with soaring ceilings and high, arching walls. Of a temple that she knew like her own heart, and a responsibility to something bigger than herself. Her sister was there. She didn't look like Rivkah, yet Ari's heart swelled with a love more powerful than the sun.

She dreamed of a world she missed and could never have.

Ari woke with an ache of longing in her chest to find Damien's side of the bed empty. Rolling over into the cold sheets, she closed her eyes and breathed in the scent of gunpowder and smoke until she could almost convince herself he was there. A small part of her was secretly thankful not to have to face him after seeing Rezek, which had left her off-kilter in more ways than one, but a larger part wanted to apologize for snapping at him the day before.

You don't owe him an apology. The Heretic all but bristled. *He should be begging your forgiveness.*

He might if you stopped making me hurt him. Ari threw back the covers, crossing the room to peel back the thick velvet curtains. A gray sky promised rain, reflecting the heaviness that descended through her. She felt half-rested, as if she'd spent the night running in place.

Or perhaps you're trying to drive him away so he won't help me, she added. *Just like you're trying to keep me from Rezek.*

That boy is dangerous, the voice hissed.

He is also my only source of truth, Ari replied bitterly. *Unless you'd like to share?*

A beat of silence, then, *Nava.*

Excuse me?

I am sharing. My name is Nava.

It wasn't the knowledge she wanted, but it was *something.* Until now the Heretic's presence had been an amorphous shadow in her mind. A name made it something else, *someone* else.

Someone Kinnish.

Ari hadn't considered the identity of the Heretics before, but with Enderlain's systematic eradication of Kinnish magic after the invasion, it'd seemed likely to her that those in possession of the Racari would be Enderlish.

It was just a reminder of how little she truly knew. What the Racari were capable of, where they'd come from, how hers had ended up with her family—even about Nava and the other Heretics. If she and Rezek were possessed, what about the other two? She hadn't seen any sign of the third Racari from the castle at Rezek's. Had he left it there when she'd fled, or did it already belong to someone?

What else? Ari pressed, desperate for more even as she recognized that the Heretic's sudden willingness to answer questions was suspicious. Was this just another attempt to keep her from seeking Rezek's help?

What would you like to know? Nava asked shortly. *My favorite color and if I eat my latkes with cream or sauce?*

Ari's stomach rumbled at the thought of latkes. There wasn't much Kinnish fare in Veradell, and though Damien's chefs would prepare anything she asked, their food paled in comparison to her mother's. She missed sitting with Rivkah in the kitchen, peeling potatoes while their mother hummed, even if her sister always found a way to slip away and leave her to do the work.

You speak oddly colloquially for someone trapped in a spellbook for over a hundred years, she said, her curiosity getting the better of her. But perhaps there was another way to handle this situation that didn't require Rezek at all. If she knew more about Nava, understood her, then maybe she could convince her to share what she was after, and they could reach a truce.

I was still aware of the world around me, in there, Nava replied softly.

Since the day I . . . Ari's response trailed off, her fingers curling into her skirt at the memory of her Saba's still body.

Blood on the floor. Blood on her hands.

Mercifully, Nava finished the thought for her. *No, we've been linked far longer than that.*

Rivkah had said their parents knew all along. She was the reason they'd kept their family separate from town, denying her and Rivkah access to their own people. They had never gone to temple, never studied the Arkala, never learned much of their history and culture.

Had they worried what she would become with such a power at her disposal? Had they been *afraid* of her?

Did you take control of me before? Ari demanded.

Once, came Nava's soft voice, *when I first awoke. After that I had no reason to, until you came to Veradell. I could not accept the way these people treated you.*

That was why the voice had been quiet until recently, when she'd begun selling golems to people who treated her like dirt. Nava had been looking out for her all this time, a thought Ari didn't know how to parse.

I . . . am sorry, for what you were denied, Nava said quietly. *I know something of that pain.*

You? Ari struggled to imagine what one of the foremost enchanters of her time, a woman who had *lived* in Kinahara, could know of being cut off from her people.

A feeling akin to mourning emanated from the Heretic. *You forget, I lived beneath the Enderlish occupation. My magic was illegal in my own land. Once, I was a Kesema. Then I was nothing.*

A Kesema? Ari repeated, the Old Kinnish unfamiliar to her.

A practitioner of Kinnish magic.

Ari turned the word over on her tongue. She'd never had a name for what she was before, something that both saddened and infuriated her. Like so much of her people's world, it had been lost in the Cataclysm.

Lost because of Nava.

So you joined the Enderlish enchanters instead, Ari thought bitterly. *And destroyed our world.*

I was trying to protect it! Fury seeped into Nava's voice, and Ari felt the emotion resonate through her. *The others—they were pursuing powers they didn't understand. Power that did not belong to them.*

Is that why you didn't reach out to Selvin yesterday? Ari pressed. *Because you didn't agree with what he was doing?*

Nava made a derisive noise. *Selvin cares nothing for me, only what helping you to subdue me would get him.*

My Racari. Ari turned from the window, studying the spellbook where it lay on her nightstand. She'd fallen asleep poring over the parts Damien had translated, seeking answers at every turn.

Do not give it to him, little lion, Nava urged. *Nothing good will come of it.*

For me, or you?

Nava's silence was a physical thing this time, and it frayed the last of Ari's patience. She went to wash and dress, her own words haunting her every movement. Her magic was her strength. It had filled the cracks in her armor like molten steel, becoming a part of her, and now the thing that had saved her was threatening to dismantle everything she'd built.

She would not allow that.

Emerging from the bedroom, she went straight for the drink cart to pour a cup of strong tea, then joined Reid where he sat behind Damien's desk hovering over a microscope.

"No, I don't know where he is," he said without looking up.

Ari swallowed back the question, feeling it lodge like a stone in her stomach. Damien hadn't even told Reid where he'd gone? At the very least he usually told them when he'd be out on house business, if not the details, but it wasn't just his reticence to share that concerned her. It was the look of suspicion in his eye, the traps he left for servants to see who rifled through his belongings.

It was the grudge he held against Mikira for her mistake.

If she told him about Rezek now, he wouldn't be able to handle it. He'd probably hunt his old friend down, and he wouldn't forgive her. All she would do was cause him more pain.

"Aren't you worried about him?" she asked.

Reid peeled back from the microscope with a look that all but screamed *please don't ask me for relationship advice.* But beneath that, she detected a flicker of unease.

"He's fine," he said half-heartedly.

She snorted. "He's not."

Reid didn't argue again, slumping into his chair with a groan. Something squirmed behind him, and a moment later an affronted Widget escaped being crushed and resettled in his lap with a glower that promised revenge at a later date.

"I haven't seen him like this in a really long time." Reid scrubbed a hand across his face.

Ari held the warmth of her tea close to her stomach. "Since Rezek." Reid's look of deep misgiving was answer enough, and she pressed, "What were they both like, before . . ."

"Before Rezek murdered Damien's mother and getting revenge became his sole reason for existing?" Reid's glib tone did nothing to undermine the weight of his words. "I didn't know them. Damien and I didn't meet until after, but from what I gather, Rezek was always a rich, pompous ass, but he was harmless. And Damien . . ."

He shrugged one shoulder, scratching Widget behind the ears. "Shira said he was always too smart for everyone else around him, and that it isolated him. Rezek was the only person who seemed to like him for it."

Had it all been a trick, a ploy to get to Damien's mother? Or had Rezek truly been his friend, once?

The suite door opened, and Damien's voice preceded him. "My decision is final. I expect you off the premises within the hour."

Reid groaned softly. "That's the second one this week," he muttered. To Ari's questioning look, he added, "People he's fired."

"Great," she sighed as Damien joined her and Reid at the desk.

He eyed the microscope. "Any progress?"

"A little, but nothing worth *sharing*," Reid replied pointedly.

Damien let out half a sigh, which for him was practically akin to rolling his eyes. "Reid."

Reid held his ground for all of a second before his shoulders slumped, and he gestured at his microscope. "I have a theory that like verillion can only grow in magic-rich soil, these cells may only be visible in the presence of magic. But I think I need a better microscope. There's a new model in from Vyna, but it costs—"

"Get it," Damien cut across him. "Whatever it takes."

Reid slunk out of his chair with obvious reluctance, vanishing into his room and leaving her and Damien alone. For the first time, Ari wasn't quite sure how to approach him. They had never argued like yesterday before, and though she wanted to apologize, she wanted him to as well. And though he kept his face impassive, she had a feeling he wanted the same.

In the end, he withdrew a gilded envelope from his jacket pocket. "I have a lead on Elidon Shaw. He'll be hosting an Eridice party three days from now."

A little of Ari's tension washed away at his openness. "That's good news."

Damien tossed the invitation onto the desk, closing the space between them. He curved over her like a sheltering wing, his fingers tracing along the line of her jaw. "Will you come with me?"

Ari leaned into his touch. Whatever uncertainty plagued her mind, her body knew this rhythm and sought the comfort of it. It wasn't an apology, but it was normalcy, and she craved that twice as much.

"Of course," she replied, and his lips found hers.

He never kissed her quickly, as if each moment they came together existed outside of time. When she was with him, his attention belonged solely to her, and she reveled in the way that he beheld her. His arms encircled her waist, his presence sturdier than steel, and she leaned into that strength as she kissed him like the apology she couldn't give.

The truth burned behind her lips, a second heat to the one coursing along her skin, but she swallowed it down with the taste of him and came up for air.

"But in that case, I'll need a new dress." She hoped her face was as steady as her voice. It wasn't a lie, per se, but it was not the main reason she needed to leave. She had a meeting with Rezek. Even thinking of him in Damien's presence felt like a betrayal, and she couldn't help feeling he could see straight through her, but Damien only smiled, reluctantly letting her go.

She hoped he'd understand, in the end. That everything she was doing, the lies, the secrets—it was to keep the people she loved safe.

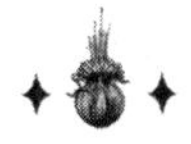

REZEK ANSWERED AT her knock, looking twice as disheveled as yesterday.

"Are you drunk?" she asked as a whiff of alcohol reached her.

He folded himself against the doorframe. "Not for lack of trying. Selvin keeps burning it off." He paused, eyes rolling upward as if hearing another voice, before he snorted derisively at whatever his Heretic said.

Stepping aside, he gestured overdramatically for her to enter. Ari eyed him as he led the way to his study, where he went straight to the drink cart, pouring a glass of whiskey. He offered it to her, and she shook her head. "Tea would be nice."

He filled a cup from the enchanted kettle on the cart and handed it to her, and she tried to slot the domesticity of the gesture alongside the feeling screaming at her not to trust him. Her gaze searched his, but there were no signs of the white that overcame their irises when the Heretics took control.

"You seem to be in concert with Selvin," she observed.

"A consequence of years together." Rezek lifted one slender shoulder and leaned against his desk again. The boy she'd known cut through a room with his presence; this one seemed content to let the world hold him up. She wondered how much of who he was in public had been an act, and then she wondered if this was too. Rezek might prefer the direct approach to Damien's more cunning one, but that didn't mean he couldn't perform with the best.

"Like you had to learn to control your magic as an enchanter, the Heretics have had to learn how to possess us," Rezek explained. "The blackouts happen if they overwhelm your body with their magic when they take control, turning your eyes white. It may be a lack of experience or on purpose, as they are capable of taking control without either of those signs."

Ari didn't know which one worried her more: the idea that Nava was test-driving her body like a new motorcar, or that she was intentionally overwhelming her so that Ari wouldn't witness what she was up to. She'd tried again to convince Ari not to come on the way here but retreated the moment Ari entered the manor.

"Exactly how long have you been . . ." Ari trailed off, remembering his reaction to the word *possessed*.

He smirked lightly. "Since I was twelve."

Her breath caught. Rezek was in his early twenties, which meant he'd been with Selvin for over a decade. No wonder he seemed so at ease with the Heretic.

Something else occurred to her then. She'd never heard anything about him being an enchanter. Which meant—"You're unregistered."

"Took you a bit longer than I expected." He swirled his drink. "My father kept my powers a secret once they manifested. The idea of a Kelbra becoming some lowly enchanter in the royal service disgusted him. That was before he discovered the Racari."

Her gaze flitted to his desk, but the spellbook was gone. If Rezek wanted access to hers in exchange for his help, then it seemed likely he'd also taken the third Racari they'd encountered in the castle. Did he have the fourth too?

"Exactly *how* did he discover it?" she asked. "The Racari were bound to the Heretics when the Cataclysm happened. Shouldn't they have been destroyed?"

The question stirred something in Nava, her presence flickering. Did she want to know the answer too, or was her reaction because she already did?

Rezek set his glass aside on the desk. "The Racari are more than just spellbooks. They're pieces of divine magic. The *Harbingers'* magic. It makes them capable of far more than we know, including the ability to survive the Cataclysm. But Selvin's theory is that once bound to an enchanter, the Racari remain connected to that bloodline."

He watched her, as if waiting for an implication to settle. It came gradually, like a half-remembered dream. If the Racari were linked to a bloodline, then—

We're related? Ari asked and felt Nava shift in response. Was that why the Heretic had surfaced moments ago? Did she not want Ari to know this?

Ari swallowed hard, trying not to let the revelation unsteady her. It didn't change anything. Nava was still using her, still a danger, and she wasn't the only one. Selvin likely had his own motivations, and the other two Heretics were wild cards. With how little history about them remained after the Burning, she knew next to nothing about any of them.

"Then your Racari," Ari began. "It came to someone else in your family?"

"A distant relative," Rezek replied, a familiar look she couldn't name in his eyes. "My father took it from him when he realized what it was and learned the secret of bloodstones from it. It was he who bound the Racari to me. All it takes is a drop of blood."

Ari recoiled. "Your father did this *to* you?"

Rezek threw back the rest of his drink in one swallow. "He thought he was making me stronger. He didn't know about the Heretic's soul clinging to the book. When I started acting differently, more violently, my father became afraid of me, and there was nothing Eradas Kelbra hated more than something that scared him."

Something Damien once said came back to her then: *That he is not the son Eradas Kelbra wanted is the worst-kept secret in Veradell. His brother was the golden boy; Rezek was a problem.*

A problem his father created and then discarded, washing his hands of the matter. For she recognized the look in Rezek's eyes now, the distance he'd created within to separate one part of himself from another. To lock away the fear, lest it consume him.

Had his Heretic sought to control him at first the way Nava did her? Their eyes turned white only when the Heretics took complete command, but there had been times when Nava hovered on the edge of it, where her thoughts and feelings and actions blended so seamlessly with Ari's, she could not tell where one ended and the other began.

How much of the Rezek she knew was truly him, and how much was the creature lurking underneath? The thought stirred another memory. Her gaze returned slowly to his to find him watching her, waiting, as if begging her to comprehend.

"I was not always in control." His voice broke on the last word, and Ari understood.

"Damien's mother," she breathed. "Did you . . ."

"I don't know." Rezek's grip tightened around the glass. "I remember . . . pieces. I remember wanting to make my father proud. I remember blood. So much blood. I remember running." He pressed a hand to his face, his fingers curling in his hair. "That's all."

The line between him and Selvin had eroded so thoroughly, he didn't know which actions were his and which were the Heretic's. Didn't know whose hands the blood of his once best friend's mother had stained. She knew the terror that instilled in someone; she felt it every time she came back to herself after a blackout.

It felt like coming undone.

A hundred questions surfaced, the first leaping out almost accusatorily: "But why would Selvin want Damien's mother dead?"

"To make me head of House Kelbra. No matter the cost." A wry smile curved his lips. "Our Ascension task was to deal the greatest blow to a rival house, but when I told my father what I'd done, he still chose my brother."

"Because he was afraid of you," she said. Then Rezek's brother disappeared, and he became head of House Kelbra anyway, and slowly carved a name for himself as heir. But how much of that had been him?

How much had been her, and how much Nava?

In that moment, she understood why she'd been so angry with Damien after the attack. It wasn't just the leftover adrenaline and burgeoning frustration with whatever he was keeping from her; it had been the way he looked at her, as if he didn't quite know her anymore.

As if he was afraid of her.

Rezek set his glass aside. "I don't know how to suppress the Heretic inside you, because I've never sought to do the same to Selvin, but I have an idea. Follow me."

Ari followed him upstairs to the workroom, drifting reflexively toward the table of enchant stones. Rezek had said there were four Godstones, but she noted only three additional baskets.

"Would you like to learn how to use them?" Rezek pointed to each basket in turn. "You already know what bloodstones do. The polished black ones are onyx, which create transformation enchantments like the rose I gave you. The colorful ones are opal, which enable death enchantments."

She recoiled. "Death enchantments?"

"It sounds worse than it is." He picked up one of the opals, turning it over in his hand. "Death is a cessation. These enchantments are similar: they stop things. Say a spell to stop weeds from growing, or a river from running a direction you don't want."

He made it sound so benign. "Can you . . . kill with them?"

"Only if you bind the stone to a living creature, the same way you would enchant an animal." He dropped the stone back into the basket. "A waste of magic when a blade will do perfectly well."

She thought about asking after the missing fourth stone, but she had a feeling that it might be why she was here. Because her Racari spoke of another stone as well, one whose power she'd never understood. Truthstones, her people called them—the stone that made golems.

And for some reason, Rezek wanted them.

Rezek retreated to his desk and opened a drawer, pulling free a thin bracelet made of tightly threaded individual stones of opal, the colors iridescent in the sunlight streaming in at his back. "I think a death enchantment is exactly what we need."

"I thought we were beyond the part where we tried to kill each other."

"Tempting, but I've had enough of Damien's revenge." There was something about the way Rezek said Damien's name that needled at her. Not a softness, but an absence of the edge that colored the way he usually spoke.

He rejoined her at the worktable, and as always, she burned verillion on instinct at having him so close, ready to defend herself at a moment's notice.

She'd taken to wearing a diamond ring so as to have ethereal enchantments at her call as well.

"Death enchantments can stop a movement, or a flower from growing," Rezek explained. "The trick will be making sure it targets only what we want, and not, say, your heart."

"Which should only be a matter of intent," Ari said, her curiosity piqued.

Rezek laid the bracelet on the worktop before her. "We should research it more before attempting anything, but yes. I suspect we could charm this bracelet to stop the Heretic inside you from surfacing, but there will be a price."

Somehow, Ari had known it would come to this. Her knowledge of magic might be incomplete, but she knew enough to suspect where this was going, and from the uneasy shift of Nava's presence, so did she.

"My magic," she said, and he nodded.

"Even I don't truly understand the bond between Heretic and host." He leaned against the table, arms folded. "A Racari can surely bond to anyone, enchanter or not, the same way any bonding enchantment would. But I suspect only an enchanter can host a Heretic's actual soul in their body."

"You mean you don't know whether my magic is my own." Rezek had known he was an enchanter long before he'd been bound to a Racari, but Ari had found hers as a young child. She had no idea if her powers belonged to her, or if they came from Nava.

Rezek shrugged, pushing off the table. "Either way, the magic is the bridge. If we suppress the magic, I suspect we suppress the Heretic."

Do not do this, little lion. Nava's voice roared to life in her head. *He will make you weak. Do you really want to lock away your power?*

Ari flinched. Of course she didn't. But she didn't know how deeply intertwined her power was with the spirit, only that using one strengthened the other, and until she could find another solution for Nava, her magic might be the price she had to pay.

Still, it tore at her to consider it. Her magic had strengthened her, saved her. Without it, she'd be vulnerable in more ways than one. The idea of locking it away made her want to say to hell with the risks. But then she remembered how close she'd come to truly hurting Damien, and she thought of the things Rezek had done at the whims of another mind, and she sealed that anger away.

He's not the one doing this. Ari's fingers closed around the bracelet. *This is your last chance to tell me the truth. What do you want from me?*

When only silence returned, Ari picked up the bracelet. "Where do we begin?"

CHAPTER 13

MIKIRA

THE TARGET BEFORE Mikira was little more than a piece of marked wood, yet it was twice as satisfying to strike as the bales of hay she and Lochlyn used to practice on.

This was nothing like that.

Where those mornings had been peaceful, the air around her now was charged with an energy so frantic, it buzzed against her skin. To her left, an archer loosed bolts into a cloth figure. To her right, a group of rebels drilled in hand-to-hand combat, the thud of bodies a now-familiar sound. Everyone around her was preparing for war.

The noise of the cavern was almost too much for Mikira after the quiet of the ranch. Her family had left that morning with the rebels' help, and the house had felt so empty, like a bone scraped of its marrow and left hollow and cold. She couldn't get Ailene and Nelda's accusations out of her head.

"You want us to do *what*?" Ailene's shrill voice had cut through the kitchen at the news.

"It's not safe here anymore," their father had said.

"And whose fault is that?" The betrayal in Ailene's eyes had nearly leveled Mikira.

"Was this your idea?" Nelda's voice had been so quiet she almost missed it. "This was all supposed to be over after the Illinir. We were supposed to be a family again, and now you're sending us away!"

Mikira winced. "I'm sorry, little frog."

Nelda flinched at the nickname. "Don't call me that." Ailene had pulled her close, and they'd stared defiantly back at her, a united front.

It'd made her heart break.

Now, Mikira forced a deep breath, weighing a blade in her hand. Lochlyn had taught her to make it an extension of her arm, but this new magic gave that concept an entirely new meaning. She had only to funnel her intent through the blade and let it go.

Hit the target, she told it, and released.

The blade leapt from her hand, zipping toward the target—and hit the edge of it hilt-first.

A low whistle sounded behind her, and Talyana approached, clapping slowly. "I'm quaking in my boots."

Mikira rolled her eyes and retrieved the blade. "I'm practicing."

"I can see why."

Atara, who stood beside them, snorted and pawed at the earth. A grin split across Talyana's face. "See? Even the horse agrees."

Shutting out Talyana's laughter, Mikira retook her position. She needed to be more specific, more intentional, until she'd gotten a feel for the magic. At least, that was how Ari had described her approach to enchanting herself. She wished the girl were here now to share her expertise, and because she always made Mikira feel a little less alone.

Focus, she told herself, fingers tightening around the hilt. *Hit the center of the target point-first.* She envisioned the path the knife would take as she gave it a command and let go.

The blade struck true.

Talyana's whistle came again, this time followed by several others and a smattering of applause. People had been watching her on and off, not half so discreet as they thought. She didn't blame them. With Atara standing at her side like a bodyguard and magical knives that leapt from her hands of their own volition, she would be staring too.

Besides, a part of her kind of liked the attention. It reminded her of why she was doing all this. Not just for her family, but for all the families like hers who had suffered beneath unfair taxes and a war they didn't want. For a life where she woke to the bustle of the ranch and went to sleep to the knowledge that she and her family were safe.

After watching them pack their bags and leave, that life felt impossibly far away. But it was only all the more reason for her to fight.

She had to bring them home.

Mikira retrieved the blade again, sheathing it and joining Talyana. "Do you have news or are you just here to torment me?"

A wicked sort of grin turned Talyana's lips. "I am always here to torment you," she said, and it felt like a promise. Mikira's cheeks flushed, and she quickly hooked her arm with Talyana's to drag her away from their growing crowd. Atara followed, nudging Talyana in the shoulder as if to chastise her.

Talyana captured the mare's nose in the curve of her hand. "Back, you beast. I promise not to damage her delicate sensibilities."

"She's charmed to sense danger," Mikira muttered drily. "You can't trick her."

"I'll just have to distract her with this, then." Talyana produced a green apple from her pocket, and Atara snatched it with the dexterity of a cat, leaving Talyana visibly shaken at how close her fingers had been to becoming snacks. Mikira laughed and patted the horse's neck as she munched happily.

Talyana's gaze brightened with delight, a look that never failed to make her appear as if she were glowing. She had a way of pulling smiles out of Mikira like a hard-won prize, looking all too pleased with herself each time she did.

Talyana cleared her throat. "As fun as this is, we've been summoned to

Eshlin's office. Without the death certificate, we need to figure out our next move for the prince." She pulled a rolled-up newspaper from her pocket. "Also, I thought this might interest you."

Mikira unfurled it to reveal the headline: "Adair on Warpath."

The tag line read: "Council of Lords strikes down tax! Find out how it affects you." Beneath it was a photograph of Damien standing before a new fountain of Aslir at Adair Manor, along with an article that described the recent announcement from the Council of Lords that both the draft tax and exemption fee had been ended.

"'Sources close to High Lord Adair claim the money will soon be repurposed to support the wider populace,'" Mikira muttered under her breath, and Talyana snorted derisively. Here was a man holding coin that rightfully belonged to her hostage with one hand while he promised to redistribute all but *stolen* funds back to the people that deserved them with the other.

"Well," Mikira began with a sigh, handing back the paper. "I did always believe him when he said he wanted to make things better."

"So long as he's the one in power." Talyana rolled the paper up and stuck it in her pocket, then knocked on Eshlin's door. The princess beckoned them in, the same paper spread across her desk with Damien's face staring up at them. She looked equally disgruntled, making Mikira wonder what impact Damien's improvements would have on the rebellion's momentum.

Eshlin folded her hands beneath her chin as they came to stand before her. "Our spies have reported back, and they think the man who attacked you worked for Niekla Dramara. I suspected she and Royce would make an attempt to find the prince themselves, but their participation is just another reason we need to move swiftly. Do we have any new leads?"

"There's the second smudged sigil we couldn't read," Talyana offered with a shrug. "Death certificates have to be signed by an undertaker, so I assume that's what it is. If we check the records of individual businesses, we can see if they have a Torren Ranier."

Mikira shook her head. "You'd have to use your authority as an Anthir sergeant, and it will tip off the others that we're looking." As of now, Talyana's involvement in the rebellion was a secret, and they needed her position's connections.

Mikira released a heavy breath. "But I have another idea."

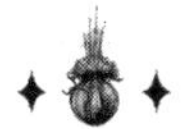

"**WHAT IF HE** never leaves?" Talyana asked from their position hidden behind a row of trees outside of Adair Manor. Atara and Talyana's horse were tied deeper into the woods, where they couldn't be seen, and Mikira was careful to stay concealed behind a row of tall bushes as she watched the front gate for what felt like the hundredth hour.

It had only been two, but the weather was chilly and threatening rain. If Reid didn't show soon, she might have to rethink her plan. The undertaker's sigil on the prince's death certificate had been nearly illegible, and the paper itself was gone, but to someone who knew what they were looking for, with an eye for images, the drawing she'd re-created might just be enough.

"He'll leave," Mikira said with a confidence she didn't feel. Reid usually completed errands himself, and he often went with Damien on house business. But there were also stretches of time when he remained holed up in his workroom and snapped at anyone who came inside.

"Are you sure you don't just want to see him again?" Talyana's voice tilted up awkwardly at the end, and Mikira turned incredulous eyes upon her. She had her hands shoved into her pockets and was poking the wet earth with the tip of her boot.

"*Now* you're jealous!" She'd imagined this Talyana armed with too many knives, not squeaky-voiced and toeing the dirt as if wishing it would swallow her up.

Talyana's eyes narrowed sharply. "I'm nothing of the sort. I just want to make sure you haven't forgotten the fact that he stabbed you in the back."

Mikira's smile faltered. She hadn't forgotten. But that didn't change the fact that when she saw him at the Vault yesterday, all her anger, all her pain, had felt miniscule in the face of longing. She missed him. His snipes, his grumpiness, his inability to properly sit in a chair. She knew she had to let him go, but it felt like carving out a piece of herself.

Whatever had existed between them . . . it had meant something to her.

"Mikira." Talyana's voice had a new intensity to it, and Mikira's head snapped toward the manor, where a figure in all black descended the front steps to a waiting coach.

"Come on." Mikira turned back into the forest, Talyana on her heel. Atara greeted them with a huff, and Mikira gave her a pat before addressing the crow perched on a low branch.

"Follow the coach," she instructed. The golem cocked its head, every bit as sharp-eyed as the woman who'd made it, and then launched into the air.

"Another part of this plan I don't like," Talyana muttered as she mounted her horse. "Eshlin trusts Shira; I do not." She nudged her horse into a trot. Atara followed, and they picked their way carefully through the trees along the Traveler's Road, following the crow.

When the coach turned off the road and into town, they fell back a little, letting the traffic of the city build up between them. Mikira kept the hood of her cloak up, not wanting any unexpected attention. Eventually the crow began to circle, before alighting on the ledge of a building on Ettinger Street. They hung back while Reid entered the store.

"It's a laboratory supplier of some sort," Talyana observed as they dismounted, tying their horses to a nearby hitching post.

"Of course it is." Mikira sighed, hoping that Reid was feeling cooperative, which was a lot like hoping a particularly dark cloud wouldn't rain. "Come on."

A brass bell dinged overhead as they entered, an older Yaroyan man at the front counter greeting them with a nod. The store was a twisting maze of haphazard shelves, stocked to the brim with curiosities and supplies that Mikira didn't know half the names of. She recognized test tubes and glass slides, beakers and burners, but there were also round metal objects with glass faces that resembled clocks, strangely shaped tongs, and long glass tubes with knobs at the end.

Her father would have loved it, a thought that stung her heart.

Talyana craned her neck in search of Reid. "Where did he go?"

Mikira thought of the blueprints they'd seen Reid clutching at the Vault and pointed down an aisle lined with microscopes. It reached all the way back through the narrow shop, stuffed to the brim, before curving sharply to the right.

Reid had just lifted a microscope down from the top shelf when they arrived. He started at the sight of them, quickly regathering himself to demand, "Now who's following who?"

"I don't know what you mean," Talyana remarked offhandedly. "We frequently visit dusty antique shops."

"It's not an antique shop; it's a—"

"Really don't care." Talyana advanced a step and Reid retreated, but the aisle dead-ended into another shelf of microscopes behind him.

"Tal," Mikira chastised softly. Talyana might not like Reid, but she didn't have to torment him.

Talyana sighed, and Mikira slipped in front of her, unexpectedly finding herself nervous. Her encounter with Reid at the Vault had been so brief she'd barely had time to process seeing him. Somehow, she'd expected him to look different, but his hair was still a maelstrom, his too-bright eyes watching her with a mix of apprehension and apology.

She hated how badly she wanted to hear him say it. To tell her he hadn't meant it and that he was sorry. She didn't want to be angry with him.

But that wasn't why they were here.

"I need your help with something." She withdrew the drawing.

Reid's expression softened for the briefest flash before he shook his head. "I shouldn't even be talking to you." He shouldered forward, clearly intending to go between them, but Talyana was faster. She closed the gap and snatched the microscope out of his hands.

"Might want to rethink that," she said.

Reid scowled. "Or what, you'll hold my microscope hostage?"

Talyana lifted it to her full height with the clear intent to smash it, and Reid lurched forward. She grinned. "So you do care about it."

"It's the only one of its kind in the shop. If you break it—" Reid cut off. The only time Reid didn't say something was when he couldn't say something, which meant that microscope was important, most likely to Damien. Breaking it would only get Reid in more trouble with him, a thought she half expected to feel satisfied by.

She didn't.

As upset as she was with Reid, she didn't hate him. If anything, she felt bad for him, knowing how ensnared he was in Damien's machinations. She wanted to pull him free as badly as she wanted to push him away to a place where he couldn't hurt her again.

Mikira forced a settling breath, then took the microscope from Talyana. "We're not holding it hostage." She gave Talyana a pointed look and jerked her head toward the door. Talyana didn't budge. Mikira stared at her until she took one step back, and then another, before drifting grudgingly to the end of the aisle. She did not look away.

Mikira handed the microscope back to Reid, who hugged it to his chest. She unfolded her drawing. "I just want to know if you recognize this undertaker's sigil?"

Reid wiped the shock from his face too late. Was it the sigil that surprised him? His gaze flicked to Talyana as if measuring his chances of escape, and he pulled the microscope closer. Then his shoulders slumped.

"It's the Ambry family's sigil," he said shortly. "Now can you call off your dog?"

Mikira nodded to Talyana, who retreated to the shop entrance, granting Reid passage through the aisle. Except he didn't move. He looked as if he were working his way up to saying something, each attempt interrupted by a deeper and deeper scowl.

"How's Ari?" she blurted.

Reid swallowed back whatever he'd been about to say. "She misses you."

"She knows where to find me." Mikira hated the bitterness in her voice, hated that she felt it even a little.

Reid gave her a mournful look. "It's not that simple."

"Nothing ever is." Mikira folded up the paper and stuffed it into her pocket, where her fingers brushed the vial. She withdrew it. "One more thing. My father took this from Rezek's labs. He thinks it's connected to why Rezek wanted him in the first place, but he couldn't figure out what it is. I thought maybe you could."

Reid accepted the vial. "I'll try."

She nodded stiffly. "Thanks for your help."

"Mikira." He caught her arm as she backed away, his fingers warm against her skin. She stared at the crow tattoo encircling his forearm. His grip was gentle, so easy for her to pull away from, and yet she couldn't bring herself to do it. Everything in her wanted to meet his eyes, to pick apart the emotions breaking in their blue depths. She could feel him watching, waiting, as if afraid a single word would send her running.

She heard him swallow. "I—"

Mikira held up a hand, drifting backward along the aisle. They'd gotten what they'd come for.

The rest she couldn't have.

"Just . . . be careful, all right?" she said, and fled.

CHAPTER 14

DAMIEN

ARIELLE CAME HOME smelling of roses.

It was absurd to be unsettled by a scent, but Damien's mind only ever went one place when he encountered it: Rezek. The Kelbra estate was flush with roses, and he and Rezek used to spend hours out in the gardens, avoiding Rezek's father.

Damien always came home stained with blood from the thorns.

The thought permeated his mind until sleep was lost to him. Instead, he studied the curve of Arielle's silhouette in the moonlight, the bow of her lips. Her breath was soft as a bird's wings against his collarbone, the sight of her more intoxicating than any drink. He longed to bridge the meager few inches and erase the strain between them.

Then he remembered the press of her forearm at his bruised throat. Remembered the shock of white that stared back at him from her eyes. Neither of those compared to the knowledge that she'd hidden it all from him.

If she could keep a secret as immense as that, what else wasn't she telling him?

The question pained him in a way he couldn't explain. It was worse than betrayal because it wasn't definitive. He couldn't draw a line through it, couldn't sort it into a box. There was no order here, only unruly emotion that threatened to undo him. So he did the same thing he always did each time he tried to control the tempest inside him—he sought an outlet.

Descending into his chair by the fire, he spent the night reading about Kinnish history. Study was one of the few things that quieted his mind, a habit he'd adopted from his mother, who would disappear for hours into centuries long past. The facts, the timelines—they imposed order onto chaos, though he knew as well as anyone that history did not always mean truth.

By the time the sun crested the horizon, he felt only marginally better. His head resembled a room packed with too many people, each one carrying on a different conversation. The upcoming Eridice party in search of Elidon Shaw and the Ranier prince. Reid's research into enchanter cells. His seat on the council and the precarious position it put him in.

He had no doubt those assassins were Niekla's or Royce's; what bothered him was not knowing if he and Arielle had been tracked, or if there was a spy in his midst. He'd relieved the valet of his position just in case, as well as the servant who'd cleaned the suite earlier that day.

He'd have to be more careful.

"Are you planning to read that book, or murder it?" Reid's voice startled Damien out of his thoughts, and he looked up to find his friend wrapped in a blanket with Widget tucked in his arms. The sun had barely risen, but even Damien wasn't certain if or when Reid slept.

He snapped his book shut. "I haven't decided."

Reid dropped heavily onto the chaise, Widget scrambling out of his arms. "Careful, that was almost a joke."

Damien's gaze tracked the cat, who took up residence atop Reid's head. "Yes, I wouldn't want to appear ridiculous."

Scowling, Reid plucked Widget from his head. "He's your stupid cat anyways."

"I didn't feed him every day and let him sleep in my bed."

"Shira made him for you."

"And gave him to you." Damien lifted one shoulder in a shrug. He'd had no interest in keeping the golem, but Reid had been recovering from a run-in with Loic that had left him scarred in more ways than one, and having the little cat around seemed to help. So he'd made the creature Reid's responsibility, and the two had been inseparable since, something he wasn't sure if Reid thanked or blamed him for.

Muttering under his breath, Reid flipped around to pour himself a cup of tea from the drink cart as Damien rose, picking up a pile of messages from the desk. The first were reports from the lesser houses below Adair responsible for running the day-to-day of their districts, but the third was unsigned, written in a code only Damien knew.

A note from his spy at the Vault.

He opened it, scanning the contents quickly, before crushing the paper in his fist. "Mikira was at the Vault yesterday." He met Reid's gaze. "Weren't you there also?"

Reid slumped deeper into the chaise, a flush of red coloring his cheeks. "I ran into her."

"And you didn't think to mention it to me?" Damien asked tightly.

"I didn't think it was important—"

"Everything is important right now, Reid." This was why he kept so much to himself. What others saw as harmless information, he recognized as weapons in the right hands. The more he knew, the more prepared he could be, and while there were a hundred reasons Mikira could be at the Vault that had nothing to do with him, it was not her presence that bothered him.

It was that Reid had kept it from him.

Reid's scowl deepened. "She was there to commission a new signet ring—happy? Should I tell you what I had for dinner last night too? Or maybe you want to tell me why you're in my living room every damn morning."

"*Your* living room?"

"Before sunrise it is." Reid jabbed a finger at the slowly brightening sky. "You're not sleeping, you're not eating, you're accusing everyone around you of being your enemy. When are you going to admit that things with Hyle and Mikira freaked you out?"

Damien was about to respond when he felt it—the line of tension running through him like a steel rod. He'd let his anger best him. Carefully he unfurled his hand and smoothed out the note. "I have everything under control."

Reid's wide eyes remained pinned on him a moment longer, before he shoved off the chaise with an inaudible mutter and stomped over to the desk, throwing himself into the chair and sliding his microscope over with enough force to scratch the wood. He thrust Widget back atop his head and bent one eye to the scope, adjusting knobs. Damien let him go, approaching the fire to feed the note to the flames.

A knock sounded, and a servant entered at his call. "My lord, Prince Darius is here."

"Oh, great," Reid muttered without looking up. "Clandestine visits from royals. Those always go well."

The servant bowed and vanished into the hallway, returning a moment later with a man whose resemblance to Rezek made Damien's skin crawl. With sharp features, pale skin, and blue eyes that bored straight through you, he lacked only his cousin's cleverness to match his appearance. Rezek had always been a challenge; Darius was child's play.

Damien gestured at the chaise. "Your Highness. To what do I owe the pleasure?"

Darius didn't sit. "I would speak to you alone." His gaze cut to Reid.

Scowling, Reid guided Widget onto his shoulder and stood, disappearing into his workroom. Only once he was gone did Damien say, "I thought we agreed not to meet in person."

"I accepted your suggestion at the time, but if I want to meet in person, then we meet in person." Darius leaned his hands on the back of the chaise.

"Your suspicion was correct. Royce remains, as always, an overconfident fool and all but took credit for the attack openly at last night's soiree. He and Niekla will be at the Lily in the Greenwark at noon."

Satisfaction descended through Damien. Darius liked to think himself above Royce, but he was just as easily manipulated. One suggestion that the assassination attempt was related to the Ranier prince, and he put all his connections to use finding out who was responsible.

"If they're willing to go to those lengths, then we need to move more quickly." Darius started pacing, his arms clasped behind his back. "We need to keep an eye on my sister as well. She's dangerous enough on her own, but I have reasons to suspect she has ties to the rebels."

That, Damien had not been expecting. "What reasons?"

Darius came to a halt. "I have evidence suggesting that she is aiding them. Bank records, clandestine meetings with people connected to known rebels. Nothing I can make a case out of, but enough to know that if you do not help me ascend the throne, she will ruin everything."

For some time, Damien had been trying to decipher Eshlin's motives, but he had always felt as though he was missing the central piece. This was why the rebels had only attacked Darius during the Illinir. But then what of her voting decisions? She had the power to change things from the inside yet remained rooted firmly in the way. Was it to throw off suspicion?

"I see you understand what I'm saying." Darius stepped around the chaise, finally deigning to sit and unbutton the clasp of his diamond-lined jacket. The vest underneath was equally garish, slivers of gemstones following the lines of the stitching in an ostentatious show of wealth.

"The rebellion is no idle threat," Damien agreed. "Have we done anything to address it?"

Darius waved a dismissive hand. "I'll be king by the end of the month, and then I can crush them."

The certainty in Darius's voice drew Damien's attention. "Your father's health is that poor?"

Darius hesitated before saying carefully, "He's unlikely to last that long, yes."

"So we can be certain the throne will be vacant at that point?" Damien pressed, all but daring Darius to say it. He was foolish enough to boast about his plans simply for the clout, but if he was implying what Damien suspected, this was no small admission.

"I'm certain." Darius lifted his chin, and Damien's suspicion solidified. There had never been an official announcement of the king's illness, nor a consensus among the nobility of what it might be. Whatever it was, in that moment, Damien was certain that Darius was the cause.

Darius sprung to his feet. "Find me the Ranier prince, Adair, and do it quickly." He turned on his heel.

Only once the door shut in his wake did Reid poke his head out from the workshop. "For the record, I could still hear everything. Is he going to be a problem?"

"He isn't a threat." Darius liked to pretend that he was dangerous, but he had always been the bark to Rezek's bite. Without his cousin at his side, he was soft.

Reid snorted. "You would call a lion bearing down on you for the kill 'not a threat.'"

"If I had gun, it wouldn't be." Damien made for the door before Reid could press any further. "I'll be back this afternoon. I have something I need to take care of."

"Where are you going?" Reid called.

Damien didn't stop as he replied, "Hunting."

THE LILY WAS a high-end teahouse at the end of Ettinger Street, made entirely of glass and ironwork in the shape of a dome. Sound reverberated off the hard surfaces, making it the perfect public place to have a private conversation, as each person's voice was lost to the next.

Damien bypassed the hostess without a word, entering a circular room with a shallow pond at the center. Countless wide lily pads dotted the water, tables secured atop them as an energy enchantment carried the lilies in a slow, steady pattern across the pond.

He spotted Royce and Niekla at a nearby table, their pad just about to skirt the edge, where a server waited for them.

Damien held out a hand for the server's teapot. "I'll take that."

The server gaped at him, handing it over and bowing swiftly before backing away. Damien faced the pond, waiting until Royce and Niekla's pad paused alongside the edge. They didn't even look up as he stepped on board, assuming he was only a servant. He dragged out a chair, letting the edges scrape, and sat down.

"What in the four hells do you think—oh. It's you." Royce looked unimpressed, but Damien could see through the act to the tension underneath. He hadn't expected this. Niekla hid her reaction much better, sharp eyes evaluating him as he plucked an extra teacup and turned it over, filling it from the fresh pot.

"I thought the three of us should chat," he said.

Royce brushed an errant hand through the air. "Oh, don't be so offended. You know how the game is played, boy."

Damien refilled Niekla's cup next, hiding his irritation at the diminutive term. "I do, which is why I spent the morning making the most of my turn." He pretended not to notice the look the two exchanged, turning instead to refill Royce's cup.

"I have little doubt whose idea the attack was, as only one of you is reckless enough for something like that, but I thought it important that you understand that you're not the only one capable of moves of that scale." Damien lifted his gaze to Royce's, savoring his growing look of apprehension. Royce was trying so hard to catch up, to predict where this was going, that he didn't notice the boiling tea overflowing from his cup.

Royce hissed and leapt from his chair as the scalding liquid spilled over the edge into his lap. The chair toppled into the water, creating a splash that drew people's attention.

Royce clutched his reddened hand to his chest. "How dare you," he snarled.

Damien set down the teapot. "You're too focused on what's directly in front of you, Royce. It leaves you wide open."

A murmur had picked up through the room, the sound amplified by the dome, but it wasn't Royce they were staring at any longer. Damien watched as Royce followed the crowd's attention out the window to a line of smoke rising in the distance.

Damien dropped a sugar cube into his teacup. "I was sorry to hear about your daughter's coma." While he wasn't directly responsible for Lady Vanadahl's misfortune, her state the result of a visit from the gambling den owner she owed money to, he was the one who'd revealed her location after she'd started using Arielle's name as a bartering chip.

He stirred his tea and picked it up, taking a slow sip. "I hope that fire isn't anywhere nearby."

At last, understanding clicked into place behind Royce's eyes. "You bastard." He seized hold of Damien's shirt, nearly spilling his tea, but fell still when Damien's gaze landed on him.

"The smoke is growing quickly," he said. "You should probably go."

Royce hesitated, clearly torn between ceding to Damien and ensuring his manor didn't burn down. In the end, he released him with a curse and leapt into the pond, wading through the shallow water to reach the edge. Two guards descended from the perimeter to join him as he hurried out the exit.

Damien set down his tea, looking to Niekla, who'd watched the scene unfold without interference. She tapped one manicured nail against the edge of her cup. "I see," she said at last. "Rezek always said you were clever, but he undersold your dedication."

Damien forced himself not to react at the notion of Rezek discussing him with these people. He could only imagine the sorts of things they said, hidden behind gilded walls.

"The idea was Royce's, but the assassins were mine. Though I assure you my participation was purely academic," Niekla continued. "I wanted to know how you would respond, and now I do."

She clicked open a white leather purse hanging from her chair, pulling free an envelope. "Consider this a peace offering."

He took the envelope, withdrawing a sketch of a death certificate for Torren Ranier.

Niekla slid back her chair, slinging the purse over her shoulder as the lily pad came to rest against the edge of the room.

"My man took the real one off of someone investigating the prince," she explained, stepping onto steady ground. "He said it was Mikira Rusel."

CHAPTER 15

ARIELLE

OVER THE NEXT few days, Ari planned her visits to Rezek around when Damien was out. Rezek had been enacting a series of experiments with death enchantments, imposing them onto already charmed objects to see if he could suppress their magic. At first, they tended to work a little too well. An enchanted clock stopped ticking. The coldbox thawed. She was fairly sure that if he tried the enchantment on her as it was now, something vital would stop and never restart.

While he worked, he let her use his workshop, and she spent the time experimenting with the Godstones. She charmed scrap metal into coins and seeds into flowers using the transformation enchantments granted by the onyx stones. Things could only become another version of themselves, preventing her from changing books into birds or hair into gold, but opening up a whole new range of possibilities that entranced her.

It reminded her of a magic show that would frequent her town edah, one of the many events Rivkah had snuck out to, leaving Ari with no choice but to follow. Ari had always thought the show silly, but she'd loved watching it all the same, because it meant she was with her sister.

She only hoped Rivkah was far away from her now.

The journey to Aversheen was nearly four days by coach, which meant she'd likely already arrived. What had she told their parents about where she'd been? Would they be proud of her or, like Ari, only thankful she was safe?

It pained her to consider, so she threw herself deeper into her studies, but all the while a thread of guilt needled at her ribs. It felt wrong exploring magic like this without Damien. It was only because of him that she'd discovered what she had. Knowing that she was here, with Rezek of all people, only made it all the sharper.

Ari toyed with one of the flowers she'd charmed from a seed that afternoon, frowning at the dirt under her nails that she'd missed that morning. She was used to it from making golems, though it had been a while since she'd crafted one. Was that why Rezek wanted the fourth Godstone? To create golems of his own?

That would mean his spellbook didn't mention it, and neither did the Racari from the castle, assuming he'd taken it.

Casually, as if she were just browsing, she began to walk the perimeter of the workshop, her eyes sliding over rows of titles, looking for a ribbed spine of leather. She barely made it a quarter of the way around the room before Rezek's voice reached her.

"It isn't here." He lifted his head. "The third Racari."

"I'm not—"

"Of course you are." He sprawled back in his chair. "I'm only surprised you didn't look sooner. But like I said, it isn't here. I went chasing after you that night at the closing ball, and when I returned, it was gone."

Ari searched his face, but if Rezek was lying, she couldn't tell. "Then you think someone in the castle has it? That they're possessed too?"

At that, Nava stirred, and Ari braced herself as she did every time the Heretic's presence solidified. She kept waiting for Nava to interfere, to ruin their experiments, but she seemed content not to draw Rezek's interest. Or, rather, Selvin's. Still, she couldn't subdue her stronger emotions, and every time Ari broached the subject of the other Racari, she seemed unable to remain completely neutral.

Rezek shrugged. "Selvin and I have no interest in the others."

Nava had suggested the same, and while nothing in Rezek's expression gave him away, his words rang false to her. He'd brought her here out of interest for her Racari; it seemed unlikely he'd be so cavalier about the other two, particularly as someone who claimed to be pursuing magical study. But Ari let him have his lie. Until she had what she needed from him, she wouldn't risk upsetting this delicate balance they'd established.

Rezek held up the opal bracelet. "Anyway, I'm finished."

A sudden doubt swelled inside her as she approached. Not only that he might have misdone the spell, but that she had missed something. That all this talk of magic and her suspicion of what he was truly after was a distraction, and the last thing she should do was allow Rezek Kelbra to place an enchanted bracelet on her wrist.

Trust your instincts, little lion. Nava's presence resounded through her in a low hum, one last plea. *Do not do this.*

My instincts tell me you're dangerous, Ari countered. *That you're keeping things from me for your own gain.*

I am protecting *you.* Nava sounded almost desperate for her to understand. *As I have always protected you. While these others are fickle and fearful, I have always been here for you, Arielle.*

The use of her real name sent a shudder through Ari. It had sounded . . . familial. The knowledge that, however distantly, they were related had lodged like a splinter beneath her skin. It made her want to believe Nava, if only so she could have a piece of her family back.

Ari's fingers curled into a fist. *Perhaps I would if I thought for a second it was truly my best interest you had at heart.*

It is the interest of all Kinnish I hold close.

What is that supposed to mean?

Something like regret reverberated down their bond, and it left Ari feeling strangely forlorn. She pushed it aside, refusing to let Nava's emotions influence her. She couldn't let this go on any longer. Not only because of the risk to the people around her, but the lying, the sneaking away. She wanted these meetings with Rezek over, and she wanted control of herself once more. She wanted to see Mikira, to hold Rivkah and never let her go.

Ari held out her hand to Rezek.

Arielle, please—

Everything inside her quieted as the bracelet slid over her wrist, a flame snuffed out by an errant breeze. It took her breath away at first and for one protracted second, she was certain Rezek had done something wrong, that he'd tricked her after all. Then she began to adjust to a body that felt suddenly foreign, her sense of her own physical limits shifting just a fraction.

Nava? she called.

The Heretic was silent; Ari didn't feel so much as a wisp of her presence.

"It worked," she breathed.

ARI RETURNED HOME that evening feeling strangely empty.

She hadn't realized how much strength her magic had given her even without her using it. Or perhaps that had been Nava's presence, and she was only feeling the absence of it. She'd tried again to reach the Heretic once she was free of the Kelbra estate, but there'd been no answer.

The relief she'd expected at their success was short-lived, swiftly replaced by a series of emotions she could hardly parse, the strongest of which was a biting sense of grief. She'd lost access to the thing that made her powerful, made her safe, and she toyed with the bracelet the entire ride home, resisting the urge to rip it from her wrist.

She didn't know if she could do this.

As the coach drew to a halt at the front of Adair Manor, she was forced to admit that it was more than just the absence of her magic that scared her; it was the realization that all her excuses, all her reasons, were gone.

Either she told Damien the truth about the bracelet, or it became another lie between them.

Emerging into the lavender-scented night, she forced one foot in front of the other, tracing the path back to their suite with growing apprehension. She'd worked over the words a hundred times, trying to find the right ones to explain her desperation, her decision, but none of them felt like enough.

The suite was quiet when she entered, an hours-old fire smoldering in the hearth. A light burned from Reid's room as it always did in the evening, but she was surprised to find hers and Damien's dark. She cracked open the door. Damien lay atop the covers still dressed in his vest and tie, one shoed foot on the floor and the other half-tangled beneath the blankets.

He was asleep.

A relief she didn't deserve twisted through her. It was early for Damien to be asleep, and the state of his clothes made it clear he hadn't meant to be. He'd chastise himself for it in the morning, if only for letting his body do something without his intention, but for now he looked more peaceful than she'd seen him in some time.

His dark hair curled across his brow, the tension so often wound along his jaw nowhere to be seen. His full lips were slightly parted, the moonlight pooling on his olive skin. She resisted the urge to run her fingers along it.

Her Racari sat on the nightstand beside him. She'd promised Rezek she would bring it to him once she was certain the bracelet worked, but now that she was free of him, could she avoid fulfilling her end of the bargain? She had no qualms with betraying Rezek Kelbra, but if she was right about him wanting her Racari for a larger purpose, she didn't think he'd give up on obtaining it so easily.

And with her magic suppressed, she was vulnerable.

Another reason she ought to tell Damien the truth. He knew how to handle Rezek better than anyone, yet she couldn't bring herself to wake him. Carefully she lifted his other leg atop the bed, straightening him. Her fingers made quick work of the buttons on his vest, and she gently slid him free of it, all but holding her breath.

A hand fell on her wrist, just above the cold press of the bracelet, and she stilled.

Damien was clearly only half-awake, his bright eyes heavily lidded with sleep, and yet she still felt pinned beneath his gaze. His grip softened, his thumb teasing along the inside of her wrist in a motion that made her shiver.

"Arielle," he murmured. "What time is it?"

"Go back to sleep," she replied, folding herself onto the bed beside him. His arms encircled her, strong and familiar and warm, and she leaned into that steadiness in the absence of her own. All the words she could not say gathered in her throat, and she let him hold her, let her body say what her lips could not, and prayed that, come morning, she would know what to do.

CHAPTER 16

MIKIRA

MIKIRA HAD HOPED her days of fancy balls had ended with the Illinir. Yet here she was, doused in a dress of deep forest green reminiscent of Rach, the Armored Bull, in honor of Eridice. The yearly holiday celebrated the Goddess Sendia's mercy, with people taking stock of the previous year and working to cleanse their souls in order to rejoin the Goddess in death.

At least, for the devout.

For the rest of them, it was an excuse to throw extravagant parties like the one she and Talyana entered now, hosted by Elidon Shaw. His family sigil was the second on the death certificate according to Shira, who had paid Alek Ambry a visit following Reid's identification of their crest. But all Ambry had done was forge the false death certificate; it was Shaw who'd witnessed the prince's birth.

She and Talyana ascended the townhouse steps alongside guests dressed in colors evoking the four Harbingers. There were long white capes of pearlescent feathers hooked over shoulders and old books tucked under people's arms symbolizing Aslir's dedication to study. Others wore Skylis masks and traveling cloaks in honor of the Harbingers' habit of disguising themselves to walk unknown among the people.

As they entered a spacious foyer, a pair of servants in black-and-white suits checked their invitations. It was Mikira's celebrity status that had landed them one and now served as their cover for being there. If she disappeared in search of Elidon Shaw, people would just think her seeking to thank their host.

The servants ushered them onward, and Mikira's chest tightened with anticipation. She wished suddenly that Reid were there. His presence had gotten her through more than one of the Illinir balls, and he had a way of making her feel ten times bigger than she was.

"It looks like the dancing has already begun," Talyana said as they entered. The townhome's central room was large, with high, arching ceilings and a space cleared for the band and dance floor. Other guests milled about in conversation, plucking food and drinks from the platters of passing servants.

"Care to make an entrance with me?" Talyana held out one long-fingered hand. She was resplendent in a crimson Skylis suit, her vest a coal black, sans jacket. Her hair fell in loose waves to her shoulders, and there was a healthy flush in her light brown cheeks from the chill fall air that made Mikira want to press a palm to her skin.

Mikira grinned, sliding her hand into Talyana's, and they emerged onto the dance floor with the next song. They flew along in time to the music, Talyana's practiced steps easily carrying Mikira's more uncertain ones. Her strong arms pulled Mikira flush so that they were chest to chest, hip to hip, and she could smell the tantalizing floral scent of Talyana's perfume.

"This is far more fun when I can actually see your face," Mikira teased, thinking of their last dance at the Vanadahl ball.

A sly grin curved Talyana's lips. "Why, do you like my face?"

Heat flooded Mikira's cheeks, and she fought to keep a straight face. She didn't know what to say. She never did, and she was starting to recognize that there was a reason for that. That flirting and smiling like this carried with it expectations she didn't know how to meet, and that she was beginning to suspect she didn't want to. She liked the banter, liked the familiarity and the closeness it brought, but that was where her interest ended.

It was an aspect of herself she'd avoided examining, afraid of what it might mean. Her feelings weren't the kind Lochlyn had ever described to her, didn't mirror Ailene's bright-eyed infatuation. It left her feeling almost . . . broken, as if some fundamental part of her was missing, and if anyone knew, they would reject her, like so many had before.

Even now it felt as if every set of eyes upon her could see straight through her, down to the raw truth underneath, but she wanted Talyana to understand.

As if sensing her reticence, Talyana's smile faded. "Kira, I . . . I owe you an apology. I should never have put you in the middle of things with Damien. I wanted so badly to get you away from him that I endangered you and your family instead."

Mikira hadn't realized how much she'd wanted that apology. She and Talyana had been so close once, attending races and riding through her family's fields together every chance they got. She ached for that intimacy, that friendship, but a part of her had still been holding on to a kernel of resentment over what happened with Damien's signet ring.

"I won't forgive anyone who hurts you, myself included," Talyana continued, pulling her through another turn. "If that means this can't be between us, I understand that, but I want you to know how much I care about you. Whatever you want from me, my answer is yes."

"This," Mikira said on instinct, desperately attempting to rein in her rising emotions. "I want this, exactly the way it is."

Her hand tightened on Talyana's, trying to impress upon her the intensity of the feelings inside her. That they might not be romantic, or even physical, but they were just as powerful, just as fierce.

The look in Talyana's eye told her that she understood, but before she could respond, the song swelled to an end and the dance broke apart. Like moths to a flame, a small crowd formed around Mikira, and Talyana allowed herself to be pushed to the fringes. It took all of Mikira's self-control to readjust, to tuck her feelings for Talyana away somewhere safe as she played her role. She absorbed their attention, her stories well practiced by now. Everyone had the same questions: How did you win the race? Where did you get Atara? Can I have your autograph?

But in between the questions were the stories people shared openly, treating her like a confidant. "I never thought someone like me could win that race," said one man in a secondhand suit. He wasn't the only one whose outfit was less than opulent among the gemstone jackets and silk waistcoats. Everyone wore their finest on Eridice, but for many it was just a stark reminder of what they didn't have.

"I heard you lost your brother in the Eternal War," said an Enderlish girl with a sympathetic smile. "I lost my sister."

These were the things she listened for. The hints that people might be as hungry for change as she was. She filed away their names to pass on as possible recruits, inviting them to tour the ranch or meet Atara, and all the while she felt as though she were floating upon a cloud, as if the sheer volume of the clamoring voices around her could buoy her above their heads.

"Mikira? Mikira!" A hand seized her wrist, and Talyana dragged her from her admiring circle. She blinked, realizing the room was nearly twice as full now as it had been before, the sun slanting in through the large windows at a new angle.

"The party is getting too busy." Talyana let go of her to survey the crowd. "We should look for Shaw and go."

Mikira nodded, scanning the room. They had nothing but the man's name to go on, and no one had mentioned him. Her eyes locked on the bartender at the back of the room, who was chatting animatedly with a woman waiting for her drink. They ought to know Shaw if he hired them, but even if he hadn't done it directly, the bartender was always the heart of the party.

With a loose, sleeveless top baring golden-brown arms and their hair shorn on each side, the top a longer silky black, the bartender looked as though they ought to be magnetizing a crowd in a brass band rather than making drinks. A patchwork black bird tattoo curled up from their collarbone around their neck, and they had several silver hoops in their ears. They wielded the cocktail shaker like a weapon, dispensing drinks with practiced ease.

When she and Talyana reached the counter, the bartender was already sizing them up.

"Whiskey, neat," they said to Talyana in a drawn-out Kenzeni accent, their dark eyes falling on Mikira. "And something a little spicier. An Orange Slice, perhaps?" Their hands were already moving, fixing the drinks before she and Talyana had even taken their seats at the bar.

"Is this Adair?" Talyana asked when the bartender set a glass of amber liquid before her.

"Top shelf."

Talyana discreetly scooted the glass away while the bartender was busy with Mikira's drink. It started with a whiskey base, before they added a dash of some dark liquid she didn't recognize, followed by a twist of orange peel and a sprinkle of cinnamon. She accepted the drink and tasted it, the whiskey far spicier than the Adair she'd tried.

"Eh?" the bartender asked with a grin.

"It's good," Mikira said with a smile.

"Nothing but the best for the best, or so I hear." Their hands were already busy making another drink. "What's it like being a celebrity?"

"A little bit like being a bartender, I think. Everyone feels like they know you and expects you to know them." She wouldn't lie and say she didn't like the attention, but the more she exposed herself to it, the more she realized that these people genuinely expected her to call on them for social engagements, or to remember their brother's wife's mother's name.

Talyana gave her a questioning look, but Mikira only shook her head, focusing on the bartender. "We were hoping you might be able to direct us to the party's host? Elidon Shaw."

The bartender poured a fizzing drink into a tall, stemmed glass.

"Mr. Shaw will be down shortly. Why don't you enjoy the party in the meantime?"

Reluctantly, Mikira picked up her drink as the bartender turned away. "We can do a circuit of the room, see if anyone knows him?"

Talyana nodded and they split up, sliding from conversation to conversation, but no one had seen their host yet. In fact, almost everyone Mikira spoke to claimed to have never seen him before. By the time she met up with Talyana on the other side of the room and heard she had a similar experience, Mikira was starting to suspect they were missing something.

Across the way, the bartender emerged from behind the counter to let someone else take over. They seized a crimson sash delicately embroidered with falling feathers from the back of a chair and wrapped it smoothly about their waist, leaving the end to dangle over their loose cotton pants, before disappearing up the nearby staircase.

Mikira's gaze switched back to the servant who'd taken over, dressed in a white-and-black uniform like the one out front, and she groaned.

"What?" Talyana asked.

"The bartender was not a bartender," she muttered. "Can you cover for me down here?"

Talyana nodded as Mikira fought through the crowd. People called out to her, roping her into conversations, but she finally emerged on the other side and made a show of looking for the bathroom as she wandered upstairs. The boards creaked underfoot, the fine wood covered in a layer of dust that belied the rich furnishings below.

The stairwell opened into a short hallway that veered left, and Mikira approached the corner cautiously. Distant voices echoed, and she peered around the wall to find a door at the end of a long hall cracked open. She crept closer, ducking into the room next door to listen.

". . . shipments will be arriving in Celair next week." That was the bartender.

"We need more, Rahzen," replied a feminine voice. "So many more."

"You wanted Kenzeni weapons, and they come with a Kenzeni price tag," Rahzen replied with a dismissive air. "That's the best I can do for you without more funds."

A quiet sigh preceded the scraping of a chair. "I'll talk to the others."

Mikira shifted deeper into her hiding place as the door opened fully and footsteps proceeded past her down the hall. Only then did she notice how bare the room was, empty of everything save a grimy desk below the window. The townhouse was huge, and she couldn't imagine Elidon used every room, but it looked like no one had set foot in here for ages.

With one hand on a knife, Mikira emerged into the hall. She'd only heard one set of footsteps, which meant the bartender was still up here. Slowly, she pushed open the door.

Rahzen lounged in a metal chair backlit by the setting sun. A second chair sat at a round table occupied by a single drink. The bartender offered her a lazy grin, not the least bit surprised to see her. "Miss Rusel," they greeted. "Do you need another drink?"

"Actually I'm looking for Elidon." Mikira scanned the room; it too was almost entirely empty and clearly neglected.

Rahzen gave her a knowing smile. "And what might the rebellion want with him?"

Mikira's hand tightened on her knife hilt. "I don't know what you—"

"Before you bother lying, you should know I'm rather good friends with Shira Adair." Rahzen lifted their drink, ice clinking against glass.

"Of course." Mikira released a sigh, but not her blade. As courteous as Rahzen was being, there was something about them that had every one of Mikira's instincts screaming at her not to let her guard down.

"Then will you let me speak to Elidon?" she asked.

Rahzen took a long draw of their whiskey, black eyes watching Mikira over the rim before they said, "He isn't here, and I'm afraid I can't help you find him."

She'd begun to suspect as much from the state of the townhouse, which meant they were yet again out of leads in their search for the prince. There had to be another way to find him. Without him, Eshlin couldn't ascend the throne, and the rebellion would have to resort to their original plan to take it by force.

You wanted Kenzeni weapons, and they come with a Kenzeni price tag. Rahzen's voice came floating back to her. If they truly were a friend of Shira's, then perhaps there *was* something else they could help the rebellion with.

"I heard you talking to that woman," Mikira began tentatively. "It sounds like bartending isn't the only service you provide."

A gleam lit Rahzen's eyes. "Ah, so this is that sort of conversation."

"Will you help us?"

Rahzen sipped their drink, the movement shifting a golden torque about their neck set with a spherical bloodstone. "Your timing is less than ideal. The Eternal War is heating up again, and as you've just witnessed, Izir is funneling weapons into the Celairen army. This could become a three-kingdom conflict at any moment, and I'd hate to be tied up at an inopportune time."

Mikira swallowed back a retort. Anger and pleading would get her nowhere with someone like this. She knew this dynamic all too well, the one where the powerful made a game of conversations that could change lives. This time, she played back.

Rahzen clearly liked attention, and their chosen profession paid well, yet they continued to risk their life as a weapons merchant. Was it just for the thrill, or something more?

"Is it only about money for you?" she challenged.

"I've done more for less." Rahzen flashed a grin that bordered on predatory, and that same uneasy feeling crept down Mikira's spine again. The merchant had no obvious weapons, but Mikira still gave her knife a command to protect her if they attacked. The blade hummed in its sheath, ready to move.

Rahzen eyed the knife as if they knew exactly what she'd done. "I'm very careful about the people I help, Miss Rusel. Even friends." They crossed their legs, toying absently with their torque. "I do not wish to sow chaos for its own sake."

Mikira relaxed a little at that. So they weren't just an opportunist snatching handfuls of blood money. That, she could work with. She thought of the people she'd spoken to today. The man who'd only ever seen closed doors in his future, the girl whose sister's life had become one of many crushed beneath Enderlain's unyielding pursuit of power. She thought of her father's silence, and her own relentless rage.

"I don't want that either," she said, and meant it. The chaos of a battle would leave people frightened. Lives would be lost, others upended. "But neither can I allow the status quo to persist because the alternative isn't easy. I've watched this city crush people like me over and over again, watched the structure be upheld in the name of peace."

Her fingers tightened on her knife handle. "The only peace being maintained here is theirs. Their lives, their fortunes, their safety. Never ours." She met Rahzen's solemn gaze. "Chaos has already been sown. It's about time the other half felt it."

She felt Rahzen's careful consideration, before they tipped their glass to her in a small salute. "Very well. I'll set something up with Shira."

Mikira nodded, retreating slowly from the room and closing the door. Deal or not, she didn't want to turn her back on the weapons merchant without a barrier between them. That apprehensive feeling stuck with her as she hurried down the hall.

She rounded the corner—and jolted to a halt as she came face-to-face with Damien Adair.

CHAPTER 17

DAMIEN

DAMIEN DIDN'T BELIEVE in coincidences.

When Niekla Dramara had told him that her man had intercepted Mikira Rusel at the Vault, he'd believed her, but still intended to verify it. Then word of her presence had been on everyone's lips the moment he entered Elidon Shaw's townhouse, and now here she was, skulking through the back halls the same as he.

He stared down at her as something slowly unspooled deep inside him. He'd trusted Mikira, seen her as a partner, even thought that they understood each other's twisted love for this city. And she'd nearly cost him everything. That feeling of helplessness that had incapacitated him as he'd been forced to watch Ari's abduction rose anew.

He had promised himself he would never be that powerless again, and yet the feeling had taken over him, so much like the day he'd watched the blood rush out of his mother like spilled wine. He'd felt useless. It was an emotion he refused to give purchase now, a weakness he couldn't afford, and he crushed it in favor of the rising heat of anger. But while his face remained impassive, Mikira's flooded with consternation.

"What are you doing here?" she asked, always so direct. He'd admired that about her once, even if her bluntness had made their delicate machinations more difficult. So few people said what they meant in his world, himself included, that Mikira's honesty had been refreshing.

Until she'd turned it against him.

Understanding eclipsed her dismay at his silence, and one hand drifted to the knives at her hip. He had no doubt she'd reached the same conclusion as he: that their shared presence here meant they were after the same thing, and neither of them was going to acknowledge it. The question was, had she already acquired the information he'd come for?

Yet when he opened his mouth to speak it, a different one came out. "Did you lie to Reid, or did he lie to me?"

Mikira looked as caught off guard by the question as he was, but it had been pestering him since his meeting with Niekla. Reid had run into Mikira at the Vault the same day she was there looking for information on the prince. What if Reid had known why she was there and hadn't told him? What if—

"I can't believe you even have to ask that." Mikira's scoff cut short his spiral of thoughts. "After everything he's done for you, you still don't trust him?"

Damien's irritation flared, leaking into his voice. "After everything I did for you, you still betrayed me." And if someone as moral and honest as Mikira could turn on him, what did that say of everyone else?

Mikira's hands balled into fists, and he wondered if she might punch him. It wouldn't be the first time her anger got the best of her. But to his surprise, she forced a breath out through her nose and released a low, scornful laugh.

"Have you ever stopped to consider that people aren't betraying you?" she asked. "Maybe you're just driving them all away."

With that, she shoved past him, descending the stairs without a backward glance. Her words remained, floating like dust particles in the dim light. What she had done, what Hyle had, what Rezek . . . *Was* it his fault?

Loic had always blamed him for their mother's death, and he'd carried a seed a guilt for years at not seeing Rezek's move coming.

If he'd been smarter, if he'd been quicker or more in control, he could have prevented all of this. Every betrayal, every wound—none of it had to happen. But this city bred competition, it bred powerful people hungry for more, it bred violence and greed and corruption, and it forced people to make choices.

He thought of Arielle, who he'd barely seen the last couple days. When they arrived at the party together, she'd looked resplendent in the emerald dress she'd had commissioned from Sinclair, and yet all he could focus on was the opal bracelet about her wrist. She claimed to have purchased it to go with the dress, but when he'd asked at what store, intending to find a necklace to match, she couldn't remember the name.

For anyone else, it might mean nothing. A forgotten detail. Except Arielle *didn't* forget. Her keen mind and perceptiveness were two of the things he loved about her. She sheared through every wall he built, straight to the truth of him. She could read him in a way no one else could, even Reid, and that feeling of being known by her . . . it was intoxicating.

Which was why he didn't believe that she would forget a name, but neither could he think of a reason she would have kept it from him. Unless she didn't want him to know where she'd truly gotten it. His mind flashed back to the scent of roses, and he nearly laughed at the absurdity of the connection. The idea that Ari would have even visited Rezek was ludicrous, that he would have given her that bracelet even more so.

Maybe Mikira was right. Maybe he was pushing her away as well, first with talk of the prince, then again after their argument outside Zivaya's clinic. She'd hardly been around the last few days, gone when he returned or always out the door for some appointment. He wanted her to tell him what she was thinking, wanted to know how the creature in the Racari plagued her.

Was it only a matter of time before she turned against him like all the rest?

"It seems I'm rather popular today," drawled a voice, startling him from his thoughts.

A slim figure leaned one shoulder against the corner wall, regarding him with mirthful dark eyes. They wore traditional Kenzeni clothes, the colors of their sash invoking Skylis's plumage, and they held a half-empty whiskey in one hand.

"Rahzen," he greeted, reeling in his surprise. "Is Shira here too, then?"

Rahzen pushed off the wall, sliding their free hand into a pocket in a languid motion. "Is that really the question you came to ask me?"

He hadn't come to ask them anything; he'd come in search of Elidon Shaw. But after inquiring about the man at the party, it'd quickly become clear that no one had laid eyes on their mysterious host. So Damien had come looking for him himself, and now here was Rahzen.

He knew only a little of the weapons merchant from their interactions with Shira, as it was Rahzen who had procured his Lonlarra revolvers for him, but he was aware of their penchant for setting up shop in abandoned buildings. It seemed this was a façade they'd been maintaining for some time, using Elidon's parties as cover.

"Very well." Damien drew a gun and leveled it at Rahzen's forehead. "Where is Elidon Shaw?"

Rahzen grinned with complete disregard for the weapon pointed at them. "I see why Shira's worried about you."

Damien's grip tightened. "I'm not in the mood for games. Tell me where he is, or I'll shoot you."

Rahzen sighed. "I'd really rather you didn't. It always makes things so messy."

"Rahzen."

"And what if I told you that I didn't know?" Their smile turned feline.

"I wouldn't believe you." Damien cocked the gun. "You wouldn't use someone's property without knowing everything about them. And if my brother is to be believed, you've been operating out of this townhouse for some time, which tells me you're very confident that wherever Elidon is, he's staying there."

He only hoped that didn't mean that Elidon was dead. Damien would be out of leads, his chances at finding the prince gone. Worse, if Rahzen had already told Mikira of Elidon's location, she could be on her way there right now. If she found the prince first, Damien's carefully constructed plan would crumble.

"Well, you have me there." Rahzen knocked back the last of their drink. "Elidon lives in the Pendron District, on a street called Thistledown. His is the third house on the left. The door bears the Goddess's mark."

Damien lowered his gun. "Is that what you told Mikira?"

"Oh, Miss Rusel and I had a very *different* conversation." Rahzen held up their empty drink, shaking the lone ice cube like a bell. "Now, if you'll excuse me, it seems I'm regrettably still sober." They turned on their heel, disappearing down the hall.

Damien holstered his revolver, trying to parse the meaning between Rahzen's words. If Mikira had come here looking for information on the Ranier prince, why had Rahzen told him and not her? There was only one other reason he could think that Mikira would have business with them, but he couldn't imagine what need she would have of a weapons supplier on that scale unless—

"Unless she's working for Eshlin," he muttered, thinking of Darius's suspicions about his sister, of Mikira's clandestine meeting with the princess at the last Illinir ball.

It seemed Mikira Rusel had joined the rebellion.

CHAPTER 18

ARIELLE

ARI FIDDLED WITH the opal bracelet.

Damien had noticed it that morning at breakfast, as he noticed everything. The excuse she'd given had been poor, but he'd let it go, and they'd climbed into the coach together that evening in silence. But as long as the bracelet continued to work, the lies would all be worth it. The blackouts would be under control, just like Damien wanted.

Like I want, she reminded herself, though a part of her was doubtful. The part that wondered how much of her strength came not from herself, but from the Heretic inside her. That wondered how lonely it would be without the presence that, for all their arguments, had been with her for most of her life, and there for her in some of her darkest moments.

A flurry of attention had greeted her, Reid, and Damien upon their arrival at the party, the crowd practically swallowing Damien whole. Since the news broke about his role in ending the taxes, the papers had been writing about him nonstop, theorizing about what he'd change next. Everyone wanted to talk to him, but he'd stayed only long enough to establish his presence before heading off in search of Elidon, leaving her and Reid to cover for his absence.

She wouldn't have minded, save for the fact that she had greeted Atara on her way in. Even now, the bond of magic between her and the golem horse thrummed—which meant Mikira was here too.

Ari's mind turned over possibilities, trying to decide the best thing to say to her, but a headache had slowly begun to gather at the base of her skull, scrambling her thoughts. She could try to avoid Mikira altogether, but the prospect of walking away from her now that they were so close felt impossible. She didn't want to run from this any longer, and if the bracelet was working, then approaching Mikira ought to be safe.

Except after everything that had happened, did Mikira even want to see her?

Ari toyed with the bracelet again, reflexively seeking the burn of her verillion to soothe her, and nearly lurched at the emptiness that she found. The unease in the pit of her stomach grew tighter, and she forced herself to breathe. From the miserable look on Reid's face, his mind was in the same place. He kept scanning the crowd and had all but worried a button off his coat.

Ari stilled him with a touch at his wrist. "She probably doesn't want to talk to us."

"Maybe she's not as angry as you think," he countered.

"We are talking about the same Mikira?"

Reid very nearly smiled, until a voice rang out. "There she is!"

As if by fate, the crowd parted to reveal two girls—one tall with her brown hair in waves down her back, the other pale-skinned and looking fresh from a fight with her hands in fists. Talyana saw them first, eyes locking on Reid like a target. Mikira followed her gaze, the flush in her cheeks draining when she realized who it was. Reid made a strangled noise, but it was too late. Talyana was already cutting toward them, Mikira whispering furiously at her side.

"This is getting ridiculous, Haldane." Talyana's voice dripped with acidity.

Reid held up his hands. "I don't want to be here either."

"Then why are you?" Mikira looked to Ari before shaking her head. "Never mind, I don't care. Let's go, Tal." Her hand curled about Talyana's, pulling her away. Ari and Reid moved after her in unison, elbowing their way through the crowd to the foyer.

"Mikira!" Reid called, and she spun.

Talyana edged between them. "What do you want?"

"To talk to our friend." Ari looked beseechingly to Mikira. "Give us time to figure this out, please. Damien is under a lot of pressure right now."

Mikira snorted. "He drew this line, Ari, not me." Her gaze cut to Reid. "You both did."

"I didn't mean—" Reid cut off, gritting his teeth. He seemed to summon the words that came next from a place deep inside himself. "I didn't tell him about the ring on purpose."

Mikira's anger faltered, and she glanced at Ari, who nodded. "Widget found it and decided it was a toy. Reid's a fool for not better securing it, but he didn't out you intentionally."

"You think that's what she's upset about?" Talyana asked incredulously. "This is so much bigger than that."

"Tal." Mikira nudged her toward the door. "Give us a minute."

Reluctantly, Talyana marched outside. In the silence, Mikira gathered herself. "You said I'm your friend," she said to Ari. "Then where have you *been*?"

Ari wanted so badly to answer, but Reid would tell Damien the moment he learned the truth. Mikira didn't even know about the blackouts, the Heretic, the growing magic that she couldn't control that had driven her to keep her distance. But more than that, she could not imagine herself explaining to Mikira that she had gone to *Rezek* for help.

Mikira's eyes softened. "Whatever it is, Ari, I can help you. I'll always help you."

Ari's jaw clenched, trapping the words in her throat. She didn't trust herself to speak, and in the silence, Mikira's disappointment only grew. She nodded once, curt, and then she was gone, the townhouse door slamming in her wake.

Ari pressed a hand to the deepening throb at her temple, glancing down at the gleaming bracelet on her wrist. She would tell Mikira the truth eventually. Her power had been suppressed, but she didn't want to tell anyone about Rezek, tell them anything, until she was absolutely certain.

"Ari?" Reid asked uncertainly. "Are you okay?"

"I'll be fine," she ground out more irritably than she intended.

A sharp intake of breath made them both turn. A reed-thin woman with a heavy layer of cosmetics had entered the foyer, her dress nearly as pale a cream as her skin.

Ari recognized her with a start. "Lady Belda."

"My, haven't you changed." Her old client's eyes slid the length of Ari's emerald dress, her eyebrows rising higher with each passing second. "I saw you earlier with High Lord Adair. I wonder if he knows what company he keeps."

"You should be careful with your next words," Reid warned her. In response, something shifted from behind Lady Belda, and the big black golem dog Ari had created for the woman months ago growled softly.

Lady Belda's thin lips twisted. "I wonder what High Lord Adair's allies would think if they were made aware of your . . . proclivities."

Ari's hands tightened into fists at the small of her back. "What do you want?"

"Another beast," Lady Belda said lightly. "I went by your shop and found it closed."

"I don't take orders anymore," Ari replied sternly. "Good day, Lady Belda."

She started back inside, but Lady Belda seized her wrist. "Did I say we were finished, girl? Just because you've whored yourself out to—"

What happened next was nearly too fast for Ari to track. The golem dog lunged, its jaws closing around Lady Belda's thigh. She screamed, and Reid pulled Ari away as the dog slammed the woman into the ground.

Ari's senses grew fuzzy, her mind addled by the overpowering scent of blood, the feel of flesh tearing between her teeth. A channel had opened between her and the dog, like the one she shared with her golems, but this was stronger, more furious, and distantly she knew what it signified, knew that this was wrong, knew what the humming rising inside her meant.

She watched in distant fascination as the dog's teeth ripped into Lady Belda's shoulder. Other than Atara and an enchant shop cat, she'd never come face-to-face with her creations after relinquishing them to their owners. She hadn't realized that the golems' loyalty still lay with her.

"Ari," Reid hissed. "Call it off!"

He must have realized what was happening, and the last thing Damien needed was any press asking why his best friend and lover had been the only witnesses to a brutal mauling. But Ari didn't want to stop. She wanted to lean into the golem's anger, its violence, and let it carry her away. For its fury was her fury, its teeth arbitrators of justice. Of a kingdom that had been torn apart, a people scattered and a way of life annihilated.

Lady Belda deserved this. *All of Enderlain* deserved this, and she would see it done. She would—*no!* She seized the bracelet, but she knew even before she touched it that it had failed. She could feel the Heretic's presence gathering inside her, a step away from taking control.

Leave. Me. Alone! she screamed, and felt Nava's answering anger like a thunderclap.

This is no less than she has earned, little lion.

Through her haze of emotion and bloodlust and power, Ari recognized that some part of her agreed with that, but she would not be made a pawn in Nava's play for vengeance. She would not lose herself.

"Stop!" Ari hissed in Kinnish just as the foyer doors flew open and the crowd flooded the doorway. The dog stepped back, its jaws crimson with blood. Lady Belda lay motionless, her dress stained scarlet like an abstract painting. Her chest rose and fell in shallow breaths.

"Her dog went rabid," Reid explained to the stunned faces.

Damien stepped free of the crowd. "Call for an enchanted coach," he said to the nearest person. Reid was already moving, tearing free pieces of Lady Belda's dress to make compresses.

Ari only stared at the blood puddling on the marble floor—then she fled into the gathering dark. She heard Damien call her name but didn't stop until she'd reached the road, sucking in a lungful of cold autumn air. The street was thick with people celebrating, and no one paid a panicking Kinnish girl any heed.

Ari swallowed a scream as Damien joined her, already removing his overcoat to set around her shoulders. The warmth enveloped her in the scent of gunpowder.

"What happened?" he asked.

"She was a client of mine." Ari was breathless. "From before. The golem protected me."

Relief flitted through his face, and she wondered if he thought she'd done it herself. Or rather, under the influence of the Heretic.

The thought sent a spike of rage through her.

"I have my magic under control," she told him, and felt the truth of it stretch. But she hadn't had a full blackout for weeks, and she and Rezek were on to something with the opals, even if this iteration had failed. "You don't need to worry about me."

"You might as well tell me not to breathe." Damien brushed back an escaped curl. She captured his hand with her own, bringing his callused palm flush with her cheek.

"I could say the same to you," she replied softly, and very nearly left it at that. She wanted things to be okay between them. Wanted the intimacy that came with knowing someone better than you knew yourself, but she could no longer deny that that feeling was slipping away.

Her hand tightened on his. "I need to know what you're keeping from me."

She knew it wasn't fair, knew that asking him to bare his secrets when she would not was selfish. But he had always made her feel like it was the two of them against the world, and the idea that there might be a wall between them made the prospect of telling him about Rezek feel unscalable.

It made her afraid of what he'd do.

His fingers curled against her face, the kind of gentle touch he reserved only for her. "I'm hunting the prince. You know that."

She recoiled, letting his hand fall back to his side. "That's it?"

"That's it."

"I don't believe you," she whispered. "What are you planning, Dara?"

His fingers sought his cuffs, straightening them as if command of something so small might regain him control of the conversation too. It was a delay, a tactic for stalling until he could find the proper words, the ones that skirted the edge of a lie.

It gutted her.

She felt her face crumple, knew that he saw every raw nerve his refusal to share had set alight.

"Arielle—" he began, apologetic.

"No. Forget it," she said, and bolted into the crowd. She let the swarm of bodies swallow her, jostling her with every step, and tried to lose herself in the sensation, the anonymity, even as her mind pulsed.

The bracelet had failed; she needed another solution, and then she would tell Damien the truth.

A stirring in the back of her mind broke her train of thought, and her nails dug into her palms. *You knew, didn't you?* she asked Nava. *That it wouldn't work. That's why you didn't try to stop me.*

I suspected, Nava returned. *But it took me time to gather enough strength to overwhelm your enchantment. You cannot lock a power such as ours away, little lion. Nor should you.*

"I didn't want to lock it away!" Ari seethed aloud. "I wanted to lock *you* away."

Eyes turned as she passed, faces folding in dark looks she knew too well. She pulled Damien's overcoat more tightly about her shoulders, hiding her necklace, and walked quicker.

You might as well try to imprison yourself, Nava hissed back. *We are the same, you and I.*

We are nothing alike.

Nava's laugh echoed through her mind. *They tried to control me too. To use me for their own gain even as they disdained me.*

Ari hated the way the Heretic's words resonated with her. She didn't want to feel a kinship with this creature. Didn't want to understand her. Not when Nava's presence was slowly eating away at her sanity, the line between the two of them blurring more each day. She wanted the spirit *out* of her before it was too late.

Tell me what you want, she demanded.

Nava's reply was soft when she said, *Soon.*

CHAPTER 19

DAMIEN

IT WAS THE second time Arielle had walked away from him.

As his and Reid's coach flew down the street, he couldn't get the way she had looked at him out of his head. The way she'd fled into the crowd as if to escape him. There were so many things he hadn't told her: his discovery of Mikira's place in the rebellion, the true reason behind his hunt for the lost heir, the way it tore at him every time he watched her walk away, knowing it was his fault, knowing he'd driven her to do it.

Have you ever stopped to consider that people aren't betraying you? Maybe you're just driving them all away.

Mikira's words cut at him, but until he was sure everything was in place, until he knew nothing could go wrong—he couldn't make himself reveal the truth, and there was a part of him, however spiteful, that wanted her to give in first. Because he was not the only one keeping secrets, not the only one out at odd hours and exhausted upon their return.

Somewhere along the way, Arielle had stopped talking to him. She'd turned inward, and a little of that fear that had lived inside her when they'd first met had resurfaced. Seeing it that day the assassins attacked had rattled him more than he wanted to admit. It made him want to wrap his hands around the throat of whoever had made her feel that way, and the knowledge that he couldn't, that what tormented her was the very thing she loved, made him feel useless.

That was part of what drew him to Arielle. Her strength, her power—it seemed impossible that someone could ever hurt her. He knew he ought to tell her his plans, knew that she would not forgive his keeping things from her again, but every time the words rose to his lips, that feeling of helplessness came rushing back, a reminder of what came of trusting.

Reid jittered nervously in his seat, glancing between Damien and the darkened city rolling by outside their window. They were both dressed in black, hooded cloaks fastened at their shoulders. Reid had been toying with the clasp the entire ride as they flew toward Elidon Shaw.

"Are you sure about this?" he asked at last. "It's not too late to tell Darius to get lost."

"Yes," Damien replied.

Reid fiddled more intently with his cloak, a look on his face Damien knew meant that he had more to say. Just like he knew the flex of his friend's jaw meant he'd decided to let it go, albeit grudgingly. He relied on Reid to check him, but he also knew how easily he worried.

Damien stopped the coach several streets over from their destination, and they emerged with their hoods raised. Enchanted lamps cut through the late evening mist, lighting their way through rows of townhouses to Thistledown Street. It was lined with smaller, single-story homes, and he counted until he reached the third. The house had a single enchanted light, illuminating the supplicating hands of the Goddess carved above the door.

"Let's go." Damien slipped on a simple black mask, Reid following suit, then knocked.

A tall silver-haired man answered the door in his evening clothes. Elidon barely had time to register the masked forms on his doorstep before they'd shoved their way inside, Damien's revolver pointed at his chest. He held up his hands, eyes switching keenly between them.

Reid kicked the door shut, and Damien waited while he closed the curtains, before indicating the couch with his gun. Elidon obeyed, edging backward until his legs struck the edge and he collapsed onto it.

"Who are you?" he demanded.

"I'm looking for the Ranier prince," Damien replied.

Elidon's lips thinned just the slightest. He was good, as Damien had expected. To have been able to get the child out of the castle and to safety, to have kept him hidden all these years—it took skill and intelligence. The same intelligence Damien hoped would lead Elidon to realize that his options were limited: the truth, or a bullet.

Damien watched the decision play out across his face.

"I can't help you," Elidon replied with resignation.

"I thought you might say that." Damien withdrew a photograph from his pocket with his free hand. "So I brought motivation."

Elidon's eyes widened with recognition of his son's face.

"You've been estranged for so long, you probably thought everyone had forgotten him." Damien tossed the photo into Elidon's lap. "But I always do my research."

He'd found Elidon's son before he'd found the man himself, had even thought he might be a lead in lieu of the one he'd pursued at the townhouse. But one casual conversation had made it clear the man knew nothing of his father, who he'd presumed dead.

Elidon's hands curled into trembling fists. It had to be difficult for a man who had spent his life protecting others to be in this position. In truth, Damien didn't like putting him in it, and he could tell from Reid's fidgeting that he liked it even less. He'd have to find a way to compensate Elidon for this. Perhaps put in a good word for his son at the bank where he worked.

"If I tell you, you leave my son alone?" Elidon asked weakly.

"I do."

The old guardsman swallowed hard. "I only have an address." He nodded at a plain wooden chest on the side table. "It's in there."

Reid retrieved the chest for Elidon, who withdrew a key from a chain beneath his shirt. He inserted the key, and Damien heard the lock click just as Elidon thrust the chest at his face.

Damien batted it aside, but the guardsman was already on him. They crashed into a low table, shattering it. His gun skittered away, Elidon's fist striking his jaw before he could get his guard up. His head rang with the blow, but he thrust an elbow at the man's temple. Elidon took the strike, but then Reid was there, driving his boot into the man's chest.

Elidon slammed into the couch. His hand went under the nearest cushion, and Damien seized his other revolver. It caught on the strap, and Elidon pulled his own gun from the couch crevice. Damien tugged again and the gun snapped free. He dropped flat to the ground a second before Elidon pulled the trigger, the bullet tearing through the front of the house.

Damien aimed and fired.

The bullet struck Elidon in the chest. Blood blossomed from the wound in an ever-growing pattern, soaking his shirt through in seconds.

Damien climbed to his feet, the revolver still aimed at Elidon's heart, adrenaline firing through him in jagged bursts.

Reid's booted toe nudged his, and Damien became very aware of his finger on the trigger, of the stillness of Elidon's body. He wasn't breathing. Bit by bit, Damien reasserted control, turned instinct to rational thought. He holstered the revolver. Secured the second one and locked it away too. Straightened his cuffs, lifted his hood. Breathed.

Reid watched him do it all with a fraught expression. With how little stomach Reid had for violence, it was an enigma to Damien how they'd remained friends. In a way, Reid was the brother Loic never had been, and it was in moments like this, when Reid pulled him back from the brink of blood and cracking bone, when he reminded him he was still human, that Damien was most thankful for it.

But looking at the still form of Elidon Dalart before him, a part of him began to doubt.

As his rush of energy waned, a new feeling took its place. A yearning to undo, to go back, a desire that often wriggled beneath his decisions, trying to force him into uncertainty. He refused to give it a foothold. Thoughts like that would only drag him backward, mire him in indecision he couldn't afford.

He had to keep moving forward.

Locking the thoughts away, he seized the chest as Reid stared mournfully at Elidon's corpse. Damien turned for the door. "Let's go."

Lights were on in the neighboring houses when they exited, their inhabitants woken by the gunshots. Reid and Damien slipped through the alleys and back to their coach, setting off before the crowd gathered.

Only once they were alone did his adrenaline fade completely, a sharp burst of pain radiating from his half-healed shoulder. He clasped it with a wince, Reid staring pointedly at him as if he expected it to prove something.

Damien lowered his hand. "We'll wait for things to calm down before we call this in."

"Is that it?" Reid demanded.

"What else do you want?"

Reid shuffled in his seat. "You said no one would get hurt."

"No, I said I didn't *want* to hurt anyone." And he hadn't. They could have taken their information and left if Elidon hadn't tried to play the hero. He should have expected it—the man's service history was full of acts of bravery—but Damien wouldn't let his death be in vain. He would make it count for something.

He flipped open the box, finding a single folded letter.

> *I write only to let you know of our new location. After what happened, we couldn't remain. Too many eyes.*
>
> *If you need us, you can find us here under a new name.*

Damien took one look at the address—and laughed.

CHAPTER 20

MIKIRA

MIKIRA BURIED HERSELF in ranch work the morning after the Eridice party, her emotions from running into Ari and the others still coursing through her. She'd expected the cold shoulder from Damien, though it stung to face him more than she'd expected. He'd never given her the chance to explain, rejecting her for a crime she hadn't even committed.

At least, not on purpose.

She hadn't known Talyana was an Anthir sergeant, and she regretted sharing the ring with her, but she hadn't given it to her in the end. Still, her actions were the reason Damien hadn't been there to protect Ari from Rezek, and if there was one thing the two of them agreed on, it was keeping her safe.

Even if she wouldn't tell Mikira the truth right now. What was happening with her, and why wouldn't she let Mikira help? Then there was Reid, who claimed he hadn't sold her out to Damien after all. She didn't know whether to believe him, but she wanted to. Every time she tried to focus on a task, her mind circled back to how he'd looked at her as if he were drowning.

"Miss Rusel?" It was one of the new stable hands, a boy whose pale face flushed scarlet each time he spoke to her. "I've finished with the stalls. Do you want me to prepare the pasture for tomorrow's new arrivals?"

"Yes, thank you." He'd barely scurried off before another took his place, seeking direction. The ranch bustled with activity, workers setting up new fences and painting old ones, others brushing down horses throughout the barn. They'd even set up a series of targets for her to practice with her knives on behind the barn, and she'd spent the morning training with their magic.

Nelda had once said she should hire a stablemaster to handle it all, but Mikira wasn't quite ready to let it go. Seeing the ranch come alive again had been like stepping into a waking dream, everything working in impossibly perfect concert. After so long struggling to survive, she wanted to bask in this for as long as possible.

She only wished her family were here to see it.

She'd tried her best not to think too much about them since they'd left, swallowing the urge to ask Jenest where the rebels had sent them. The less she knew, the better, but it ached not being able to share the ranch's revival with them.

Soon, she told herself. When the rebellion had succeeded, when it was safe, her father and sisters would come back.

They'd be a family again.

By that afternoon, she was sweat-soaked and exhausted, but knew she needed to check in at headquarters. Talyana had returned last night to deliver a preliminary report about Rahzen and Damien, promising to join her that morning, yet the sun already shone overhead. She'd probably been waylaid by an assignment or stayed too late at her parents' house last night after the party.

After showering, Mikira saddled Atara and set off for the city. She let Atara pick her way through the bustle, only vaguely aware of the whispers trailing in their wake. She was so used to them by now that they were as much a part of the background as the humming wind. It tossed the loose strands of her braid about her face, the air thick with the scent of promised rain. People hurried along the sidewalks, anxious to reach their destinations before the storm broke.

A man holding a newspaper over his head nearly crashed into Atara in his haste, and when he glanced up at her, something like terror flashed through his gaze. He stumbled through an apology before darting across the street.

"I'm telling you, that's her." A voice nearby drew her attention. "Look at the horse."

Two men eyed her from the sidewalk, glancing between her and a newspaper. Unease pooled in Mikira's stomach, and she nudged Atara onward. The mare's ears twitched backward, as good an indication as ever that Mikira's instinct about the men was right.

They rounded the next corner and nearly plowed straight into a draft line, a row of despondent faces staring back. Mikira mumbled an apology and drew Atara along the road, the press of eyes following them.

"Mikira?" a voice called. "Mikira Rusel?"

The line of draftees perked up, more than one exchanging muttered remarks. She watched recognition dawn in their eyes like a catching flame, but where once she had seen excitement and respect, all that gazed back at her now was cold, depthless hunger.

A woman from the draft line seized her arm, nails digging into Mikira's skin. "He can get me out of this." She said it like a prayer. "He can save me."

Mikira couldn't wrench free. "I'm sorry, I don't—"

"She's mine!" A young boy jostled the woman, breaking her grip. Mikira tried to scramble away, but hands were reaching for her from every direction.

Atara reared, her high whinny sending the crowd shrinking back. The moment her hooves struck stone, Mikira urged her into a canter. They swiftly left the mob behind, barreling down the King's Road until they reached Tea Street.

The rain had begun, and Mikira tugged the hood of her riding cloak up, nudging Atara down a nearby alley that connected to the enchanted tunnel entrance. What had those people wanted from her? They'd seemed half-possessed.

It was then that she saw the poster.

A black-and-white photo of her standing alongside Atara was printed at the top, and below that in clear black letters:

WANTED: MIKIRA RUSEL
For suspected rebel ties,
by order of High Lord Adair

Everything went cold.

Damien had taken the fame she'd earned with blood and sweat and turned it against her, exposing her as a rebel. And those poor, desperate people in the draft line had thought they could barter her to save themselves. She quivered, her adrenaline cooling into an icy chill.

In that moment, she longed for the days before the Illinir, when she could merge into the city streets without a second glance. No one cared about her name or what she was doing there, and at the end of the day, she returned to the warmth of her home, listening to Ailene complain about boys and Nelda cooking in the kitchen while her father pored over some old book.

She wanted it so badly it hurt.

But she could never go back to the ranch now; it was the first place people would look. With one move, he'd taken what was left of the home she'd painstakingly rebuilt and erased one of the rebellion's greatest weapons.

She was useless now.

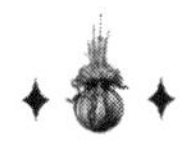

ESHLIN ALREADY KNEW by the time she reached headquarters.

Mikira's own face stared back at her from the wanted poster on the princess's desk, Shira a silent presence at her side.

Eshlin sank back into her chair with a heavy gaze. "Did you do this on purpose?"

"What? No." Mikira looked between her and Shira, whose face was inscrutable. "You think I'm some sort of double agent?"

"You were close to Damien Adair before now." Eshlin steepled her fingers. "Perhaps he asked you to spy on us, and then sabotage your usefulness once he had what he needed. Or perhaps he made you? You have a history of ending up in tight spots with the nobility."

Her nails dug into her palms. "Tight spots that I have spent every waking moment of the last few years fighting my way out of. I would never jeopardize this!"

Something shifted across the princess's shoulders, and the golem snake filtered into view. Its tongue flicked in and out, as if measuring her words, and at last the princess nodded.

It's charmed to detect lies, Mikira realized.

"I had to ask." Eshlin's voice softened. "I am sorry, Mikira. I know how much helping us has meant to you."

"I can still help," Mikira said, sensing where this was going. "I might not be able to be the face of the organization, but I can still fight."

"You're too recognizable," Shira countered gently, unfolding herself from the sill she sat on. "If the wrong person spots you, you'll be arrested."

"What about Rahzen?" Mikira protested. "They—"

"I have a meeting set with them for this afternoon," Shira cut in. "I don't know what you said to convince them; they even turned me down when I asked. It's a job well done, Mikira, but I'll handle it from here."

Mikira sought the words to convince them and came up empty. Everything was slipping through her fingers. Her fame, her family, her opportunity to change everything. But there had to be a way for her to fix this. A way to prove that she could still be useful.

The door to the office burst open, and Jenest swept in, out of breath. "It's Talyana. She's been attacked."

CHAPTER 21

ARIELLE

ARI LEFT BEFORE Damien woke.

He'd been out late with Reid, returning in the early hours of the morning, and so he didn't notice as she crept from the room. His coat was still lying at the foot of the bed where she'd left it, and she slid it on at the sight of rain and walked into town, hiring a coach to take her to Rezek's.

You are making a mistake, Nava warned as she emerged to the scent of roses, but it was half-hearted. The Heretic knew that Ari wouldn't listen to her. Not when success meant smothering the spirit entirely. If after all this she failed, if she had to tell Damien what she'd done with nothing to show for it—she closed her eyes briefly against the thought.

It wouldn't come to that.

Ari ascended the stairs, not bothering to knock. After spending hours alone with him, the threatening veneer of Rezek Kelbra had worn thin, and she'd come to realize the boy beneath was barely a boy at all, more an amalgamation of broken pieces.

She burst into the library. "Rezek?"

He appeared at the railing above, frowning down at her. "You know, I've had people killed for less than barging in unannounced."

Ari ignored him, joining him on the landing. She shoved the bracelet into his chest. "It didn't work."

He clasped it. "I said it might not."

"Well, do you have any other ideas?"

His lambent gaze slid along her in a way she couldn't identify. "You're wearing his coat."

Suddenly Ari was starkly aware of Damien's scent, its incongruence with her surroundings. For the first time, she truly imagined herself telling him where she'd been and with who. She pictured herself trying to explain why she'd done it, and watching as the wall descended behind his eyes, shutting her off for good.

Damien might never forgive her for this.

Rezek stepped toward her. "He doesn't know, does he?"

"That I've asked the man he detests more than anything for help?" Ari scoffed. "Is that a real question?"

Something strange overcame Rezek then, a sort of readjustment that made her wonder if all this time, he'd thought that Damien knew he was helping her. What did it matter to him? Had he been enjoying the idea of Damien struggling with the fact that the woman he loved had no one else to turn to but him?

Rezek's expression went suddenly cold, and he turned for his workshop. "There is one thing we haven't tried. Your Racari, do you have it with you?"

A chill shuddered through her. She'd known Rezek's true target was her Racari—he'd never hidden that—but she couldn't shake the feeling that he'd led her to this point. That he'd waited until she was at her most desperate, until she had no other choice. Had he known all along the bracelet wouldn't work?

"I don't," she replied carefully.

"Summon it." Rezek dropped into his desk chair. "It may contain information about enchanting that even we don't know. It's the only idea I have left."

"Summon it?" she asked.

"Through the bond." Rezek pointed at the spellbook at the corner of his desk. It vanished, reappearing in his hand.

Understanding struck her as she remembered the times she'd tried to do away with the spellbook. "I thought it was an enchantment never to get lost, but I must have been accessing the bond without realizing."

Rezek nodded. "Focus on it. Pull it toward you, and the Racari will come."

Ari hesitated. She was certain that Rezek wanted her spellbook for more than academics, but without proof, she couldn't ignore the chance that her answer lay inside it. Still, if she was wrong, if she handed Rezek exactly what he wanted—well, the things Rezek wanted never tended to go well for her and the people she cared about.

It was bound to her, though, and if he took it by force and she fled, she could just summon it again.

Drawing a quiet breath, Ari pictured the Racari where she'd left it: sitting on her nightstand. The familiar thrum of magic came to life, a gentle tug jerking from somewhere deep inside her chest. Seizing hold of it, she pulled, and the Racari materialized in her hands.

She held it close. "What do you really want with it? And don't tell me that you only want to help me. As you've said, I've been spending a lot of time with Damien."

His lips twitched in a rueful smile. Then his gaze flitted aside, the telltale sign he was listening to Selvin. Between one blink and the next, his eyes came alight with an uncanny white glow, and Ari's skin prickled. Was that what she looked like when Nava took control? Like a god reborn?

"Selvin," she said softly.

The Heretic inclined his head. "Follow me, and I will answer your questions."

He led her downstairs to the empty manor, the soaring corridors echoing with their footsteps. There were windows that had been abandoned half-cleaned, trays of food and teapots piled inside a brief glimpse of the kitchen, cobwebs gathered in every corner. The whole place had the air of the forgotten, until they reached a door at the end of a hall.

It had a presence about it that made her want to go the other way.

"My interest in magic has always been purely clinical." Selvin opened the door, revealing a descending staircase. "I wanted to push the boundaries of what was possible. To know magic's strength, its power. Something I imagine you understand."

Cold air curled against her skin as she followed him down to a small stone room. Her body recognized where she was before her mind, and she burned verillion on instinct, seeking its security and warmth as Selvin led her into the dimly lit dungeon corridor.

The sharp edge of iron digging into her wrists, the press of Kyvin's knife against her skin—they came flooding back to her in full force, pinning her in place. The air had the same rotting scent to it, the distant sound of scraping claws and quiet moans reaching through her addled mind.

Selvin paused to look back at her. "Oh yes, I forgot. You have been here before. Is that going to be a problem?"

The question startled her back to herself. It wasn't the cruelty of it; it was the sheer distance from which he asked it, as if he didn't have context for things as trivial as fear and pain. For the first time, Ari had the distinct and unsettling sensation that she was talking to a creature that she couldn't begin to understand.

Selvin lifted a brow, and she took a steadying breath, focusing on the burn of the verillion. "I'll be fine." She stepped after him.

He didn't move right away, as if still waiting for something. "You do understand, don't you?" he asked, and she remembered what he'd been saying about his pursuit of magic. Of power.

Blood on her hands. Blood on the walls.

Her curiosity had taken her down dark paths before. Even now, it drove her forward. Without his promised help, would she still be here, asking questions in the dark?

"I do," she said, and wondered what that made her.

Seemingly satisfied, he led her onward. "I've watched you these last few days, Arielle. I've seen what magic means to you. You are a kindred spirit, a true enchanter, but you should be at the height of your power, not just discovering it. It's blasphemy what these people have done to us."

"Blasphemy?" she asked as they progressed along empty cell after empty cell.

Selvin's lip curled. "How long have you been contained? Controlled? You're more powerful than most of this continent, and yet you're the one who's forced to hide? To fear?"

Be silent. Be careful. Don't give them any reason to see you.

Ari shivered. It had been a long time since her mother's voice had infiltrated her thoughts. Not since she'd banished the fear that used to simmer constantly in her gut, replaced by the burn of magic.

The noises grew louder. Strangled snarls, grinding teeth. The scrape of metal against stone. Her lips hovered over the words of a binding, ready to enchant herself.

"Enchanters are pieces of the divine." Selvin's voice grew more fevered. "We should not be subjugated by this world. We should rule it. But to rule, I require an army."

They came to a stop outside a solid iron door with a small, hinged plate set in the center. Selvin flipped it open, revealing more darkness beyond. But the longer Ari stared, the more she began to see. A shape formed in the shadows; human, but not. It had long, curving fangs and an arching back tipped with spikes. Fingers that curled into claws and hair that resembled fur. As she watched, one piercing green eye peeled open, the pupil slitted like a cat's.

Then a snarl unlike anything she'd ever heard ripped from the creature's throat and it launched itself at the door, slamming into the iron with utter ferocity. Ari flung herself back into the far wall, but another roar rent the air, and she barely pulled away in time to avoid the swipe of a taloned paw.

Bit by bit, the dungeon came to life, creatures behind every iron door awakened by the first one's call. Razor-sharp claws jutted out through the barred windows alongside feathered paws, the creatures' cries half-human, half-animal in their anger and anguish. How many of them *were* there?

Selvin turned his back to the beasts, unfazed by her rising panic. "I will use my army to reassert the dominance of enchanters. We will be free to practice our magic how we choose, free to push the boundaries of power. But my chimeras are incomplete."

His eyes dropped to her hands. "I require the fourth Godstone."

Because his creatures were nothing more than wild animals, nothing like the keen intelligence of her golems. Not without the final stone. Truthstones, her Saba had called them, but the truth was not what they granted.

They granted life.

They granted *souls*.

Nava's voice was barely more than a whisper when it came: *Run.*

Speed flooded Ari's body with a spell, and she dashed back the way they'd come. Then Rezek was before her, except it wasn't truly him—the boy she knew was gone, overwhelmed by the ancient creature wearing his skin, and it stared down at her with cold rage.

"I thought you would understand," he seethed. "I should have known better than to expect a child to comprehend my vision. You are too young. But I expected better of you, Nava."

Ari felt the spirit within her come alive, felt her own mind retreat, and she clawed with everything she had to hold on as Nava spoke through her lips, "You could never see past your own ego, Selvin."

A jagged snarl split across his face. "I was content to let you hide in this girl's body. I thought perhaps you were frightened after what happened to us before, and I had no need of you. But I will not stand for you to interfere."

Nava laughed, the sound at once Ari's and unlike it in its cruelty. "You fool. I stopped you once; I can again."

At that, the anger encasing Selvin's expression melted into something cold and terrifying. "It was you," he breathed. "You were the reason my experiment failed."

"It was failing already," Nava spat. "It was too much magic. It overwhelmed you—I only made sure of it."

A hand cracked across Ari's face, the pain jolting her fuzzy mind into focus. With a cry, she seized control of her body back from Nava and burned verillion to fuel her speed, shooting past Selvin. He seized her arm, thrusting her into the wall with inhuman strength. The air rushed from her lungs in a heaving gasp, and then he was pressing a forearm against her throat, his white eyes nearly blinding.

"You are a century too young to compete with me," he snarled. "You should have let Nava stay in control."

She pushed against his arm with all her strength, but it wasn't enough. Her lungs were beginning to burn. A memory of another time flooded her mind, of two men breaking down her door and taking everything she had, of being so utterly, impossibly helpless.

He tore the Racari from her hand.

Give me back control. Nava's voice was frantic. *Arielle, release me!*

Ari knew she ought to listen, knew Nava's skill exceeded her own, but another part of her was equally certain: if she gave in to Nava now, she would lose herself forever.

Then Selvin's eyes flickered—once, twice. Blue overtook the white, until it was Rezek she was staring at, Rezek who was slowly killing her.

With a lurch, he ripped his arm away from her. Air dove back into her lungs, and she clutched her throat.

"Run," Rezek rasped. "I can't hold him long."

The white light was already returning to his eyes. Still, she didn't move. Some traitorous part of her didn't want to leave him here like this, his body at the mercy of another's mind.

But she was no match for Selvin, and so she fled.

CHAPTER 22

ARIELLE

ARI WILLED HER coach to go faster, trying and failing to keep her spiral of emotions at bay. She couldn't get the images of the chimeras out of her mind, nor the feeling of Selvin's overwhelming power as he ripped her Racari away. She'd tried to pull it back to her, but the link was quiet. He had to be suppressing its bond to her with a death enchantment.

I told you that you were making a mistake. Nava's voice had an edge that sounded almost like concern.

You've told me nothing, Ari thought back, feeling hollow.

She expected the Heretic to disperse after that, always quick to run whenever Ari challenged her, but the presence remained.

Very well, Nava said. *I'd hoped to wait until things were further along, but if you're going to insist on nearly getting yourself killed, I don't have much of a choice.*

Ari pushed herself up in her seat. *What is it?*

You already know that I'm Kinnish, but what you don't know is that I was never actually a part of Selvin's group. Not truly.

They were not my friends, the Heretic had said. Ari had thought she'd meant now, after so many years apart, but she'd meant from the beginning.

Before Enderlain's invasion, I worked at the Royal Temple as one of the Head Sage's four Kesema. It was our responsibility to protect the Racari, which we housed inside the temple.

The day the Enderlish descended upon the capital, the Sage sent us fleeing with the Racari. I was the only one who made it.

Ari could picture it too easily: Nava escaping with the book clutched to her chest, the chaos of the invasion unfurling around her. She must have thought her world was ending. In so many ways, it had.

The other Racari were gifted to our three conquerors, who began to make a name for themselves in their pursuit of godlike magic. By then, those of us from the Royal Temple who survived had begun to regroup, led by the Head Sage, who instructed me to bind the surviving Racari and infiltrate Selvin's group.

Nava's voice tightened. *Selvin's ideology was dangerous. He saw enchanters as more than human, and he intended to force those beliefs on others. He announced a public demonstration of the power he claimed to have discovered. Even I had no idea of what he intended to do, or I would have stopped him long before the moment.*

Unease trickled through Ari as Nava said, *He tried to absorb his Racari's magic.*

"What?" Ari asked in disbelief. "Is that even possible?"

Perhaps, but he was not powerful enough to do it. Magic is amplified through us, our bodies the conductors, and he was trying to take in a piece of the divine. A god's power. He was spiraling out of control, and when I attacked him, trying to stop him . . . it was too much. His magic erupted. Until now, Selvin had no idea I'd betrayed him.

This was the truth of the Cataclysm, laid bare at last. This was what had destroyed her people's home, what had led to her possession a century later.

Now Selvin is trying to complete what he failed to before. Nava's voice hardened. *He wants to become a god.*

Ari sank back into the bench, Nava's words too large to comprehend. She barely noticed the coach rolling to a stop outside Adair Manor, barely felt anything but the hot breath of that chimera on her skin.

She had to tell Damien the truth. This was something she could not handle alone.

The more people you involve in this, the more difficult it will become, warned Nava. *I can handle this myself.*

Using me? Ari snapped back. *You failed once before. What makes you think you can truly stop him this time?*

At the Heretic's silence, Ari released a snarl of frustration. She ducked out into the drumming rain and made a dash for the suite, where she flung open the door to find Reid at the desk and Damien reading in his chair by the fire. His gray eyes cut straight to her with an intensity she had always craved but that felt unbearable now.

"Arielle." He met her halfway as she descended the stairs. There was something new in his expression, a remorse she'd never seen him wear before. "I've been waiting for you all morning. I—"

"Wait, please," she cut in, her stomach turning. His voice was soft and heavy and full of a regret she did not deserve, not until he'd heard the truth. "I have to tell you something."

He waited, and Ari thought she might be sick. The idea of saying what she'd meant to now felt akin to sticking her hand in a burning flame, but if she let it go any longer, it would grow into something too large to be handled.

"The Heretic isn't possessing the Racari." She swallowed hard. "It's possessing me."

Understanding settled slowly across Damien's face. "When did you realize this?"

"At the closing ball."

"And you didn't—" He cut off, regathering himself. "No, I understand why you didn't tell me. I've been . . . distracted."

He had been. Distracted, and angry, and mistrustful, to the point that even if she hadn't gone to see Rezek, she wasn't sure she would have approached him with this. Not until now, when he'd looked at her like the Damien she remembered.

Now, when it was too late.

"The Heretic took control of me that night," she said tightly. "When I came to, I was standing in an unfamiliar part of the castle . . . and Rezek was there."

Like a struck match, his eyes came alight, and he said with barely tethered fury. "Rezek?"

She wanted to stop there, to tell him that was the end of it, but someone had to know what she'd seen in those dungeons. Someone had to help her stop him, and no matter how this conversation went, she knew Damien would do at least that much.

"He's like me, Damien. He's bound to a Racari."

Damien recoiled, and Reid only shook his head as he said, "Rezek's not an enchanter."

"He is. His father hid his powers. But that's not why I'm telling you this." Each word grew thicker, more difficult to voice. "He offered to help me."

It took only a moment for him to extrapolate her words. That quick mind she'd always loved jumped swiftly from conclusion to conclusion, his expression shuttering with each passing second until he said, "That's where you've been going all this time. You've been with him."

Shame burned hot and sharp in her veins, but she did not look away. "Yes."

She expected Damien's fury to explode across his face, to watch his neatly coiled control come undone. For an instant, his hand twitched, as if it might curl into a fist. Then a cold, impossible calm settled over him, and he brushed past her toward the drink cart. In the silence the only sound was the clink of glass. Even Reid was still, watching the two of them as if afraid a single movement would shatter the scene.

She couldn't stand it. "He said that he could make the blackouts stop. That he knew what was happening to me." Her voice broke. "I just wanted answers, Damien. I *needed* them."

"Then you should have come to me!" Damien hurled his glass against the mantel. It shattered, spraying whiskey across the stone.

"You've been impossible to talk to!" Ari shouted back. "Everywhere you turn you see a new enemy."

"Clearly I've been right to. Hyle, Mikira, now *you*?" The last word was breathless. She wanted to rally against it, to fling the blame back upon his shoulders, but there was a pain in his eyes she'd never seen before, and it turned her words to ash.

"You went to *Rezek*, Ari."

She forced a deep, shuddering breath, and sealed away her reply: *I didn't have a choice.* "You need to know what I saw there. It's magic I've never seen before, using new stones like the bloodstone. He called them Godstones."

She wasn't even sure if he was listening. He was staring at the shattered glass as if sifting through the pieces, looking for something he'd missed, but she had to try.

"He used them to make vicious creatures he called chimeras," she persisted. "They looked like they were human, once. But he's building an army, Damien. Or rather, the Heretic possessing him is."

At that, Reid drew a breath as if suddenly coming back to life. "He's possessed too?"

"He doesn't call it that, but yes."

"Great. That's just perfect." Reid slumped into his chair, cradling Widget close.

Damien still hadn't moved. She'd forgotten how still he could be, how quiet. When he finally did, he only straightened his vest and ran one hand through his hair, tucking the curls back into place. "I can handle Rezek. Not now, but soon."

"How?" Ari asked, but Damien only straightened his cuffs.

"Is that all?" Damien was already striding for the door. "I have a meeting."

"Damien!" She caught his arm as he strode past and nearly recoiled at the tautness of his muscles. He pulled his arm free, oh so carefully. But that was who he was, wasn't it? Careful. Controlled. Everything attached to its string and dancing to the tune he'd set.

This time, she let him go.

He'd just reached the door when the words came bubbling up from inside of her. "I'm not the only one who's been keeping secrets. And you wonder why I didn't think I could tell you? You've never trusted me the way you claimed to, not really."

She expected some acerbic retort, the sort of thing he'd say to Mikira. But his fingers only curled on the door handle, then went slack.

"No," he said softly. "But I did try."

Then he was gone.

CHAPTER 23

DAMIEN

DAMIEN DIDN'T HAVE a meeting.

He'd lied without even meaning to. Instead, he went straight to the barn, saddled Eilora, and galloped down the nearest trail. The roaring wind drowned out the maelstrom of his thoughts, and he focused only on the ride.

As the path gave way to a small clearing alongside the bank of a stream, he let Eilora fall into a walk and slipped off her back. He'd taken his jacket off in the barn, but even the vest and collared shirt felt too much now. He undid the vest and tossed it into the grass, rolling up his sleeves to the elbow.

He offered to help me with my Heretic.

Damien drove his fist into the nearest tree hard enough to split his knuckles. The pain radiated up to his injured shoulder, and he fixated on it, desperate for something to give order to his mind. When Arielle had swept into the suite, he'd been prepared to apologize to her, to tell her everything he'd discovered with the prince and now—he swallowed hard. He'd known something was wrong, but he'd given her the benefit of the doubt. He should have listened to himself, should have known better than to trust her so fully. To trust *anyone.*

Of all the people she could have gone to, why did it have to be Rezek?

He could imagine the satisfaction that must have curled through his old friend when Arielle showed up at his door, the knowledge of how much this would anger him. That he could help her had probably been a lie. He'd identified Damien's weak spot and struck at it, the same as he'd done a hundred times before.

Damien's fingers sought his mother's pocket watch, but it'd been tossed to the ground with his vest. Only then did he realize where his subconscious had brought him. Across the trail, a dirt path followed the rise of a small hill. His feet were carrying him along it before he made the decision to move, the hill cresting before giving way to a shallow valley. A wrought-iron fence surrounded a section of grassland, the earth dotted with wildflowers save for a handful of dirt plots with headstones.

He came to a halt between his parents' graves, his mother's old and stacked with stones, his father's fresh, the dirt tilled dark. He stared at them and wondered what his parents would think of the choices he'd made, the plans he'd laid. A part of him wanted so badly to know; another recognized that it didn't matter.

What was done was done, and there was no going back now.

He watched the blood run in rivulets down the back of his hand, feeling more on edge than he had in years. Being bested was one thing—he would always find a way to respond. But being betrayed? First Hyle, then Mikira, and now Arielle. After Rezek, he had sworn he would never be fooled like that again, and yet here he was, a fool thrice over.

He closed his eyes, memories of Arielle coursing through him. The low murmur of her voice as she read. The feel of her lips against his skin. The way she looked at him, as if she truly *saw* him, and not the mask he wore. Things had been strained between them before, but never like this. This was agony. This was bereavement. It was desolation of the cruelest, most bitter kind, and it would ruin him if he let it.

Everyone thought he was so calm, so controlled. They didn't know the turmoil that roared endlessly beneath his skin, a flame that drove him relentlessly forward. They didn't know how close it blazed to the surface. He allowed himself one moment more to burn. For one slow breath, he let the anger wash over him, sharp and hot and biting. Then he sealed it all away.

He had work to do.

REID WAS WAITING for him when he returned to the room with his vest and jacket slung over his shoulder. He hadn't moved from his spot behind the desk, a nervousness to him Damien didn't have the energy to explore.

"How was your meeting?" he asked in a tone that clearly said, *you didn't have one.*

Damien's returning look was enough to put an end to the conversation. Then he noticed Reid's fingers tapping atop his notebook, and he realized it wasn't nervousness, but excitement.

He descended the steps. "What did you find?"

Reid nodded at his microscope. "See for yourself."

Damien joined him, peering through the lens at a series of hollow-looking circles alongside a larger, denser sphere. "What am I looking at?"

"A kind of blood cell. One present in enchanter blood only. Watch." He heard Reid take a stopper out of a glass bottle. "I'm putting a drop of liquid verillion on the slide."

As Damien observed, the verillion spread through the blood sample. As the liquid contacted the larger cell, it absorbed it, coming alight with a soft, golden glow.

Reid had done it. He'd done it, and—Damien's mind stalled, before thoughts of Arielle came rushing back. Shira had warned them against pursuing the power of the Racari from the beginning, and they hadn't listened. Now the power Arielle had so desperately sought was consuming her, and as angry as he was, he still wanted her to be okay.

That thought felt like a betrayal of its own.

Reid stared at him with mounting trepidation. "Ari left, Damien. She packed a bag and took a coach."

Damien closed his eyes. He should go after her. He should apologize and share what they'd discovered. He should—No. This would not unravel him. He wouldn't let it. She'd made her choice; he should be done with her, even if the idea of trying to separate himself from her felt like tearing himself in two.

There was no room in what was to come for people he couldn't trust.

With every ounce of control he possessed, he strangled his emotions into submission and locked them away. "It's for the best."

"No, it isn't!" Reid slammed his hands down onto the desk. "None of this is. Not for you."

"This isn't about *me*." Damien thrust his jacket and vest onto the desk, scattering glass slides. "That's what none of you understand. What I'm trying to do—it's bigger than that."

"Well, it isn't to me." Reid's voice came out shredded, and Damien realized what he'd mistaken for anger was something else entirely. Reid wasn't mad; he was *scared*, an emotion he usually buried so deeply behind scowls and bitter commentary that it was easy for Damien to forget that Reid wasn't like him.

He didn't want to fight.

Reid's shoulders flagged, his passion ebbing along with them. "I've stood beside you for every move you've made, but I won't help you dig yourself in any deeper."

"Then leave." Damien said it before he could think. Before he could realize that Reid had nowhere else to go, and that putting him back out on the street, a place he'd barely survived once before, was tantamount to stabbing him in the back. He wanted to draw the words back, to say he didn't mean them, but Reid was staring at him as if he didn't know him any longer, and all he wanted was to be alone.

Because he *was* alone; that much was clear to him now. If even Reid would abandon him, then he had to let him go.

He had to let them all go.

Reid went straight for his room. Damien heard the zipper of a bag, things being shoved inside. He didn't move, just waited. Reid reappeared, stomping over to the desk to scoop up Widget and tuck him onto one shoulder. Only then did he hesitate.

For one selfish moment, Damien thought he might apologize. That as quickly as this fight began, it would be over, and Damien wouldn't have to watch the last person he had left turn his back on him. Then Reid pulled a vial of clear liquid out of his pocket, and the moment passed.

"You should know that the enchanter blood cell isn't the only thing I've been looking into," he said. "This solution contains a mixture of flecks of bloodstone and other gemstones, traces of verillion, and what I'm pretty sure is animal DNA. It's probably what Rezek is using to create the chimeras Ari mentioned; I think it bonds enchanter cells."

It took a second for the pieces to click before Damien said, "Then the unlicensed enchanters that Rezek has been funneling out of the Anthir . . ." He'd been using them in his experiments, injecting them with the serum to transform them into chimeras.

Reid nodded once, curt. "I don't think it's just them, though. Like any other trait, some people carry the genetics of enchanting without actually manifesting the power. He's probably gone after their families too. There's no telling how many of them there are."

A dark, insidious feeling uncurled beneath Damien's skin. "Did Arielle give you that?"

Reid snorted, his face hollow. "Mikira did, when I saw her at the Vault. And no, I didn't tell you, because you probably would have chucked it against a wall out of spite, and it's the only reason I even figured out the enchanter cell. But here." He thrust the vial into Damien's chest, and Damien clasped it reflexively. "Since everything in the world is your responsibility, you can have this too."

With that, he shoved past him toward the door.

Damien's fingers tightened around the vial, the need to defend himself rising suddenly. "I can save this kingdom from itself, Reid. I know I can. But not as I am now."

Reid stopped at the top of the stairs but didn't turn. His voice was nearly too quiet to catch as he said, "I don't care about this kingdom, Dara." He peered back solemnly. "Who's going to save you?"

Then he was gone.

CHAPTER 24

MIKIRA

MIKIRA WOKE STIFF and sore from the chair she'd fallen asleep in beside Talyana's bed. They were in the rebel infirmary, Talyana occupying one of several beds in the otherwise empty room. Her left forearm was bandaged, and her skin was pale, but she was alive.

Mikira heaved out a breath at seeing her awake. "Thank the Goddess. What *happened*?"

The doctor had given her so little information, only that another rebel had found Talyana collapsed in an alley. From her symptoms and the needle mark on her arm, he'd suspected poison and administered a general antidote, which appeared to have worked.

Talyana reached into her jacket pocket and pulled free a note, tossing it to Mikira. "A message from your old friend."

A deepening sense of dread stole over Mikira as she unfolded the note. It was blank, save for the lion's head crest stamped into black wax in the center—House Adair's new sigil.

"That bastard." Mikira had known from the beginning that it was a risk getting involved with Damien, but she never would have imagined that things would turn out this way. Not long ago, she'd done everything she could to keep from betraying him, to be worthy of his trust—now she wished she'd let him burn when she had the chance.

Her anger surprised her, not because it was new, but because for once, it wasn't born of fear. Things like this used to shake her to her core. When had that changed? With the press of a thousand eyes at her back, holding her aloft? Or was she merely a product of unyielding pressure, forced to become something stronger?

Something unbreakable.

"That's not all." Talyana fiddled with her blanket. "He got me fired from the Anthir."

"Oh, Tal," Mikira said softly. She knew the feeling of having everything you'd worked for swept out from underneath you. Damien had done the same to her. She'd paid the ranch hands for the month, so the horses would be cared for, but all the progress she'd been making, the work she'd put into reestablishing the Rusel name—he'd destroyed it. The rebellion was all she had left.

Either they succeeded, or everything Mikira loved would remain lost to her forever.

Mikira stood, drawing Talyana into a hug and held fast with all the strength she had. Talyana leaned her head against Mikira's with a sigh. "Well, how was your day?"

Mikira released her with a snort, settling onto the edge of the bed as she explained that Damien had exposed her as a rebel and Eshlin's subsequent decision to take her out of the field.

"That absolute—urgh!" Talyana threw back her covers, swinging her legs over the other edge of the bed.

Mikira spun off her side, holding her hands up to corral her back. "What are you doing? You shouldn't be getting up right now."

"I'm fine." Talyana ripped the bandage off her arm as if to prove it, revealing bruised skin and a small scab but nothing more. "Come on."

She marched across the infirmary and threw open the door. Mikira trailed her back to Eshlin's office, where Talyana knocked until the princess called them in. She and Shira had their heads bent together over a map of the city, and Eshlin glanced up as they entered. Mikira couldn't tell which of them she was less pleased to see.

"You should be resting," the princess told Talyana.

"And with all due respect, Mikira shouldn't be punished for what Damien did." The edge in Talyana's voice surprised Mikira. Talyana respected Eshlin, respected the chain of command, and yet she looked one second away from unloading on the princess. "This isn't right."

Eshlin sighed, setting down a pen she'd been marking the map with, but before she could reply, Jenest appeared in the open doorway. "An anonymous tip came into our soup kitchen in the Fairfield District. Someone claims there's a retired royal guard living there who knows the location of the Ranier prince."

"Let me go." The words leapt from Mikira's mouth, and Eshlin frowned, but she continued, "This might be a trap. Why else would someone deliver that information unless they already thought the rebels would be looking for the prince? It could be Damien trying to draw us out. At least if it's me, no one else's identity will be exposed."

Eshlin looked to Shira, who inclined one shoulder. "She makes a good point."

"Let me do this," Mikira pressed. "Let me help."

Let me show you I can still be useful.

Eshlin regarded her shrewdly, her golem snake shifting restlessly about her shoulders. Then she nodded. "Very well. Good luck."

TALYANA INSISTED ON coming too despite her and Eshlin's protests, and they rode in silence until they reached a nondescript house with shuttered windows. Though the rain had let up, the street was eerily quiet, the house dark.

Mikira dismounted, touching one of her knives. *Defend my back, but don't hurt anyone,* she commanded, and it levitated behind her. Talyana tried the door handle, and it swung open with the creak of rusted hinges. The scent of decomposing flesh hit them both, and they covered their noses.

A body sat on the couch, rotted nearly beyond recognition.

The nausea that welled in Mikira's stomach was nothing like she expected it to be. The last time she'd seen a dead body, she'd retched for hours. This time she only stared and saw Gren's unseeing eyes, his wrinkled, pale face splattered with blood. The sight pulled her down, like the draw of an unceasing chasm. Iri's dying scream. A knife parting flesh.

". . . like verillion." Talyana's voice was muffled through her fingers, but it pulled her back from the brink, to the realization that whatever knowledge this man had on the Ranier prince had died with him, along with her hopes of fixing things.

Then she latched on to what Talyana had said. The way the body's flesh had sunk in on itself, the wrinkled, scabbed state of its skin—she recognized them. These were the effects of a verillion overdose, the user's body rotting from the inside out.

Like her mother had.

Now Mikira felt sick, but Talyana only crept closer to the bloated face, waving away several flies. Then she recoiled.

"Tal?" Mikira steadied her with a hand on her arm.

"I know him." Talyana's voice trembled. "He was a friend of my father's. They served in King Ranier's retinue together before the Zuerlins took the throne."

"Were you close?"

Talyana shook her head. "I haven't seen him in years, but my father will be devastated." Her gaze slid around the ruined house, from the shattered table to the blood-soaked carpet.

"Kira," she said suddenly. "His ring."

Mikira peered closer. A signet ring encircled his right pointer finger, the design a *D* with waves on either side. "It's the symbol from the prince's death certificate. He's the other person we were looking for."

Talyana tugged on her arm. "We should go. For all we know this is a setup and the Anthir will be here any second."

"Wait." Mikira crouched down by the shattered table, digging something out from beneath a wooden leg. She held it up to the dim sunlight escaping through the moth-eaten curtains. It was an unfired bullet.

Steeling herself, Mikira looked again at the desiccating corpse, at the spot on its chest where a fist-sized hole was nearly masked by caved-in flesh.

"He was shot," she said, proffering the bullet to Talyana. "I think someone injected him with a high dose of verillion to cover it up."

Talyana took the bullet with growing apprehension. "These are only used in one kind of gun, Kira."

Mikira sheathed her knife. "Let's go."

They fled the house, remounting their horses and sending them into a canter toward Canburrow Square. Mikira's unease grew with each strike of Atara's hooves. Only a handful of people in Veradell even owned guns, fewer still with Lonlarra revolvers since the Celairen factory was burned down in the Eternal War.

Everywhere she turned, Damien was already there, one step ahead of her.

They slowed once they'd reached Ashfield Street, enough distance between them and the house for the scent of rotting flesh to finally leave her. Talyana was clutching the bullet with white-knuckled fingers, her fury flushing her skin.

"We have to report the body somehow," she said. "Make sure he's buried properly."

Mikira nudged Atara northward. "You go. I need to talk to someone."

Reid had recognized the Ambry family sigil on sight. Was it because he'd been raised alongside undertakers like the Ambrys, or was it because he already knew it? If Damien had found Elidon first, there was no telling how close he was to the prince. But if Reid had been willing to tell her about the Ambrys, maybe he would tell her what else Damien knew.

Maybe she could still reach the prince first.

Talyana stared, expecting more, but if she knew where Mikira was going, she'd try to stop her, or worse, come with her. Damien had already attacked Talyana once; Mikira wouldn't risk her again. But if Reid knew the prince's location, he was their only chance of avoiding war.

As if sensing her thoughts, Talyana angled her horse so they were face-to-face. "Don't do this, Kira."

Mikira drew back. "Do what?"

"Try to shoulder everything alone!" Talyana gestured at her. "You don't have to prove anything."

"I'm not—You think I'm doing this for *pride*?"

"I think you've spent so long fighting for every inch that you don't know how to stop and ask for help," Talyana shot back. "Let me *help* you."

People were staring at them now. Mikira tugged her hood farther down, thankful for the way it hid her warring emotions. She didn't know how to explain her desperation. To fix things, to keep the people she cared about safe, to survive. Didn't know how to say that Talyana was the only thing Damien hadn't taken from her, and she would not make her a target.

Didn't know how to say the words Talyana wanted to hear.

"I don't need help," she replied gruffly. "What I need is to stop Damien Adair from ruining everything again."

A bell rang out, shrill and piercing. Every head turned as bell after bell answered the call from the Sendian churches throughout the city. Whispers carried throughout the street, a passing murmur of the same knowledge.

The tolling only meant one thing.

With a look from Talyana that promised this conversation wasn't over, they kicked their horses into a canter. A crowd had already gathered in Canburrow Square by the time they arrived, where a pulpit had been set up on the platform. Castle guards swarmed the base, holding back the tide of people in a near-perfect mirror of the royal address she'd attended with Ari.

Talyana nudged her. "It's Eshlin."

The princess was ascending onto the platform alongside her brother, each dressed head to toe in black, a veil shrouding the princess's face. Behind them came the four greater house lords, Damien surveying the crowd as if memorizing each and every face.

Mikira ducked her head as Princess Eshlin approached the pulpit, where a charmed microphone waited. The crowd quieted as she removed her veil to reveal tear-streaked cheeks.

"People of Enderlain," Eshlin's voice rang out. "It is with a heavy heart that I announce that the spirit of my father, King Theo, has rejoined the Goddess in the next world."

CHAPTER 25

DAMIEN

THE KING WAS dead.

He was dead, and Damien was almost certain that Prince Darius had killed him. The timing was too suspect: He'd informed Darius that he'd located the Ranier prince yesterday, and now the king was dead, leaving the throne vacant and the Ascension task on the precipice of being completed this morning?

No matter. Damien needed the king gone for his own purposes; he would just have to ensure that Darius didn't become a threat to him next. It wouldn't be difficult; the prince was an easy opponent, and Damien longed for things to funnel his focus toward. Darius, the chimeras—anything that kept him from thinking of the quiet of his suite.

He'd barely slept last night, his dreams riddled with images he struggled to forget. Mikira slipping his signet ring from his finger as cell bars rose up around him. Reid with his bag hefted over his shoulder, walking away from him in an endless march.

Arielle, with her arms around Rezek.

He'd woken from that one in the dead of night with a longing so strong, he'd ended up at the drink cart with a glass of whiskey he nursed until morning.

Exhaustion riddled him to the core, but he refused to let it slow him as he approached the council chamber for today's meeting. He nodded to the guards, entering to find Prince Darius pacing the length of the room. His blond hair had been slicked back, his brow set with a circlet of elegant gold. He'd replaced his garish jacket with something twice as sleek and equally expensive, the gemstones threaded into the very fabric in a way that made the prince radiate when the light struck.

He'd fashioned himself a king.

"There you are, Adair," he said as the door clicked shut. "Is everything in order?"

Damien's gaze tracked across the room. There was no one else here, but that didn't mean no one was listening. "Yes."

"Where's the—"

"Not here." Damien cut him off with a pointed look. He'd convinced Darius to let him handle the Ascension entry, explaining that he had the prince somewhere safe and the less Eshlin and the others saw this coming, the better.

Darius drew himself up, hands clasped behind his back once more in a pose Damien was beginning to suspect he struck intentionally. "Mind the way you speak to me," he said lowly. "Things are about to change."

You have no idea, Damien thought as the chamber door swung open.

Eshlin swept in, her gaze narrowing on her brother. "Have you finally deigned to grace us with your presence, baby brother? You're a bit behind, but I'm sure we can catch you up."

Darius's grin was sharklike. "Tease all you like, sister. For once, you're the one who's behind."

Damien subdued a flicker of annoyance. It was just like Darius to preen over a victory that wasn't secured yet. He never had been very good at this.

"You'll have to be more specific." Eshlin rubbed her temple with no small amount of irritation as she took her seat. "I beat you so frequently I've lost track of the game."

"Soon, darling sister."

Neither was the picture of grief, not that Damien expected it of them. Darius was likely the cause of the king's death, and Eshlin was quite possibly a rebel. Still, the king's body wasn't even cold, and they were already fighting over the scraps like dogs. If ever he needed proof of this kingdom's failure, it was before him.

The door opened as Damien sat, Niekla and Royce entering together, Cassian a few moments behind. Niora was the last to arrive, and she wasn't alone.

"What are you doing here?" Eshlin asked as the Vault's liaison entered after Niora, a briefcase clasped in his hands. He was sweating profusely, pulling at his collar in a nervous tic, and Niora's face was grim. Four impassive royal guards flanked them.

Darius shifted, his excitement all but proclaiming what was to come. Eshlin's shrewd eyes absorbed it, understanding dawning a moment before Niora took the briefcase and set it upon the table, announcing, "Someone has entered a bid for the Royal Ascension."

Eshlin's head whipped toward Darius, who grinned. Royce whispered something furiously to Niekla, who shushed him, while Cassian watched the whole thing unfold with a growing weariness. Niora, the steady eye of the storm, unlocked the briefcase and removed the royal crown. Formed of intricate layers of silver in a branching pattern, it had a large bloodstone set in its fore.

Darius stepped forward, his chest thrust out and his eyes alight, but it was not toward him that Niora moved.

She came to stand before Damien.

The others went silent, confusion blooming across Darius's face like a stain. Damien relished their uncertainty, each waiting for the scene before them to make sense. None of them could have seen this coming. He'd played it so carefully, kept the real truth only to himself. It may have cost him everything, but now—*now* was the moment that made it all worth it.

"What is the meaning of this?" Eshlin demanded at last.

"Yes." Darius's voice had gone hoarse. "Explain yourself, Adair."

Damien withdrew a small switchblade from his pocket. "The task your father set was to locate the Ranier prince and bring him in. A task that is open to anyone of royal blood."

"Which you are not." Eshlin eyed the knife as if expecting Damien to attack.

Darius was shaking his head. "That isn't what he means. He was working for me. This is just a misunderstanding, isn't it, Adair? *Adair?*"

Damien ignored him, unbuttoning the cuff of one sleeve and executing a shallow slice across his forearm. He handed the blade to Niora, who addressed the room. "As you know, the crown is enchanted to detect royal blood."

She touched the crimson tip of the blade to the bloodstone—and it came alight.

Damien had one moment of perfect, blissful satisfaction, before accusations filled the air.

"It's a lie!" Darius jabbed a finger at Damien. "This isn't possible. What have you *done*?"

"You've cheated." Royce clutched the arms of his chair with a white-knuckled grip, all but trembling where he sat.

"But that would mean . . ." Eshlin's brow furrowed as Damien took the knife back from Niora and flicked it shut. "You're the bastard prince."

Darius charged toward him, but two of the guards closed ranks between them. The prince paled with indignation. "Move," he commanded, but the guards held firm, their hands on their sword hilts.

"They aren't yours to command any longer," Damien said smoothly, and stifled a smile at the look of helpless fury on Darius's face. It was almost as satisfying as the realization playing across Royce's. He'd tried to kill the next king of Enderlain, but Damien would get to him in time. He'd get to them all in time.

"A trick?" Niekla suggested, and Damien pushed up his sleeve, revealing the cut along his forearm, just like they expected to see.

What he didn't show them was what rested above it.

An inch higher was a blood packet, strapped to his left arm and filled with the Ranier prince's blood. One he'd pricked with the knife after cutting his own skin, both trails of blood now dripping down his arm. He pulled a kerchief from his pocket, pressing it to the real wound.

"Your mother was King Ranier's mistress?" Eshlin was the only one of them who seemed more suspicious than shocked. The rest he could deal with blindfolded; Eshlin he would have to be careful with.

He tilted his head. "Does that surprise you? King Ranier was known for taking mistresses."

Never mind that his mother hadn't been one of them. It was the only part of this plan that Damien detested. His mother deserved better than this, but for his plan to work, everyone had to believe Damien was of royal blood.

I'm sorry, Mother, he thought. *But I promise to fix it. To fix all of it.*

Darius trembled, radiating indignation. "I don't care if you are who you say you are. You cannot turn yourself in and claim the crown in turn. It must be against the rules."

"It's not." Niora clasped her hands at her waist, unshakeable. "And the crown does not lie."

Cassian's chair scraped against the ground as he stood. He acknowledged Damien with a look before dropping into a bow. It only incensed Royce, who gestured uselessly at him and made an indignant noise. After a moment, Niekla followed Cassian, no doubt recognizing the wisdom in saving face now and fighting later.

Royce gaped as if they'd lost their minds. "This can't be happening. I won't. I refuse."

"This isn't over," Darius spluttered, his pseudo-crown askew on his brow. "You'll be king in name alone. My father has only just died; you can't truly be coronated until the fifth day of mourning has passed. I'll prove you're lying by then, and I'll make you regret betraying me."

Eshlin hadn't bowed either, staring him down with full-blown challenge in her eyes. Around her neck, something undulated, and Damien caught a glimpse of a forked tongue flicking free. Each of them sought a counter, but there was nothing they could do.

Satisfaction thrummed through him. After months of planning, everything had come to a head. Now he had the power to make a difference. To change things for the better, like he'd promised he would. Only the absence of Arielle and Reid soured that knowledge. They should have been here by his side, but they had made their choices.

He would do this alone.

Niora faced Damien with the crown in hand. He lowered his head, the weight of the kingdom settling upon it. He rose to the sound of Niora's voice.

"I give you the next king of Enderlain."

✦ PART 3 ✦

Still, there are stories—stories of magic from a forgotten time.
Of enchantments that can stop a man's heart, and others that can tie two together.
Of a creature that can change its face, and another that glows bright as a star.

CHAPTER 26

ARIELLE

ARI LAY ON her cot at her old workshop and thought of Damien. She'd spent the entire night replaying what had happened over and over again, until predawn light illuminated the dust motes in the air. Already she longed for her and Damien's bed, for the sound of his quiet breathing beside her. But she needed space. Space to process the look of soul-splintering betrayal that had wrecked his face, the shame and the guilt writhing inside her.

She wanted more than anything to take it back, to undo it all, but the die had been cast, and she had to deal with the consequences.

Oh, little lion, Nava consoled with a gentleness that hurt. Ari didn't want her pity. She deserved this pain, this destruction. She deserved to wallow in it until it consumed her, even as her rational mind screamed at her that she couldn't stay here forever, that telling Damien the truth had not changed it. She needed to do something, but she wore her exhaustion like a second skin, and all she wanted was just a moment to herself. One breath to let everything go and sink into oblivion before she had to face it all.

Is this the part where you say, I told you so*?* she asked. *I have no desire to inflict more pain.* Ari scoffed, but Nava pressed on. *I only ever wanted what was best for you. I see so much of myself in you, Arielle. You deserve happiness.*

As much as she wanted to refute it, this time, Ari believed her. Whatever other plans the Heretic had, whatever secrets she was keeping, there was also a part of her that cared for Ari, that understood her. And as much turmoil as she had caused in Ari's life, as much as she wanted to be free of her, Ari couldn't deny that she had also given Ari strength. Solace.

With Nava, she was never truly alone.

Nava started humming. It startled Ari at first, making her think the Heretic was about to take control, before she recognized the song. It was a Kinnish lullaby her mother used to sing to comfort her when she woke from nightmares, a folktale about the lion who befriended the moon.

The song encircled her, as close to an embrace as the spirit could offer, and with nothing left inside to hold her together, Ari let it. She descended into the vibrations, let them permeate her mind, body, and soul, and carry her away to a place where the pain could not reach her.

She dreamed of the girl that was not Rivkah again, of sitting with her on a white stone terrace overlooking a city rich with life. They picked pomegranates apart with their nails, digging out the crimson seeds within and laughing as the juice stained their fingers.

Then the first horn sounded.

Ari went still, her body drawn like a marionette by its strings. By the second horn she was on her feet, her sister's hand in hers, dragging her stumbling into the temple. Because it was a temple, she saw now, larger and grander than any she'd ever entered. Her sister was calling after her, asking what was wrong, but the fear writhing in Ari's gut wouldn't let her answer.

By the time they reached the temple stairs, the third horn had blown, and smoke was rising on the horizon. Congregants fled into the streets, Kesema shouting orders to any within earshot, but all Ari could think of was her sister.

"Go straight home," she told her. "Don't look back."

She released her sister's hand—and drew her sword.

Ari woke with a start, the dregs of the dream still lingering. It had felt so real, real enough that she could still feel the heft of the sword in her hand. She flexed her fingers; they were sore, and when she peered closer, she swore the dirt underneath her nails was actually clay. The late-afternoon light filtering through her moth-eaten curtains told her that she'd slept straight through the morning into the afternoon, and yet she felt more tired than ever.

A loud rapping on the door startled her, and she realized belatedly it must be what woke her. Was it Damien, come to apologize? Or Rezek, seeking to ensure she didn't go spilling Selvin's plans?

Rolling out of bed, she went straight for the store of verillion she'd brought from Damien's. She ate a handful and burned the plant, muttering a binding for strength before she thrust the door open.

"Rivkah," she breathed. Her sister was dressed in fresh clothes, her hair still wet from the bath. Wherever she'd come from, it was most certainly *not* several days of travel from Aversheen. "You never left."

"Technically, I never said I would." Rivkah gave her the bashful grin she reserved solely for when she knew she was in trouble. "Also, I brought rugelach."

Ari sighed, stepping back to let her in. "I should have known better." There was little that could stop Rivkah once she'd set her mind to something. Ari should have hired an escort to make sure she truly left. "How did you find me?"

Rivkah plopped down on her bed, drawing her messenger bag into her lap and pulling out a foil-wrapped package that smelled of cinnamon and chocolate. "Shira told me."

"How—never mind." Ari dragged a hand down her face, coming to perch on the worn stool at her workbench. "I'm really happy to see you, Riv, I am, but I told you that it isn't safe for you to be around me. You need to go home."

"And I will, as soon as I've showed you this." Rivkah set the rugelach aside and opened her travel bag, digging until she found a piece of wrinkled paper. Ari took the paper before retreating to her corner. On it was a list of family names in Rivkah's messy scrawl.

Kadar
Kelbra
Ranier
Levair

Rezek had told her that he and Selvin suspected the Racari to be tied to family lines, which explained her and Rezek's names. The third Racari belonged to someone in the castle, where the Raniers had once ruled. Which meant that Levair had to be the family name of whoever had originally possessed the fourth Racari.

"We can go find them together." Rivkah's enthusiasm bubbled out with her words. "Maybe they can—"

"No." Ari cut across her, folding the paper and tucking it into her skirt pocket. "You can't get involved in this. It's too dangerous."

Rivkah shot to her feet. "I'm not a kid anymore, Ari. I can—"

"No!" Ari's voice erupted, Nava's presence flickering to life at the burst of emotion. She felt the humming of the Heretic and forced a deep breath, clasping her trembling hands in her lap. She couldn't let her fear control her, not now.

Rivkah stared at her. Ari couldn't remember a time she'd ever raised her voice to her sister, but she couldn't bear the thought of her getting hurt. It wasn't just Ari that was dangerous anymore; it was this entire city. There was no telling when Selvin would unleash his chimeras, and there were still two Heretics unaccounted for.

Ari pressed her face into her hands, reeling in the urge to scream until everything inside her settled. The press of thin arms nearly startled her, but her body sank into Rivkah's embrace of its own accord, a reflex ingrained into the deepest parts of her. This was the safety and solace she craved, the life she'd left behind.

"I'll go," Rivkah said simply, and Ari's relief nearly took her breath away.

Her sister held her a moment longer before pulling reluctantly back, her dark eyes heavy. "I don't care what you've done or what you're going to do, Ari. I'll love you no matter what."

Ari's throat bobbed. "We'll see each other again soon. I promise."

Rivkah nodded. "I know."

Picking up her bag, Rivkah slipped out the door, leaving the rugelach behind. In the silence, Ari made herself a promise too. She would find a way to get Nava's soul out of her body, and then she too would go home.

She would not abandon Rivkah again.

Nava stirred in the recesses of her mind, her voice soft. *Perhaps it is time you knew the truth.*

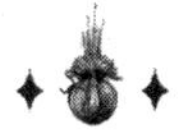

"**WHERE ARE YOU** taking me?" Ari asked the Heretic for the third time that afternoon.

Nava had ignored her initially, but now her voice came floating back. *We're nearly there.*

When she'd agreed to hear the Heretic out, she hadn't thought it would involve a trek. A coach had taken her from Rathsborne to the Barkheath District but refused to go any farther when they neared the Silverwood. Most of the land belonged solely to the crown, and trespassers would be arrested. So she'd been left to walk the last few miles, burning a steady supply of verillion for energy.

The road crested a small hill, the tops of the forest's trees visible beyond. Their leaves were a sort of silvery green that gave them a metallic texture, the trunks smooth and gray. The closer she got to the forest, the more she sensed a familiar humming, though faint.

They're cyrasi trees, Nava said, sensing her curiosity. *Gifted from an old queen of Yaroya, before they turned to an elected council to rule. Like verillion, they can hold magic, but there is very little power left in this soil.*

No wonder the royal family kept the land for themselves; it had once been worth a great deal, and still could be, if the trees were harvested for magic.

"I didn't realize there were other plants that could do that," Ari replied.

There is much about magic that you don't know. Take that path to your left.

The road diverged into an overgrown footpath, barely visible among the knee-high grass. It carried her beneath the boughs of the wood, far enough on the outskirts that she didn't think the royal guard would be patrolling the area, but she kept her verillion burning just in case. With the canopy of trees above, light was faint along the forest floor, but she picked her way along the path without snagging her skirt on nearby bushes.

There.

Just ahead, the remains of a once-large building loomed in a clearing. Its outer walls were crumbling into each other, its roof more holes than not, but in the elegance of the carvings and the simple gilding of what remained, Ari realized what it was with a sense of foreboding.

"A Kinnish temple," she said quietly, thinking of the one from her dream. "Out here?"

This was once a Kinnish settlement, not long after the Cataclysm. It was attacked by a mob from Veradell. This temple is all that remains.

"Attacked?" Ari breathed. "Why?"

What reason would be good enough? Nava returned bitterly. *Perhaps they thought the Kinnish here for revenge after what happened in Kinahara and were afraid, or they thought them remnants of the cursed magic that destroyed their own home and were afraid, or perhaps they themselves did not truly know the answer, only the fear of something different. That is what fear does, Arielle: it makes monsters of us all.*

Ari's hand closed around her Saba's necklace, Aslir's fang cold against her warm skin. How many other Kinnish faced this same hatred upon their arrival, their presence the fault of the very people who rejected them?

I joined Selvin because I knew that if he attained the power he sought, it would be my people who suffered, my people who bled in his pursuit of godhood. He wanted to take our power and pervert it, to do things no enchanter ever should, and I'd had enough of Enderlain mining us for their own profit.

Ari thought of the chimeras in Rezek's dungeon. "And now Selvin is trying to finish what he started."

As will I. Nava's voice was grim. *Let's go inside.*

The temple's steps creaked beneath Ari's weight but held, and she pushed open the front door into a cavernous room that must have once been the main sanctuary. The rows of benches had been nearly demolished by the falling roof, wind and rain doing the rest, but the platform ahead where the sacred scrolls once would have been housed and the Sage would have read from the Arkala was still in one weathered piece.

What was on it made her stop cold.

Barrels and barrels of dirt, pots of clay, and bowls filled with shining verillion. Tiny glass jars with gemstones scattered along a worktable, and in the center, an elegant female statue with thickset features, a broad brow, and long hair bound in a braid.

A golem.

The sense of unease that had been following Ari for days suddenly clicked into place. The dirt under her nails. The nights she felt half-rested. The blackouts hadn't stopped; Nava had just gotten better at taking control. Had she been going out at night, returning Ari home before dawn each morning?

"You've been using me . . . to build this." Her voice was a whisper, but it carried easily through the silent hall. "Every time you take control, this is where you go."

Only the last few times. It took several tries for me to figure out the process, and I could only maintain it for so long. But the more you used your magic . . .

"The more our connection grew." That, it seemed, Rezek had been correct about. As she grew stronger, so too had Nava, and thus her command of Ari's body. A shiver coursed through her. The idea that her body was not entirely her own had been haunting her for weeks, but to have it proved, and in such alarming fashion, made her want to rip the Heretic from her bones.

"This is your plan, then?" Anger edged into Ari's voice in place of the fear that wanted to take root. "Build yourself a golem body?"

You said you wanted to be free of me.

"I do." Now more than ever. Her pursuit of her magic had begun as a means of controlling it, of ensuring that she never hurt anyone she loved again. But she'd lost herself to the power, to Nava's bloodlust, and the thing that she'd worked so hard to turn into her strength had instead become her greatest weakness.

Seeing Rivkah's face again had made that all painfully clear. Until she was free of this power, she could never go home. Never be safe.

Well, this is how we do it, Nava replied. *My soul is bound to you via the bloodstone in my Racari. When you bled on it as a child, it linked you to the book, where my soul resided, and I was able to use that link to transfer myself to you.*

Ari approached the platform as Nava spoke, each word making her more uneasy.

If you place that bloodstone in the golem I've created, then bring it to life with a truthstone, I can use that bond to take possession of the golem. But I must transfer myself to the stone before you bring the golem to life.

"Which is why you need me to do the spell." Ari came to a halt before the golem. Could she let Nava transfer herself, then leave the golem inert? No—she and the Heretic were still bonded. Just as Nava could move to the golem, she could move back.

If Ari wanted control of herself, she had no choice but to comply.

Only a few details remained to be finished; it wouldn't take her long to do the last of it, and she could cast the spells easily. Then she would be free of Nava's influence, free of her control and her thirst for blood. She could find Rivkah before she left the Drowned Crow and tell her everything, and maybe, just maybe, she could go home.

But then what of Nava and Selvin?

The last time the Heretics fought, their magic grew so out of control that it resulted in the Cataclysm, killing thousands and making Kinahara uninhabitable for generations to come.

How did she know the same wouldn't happen again?

If Selvin succeeds with his plans, he will become a god, Nava said quietly. *Who do you think will suffer most at the hands of the man who drafted the legislation that outlawed Kinnish magic, even as he drew from it?*

Ari's breath caught. "Selvin did that?"

He was once the head of the Sendian Church. It was his laws that crushed our people's magic, and if he succeeds now, he will do far worse than that.

The feeling that she'd stepped into something decades in the making crept over Ari. The history she'd read about, the people who felt like myths, were as real as any truth, and their story was yet unfinished. A story she was now a part of, a story she could shape, but to what end?

I had a sister too, once. Ari could feel what it cost the Heretic to say this, her pain fresh as a new wound. *She was always following me around, a constant shadow. At the time, it frustrated me. She was always underfoot, always asking questions I hadn't the time to answer. I was busy ingratiating myself to Selvin and the others, too busy for—*

Nava's voice hitched. *For her. The Cataclysm took her from me.*

There was a hollowness to her voice that scraped at Ari, at the absence of Rivkah from her life. She had only been separated from her sister for a year. What would it feel like to lose her for a century?

The emptiness of her dreams came back to her, the heart-wrenching ache of something lost. They weren't *her* dreams, she realized. They were Nava's. Nava's memories, Nava's pain. Just as the Heretic had lived Ari's life through her eyes, their connection had shown Ari the agonizing truth of Nava's.

Because of Selvin, I lost everyone I ever loved. Nava was but a spirit, and yet

Ari knew that if she could, she would be crying now. *My entire kingdom was destroyed. My home. All for these people's greed and lust for power. If Selvin accomplishes his goal, if he reaches godhood and lifts enchanters up on his shoulders, he will do the same to the people you care for too.*

Nava's voice hardened. *He will take everything from you. Let me stop him, little lion. Before it's too late.*

Ari's nails dug into her palms. The emotions coursing through her were as palpable as a storm wind, and she couldn't separate what was hers from what was Nava's. Didn't know if there was even a difference anymore. She had not lived Nava's hardships, but she felt her anger, her pain. She understood that need to be strong, to prove yourself in the face of your fears.

To dismantle the ones who instilled them.

In a way, Nava had taught her that rage. That power. She had given her a strength she'd sought her entire life, and now in return, she asked for this.

Ari swallowed hard. "He took the Racari, remember?"

By now Selvin would have the information about the truthstones that he'd been seeking. His chimeras would no longer be mindless creatures, but beasts tied to his command, as a golem was hers. Soldiers designed to kill.

Selvin likely has a suppression enchantment on it, but he was never half the enchanter I was. We are stronger than him, Arielle.

Ari flexed the tension from her fingers. "What do I need to do?"

Focus on the bond between you and the Racari, the same way you did at the Kelbra estate—then pull *with all your strength.*

Ari hesitated. It wasn't that she thought it wouldn't work, but that Nava had taken so long to tell her this. She could have summoned the book back right away, or else instructed Ari to do it, but she'd let Selvin keep it. Just like she'd let her think the bracelet would work, only to shatter that hope.

You drove me to this, didn't you? Ari demanded with sudden clarity. *You made me desperate to get you out, tried to isolate me, so that when I was faced with this choice, I wouldn't deny you. Why? What is all of this for? What are you planning?*

Nava was silent for a moment, and when her response came, it was devoid of all emotion. *Make your choice, little lion.*

Ari thought of Rivkah's hopeful face, of everything her sister had done to find her. Of Mikira, and the distance between them made of silence and secrets. Of the press of Damien's throat beneath her arm and the hot, sticky sensation of blood coating her skin.

She had to do this.

Closing her eyes, she imagined the Racari, the rough texture of its pages and the hum of magic buried in its core. She felt the link between it and her, a steady rope of magic that she drew toward herself. As before, it resisted, but she pulled harder. A humming rose, Nava's strength joining hers, until with a whoosh of sound like the flutter of wings, the Racari dropped into her outstretched hands, bound in a string of opals.

She felt Nava's satisfaction curl through her as she ripped the opals free. *Well done. Now we only need a truthstone.*

Ari tucked the Racari into her satchel. "I can get you one."

But more importantly, she had a plan, a plan she could only enact with the help of another. And there was only one person who could help that Ari knew would not turn her away. Who once would have put aside everything to help her.

She only prayed she'd listen.

CHAPTER 27

MIKIRA

MIKIRA RAN A brush along Atara's back, the repetitive motion soothing her anxious energy. She and the rest of the rebels were on lockdown while Eshlin dealt with things at the castle in the wake of the king's death, and it felt as if the entire cavern held its breath.

Some were optimistic that the princess could somehow seize power in the absence of a ruler, that perhaps they could still avoid bloodshed, but if Damien was truly looking for the prince too, Mikira had no doubt he would eventually succeed where they had failed.

They would have no choice but to fight.

The cavern walls were lined with crates full of weapons from Rahzen's first shipment, and plans were already laid to up recruiting in preparation for an attack. They stood in stark contrast to the processing table nearby, where a newly arrived family fleeing the draft was being handed blankets and food.

Atara, half-asleep and full of apples the rebel children had fed her, suddenly perked up. She nudged Mikira with an urgent whinny.

"Whoa, easy, girl," Mikira soothed, but the horse only herded her more intently, and Mikira allowed herself to be guided to the front of the cavern. Atara tossed her head toward the door, whickering, until Mikira eventually gave in and secured her tack. By the time she was on Atara's back, the horse was practically dancing in place, and she barely had her feet in the stirrups before Atara took off down the tunnel.

"Atara!" Mikira shouted, but the mare barreled onward.

Two guards were playing a game of cards at the protection barrier, and both leapt up at the sound of pounding hooves.

"Sorry!" Mikira called as their cards went up in a gust of wind.

She gave Atara her head, letting her find her own way toward whatever was drawing her onward, until they emerged into late-afternoon sunlight on Ashfield Street. Only then did Atara slow, picking her way more carefully through the crowded thoroughfare until—Mikira balked.

Standing at the edge of an alley, her dark eyes like a beacon Mikira couldn't help but answer, was Ari.

The girl waited until their gazes locked, and then she disappeared down the alley. Atara followed, taking several turns before Ari faced them.

"Did you just summon me using my horse?" Mikira asked.

"It seemed the most direct route." Despite her humor, Ari looked exhausted, her dark curls wild with frizz and deep shadows gathered beneath her eyes. Clay caked her fingers and splotched her clothing. Still, she smiled when Mikira dismounted.

"It's good to see you," Ari said to them both, and Atara nickered, pressing her nose into Ari's hand.

"You too." Mikira attempted her own smile, but it faltered in the face of things unsaid. She still didn't know why Ari had withdrawn, and a part of her wanted to lay Damien's sins at Ari's feet and demand answers, even as she recognized that his choices were not her fault.

Ari fiddled with the strap of her messenger bag, looking equally uncomfortable. "I know I'm probably one of the last people you want to do any favors for right now, but I could really use your help."

That, Mikira had not been expecting. She'd half thought Ari's presence had something to do with the king's death or the location of the Ranier prince, but now that she thought about it, it was odd that the enchanter hadn't been with Damien at Eshlin's address.

Yet another thing she had missed. The two of them had once been close enough to share dreams of strength, of safety, and now it stung to see the distance that had grown between them. She'd never wanted this, not even after Damien had cast her from their lives.

"I know I owe you answers, and I'll give them to you," Ari said into the silence. "But more than that, I owe you an apology. I should have been there for you, Damien's ridiculous grudge be damned."

It was the closest to a curse Mikira had ever heard the girl speak, and it drew a smile to her lips. Some part of her had known that Ari didn't agree with Damien's decision, but it felt good to hear it.

"I could have come to you too," Mikira admitted in return. "Damien's ridiculous grudge be damned."

For all she'd stood up for herself over the last couple weeks, she'd failed to do the same for her friendship with Ari and, she admitted to herself now, for Reid. Rather than try to fix things between them, she'd let them fray, so used to being cast aside that it'd never occurred to her that sometimes, broken things could be fixed.

Ari took a tentative step forward, and Mikira leaned toward her as Ari wrapped her in a hug. Mikira squeezed as tightly as she dared until Atara's nose shoved between them, nearly knocking them off-balance. An unexpected laugh burst from Mikira's lips, and they both grabbed hold of the horse's neck with one hand to steady themselves.

Ari grinned. "Aren't you the jealous creature."

"You don't know the half of it," Mikira muttered, and though that was truer than she wanted it to be, it also felt like an opportunity. Something she could change. "The last few weeks have been . . . a lot."

It was not until Mikira saw the openness in Ari's expression, that thoughtful consideration, that she realized just how badly she'd missed her. No one else listened the way Ari did, not only with her full attention, but with more compassion and understanding than she sometimes deserved. She'd been so quick to understand them all, to know them, and it made Mikira feel seen in a way that reminded her of Lochlyn.

And like a late night spent with her brother lying out in the pastures beneath the stars, she told Ari as much as she could: about her father returning home, only for her family to leave; about her reconciliation with Talyana, and the way their friendship had grown; about the intoxicating buzz of being Mikira Rusel, youngest Illinir winner in history, and how it had felt to have that turned against her.

Ari didn't so much as blink at the revelation that Mikira had joined the rebellion, nor the bitterness that entered Mikira's voice when she spoke of the things Damien had done to her and Talyana. Rather, something incredibly forlorn crossed her face, and she shook her head.

"I'm sorry, Kira," she said. "Damien's been . . . worse, lately. I know he's planning something, but he won't share. Ever since things with you and Hyle, he sees enemies everywhere he looks. It's why I've returned to my workshop for a while."

That explained why Ari hadn't been with Damien at Eshlin's address, but not why the girl looked half-dead on her feet. If Damien had done anything to hurt her, Mikira was going to wring his neck.

"You said you needed my help," she said. "What's wrong?"

A beat too long passed, in which she swore Ari was listening to something. Her brow furrowed, a decision settling across her face. "There's a lot I haven't shared. I'll tell you, but I need to you to know, it could be dangerous."

A sensation Mikira couldn't quite name dripped down her spine, the feeling that something inevitable was creeping closer. Part of her wanted to turn away from it, to climb back into Atara's saddle and send the horse flying home, but she would not turn her back on Ari.

Mikira steeled herself. "What do you need?"

"A hand up, for starters." Ari nodded at Atara. "The rest I'll tell you on the way."

CHAPTER 28

ARIELLE

ATARA'S MASSIVE BODY swayed beneath them as they followed the Traveler's Road toward the Silverwood in the gathering dusk. Along the way, Ari told Mikira everything about the Heretic possessing her, her lost time, and her visits with Rezek, thankful that she couldn't see the other girl's face. Still, she could feel the tension in her muscles, the stiffness to her seat, but Mikira did not interrupt, did not tell Ari to dismount and deal with this herself.

She'd thought about enacting her plan alone, but the stakes were too high to risk failure, and Mikira was the only one who could help that Ari had thought wouldn't turn her away.

Mikira had defended her before she knew her, risking herself to keep Ari safe. Ari knew people thought her brash, that Damien believed her quick tongue and impulsive nature a weakness, but Ari recognized it all for what it truly was: someone who cared so deeply and so fully that she would do everything within her power to protect not only those she treasured, but anyone who needed her.

It was a selflessness most could never hope to aspire to, a strength Ari did not possess, and she loved Mikira for it.

"The creatures in his dungeon . . . They weren't human, Kira. Not anymore." She fell silent with the end of her story. In it, she could sense Nava's displeasure. She'd been hurrying Ari onward ever since they'd completed the golem that morning and Ari had secured a truthstone from her old supplier.

Why are you telling her any of this? Nava demanded. *Why bring her here?*

The Heretic had been asking such questions relentlessly since Ari had sought Mikira's help, and Ari remained resolutely silent. It had been a risk, involving Mikira, but Nava needed Ari to do the spell willingly. As Ari had hoped, it seemed the Heretic wouldn't interfere with what she did prior to that, but Nava would know that she was planning something.

They were like two card players staring each other down over the table, each daring the other to make a move or fold.

"I can't believe I'm saying this," Mikira ground out. "But I agree with Damien. *Rezek*, Ari? You should have known better than to trust him."

"I didn't trust him! I just . . . understood him more than I thought I would." She winced, knowing that wouldn't improve Mikira's opinion of the situation. "I'm not even sure how many of his actions are his own. He's been possessed by Selvin for a very long time."

Ari could practically feel Mikira weighing her words. She, like Damien, had lost people to Rezek's cruelty. She'd spent the last few months clawing for her freedom from the man, and now Ari was telling her maybe he's not really that bad and it's not his fault? If their positions were reversed, she wouldn't want to hear this either. Besides, Selvin couldn't have been in command the entire time. Rezek was responsible for some degree of his actions.

"These . . . chimeras," Mikira began again at last, pointedly leaving the topic of Rezek's behavior behind. "How many were there?"

"I didn't get an accurate count." The Kelbra dungeon wasn't small, and the noise of the chimeras had been thunderous. Who knew how many had been packed into each cell, or if Rezek had more stationed throughout the city? Ari's skin prickled, and she released Mikira to rub the warmth back into her arms. "They were human once, Kira. But what's left of them . . . I don't think Veradell is prepared to fight something like that."

"You said Damien knows about them, right?" Mikira asked, and Ari nodded. "My personal feelings aside, there's no one I'd trust more to handle something like that. A complex magical problem connected to Rezek? There's no way Damien will let him win."

Ari let out a weak laugh, caught between amusement and exasperation. "I suppose you're right."

Mikira peered at her over her shoulder as she slowed Atara to a stop, the edge of the Silverwood looming before them. "You still haven't told me what any of this has to do with why we're about to get ourselves arrested or shot."

This is none of her concern. Nava tried to dissuade her once again. *Tell her to leave you here and turn back.*

Ari ignored the Heretic. "Follow that footpath. I'll show you."

Mikira obeyed, and soon they were beneath the cover of the trees, the setting sun slanting through the sloping branches. By the time the temple came into view, Nava's irritation was a physical presence in Ari's mind. She couldn't read Ari's thoughts, so she couldn't know for sure what she had planned, but she still had insight into Ari's emotions.

She had to play this carefully.

"What is this place?" Mikira surveyed the crumbling structure.

"An abandoned Kinnish settlement that was destroyed not long after the Burning," Ari replied with an unexpected bitterness. "The temple is all that remains."

Mikira winced. "And we're here because?"

Ari drew a quiet breath and let it out. "Because I'm giving Nava her own body. To get her out of mine."

This time, Mikira twisted around in her seat to gape at her. "But you just said the last time Selvin and Nava fought, it destroyed an entire kingdom."

Ari slid down from Atara's back and drifted toward the temple. "I can't keep sharing my body, Mikira. Nava doesn't care who she hurts or who she kills. If I don't do this, she'll find another way, and I'll be responsible for even more death."

Mikira dismounted, clutching Atara's reins. "You'll be putting all of Enderlain at risk."

They deserve nothing less, Nava hissed. *None of this would have ever happened if the Enderlish hadn't been full of greed and lust for power.*

Ari gave her a mournful look. "I can't end up like Rezek."

If she couldn't gain control of her magic, if she couldn't wash the blood from her hands, she could never see Rivkah again. Never be free of the fear that she might hurt someone else.

"Please, Ari. Don't." Mikira edged toward her. Ari had hoped for this, planned for it. Mikira was too selfless a person to let her risk so many lives, and Ari would need her for what came next.

"I'm sorry." Ari dashed up the temple steps, slamming the door and locking it. Mikira's shouts followed her up the platform stairs, where she pulled the Racari and truthstone from her satchel and grabbed a fettling knife from the workbench, prying the bloodstone loose.

Yes, Nava said, her excitement growing. *Yes, Arielle!*

She pressed both stones into the golem—the bloodstone into its heart, and the truthstone into its forehead—then smoothed over the clay. The temple shuddered with Mikira's pounding fists, its weary structure barely standing.

"Ari, don't!" she screamed. "We can find another way!"

"This is the only way," Ari whispered, and picked up the Racari. In a rush like a heavy sigh, she felt Nava leave her for the stone. All at once her body felt heavier and closer to her than it had ever before, as though she had not truly been whole until this moment. She nearly staggered beneath the sensation, but Mikira's pounding had stopped, and she knew the girl had gone searching for a weak spot to break through.

Beginning the spell, Ari walked about the golem, white light flowing from her lips to the statue. As she neared the end, she heard banging again, but closer now. The wall was bowing in a thin spot nearby, the wood cracking. A hoof came through the siding. She reached the end of the spell and the golem transformed.

Clay became flesh and hair and bone and muscle. As the wall came apart behind her, Nava took her first breath. Atara's strength carried her through the hole, and Mikira swept in behind, blades raised. They were too late to stop Nava, but for Ari, they were just in time. She'd known she wouldn't be able to handle Nava on her own, so she'd sought someone she trusted to watch her back.

Ari muttered a binding for strength that coursed through her body. "I bound your soul to that body," she told Nava, who barely seemed to notice either of them. She was inspecting her fingers, flexing them one by one with growing wonder. "You'll never possess me again."

Nava's head tilted one way, then the other, her neck cracking. "I don't need your form any longer."

"Except now you're vulnerable. Now you can die." Ari lunged at Nava with the fettling knife, weeks of pent-up confusion and anger driving her enhanced strength. She drove it straight into Nava's chest.

The woman's eyes went wide with shock, her lips parted in a silent realization. "So this is pain. I'd forgotten."

Then she backhanded Ari with inhuman strength. She hit the ground hard enough to crack the wood, pain radiating through her shoulder. A whinny cut the air, and then Atara was racing for the platform, driven by her innate need to protect her creator.

"Atara, no!" Ari yelled, but it was too late.

Nava spun on the golem, and with a wave of her hand and centuries of practice behind her power, she dissolved the horse back into clay that crumpled. A surge of energy dove back into Ari—Atara's magic coming home. She retched over the edge of the platform.

Mikira's shriek tore through the hall. Her knives leapt from her hands, flying toward Nava. The Heretic didn't even bother to dodge. The knives sank into her body, and she plucked them free, the wounds healing instantly.

Ari's nausea redoubled. This was why Nava had let her retrieve Mikira. She'd protested just enough to make Ari confident in her plan, but she'd never truly been threatened. She'd known they'd be no match for her, even together.

"You can't kill me." Nava clutched the blades even as their enchantment warred with her unnatural strength, trembling in her hands. "Even if you could find a way, you wouldn't, little lion. If I die, you lose your magic."

Ari stilled.

Nava gave her a pitying look. "You weren't born an enchanter. Your magic came from me. Without me, you'll have nothing. We are still connected, you and I."

Ari pushed herself up to her knees, the Heretic's words spinning with her dizziness. Was that really true? Did stopping Nava mean losing her power? Her strength? But letting her go . . . Ari swallowed through the thickness in her throat. "I won't let you destroy Enderlain like you destroyed Kinahara."

"I *protected* Kinahara!" Nava thrust Mikira's knives into the earth down to the hilts. "Its destruction was Selvin's fault, and now that he is free, he will seek out his compatriots to expand his power, and I will stop him again. I will see that he pays for what he's done."

With inhuman speed, she fled through the hole Atara had created.

In her wake, Ari's vision blurred, her dispersing adrenaline leaving a gaping chasm of exhaustion. The last thing she saw before she went under was Mikira collapsing to her knees as she wept over Atara's body.

CHAPTER 29

DAMIEN

THE CASTLE HAD a private gun range.

Set at the very back of the property and furnished with more types of guns than Damien had ever seen, it was the perfect place for him to clear his mind. With each crack of a fired bullet and burst of power that radiated up his forearm, the chaos of his mind began to settle.

He'd given the other council members the day to collect themselves. It would be impossible to get anything productive done with three of them all but planning his death, and he'd needed time to prepare something of his own, so he'd released them with a command to return for an emergency meeting that evening. But with the sun descending outside the range windows, he was restless to put things in motion.

He'd tried returning to the manor, but he'd barely made it a step into the suite before the urge to look for Arielle or Reid struck. It was like a reflex, a magnetism that he couldn't fulfill, and the simple fact that he wanted to only set him more on edge. Against his will, his mind spun a hundred questions: Where had Arielle gone? Who was she with?

The idea that she might not be staying at her workshop at all, but rather with the man he despised above all others, was a thought he couldn't shake.

No, she wouldn't have gone back. Not after the way things had erupted between them. She wouldn't do that.

Would she?

Damien opened his revolver. Reloaded. Straightened his cuffs. Funneled every last bit of simmering rage at the thought of Rezek anywhere near Arielle through every benign action he could think of and—no. He shouldn't even be thinking of her. He had to stop thinking of her. She was a distraction, a liability, and the next few days would be perilous enough as it was without his full attention upon them.

And yet . . .

He fired, centering himself on the strength of the recoil through his arm, but it only drew forth more thoughts of Rezek. After all, it was he who had taught Damien to shoot. They had stolen one of Eradas's revolvers and snuck into the verillion fields, where Rezek's brother had set up a target.

Rezek had shown him the parts of the gun, the bullets, the mechanism—and then he'd pointed it straight at Damien's head.

Rezek's lips had curved into a smile he would one day come to hate, but that at the time felt like a secret between them. "Remember," he'd said. "If you going to point a gun at someone, you have to be ready to use it."

He'd pulled the trigger, and the empty gun clicked. "Bang."

He'd loaded it after that, teaching Damien everything from how to hold it to where to put his feet.

The next day, he'd killed Damien's mother.

A throat cleared behind him. "High L—I mean, Your Majesty?"

Damien sealed his rising emotions, turning to find a servant in a low bow. "High Lord Adair is fine for now." He wasn't truly king, not yet. Not until the fifth day of mourning was at an end, and he was rightfully crowned by the head of the Sendian Church.

The servant straightened and held out a folded paper. "We received a report of the nature that you asked us to look out for. A group of dockworkers in the Westmire were found dead early this morning down by the Grey. They appeared to have been mauled."

Damien holstered his gun, taking the note from her. The rest of the message detailed several eyewitness accounts, each claiming to have seen a different animal: a tiger, a feathered scarling, the scales of a desert lizard.

He crumpled the note in his fist. "Rezek."

Was he already making his move? Arielle hadn't said when or where the chimeras would strike, or even what Rezek's goal was. Or rather, Selvin's goal. Arielle had spoken as if Rezek was an unwilling participant, but his old friend had always had a thirst for power.

He wasn't meant to meet with the council until evening, but if Rezek was putting his plan into motion, he had to act now.

And he *would* stop Rezek.

"Summon the other council members back to chambers," he told the servant, pocketing the note. "Then send a message to Inspector Elrihan to join us. You'll find him in the king's office." She bowed as he strode by, two guards peeling off from the doorway to follow him.

It felt strange having them at his back, but with Darius's bruised ego and Eshlin's hungry eyes, he didn't trust them not to try something. He'd vetted most of the palace security in the last few weeks, and he was confident the two with him were loyal, but he kept his guard up. For Reid's and Arielle's abandonment had emphasized what he already knew: he could trust no one.

"Adair!" Prince Darius's voice erupted along the towering corridor. He'd been pacing outside the council chamber, his skin flushed an angry red. The prince had tried to corner him after the meeting earlier, but the guards hadn't let him close enough; Damien had suspected he'd try again.

"Listen carefully," the prince began. "I—"

"Do you really want to do this?" Damien cut in, and Darius balked. Even now, it startled him that Damien would be anything less than deferent toward him. "I've won the Ascension by legal means, Darius, and I won't suffer threats."

He stepped closer, dropping his voice low enough that the guards couldn't hear. "If you insist on pushing the matter, I'll have to have to discuss the unusual timing of your father's death with Inspector Elrihan. My mortician is well-versed in poisons; I'm sure he'd be able to decipher what it is that killed him."

The color drained from Darius's face, his mouth opening and closing like a fish gasping for air. Damien had known the prince would be a problem, known he'd have to do something about him, even eliminate him if need be, but he didn't want to hurt anyone if he didn't have to.

"Keep out of my way, and we won't have a problem," he instructed.

Finally Darius swallowed whatever he'd been about to say. A little of his fury lingered, but a new wariness had overcome it. Perhaps he wasn't as much a fool as Damien thought.

Sweeping past him into the chamber, Damien took his customary seat. Darius didn't follow, but shortly afterward a harried-looking Niora bustled in, likely pulled from some other duty for the impromptu gathering. The others followed in spurts, Royce's fury just as palpable as it was that morning, whereas Niekla's face was drawn inscrutably tight.

Cassian remained impassive, but Eshlin . . . The princess watched him as if she knew exactly how to take him apart. She was the real threat, not her brother, and while the ideal move would be to expose her as a rebel, he didn't have any proof. His word carried a weight it never had before, but if he accused her without evidence, it would look like exactly what it was: him eliminating his political opponents.

"Care to tell us why we've been summoned, *High Lord Adair*?" Eshlin settled into her chair with a grace that belied her underlying rage.

"Simple," Damien replied. "I want to end the Eternal War."

Royce sputtered over the glass of whiskey he'd poured himself. "Excuse me?"

"We're all heavily financially invested in the war," Niekla observed with her hands folded in front of her mouth. "You can't honestly expect us to end it."

"I told you." Royce slammed down his glass. "I told you this was what he'd do. He's been trying to undermine us from the beginning. He—"

Damien pushed back his jacket to reveal one Lonlarra revolver, and Royce's mouth snapped shut. "Be very careful with your next words, High Lord Vanadahl," Damien warned. "My patience with being called a traitor runs thin."

"You do nothing without reason." Eshlin lounged back in her chair, gesturing for him to speak. "So tell us why."

Even now, the princess managed to maintain the façade of control. Calming the others, entreating him to speak. Until he'd been officially crowned, his power here would be tentative, which meant he needed the others on his side if he was going to stop Rezek.

"Because we're about to face a greater threat here in Veradell." Damien withdrew the vial Reid had given him from inside his jacket, setting it delicately upon the table. "In this vial is a solution that when injected into an enchanter, or someone descended from one, transforms them into a mindless beast called a chimera. These creatures—"

A snort of laughter cut through his words. Royce pressed a ruddy hand to his face as if to silence it, but his mocking grin showed between the slats of his fingers. "Have you lost your mind?"

Eshlin had a similar smile, and even Niekla's expression had softened into amusement. Only Cassian maintained a show of respectability, offering Damien a look of utter befuddlement. "I'm sure High Lord Adair has an explanation," he murmured.

Damien forced a measured breath. He'd known this wouldn't be easy, that the others likely wouldn't believe him, but he'd been hoping they'd prove him wrong, if only so he didn't have to resort to his contingency plan.

"This isn't a laughing matter," Damien pressed. "These chimeras are the product of ancient magic once used by the Heretics, the souls of which are occupying human hosts. Rezek Kelbra is possessed, and under the Heretic's direction has created these chimeras—"

This time, Royce made no attempt to hide his laughter, and Eshlin's lips curved with a wry smile. "Your paranoia is getting out of control, High Lord Adair," she said. "You can't possibly expect us to believe this. It sounds far more like a personal vendetta."

"And if I have proof?" Damien asked.

Eshlin gestured at him. "By all means."

Damien hesitated, searching the faces of the others for some sign of understanding, anything that would let him progress with words alone, but they all only stared back at him, a united front. Resigned, he pushed back his chair with a nod to the guard stationed inside.

The guard opened the door and Inspector Elrihan, a bearded, broad-shouldered man bedecked in the formal blue-and-white uniform of the Anthir, entered. He towed another man after him by a chain connected to a pair of shackles. The prisoner's clothes were worn and threadbare, his skin pale from lack of sun.

"This man is a condemned murderer and registry evader," Damien explained to the cautious looks of the others. He picked up the vial of solution as Inspector Elrihan withdrew a syringe. "The Inspector's syringe is filled with this liquid."

"What is it?" the prisoner demanded, beginning to struggle anew in his bonds. Two guards stepped up, each taking him by an arm.

"High Lord Adair . . ." Cassian began cautiously, no doubt sensing where this was going. By the looks of the others' faces, they did too, but none of them raised their voice to stop him.

Damien looked to Cassian. If he believed him now, if he wanted to help him convince the others, Damien would stop. But he would also do what was necessary for them to understand the threat they faced. He might not be certain of Rezek's plan yet, but he knew without a doubt that where Rezek went, death followed. He wouldn't put it past him to hold the city under siege to regain his house's status, or simply to raze it for the sake of petty revenge.

When Cassian only looked on helplessly, Damien nodded to Inspector Elrihan.

Elrihan injected the prisoner.

At first, nothing happened, and the man's wide eyes slowly slackened. Then he went still. All at once, every inch of his body began to strain, his mouth opening in a silent scream. The sickening crunch of bone rent the air, and one shoulder popped from its socket, then the next.

Royce stumbled from his chair as Niekla watched in frozen horror, and Cassian's skin turned a sickly hue. Only Eshlin watched with rapt fascination as the prisoner jerked into a sudden hunch, his waxy skin taking on a rougher texture that slowly began to resemble a lizard's leathery skin as his face elongated into a beak. A tail sprouted behind him, the end ballooning into a club-like shape.

With each second, his body morphed and bent and twisted until what stood before them wasn't human at all. Poised on four clawlike feet with a leathery face ending in a bird's beak and a tail lashing with agitation, the chimera raised its head and let out a screeching roar.

"Goddess save us," Royce whispered.

The chimera let out another bone-chilling call and, with the strength of ten men, broke the chains that bound it. It lurched forward, beak-like jaws snapping for Cassian—before a bullet caught it in the side of the head.

It collapsed, twitching once before going still, and Damien lowered his gun.

"There is currently an army of these in the city," he said. "We need our soldiers home as quickly as possible, and we need to put together a strike team to send to Rezek's. Now."

This time, no one argued.

CHAPTER 30

MIKIRA

MIKIRA STARED AND stared at the heap of clay that had once been Atara.

With the Heretic gone, she'd just managed to drag the unconscious Ari over to a section of stable wall, then collapsed with the enchanter's head in her lap. She'd been unconscious for hours, and in that time Mikira must have slept. She didn't remember it, but morning light was now streaking in through the ruined temple, and all Mikira could do was stare.

She kept seeing Atara fall apart before her eyes, reduced to desiccated clay with a sweep of Nava's hand. There hadn't been anything she could do. There never was. She couldn't protect her family, couldn't keep her friends safe, couldn't find the lost prince.

She couldn't save anyone.

The tears she wanted to fall wouldn't come. This feeling was too familiar, her body too used to the shock and the pain. It simply nestled down inside her alongside the other scars, another mark of her failure.

Bit by bit, she realized she was still clutching one of her knives. She didn't remember retrieving it, but she clung tighter to it now. The power that Nava displayed had been on a level unlike anything she'd ever seen.

Unlike anything anyone had seen in a hundred years. Now she was free to roam Enderlain as she pleased, and a being just like her possessed one of the vilest men she knew.

The city was on the brink of civil war, collapsing beneath the weight of its own corruption, and now they had two demigods to deal with.

"Mikira?"

Ari sat up gingerly, one hand pressed to her head. She took in the destruction with a measured stare that grew slowly wilder, before landing at last on Atara. Her olive skin paled, and she looked like she might be ill before she tore her gaze away, letting it rest at last on Mikira.

"Are you . . . okay?" The look on her face was cautious, the guilt equally plain.

Some delirious part of Mikira wanted to laugh at the question. She didn't think she would ever be okay again. First Iri, now Atara—she was a curse, a poison to her family's legacy. What if all her attempts to save her family's ranch, their lives, had only dug them a deeper grave?

When at last she summoned the energy to respond, a question escaped. "*Why?*"

Ari adjusted so her legs were folded under her. "I thought you could help me stop her once she was free. I didn't know she'd be so powerful."

"We could have found another way," Mikira protested, unable to let go of the what-if. She curled her knees up to her chest against a pain she couldn't stop, but there was no protecting herself from something so deep inside her. Lochlyn, her mother, Iri, Atara . . . They became an invocation inscribed along the ridges of her heart.

"I couldn't do it any longer." Ari's voice wavered, and she wrapped her arms about herself. "She was consuming me. I could feel myself slipping more every day. And the things she made me do . . . If I didn't release her, I would have lost myself to her. I'm so sorry, Kira."

It was the most vulnerable Mikira had ever seen her, and she realized now that she'd taken Ari's strength for granted. She was always so calm, so composed, that the idea of her falling apart felt impossible. But maybe she'd only ever seen what she wanted to see. Ari's grace, her beauty, occupying the spaces Mikira didn't know how to navigate. She'd built Ari up into something unattainable.

She hadn't realized that Ari was breaking too.

Mikira worked the stiff fingers of her right hand free of the knife handle and pulled Ari close. The other girl enveloped her, a shudder coursing through her. They sat that way for a moment, the gentle fall winds through the temple cracks their only companion. She focused on that strength, on Ari's presence, and let it seal over the fissures inside her. She would not fall apart now, not when they faced so much.

She would not let Atara's death be in vain.

"We'll fix this," she said, pulling free of Ari's arms and squeezing her hand.

"I know." Ari clasped it back, then staggered to her feet, drawing Mikira up with her. "I can feel Nava, though the connection is faint. She's somewhere in the city, but I think she's the lesser threat right now. I think she *wants* Selvin to enact his plan for some reason. That's why she didn't help me summon back the Racari before she needed it: so that he'd have time to get what he wanted from it."

Mikira picked up her knives, sheathing them. "She also said he's free. What does that mean exactly?"

Ari offered her an apologetic smile. "I know someone who can help us, but you're not going to like it."

***NOT GOING TO** like it* proved to be a massive understatement. By the time they'd walked back to the Traveler's Road and caught a hired coach at the outskirts of the city, Mikira was still fuming at the idea. Only the recognition that without him they were missing vital information kept her from leaping from the coach.

"Rezek," she seethed as the coach carried them through the open Kelbra gates and around the circular drive. "I'm never going to be free of him, am I?"

"He's not quite the person you remember." Ari opened the coach door. "You might actually enjoy this."

Mikira highly doubted that, but she followed Ari inside nonetheless. Ari muttered a binding, likely charming herself for strength, and Mikira drew her knives, instructing one to float behind and defend their backs while she clutched the other.

From Nava's words, they suspected that Selvin no longer possessed Rezek, but they were both prepared to flee should they instead find themselves faced with another Heretic.

A hallway deposited them in a cavernous library, and Ari led her up a spiral staircase in the corner, opened the workshop door, and stilled.

The place had been torn apart.

Books lay strewn across the floor, bent at awkward angles like broken limbs, pages and pages of notes littering every surface among a sea of glistening glass. One worktable had been split clean in two, fresh air streaming in from a shattered window.

And sitting in the center of it all, like the eye of a hurricane, was Rezek.

The knees of his long legs were bent up to his chest, his face buried in his hands and fingers twisted in his copper hair. It'd come free of its tail, shrouding his face.

Ari was wrong—Mikira didn't enjoy this. She wanted to. She wanted to revel in seeing Rezek undone, defeated, crushed, all the emotions he'd driven into her like rusted nails, but all she felt was a deep, yawning exhaustion. That after all he had put her family through, all the pain he had caused her, he was just another broken piece like her.

“What happened?” Ari drifted cautiously into the room, Mikira on her heel.

Rezek didn’t move. For a moment, she thought he hadn’t heard. Then, in a quiet, strained voice, “He left.”

“Who left?” Mikira asked.

Bit by bit, Rezek lifted his head, letting it fall back against the grandfather clock behind him. The whites of his eyes were strained red, his pale cheeks flushed.

“Selvin.”

Mikira glanced over her shoulder at the library below. They were alone, that she was sure of, but the way he’d said that . . . she half expected to find Selvin standing at her back.

“How?” Ari asked.

Rezek dropped his head into his hands. “Your Racari was the key to everything. The life stones. Before, his chimeras were wild animals. But with those stones he could make them think, make them obey, and he could create one for himself.”

A chill prickled Mikira’s spine. Selvin had made himself a body, the same way Nava had.

He truly was free.

“Is he still here?” Mikira kept her back pressed to the doorway so she could see into both rooms at once.

Rezek shook his head. “He took the chimeras with him. The cells are connected to the underground tunnels. He needs them spread out. Needs them hungry.”

“For what?” Ari asked. When he didn’t answer, she crouched down before him. “Hungry for what, Rezek?” But he wouldn’t look at her, only kept shaking his head and muttering something Mikira couldn’t hear.

Ari seized his wrists, pulling them away and capturing his gaze. “He said he wanted to rule. The city? Enderlain? What’s his plan?” But Mikira could see the truth in Rezek's eyes: his loyalties lay with the Heretic that had been by his side for years. He would not betray him.

It almost made her laugh, the idea that their world might come crumbling down because Rezek Kelbra suddenly decided to have morals. Here was a man who had torn lives apart and reveled in their destruction, only to have his own life disintegrate in turn. Now all he could do was try to clutch the remnants as they slipped through his fingers.

"It's too late, little mouse," he whispered. "Too late for us all."

CHAPTER 31

ARIELLE

"WHAT DO YOU want to do with him?" Mikira jerked a thumb over her shoulder at Rezek. They'd left him where they'd found him and retreated onto the landing to talk.

"I want to try and get more out of him." Ari leaned against the railing. "He's our only source about Selvin's plans, and I think he might know more about the other Racari than he's letting on. Finding them has to be a priority; the last thing we need is two more Heretics."

Mikira nodded grimly. "I should report back to the rebels. They need to know what's going on, and they might be able to help us locate the other Racari. We could bring him?"

"I don't think that's a good idea." Ari had a sudden image of trying to scruff a feral cat. "He's bound not to be cooperative, and there's no telling what they'll do with him, or me. As far as they're concerned, I'm loyal to Damien."

"Are you?" Mikira peered up at her.

Ari tried not to focus on the way the question stung, nor the torrent of emotions it unleashed. Damien's actions had hurt her, and she still harbored a kernel of resentment toward him for that, but she was also partially responsible for the wall that had risen between them. Her distance from him had only made that clearer, alongside an insatiable need to see him again.

Angry or not, she loved him.

"Yes," she said simply.

Mikira looked as if she wanted to say something more, and it surprised Ari when she didn't. She looked at the girl more closely, at the bone-deep weariness lining every inch of her, and swallowed back another apology. There was nothing her words could do now; she only wished she could carry a little of Mikira's pain for her, that she had not been the cause of so much of it herself.

Mikira drifted toward the stairs. "Then you handle Rezek. I'll meet you back at your workshop in a couple hours."

Ari watched her go, her own exhaustion catching up to her in the silence. Her head still ached, but more than that, she felt different in a way she couldn't parse. In some sense, she was lighter, as though finally having shed a weight she'd carried her entire life. In another, she felt empty, as if the space it had occupied inside her was now hollow. It felt like loss, like looking for something she'd just been holding, only to remember it was gone.

Who was she without Nava? Herself, and yet not at all. The Heretic had been with her from nearly the beginning. Now she was gone, and with her, some fundamental surety. The confidence, the *power,* that Ari had acquired—without Nava, she felt in danger of losing it too.

Your magic came from me. Without me, you'll have nothing.

Had Nava been telling the truth? Had the magic in her veins feeding her always belonged to the Heretic?

Could she give it up?

Ari took a steadying breath. If that was true, stopping Nava meant losing her magic, the one thing that quelled the constant fear, that made her strong. But letting the Heretic live could mean Enderlain's destruction. If she came up against Selvin again, another Cataclysm would destroy everything.

Carefully she sought the bond she had with all golems, and felt the connection between her and Nava stir. It was only long enough to get an impression of sooty brick buildings and river air before Ari shut it down, not wanting to draw her attention. There was no telling how long Nava would wait before confronting Selvin, though Ari suspected the Heretic was in a similar predicament to her own: they were both adjusting to this new situation.

Ari picked her way through scattered gemstones and overturned vials until she stood before Rezek. The sight of him pulled at some traitorous part of her, the one that looked at him and saw only Damien, the hurt in his eyes when he learned what she'd done.

"He's the only one who was always there." Rezek spoke as if to thin air. "The only one I couldn't drive away."

"He used you," she said, unrelenting. "Like Nava used me."

They were but pawns in a game of gods. Selvin had needed the truthstone from her Racari to turn his army of chimeras from wild animals to beasts under his command, and to create a body for himself the way Nava had. And for some reason, Nava had let him. Did she want to face him down in the flesh? Look him in the eye before she took everything from him?

Rezek's blue eyes slitted. "He cares about me. I've known him half my life."

"Like you've known Damien?" She couldn't help the sliver of satisfaction at the way he flinched, but now wasn't the time for personal vendettas.

Ari placed her hands on her hips. "Get up, Rezek."

He slid his arms across his stomach, looking away from her. Out of patience, Ari charmed herself for strength and hoisted him to his feet. He stumbled, catching himself against the wall.

"How dare you—"

"You're pathetic." She shoved him back into the bookcase. "If Damien could see you now, he'd wonder why he'd ever bothered to get revenge against such a spineless, worthless little man. I thought you were supposed to be somebody. But you're just an empty vessel, aren't you? Selvin made you everything you were."

Rezek's jaw coiled tighter with every word, and Ari nearly smiled at how easy he was to wind up. He was used to having claws and teeth and the power of a greater noble house behind him. Reminding him just how small he'd become seemed like a good way to snap him out of his stupor.

"If you say one more word, I'm going to peel the skin off your bones," he hissed.

"You've used that one before. Try again."

"Ari—" Rezek cut off when she closed the distance between them, all traces of her earlier amusement gone.

"Selvin's gone, Rezek," she said, and watched his anger break into something starker. A conflicted mourning that reflected her own. "You need to decide what you're going to do next."

He gazed at her as if she'd come to end him. Some part of her wondered if she should. For what he'd done to Mikira, to Damien, to her. For what he'd unleashed.

But looking at him now, she knew there was nothing more she could do to him.

Ari stepped back. "I, for one, want to know where those other Racari are. Is finding them part of Selvin's plan, or will you help me with that at least?"

Something shifted behind Rezek's eyes, and he averted his gaze. "Selvin doesn't care about the fourth Racari."

"But he cares about the third, which is why you lied to me about it vanishing from the castle."

Rezek only set his jaw, confirming her suspicion that whoever had the third Racari, it was exactly who Selvin wanted it to be. But why didn't he care about the fourth the same way? He'd been content to leave Nava out of his plans; did he feel the same about the fourth?

"I have a lead on the last Racari," Ari told him. "It belonged to the Levair family at the time of the Cataclysm."

Rezek's gaze snapped to hers. "Levair?"

"You know the name?"

"I'm surprised you don't." He looked vaguely ill. "It was Chava Adair's maiden name. Damien's mother."

CHAPTER 32

Mikira

MIKIRA WALKED BACK to the rebel headquarters.

Having used what little coin she and Ari had to get to Rezek's, it was her only option. Her feet ached from the miles-long journey by the time she neared the tunnels, but the exercise had done her good. Visiting Rezek had put her on edge, and that was on top of everything else that had happened.

She couldn't get the image of him crumpled to the floor out of her mind, where it etched itself alongside the sight of Atara turning to clay. She kept finding herself looking for the horse, as if she might find her just over her shoulder, a thought that nearly staggered her each time. But she buried the fissuring pain a layer deeper and kept walking.

The rebellion had to know about the Heretics. Had to know that there was a threat even greater than the system they fought brewing beneath their very feet.

Mikira entered the main cavern to the clatter of hundreds of voices, the space more densely packed than she'd ever seen. She had to fight her way toward Eshlin's office, every press of another's body a reminder that once, they would have parted for her at the sight of Atara, so much quicker to recognize her with the horse at her side.

Without her, Mikira felt half-formed. Was she really Mikira Rusel, youngest Illinir winner in history, without the horse that had gotten her there?

"Damien has ended the Eternal War, our *main* driver of support." The lethal edge of the princess's voice reached Mikira through the cracked office door. "He's effectively destroyed our platform, and in a few weeks' time, half the kingdom's military will be back outside the city."

Mikira silenced her gasp of surprise. A mix of shock, relief, and a gratitude she didn't want to feel cascaded through her. The war that had ruled so many of their lives, that had taken Lochlyn from her, was over. Ended by the man who'd cast her aside, attacked Talyana, and exposed her as a rebel . . . but who had once promised her that he intended to see this kingdom change, and had kept his word.

She didn't know what to make of the sense of relief at knowing that at least that had been true.

"He's also ended one of the worst brutalities of this kingdom's rule." Shira kept her voice light, but Mikira sensed the tension underneath as she hovered just out of sight. "Clearly his goals are at least partially aligned with ours. Perhaps if we approached him with your plan to dismantle the house system—"

Talyana's sharp laugh cut across her. "Damien Adair? Relinquish power? It doesn't matter how many good things he does. He's still a part of a broken system, and one day someone else will take the throne from him, and we'll be right back where we started. And that's *if* he doesn't put us there himself."

The *throne*?

Mikira stepped into the office doorway, and Talyana's face lit up as she flung her arms about her. "Thank the Goddess you're okay!"

Mikira hugged her back, wishing she could stay in Talyana's arms indefinitely. "Why wouldn't I be?"

"Because you are on Damien Adair's list of enemies, and he just became king." The princess's visceral rage was obvious as she paced the length of the office.

Mikira cringed; so she hadn't heard wrong. "How in the four hells did he manage that?"

"My brother is claiming to be the Ranier prince." In contrast to Eshlin, Shira's voice was cool and calm, though there was a tightness to her lounging posture that looked out of place on her. "It's a lie."

"Of course it's a lie!" Eshlin roared, and the snake about her shoulders flickered into sight as if startled. Her fury was a living thing, so unlike the princess it felt like a mask she'd donned—or one she'd suddenly dropped. "But without knowing how he orchestrated it, I can't prove it, and I can't force a retest without proof."

Mikira's mind spun like a wheel seeking traction. If Damien was claiming to be the prince, if he was *king*, that meant he'd somehow tricked the bloodstone in the crown into accepting him, then presented himself as the Ranier prince to fulfill the Ascension task. It was a clever plan, but whose blood had he used to prove it?

Eshlin returned to her desk but didn't sit, buzzing with the agitation of a hornet swarm. "We have no choice but to take the throne by force now."

Shira shifted uneasily. Mikira didn't think anything could make the woman anxious, until she realized the full extent of Eshlin's proclamation.

Take the throne—*from* Damien.

"We can use this," Eshlin said as if to herself, then louder. "We need to capitalize on the turmoil this will cause. People will be uncertain of the future, anxious to see how his reign will impact them with so many sweeping changes happening at once."

"That will be difficult to do if my brother insists on making positive changes that mollify the people's anger." Shira's glib tone contrasted with the downward curve of her lips. It was the most Mikira had ever seen her betray her thoughts, but Eshlin was too preoccupied to notice.

The strangeness of her behavior gnawed at Mikira, but she recognized the pressure the princess was under. The choices she made would have ramifications for the entire kingdom; of course she would be upset at Damien's interference.

"He's not the only one who knows how to play this game." Eshlin ran a finger along the edge of the map on her desk. "I will figure out the right messaging. We must do everything we can to continue to discredit the monarchy and noble houses lest the people's frustration with them lose momentum. We need them behind us."

"He's ended the Eternal War, Eshlin," Shira pressed. "*Messaging* won't be enough. Perhaps we should give him a chance. If he can truly fix this city from within, then—"

"No," Talyana cut in. "We can't leave him in charge. We can't leave *any* one person in charge. If it's not Damien that fails, it'll be whoever comes after him. And I'm willing to bet it *will* be him."

"She's right," Mikira said gently. Even if Damien wanted to improve things, he still had to work within the confines of the council, a system that had only ever worked to profit itself. They needed something different, something where voices like hers and Talyana's were as equally heard as Shira's and Eshlin's.

But none of that would matter if there wasn't a city left to govern.

It was starting to feel as if every direction she turned, a new problem arose, and every part of her felt full to bursting trying to contain it all. Yet she recognized that these issues were connected. They couldn't abandon their plans to create change in Enderlain when they were so close to success, but a divided Enderlain could not fight the Heretic threat.

And as much as it pained her, after what she'd seen Nava do, she couldn't deny the Heretics were the more immediate danger.

She lifted her head. "But we have a bigger problem than Damien Adair."

Eshlin gave her an incredulous look, but Mikira quickly explained about

Nava and Selvin being released, Selvin's chimera army, and the impending battle between them. She half expected them to laugh, but Eshlin listened with a quiet intensity that bordered on zealousness. She'd never seen the princess like this, almost unhinged. Even Shira watched her with a furrowed brow.

She's lost everything she's worked for, Mikira thought. *You know how that feels.*

"I don't know how long we have until Selvin's army is ready," she concluded. "But we'll need military aid to stop him."

"Perhaps we can convince Damien to help us." Shira fiddled with a small throwing knife, affecting a disinterest Mikira didn't believe. "We deal with Selvin first, then the throne."

"No." Eshlin's tone brooked no argument, though her adamancy surprised Mikira. Didn't she understand the threat the Heretics posed? "I will not weaken our forces on distractions and leave the fate of the kingdom in that boy's hands. As far as I'm concerned, this is even more reason we need to take control of the throne. For all we know he's in league with Rezek."

Shira sheathed her blade with a decisive *snick.* "He would never."

"They were inseparable, once," Eshlin hissed with a curl of her lips. "Those kinds of bonds are hard to kill."

"I don't think—" Mikira started, but Eshlin held up a hand.

"I'm not interested in your advice right now, Miss Rusel. In fact, I'm starting to think my earlier suspicions about you and High Lord Adair weren't far from the truth. From now on, I want you to stay in headquarters."

Mikira gaped at her, but it was Shira who protested. "Is that wise?" She asked it almost offhandedly, but she was studying the princess with an intensity that made Mikira think she wasn't the only one taken aback by Eshlin's unusual anger. The princess had always seemed so poised, so controlled. Mikira wanted to believe it was just shock at Damien's sudden Ascension, but she couldn't dispel the pit forming in her stomach.

"It's an order." Eshlin swept forward, pausing in the doorway. "Shira,

I want regular rallies scheduled from now until the fall solstice two days from now. We need to make our presence known and get our message out. And Miss Rusel? This time, do not disobey me."

Mikira watched her go, at a loss for words as the princess surged among the crowd, heading for the platform to address the rebels. Shira trailed after her, pausing only long enough to pat Mikira reassuringly on the shoulder.

Then it was only she, Talyana, and the mistakes she couldn't undo.

Eshlin had not taken her warning seriously. She refused to turn her attention away from Damien, and now Mikira was stuck under house arrest again, unable to aid Ari with the Heretics or warn her help wasn't coming.

"Don't listen to her, Kira." Talyana laced their fingers together, squeezing tight. "You've put your life on the line for this cause. People know that. I know that. The princess is just dealing with too much."

Mikira choked down a laugh. The *princess* was dealing with too much? Why was it that everyone around her was falling apart, but she—*she* had to stay strong? She had to carry the weight, the expectation, the failure when it all went awry. For once, she wanted to drop it all, to let it crash and shatter and scream.

She could walk away. Could leave this responsibility to Eshlin and Shira. She could find her family and leave Veradell and its twisted games far, far behind, where its great houses could never reach her.

Maybe then she could finally breathe.

"Kira?" Talyana pulled their clasped hands up and pressed her lips against the back of Mikira's hand, the sensation cutting through the suffocating panic descending through her.

Then Talyana's brow furrowed, and she asked, "Kira, where's Atara?"

Something inside Mikira splintered. She could barely get the words out in between sobs, and then it was all she could do to breathe while Talyana held her with a fierceness she didn't deserve as, in the background, Eshlin's voice ignited a crowd.

CHAPTER 33

ARIELLE

ARI HAD NOT been raised religious. Even in the past few months, after she'd finally been given access to information she'd long sought about her heritage, she hadn't begun attending temple, didn't pray to the Harbingers each morning and night. She believed they existed. How could she not, with a piece of the divine in her possession? But she did not believe *in* them, not the way her Saba had.

Or at least, she hadn't before.

But as Rezek dug through his records on the Adair holdings, tossing papers over his shoulder with the reckless abandon of one who had no thoughts of the future, she felt as though she were being guided by an unseen hand. She turned slowly about the workshop, unable to shake the feeling that she would catch the glint of Lyzairin's sapphire scales or find a set of golden lion's eyes watching her from the dark.

They're real, Ari.

"Nava said the other Heretics were Enderlish," Ari said, still attempting to process the revelation that Levair was the maiden name of Damien's mother. "I thought his mother was Kinnish."

"Who knows?" Rezek dropped another handful of documents at his feet. The sheer amount of information he had stored away on the Adair family unnerved her, though she had a feeling Damien had equally as much gathered about the Kelbras.

"A lot of Kinnish adopted Enderlish-sounding names after the invasion," Ari pondered aloud. "Levair could have once been Lev."

"I really don't care." Rezek pulled free a folder with a satisfied grin, proffering it to her. "Everything I have on Shira Adair."

Ari took it, spreading it open on one of the worktables. It was only a theory, propagated by Shira's odd reaction to her Racari on the night that she helped bring Atara to life. She'd been afraid of the book, telling her and Damien they ought to leave it be. Ari had ignored her, like she had ignored her Saba, too ensnared by the power the Racari offered.

Could she really blame Damien for doing the same? He'd seen an opportunity to strengthen himself and taken it, building influence throughout the city, dueling with the council, hunting the Ranier prince. She didn't begrudge him that. She *understood* that. What tore at her so deeply was that he'd felt the need to keep her at arm's length while he did it.

Now here she was with Rezek again, validating Damien's every apprehension, but she didn't know what else to do.

"The Dark Horse seems too obvious a place for Shira to keep the Racari if she has it." Ari flipped through the documents. "And their family's country house is too far for easy access."

"*If* she even has it." Rezek had begun surveying the spines of books on his shelf, flipping one after the other out to the floor, each one an unraveled thread, as he slowly deteriorated. At this rate, he'd self-destruct before he could tell her anything useful.

"Help me look." She cut the stack of papers in half and held them out.

Rezek leveled her with a narrow-eyed stare. "I don't take orders, least of all from you," he said, but accepted the stack nonetheless. He let the pages flutter to the floor as he sorted through them, and Ari did her best to ignore him as she paged through her own.

Shira's reach extended farther than she'd realized. She was responsible for all of House Adair's verillion and its trade, the Dark Horse pub, both of their estates, and a series of shops and other businesses throughout their district that she appeared to sponsor or share ownership in.

Ari turned to the next page and stilled at the business name printed at the top. One whose familiarity to Shira would make it a trustworthy location to store something important, whose location she frequented, and whose proprietor she was friends with.

Ari set down the deed to the Drowned Crow with a dawning realization. The smoke-stained bricks she'd glimpsed Nava near earlier, the scent of the Grey on the air.

She'd been heading toward the Westmire.

Ari's throat constricted. "Rivkah."

THE DROWNED CROW was clear across town, but their coach moved faster than Nava's feet could carry her. Ari kept checking the bond between them, feeling Nava's presence on the move. She caught a glimpse of the familiar stained-glass windows of the Whispering Rose. Saw her own workshop pass out of the corner of Nava's eye.

She was after the fourth Racari.

The Racari that had been in the Adair family for generations. That Shira had kept hidden, perhaps even bonded to, stored in the Drowned Crow for safekeeping. The very inn in which her sister had been staying. Had she left as she promised? Was she safe, or straight in the warpath of a vengeful Heretic?

"I don't understand why I had to accompany you." Rezek's annoyed voice jarred her back to the moment.

"Because I'm not letting you out of my sight," Ari returned, swallowing back a comment about how he hadn't been that hard to convince. She suspected that without Selvin, Rezek had been set adrift. He didn't know what to do anymore, and so had come with her willingly. She was also fairly certain that if she acknowledged that fact, he'd do the opposite out of spite.

In many ways, he and Reid weren't very different. Damien certainly preferred a certain type of friend.

Rezek muttered something that Ari shut out, refocusing on Nava's location—and found the link utterly cold. Was Nava blocking her somehow? But then she had to know that Ari was watching her and on her way.

"Can't this thing go any faster?" she demanded.

"It's already at top speed," Rezek replied as they took a sharp corner, both sliding into the coach wall. He grabbed the handle at the top of the door. "Which, I might add, is highly dangerous."

"I don't care." Ari pressed her face to the window, spotting Roughshaw Bridge just ahead. They were nearly there. Every inch of rapidly shrinking distance felt too far, too long, and by the time the coach screeched to a halt outside of the Drowned Crow, Ari was ready to burst.

The inn's front door had been broken down.

Ari leapt from the coach, enchanting herself for strength and speed as she went, and darted inside. Vix, the inn's proprietor, was unconscious beside a knocked-over table. They appeared to have tried to stop Nava, who now crouched over another prone body, a book with pearlescent ribbing clutched in her hands.

Nava straightened at her arrival, revealing the face of the unconscious person.

"Rivkah!" Ari screamed. She launched herself at Nava, who darted aside with equal speed. Ari collapsed at Rivkah's side, reaching for her sister's pulse. It beat strong, but there was a wound in her side leaking blood.

Ari spun on Nava, surging to her feet. "What did you do?"

Nava's brown curls were a tangled mess, her olive skin speckled with blood. "The girl refused to part with the book. She's a clever one. She must have gone searching for the Levair family descendants the moment you cast her out. She realized its location before any of us and had even removed it from its hiding place."

The Heretic's gaze strayed to the unconscious Vix. "She only revealed she had it to stop me from killing that one. Even then, she did not want to give it up."

"So you tried to kill her?" Ari's voice broke.

Nava closed her dark eyes with a sigh, the heavy features of her angular face softening. "I did not want to harm her. She reminds me of my own sister."

Ari's fists trembled at her sides. "I know that you let Selvin finish his chimera army on purpose. For some reason, you want his plans to progress."

Nava regarded her with deep misgiving. "I told you that I would make him pay, but to do that I need him to begin anew what he started before."

His pursuit of the gods' powers. She was waiting for Selvin to attempt absorbing the Racari again so that—Ari's mind stalled on the realization. Nava had never wanted to keep her from Rezek. She'd protested just enough to convince Ari she was on to a solution, then let it all play out. Because she *wanted* Selvin to have their Racari. Wanted him to get the truthstone.

"You're going to attack him like you did before," Ari said. "You're going to cause another Cataclysm."

"He may very well cause one of his own if he fails to absorb the Racari." Nava shrugged one shoulder. "I am simply going to make sure that happens."

"And the fourth Racari?" Ari demanded. "What's so important about it that you'd hurt my sister?"

Nava clutched the spellbook to herself almost possessively. "I never told you how I infiltrated Selvin's group," she said. "Another of the members was a friend of mine, and she convinced Selvin to accept me."

"You said the Racari were gifted to the Enderlish." Ari pointed at the book. "That belongs to a Kinnish family."

"Morgaren *was* Enderlish," Nava replied bitterly. "But she was also Kinnish. She was the daughter of an Enderlish diplomat and a Kinnish general. Her parents were imprisoned after the invasion, and Morgaren was bound to the Racari as a political maneuver. She was paraded around the kingdom as a means of convincing Kinnish citizens that their conquerors were fair and reasonable, and all the while her parents' lives were at risk should she refuse to cooperate."

Nava peered down at the spellbook with a gentleness out of place on her rough features. "I simply want to ensure she does not become Selvin's pawn again."

She loved her, Ari thought with sudden clarity. That look in Nava's eye; she knew it, the fierceness with which it burned. Nava truly cared about the soul bound to that book, but Selvin had no interest in it. Did Nava not know that, or was there more that she wasn't sharing?

A gun fired.

The bullet caught Nava through the neck. She lurched, nearly dropping the Racari. Ari lunged for it, but the Heretic swept out an arm, catching her in the ribs. She crashed into a table and felt something break. Her verillion rushed to heal the bone as she gasped, coughing up blood.

Rezek fired from the doorway again, but Nava was ready for him now, her injury already healed. She flung a chair at him, forcing him to step aside, and then met him at the doorway, pinning him there by the throat.

"I ought to take you apart for all the pain you've caused her," she hissed as Rezek struggled to pry free her arm. "You served Selvin willingly. You deserve to die."

Ari staggered to her feet, her broken rib sealing back together. "Let him go!"

Nava didn't seem to hear her, her dark gaze growing more fervent with each of Rezek's gasping breaths. Then, abruptly, she released him, letting him crumple to the floor. "But that's what you want, isn't it, child? To die."

Rezek stared up at her like a mourner before his god, and Nava turned her back on him. "Enderlain will pay," she said to Ari. A promise. A prayer. "They will all pay."

Then she was out through the door, the fourth Racari clutched under her arm.

Ari smothered the urge to go after her. She couldn't stop her, not alone, and Rivkah needed help. She checked that Vix was still breathing and not seriously injured before returning to her sister, pressing a clean bar cloth she'd found against her wound.

No sooner had she than Rezek's broken voice came from the door. "Ari."

Flaring her verillion, she leapt to her feet and spun. Just as quickly she stilled, spreading her fingers in a show of yielding as a flood of people in cream-colored fatigues entered the inn, rifles leveled at her.

The leader's eyes landed on her. "Take them both."

CHAPTER 34

Damien

THE SCENT OF gore flooded the air.

Damien resisted the urge to cover his nose, knowing everyone in the decimated pub was looking at him for direction, for strength. The constables by the door were barely steady on their feet, and Inspector Elrihan's face had taken on a sheen of sweat by the time he finished explaining the scene.

It was a chimera attack.

The entire pub and its patrons had been ripped to shreds, pieces scattered across the blood-slicked floor. Even from a cursory glance, Damien could tell the carnage didn't match the body count. This hadn't been a random strike—it had been a feeding.

One of the beasts responsible lay in a pool of its own blood, a knife jammed into its scaled canine head. The rest had escaped whatever way they'd entered, leaving clawed prints of crimson in their wake.

"Sir, there's an entrance to the tunnels down here," called a constable from the cellar doorway. They pointed back down the stairs. "The blood trail disappears into it."

Inspector Elrihan looked to Damien. "Give me half an hour to muster a force and we'll follow that trail, Your Majesty."

Damien didn't bother to correct him. Only two days remained between him and the throne; the more people used his new title, the more authority he garnered in the meantime. "Do it. But scout only, Inspector. Do not engage with the beasts."

Elrihan inclined his head, departing to relay orders as a familiar voice emanated from the front door. "Look, I just want a sample," it said with tangible annoyance. "Ask whoever you have to if you want, but they're just going to tell you to get out of my way."

A part of Damien wanted nothing more than to disappear into that tunnel after the chimeras, but he forced himself to the front of the pub instead, where Reid was scowling at the two royal guards blocking the door. His dark expression broke at the sight of Damien, the decision whether to stalk off or hold his ground playing out across his face.

In the end, he folded his arms and muttered, "Oh. *You're* here."

Damien nodded to the guards, and they took up position inside the pub while he emerged to join Reid. The usual shadows under his eyes looked worse, his skin a shade paler than normal, and Damien had to quash the urge to tell him to get some sleep. Reid's well-being was none of his business any longer.

"I take it you heard about the attack?" he asked instead.

Reid averted his gaze, as if finding something particularly interesting in the pub wall. "The whole city's heard of it, *Your Majesty*."

So that news had reached him as well. A formal announcement had been made to the populace, along with the date set for his coronation, but Damien had been intentional about not making a grand affair of it. He didn't want the people associating him with the garish nobility they despised.

"Reid," he said shortly. There were few people in this city who could prove he wasn't the lost prince, and Reid was one of them. Not long ago Damien wouldn't have cared about that, but after how things had ended between them, he didn't trust Reid not to expose him out of some misguided sense of concern.

Reid held up his hands. "Oh, don't worry, I have no intention of getting in your way. You're doing that just fine on your own."

Before Damien could respond, something soft and warm pressed up against his leg, and he looked down to find Widget attached to his ankle. Reid snatched up the little cat and tucked him into the oversized pocket he'd sewn into his jacket.

"Look, I just want a sample of the chimera's body and then I'll leave," he said. "If you really care about this city—"

"You can take whatever you want," Damien said. In truth, he'd been considering whether to ship the corpse to Reid despite their dispute, knowing he'd be unable to resist investigating it. There was no one else whose skills Damien trusted enough to find something useful, even if he no longer trusted the boy they belonged to.

Reid regarded him as if he expected more, but Damien only gestured into the pub. Reid shifted forward a step, then another, each small moment an opportunity Damien refused to take. He could practically feel Reid's intentions; he wanted some sign that what had broken between them wasn't damaged forever, that it would be just another argument forgotten between friends.

But Damien didn't know how to do that. He didn't know how to separate the gutted, knife-wrenching feeling that spiked through his stomach when he looked at Reid from the feeling of Arielle saying Rezek's name from the sight of his mother's blood pooling around her.

He didn't know how to go back, only forward, and if he had to do that without Reid by his side, then so be it. Reid had drawn that line, not him, and he would not be the first to cross it.

"I haven't seen her." Reid hovered in the doorway. "Ari."

Damien's jaw clenched. "I didn't ask."

"Yes, you did." Reid peered over his shoulder at him with one solemn blue eye, and for an instant, all Damien could see was Rezek. This too was his fault. He'd driven Damien to this, and whatever his plans were, whatever he sought to accomplish, Damien would tear it to pieces.

"Let him in," Damien ordered the two guards. "I'm leaving."

The guards followed Damien to his waiting coach. Only once he was alone inside did he press his palms to his eyes, the images from inside the pub singed into the backs of his lids. They kept transforming, until every face he'd seen became his mother's, until the chimera reflected Rezek's solemn smile, and Reid's words were all he could hear.

Who's going to save you?

He didn't need saving. He could do this himself. The strike force the council had put together would be at Kelbra Manor by now, where they would hopefully find Rezek—and answers. If they could stop the man himself, then they could corral the chimera threat, and then Damien could focus on improving things like he'd promised.

The coach shook, then diverted unexpectedly to the left. Bracing himself against the door, Damien flipped open the front window to the bench where his guards rode. "Why have we changed course?"

"Rebel rally, Your Majesty," one of the guards responded. "The street is full of people."

Damien closed the window, retaking his seat. The coach was nondescript, the guards dressed in plain clothes, so no one would pay them a second glance, but the rebels' very presence needled at him. He'd put a stop to the draft and exemption taxes, ended the Eternal War—and yet still the protests continued?

Between the rebels and the chimeras, this city was poised to tear itself apart.

The coach rolled to a stop at the castle, and he entered to find a servant waiting anxiously for him at the door. She bowed before giving him a letter, which he quickly scanned with growing dismay.

It was a report from the strike on Rezek's: the manor was empty.

Not a single chimera remained in the dungeons below, though there'd been plenty of evidence of their presence. It was what the team had found in Rezek's upstairs office that captured Damien's attention, though. The floor had been littered with documents about House Adair. Was he one of Rezek's targets?

No matter his target, his plan was already in motion, and if the massacre at the pub was a sign of what was to come, they had to focus the entirety of their energy on the chimeras, and they had to do it now.

"Tell the team to search the city, starting from the center and working outward," Damien told the servant. "We have to find Rezek, no matter the cost."

KING THEO'S OLD office had the air of a museum to it, filled to the brim with an extensive collection of maps framed along the walls, and even more explorers' tools that had never seen a day of use. Damien planned to change all of it in time, if only because the clutter made him feel as though he'd stepped into someone else's life, but for now he settled in the leather armchair behind the great oak desk, and waited.

The other council members arrived together as if to present a united front. A move meant to command power, the same way Damien had forced them to come to him in the office instead of the level playing field of the council chamber.

The simple fact that they'd responded to the summons should have satisfied him, yet even it felt oddly hollow, and it was not until he caught himself seeking Arielle's gaze yet again that he allowed himself to accept why: he wanted her here, by his side. He wanted her to see what he'd accomplished, to understand why he'd done what he had. To explain that things would be different now, that he had the power to keep her safe.

He wanted to let himself have that—and then he reminded himself what she'd done. Again and again he reminded himself, until that feeling withered into nothing.

Only Cassian sat in one of the chairs opposite him, Royce and Niekla remaining poised near the exit.

Niekla surveyed the room with calculating eyes. "Eshlin?"

"Has not been informed of this meeting," Damien replied. If the princess truly was a rebel, he didn't want her influencing their decision today. He'd left Niora out as well, making this meeting less than official. "I called you here to discuss the rebellion."

The implication landed with Niekla and Cassian, though it took Royce a moment longer, at which point he let out a short laugh. "You know, that actually makes sense. I've never trusted that woman."

"You never trust anyone," Cassian replied lightly, and Damien nearly flinched. Cassian wasn't talking to him, and yet he hated the parallel it drew between him and Royce, even superficially. He was nothing like the selfish aristocrat, determined to milk this city for all the blood money it could grant him, and yet the idea still seethed beneath his skin.

He pushed the conversation onward. "The point is, the rebellion is an even greater danger now than they were before. We can't fight them *and* the chimeras with our limited forces. Every resource they pull from us is one less focusing on Rezek."

"I agree," Niekla said without preempt. "If we're going to protect Veradell from the chimera threat, we have to neutralize the rebel one."

Royce shrugged a dismissive shoulder. "So crush one of their rallies. Show them what happens when you play at being a traitor."

"They aren't traitors," Damien returned. "They're innocent people who have been treated like trash by a system that cares nothing for them. They want change, and we can't fault them for that."

Royce bared his teeth in a grin. "Watch me."

"I agree with you, High Lord Adair," Cassian said diplomatically, his heavy brow pulled downward. "But the circumstances are unusual and extreme. You said yourself that they are preventing us from focusing fully on the chimera threat. If we can't handle Rezek with the rebellion gathering steam, then we must find a way to stop them."

Damien didn't believe for a second that any of them wanted to neutralize the rebels for the sake of the city. They saw an opportunity to crush something that threatened them and took it without question. But neither could he refute their logic. If the choice was between the rebels and the kingdom, wasn't it his responsibility as king to choose the whole?

Damien pressed a hand to his temple. "I want warnings posted, giving them until tomorrow evening to clear the streets," he said. "If they don't listen, then we do it your way."

CHAPTER 35

MIKIRA

MIKIRA FELT LIKE a prisoner.

Eshlin had even gone so far as to assign Jenest and another rebel to watch her, all but declaring Mikira the enemy. At least Jenest had the decency to pretend she was just keeping Mikira company.

"Ooh, good shot!" Jenest cheered as Mikira hit the center target with her knife. She'd spent the entire day yesterday practicing with the blades' magic, and this morning found a simple strike to be almost reflexive now. A crowd had gathered, drawn by Jenest, who had taken it upon herself to moderate Mikira's training exercise as if it were one of her races.

"What else can the great Mikira Rusel do?" she asked of the spectators. "Perhaps call the knife *back*?" She barely had the words out before the knife came flying at Mikira, landing hilt-first in her outstretched palm to the muted cries of surprise from the crowd.

Jenest was only trying to make her feel better, but she'd much rather have been alone. She felt like a rusted knife someone had shoved into the back of a drawer. After everything she'd sacrificed, everything she'd worked toward, she'd been demoted to little better than a child to be supervised, unable to do anything to help. Eshlin hadn't even let her send a message to Ari, who was likely worrying about her failure to return.

She had to find a way out of headquarters, a thought that only reminded her of the horse she didn't have.

A chorus of whispers radiated through the cavern, and Mikira stopped short of her next command to the knives at the sight of Eshlin, Shira, and Talyana cutting their way through the cavern toward Eshlin's office. The three of them had gone out early that morning on business to which Mikira was no longer privy, and they moved now with an urgency she recognized.

Something had happened.

"Let's all move to the archery range for the next performance," Jenest called atop the murmur. "Then you'll see what these knives can really do."

Mikira was about to protest when she met the gleam in Jenest's eyes—a second before the gawking crowd all but swallowed up the other rebel, freeing Mikira to move as she pleased. Seizing the opportunity, she ducked around the flowing mass of people and behind the makeshift stage, coming up outside the office.

The door was closed.

She was just about to risk pressing her hear against it when it flew open and Talyana ground to a halt, the anger in her face receding. "Kira—"

"Bring her inside," came Eshlin's order.

Talyana hesitated, her eyes wide with warning, but whatever the princess wanted, Mikira had no intention of running from it. She gave Talyana a small nod, then slipped past her.

Shira occupied her usual perch on the windowsill, face unreadable, while Eshlin smoothed out a crumpled flyer on her desk. She wasted no time before explaining, "The council has issued an ultimatum to clear the streets. Instead, we'll host a rally. This is our opportunity to show the people how little the system cares for them."

"Eshlin wants to give the rebellion a face." Shira's tone was carefully neutral. "A tangible opponent Damien can't resist crushing."

Mikira swallowed hard. "Me."

"You don't have to do this," Talyana said, but Mikira was already shaking her head.

"Damien was my sponsor," she said. "If I come out against him, they'll talk." It would be so easy to paint the picture of the innocent ranch girl taken in by the selfish noble who wanted to be king. She'd become another stone he stepped on to get to the throne.

It would also enable her to leave the compound.

Shira evaluated her with that steady gaze that never failed to make her feel leagues behind. "You will become even more of a target than you already are."

"You'll be putting yourself in danger," Talyana protested, seizing Mikira's hand as if to impress her concern into her palm.

Mikira felt herself tremble. For so long, people had told her to back down, to control herself, but she was so tired of not fighting back. Of being the one to acquiesce, to fix instead of break. She was not the same helpless girl who had been dependent on Damien, and he was not the only one who could wield clout like a weapon.

She knew the power of her name, and she would use it.

"I won't sit here and do nothing." Mikira squeezed Talyana's hand. "I have to act."

"You understand what it is we're asking?" Eshlin's hands pressed into her desk. "With the end of the Eternal War, we can no longer rely on word alone to smear Damien's name. We must give him something to fight. Something to crush."

For an instant, Mikira could have sworn there was a spark of excitement in the princess's eye. As if the thought of the bloodshed to come thrilled her. She relinquished the idea just as quickly; Eshlin was passionate about their cause, nothing more. Why else would she be risking her life to unseat her own family?

Mikira lifted her chin. "I understand."

THEY CHOSE CANBURROW SQUARE for the rally.

They spread the word shortly before the impending meeting using Jenest's underground racing channels, Eshlin's and Shira's contacts, and by papering the town with flyers. It felt good to see them slapped over the top of the old war recruitment posters, the rebels' symbol of the Goddess's hands interlaced together in a sign of partnership.

The stage that had been used for performances during the Illinir was still up, and Mikira paced along behind it. A crowd had already begun to gather out front; it wouldn't be long before it drew the Anthir's notice—just as they'd planned.

"Are you sure about this, Kira?" Talyana asked for the third time, and though part of Mikira felt a surge of warmth at her concern, the other wished she would stop asking. Each time she did, it chipped away a little at Mikira's confidence. Because she *wasn't* sure. Not only because they were risking people's lives, but because there was no going back after this.

Today, the rebellion announced itself in full force. Today, they declared war.

Something in her twisted at that. The kingdom had only just received the news that the Eternal War was over. The streets had been overflowing with people celebrating for days. Half the crowd here had mugs of ale in hand and no idea what was about to happen. They'd surrounded the perimeter with rebels, had plans to ensure the innocent could safely flee, and yet this felt at once like a mistake and their only option.

If they didn't capitalize on people's hatred of the throne now, the rebellion would lose momentum. And no matter how many changes Damien made for good now, she'd seen firsthand how easily his favor could change—and he actually cared about this city, unlike the others. What would happen when someone else ascended the throne?

A part of her wanted to give him a chance, to trust him again, but he was only a symptom of a larger problem, a cog in a system that permeated every facet of her life. And until things with him were settled, Eshlin wouldn't focus on the chimeras. If Selvin's plans came to fruition, he'd become a god of unimaginable power, and to stop him, Nava risked another Cataclysm.

She thought of Elidon's decaying body, of her mother's giving way to the verillion rot. How many more would die like that before this was over?

"I'm sure," she said after too long a pause.

Talyana stepped toward her, capturing Mikira's face in her hands with a touch so soft it sent a shiver through her. The surety of her presence was like a drug, a lifeline. Mikira clung to it, and Talyana held fast to her, pressing their foreheads together.

"Be careful," she whispered.

Then Jenest was giving her a two-minute warning, her enchanted loudspeaker in one hand and her Lyzairin mask in the other. She barely heard Jenest announcing her to the waiting crowd, her thoughts on the absence of the horse that should be at her side. The people would be expecting them both. Eshlin had even tried to get her to take a look-alike, but Mikira had refused.

Atara deserved better than that.

She deserved vengeance, and that was exactly what Mikira would get her as soon as this was over. Jenest had strict orders to bring her back to headquarters, but once the riot began, she would use the tumult to escape and find Ari so they could handle the Heretics together.

"Without further ado, I give you the youngest Illinir winner in history, Mikira Rusel!" Jenest's voice was lost to the cheering of the crowd as Mikira forced one foot in front of the other. Up the rickety wooden steps, down to the enchanted microphone in the middle of the stage, where a hundred pairs of eyes fell upon her.

Enchanted lights had been set at regular intervals, beating back the encroaching night. She surveyed the crowd, from the children pushing to reach the front for a better view to the adults linked arm in arm, to the rebels at the perimeter keeping a lookout for the Anthir so people would have time to escape.

Then she started talking.

"I want to tell you a story." Her voice radiated through the square, and the cheering quieted to a murmur. "About a girl and a dream."

She wrapped her hands around the microphone stand, anchoring herself in place. "All my life, I've only ever wanted one thing: to race. I grew up idolizing riders Arabella Wakelin and Alren Zalaire, and yes, Keirian Rusel."

A whistle rose from the crowd at her father's name, and she gave them an answering grin. "But that world wasn't made for me. It was closed to me by someone who wanted something that didn't belong to him, and then used it against me. I was forced to enter the Illinir in order to save my family's ranch, where I witnessed racing's true brutality."

This was the story that none of them knew. They saw only the girl who had risked it all and won; they had no idea the consequences if she'd lost. The years spent ground beneath the Kelbras' boots. The fear, the isolation. But she told them about it now. About how the stress drove her mother to smoke, until the verillion ate her away from the inside out. About the crushing taxes, and her foolish attempt to appeal for help.

About her father, and Lochlyn—and Iri.

About everything she'd lost to the nobility and their games. And then she told them about Damien.

"He used me," she said to the now-silent crowd. "He made me a pawn in his bid for power and tossed me aside when I was no longer necessary. Everything he's done, he's done selfishly, because there is nothing Damien Adair cares more about than himself."

It felt good to say, even as some part of her recoiled at the lie. Because as much as he'd hurt her, as angry as she was with him, she didn't truly believe that. But she also knew that Damien would do whatever necessary to hold on to his power. He'd made that clear to her the day he excommunicated her.

Tonight, they needed him to prove it.

The crowd was murmuring now, and Mikira pulled free the microphone, walking nearer to the edge of the stage. "I know many of you think the worst is behind us. That a king who would end unfair taxes and an even more unjust war is a king you can believe in. But I believed in Damien Adair once before, and he burned me, like he will burn all of you."

The words were coming faster now, sprouting from a place rawer and full of more pain than she'd realized. "At the end of the day, Damien Adair is just another body on the throne. Another noble seeking to control you. We don't need a new king—we need a new *system.* One where your voices are heard, where you make your *own* choices."

It was not until the answering roar of the crowd came that she realized it had nearly tripled in size—and they were not alone. The rebel scouts on the perimeter were signaling frantically that it was time to go, and she spotted Jenest waving for her to leave the stage. Talyana waited beside her, her horse's reins in hand.

But Mikira's eyes had snagged on a face in the crowd, on a set of steel-colored eyes with an army of constables at his back.

Damien Adair.

Mikira held his gaze as she said, "The rebellion has come."

Then the screaming started.

Some part of Mikira had been hoping they would be wrong. That Damien would let the rally continue rather than risk innocent lives in his attempt to maintain control. But as the Anthir descended in full force, swarming around him like a tide about an uncaring stone, that hope withered to dust.

The rebel soldiers did their best to keep them at bay while the spectators fled, but the Anthir overwhelmed them. The crack of gunfire split the air, cries of pain echoing alongside the chorus of screams. A fleeing woman tripped, trampled by the frenzied crowd. A child near the stage wailed for his father, who lay unmoving.

Mikira reached for him, but then Jenest was dragging her offstage. She lost sight of the child as the tumult swallowed them up, and Jenest flung her at the horse waiting for her in a side alley. "Go! We'll take care of it."

Everything in Mikira railed at the command, but the rebels closed ranks between her and the crowd, and her window of escape was rapidly narrowing. Swallowing her rising bile, she swung up into the saddle and sent the horse flying. She heard Talyana shout her name, but she didn't slow, riding in a full-out gallop until she'd put a chunk of distance between herself and the rally. Only then did she bring her horse to a walk.

Hoofbeats drew Mikira's gaze over her shoulder as Talyana came galloping into view. She reined in her horse beside Mikira's.

"What in the four hells are you doing?" she demanded.

Mikira urged her horse onward in a trot. "I can't go back to headquarters yet. Ari was expecting me to bring help."

Eshlin would be angry that she'd broken rank again, but Mikira didn't care. Since Damien's Ascension, the princess hardly resembled the benevolent, welcoming woman Mikira first met. Her fervor for the throne shook Mikira's belief that at the end of all this, she would simply turn over power.

"Eshlin said—"

"I know what Eshlin said." Mikira twisted in her seat to face Talyana, who had urged her horse after them. "Eshlin is wrong, Tal. She refuses to see that the Heretics are the bigger threat. She's obsessed with the throne."

Shouting echoed from the way they'd come, the chaos of the riot spilling out into the neighboring streets. It'd consume half the city at this rate, a powder keg set alight by her speech. After this, there was no way that people would see Damien as their hero king come to save them. They would see only a man who would do anything to maintain power.

Maybe then Eshiln could take the throne. Maybe then, with Damien defeated, she would face the true danger in their midst.

Talyana bit her lip, glancing nervously back toward the square. "Look, I agree that the Heretics need to be dealt with, but things are only going to get more dangerous now. We should head back to the compound and regroup."

"You go. I need to check in with Ari."

Talyana's expression hardened. "Then I'm coming with you, and don't you dare try to tell me no."

The words died on Mikira's lips, a swift sense of relief flitting through her. She nodded. They took off together, following the road south toward Ari's workshop. The building was dark when they arrived, but Mikira still dismounted and rapped on the door. When no one answered, she tried the handle and found it unlocked.

It was empty.

Talyana joined her after hitching the horses, getting a lantern going as Mikira searched the room, hoping for a note or some indication of where Ari had gone. But if she'd returned to the meeting point since Rezek's, there was no sign. Had she gone after the Heretics alone?

"We have to find her." Mikira forced a steadying breath against her rising panic.

"How?" Talyana countered. "It's late, you're exhausted, and there's a very high chance she'll show up here sooner or later."

"If Rezek hasn't done something to her." Mikira dropped onto the cot, burying her face in her hands. She never should have left Ari alone with Rezek.

Talyana wrapped an arm around her waist. "From what I know of her, she's more formidable than you're giving her credit for."

Fatigue slammed into Mikira like a ram, and she let herself melt into the warmth of Talyana's body. Her mind told her she needed to act, but her body felt sluggish, and the thought of sleep was difficult to ignore. As was Talyana's logic. If Ari was safe, it was likely she'd return to the workshop that evening.

"Okay," she said. "We'll wait here. For now."

They tended to the horses before returning to the cot, where the realization that Atara would not be there to alert them to danger hit Mikira like a sucker punch. Her throat swelled up, and she forced herself to breathe through it, well accustomed to the process. It had been the same with her mother, and Lochlyn, and Iri—flits of sudden grief that caught her unaware.

She had to ward them off, lest they pull her under.

Drawing one of her knives, she commanded it to guard the front door. She curled up facing Talyana's back, eyes tracing the network of freckles that dotted her skin. Sleep tugged at her, but she wanted to remain awake and on watch for Ari, so she started counting the freckles. She'd reached fifteen when her gaze snagged on something, a dot unlike the others that pulled at a half-formed thought.

She knew it was important, but her eyelids had grown heavy and her mind fuzzy, and before she could resist, she was asleep.

CHAPTER 36

DAMIEN

DAMIEN FELT LIKE a loaded spring as he paced across the king's office the morning of his coronation, waiting for news of the night's riot. He'd wanted to approach the situation with more tact, knowing that cracking down on the rallies would only lend the rebels credence, but he couldn't afford to let them continue unchecked with the chimeras on the loose. Already he'd received two more reports of the beast's bloody attacks, and the sun had barely risen.

Still, for every citizen that raised a cup to him for ending the Eternal War, there would be another recounting the rebels' words, now more than ever after the Anthir's intervention. He'd given orders that only the rebels be targeted, the innocents left untouched, but things had spiraled so quickly out of control.

A knock sounded at the door, and Inspector Elrihan entered at his call, bowing deeply. "Your Majesty, the last of the rally has been rooted from the streets. There was no sign of Mikira Rusel."

Damien's hand curled into a fist. He'd exposed Mikira as a rebel to restrict her movements; he'd never thought she'd put herself front and center. The girl he'd known wouldn't have been able to step on a stage and rally an entire crowd—not unless she truly believed it was the right thing to do. And when Mikira believed something, people believed her in turn.

He had.

How many would join the rebel cause as a result? How many now saw him as the monster she'd painted him as? She was a bigger threat to him than he'd realized, and if she was going to put herself in his line of fire, then he would take the shot.

You said no one would get hurt. Reid's voice leapt to life in the back of his mind, but he buried it. He had played with half measures long enough. He would not let the rebellion ruin everything he'd strived for, would not let all he'd sacrificed be in vain. If that meant tearing Enderlain apart to find the rebels, then he would just have to rebuild it when he was done.

He knew Ari might not forgive him, that Reid would look at him and see a man changed, but they weren't here.

He was all that remained.

"Ensure every rebel rally is met by force," he instructed Elrihan. "Arm every Anthir constable you can with guns and set them to patrol the streets at all hours. Then put a bounty on Mikira Rusel's head."

He grabbed his jacket from the back of his chair. "I want her brought in—dead or alive."

BY THE TIME Damien reached the room in the castle he'd taken, he'd undone his vest and unbuttoned his shirtsleeves, his jacket slung over one arm. It was hours now until his coronation, and he needed a moment to let his thoughts rest. But he barely made it a step inside before he came to an abrupt halt.

Curled up in an armchair in front of the fire was Shira.

She had that same romance book in her hands from the day of his Ascension, though he knew she'd finished it several times over by now. It was practically falling apart along the spine, but her eyes flitted along the page with the earnestness of a new reader.

His gaze flicked to the two guards in the hall, who hadn't warned him of her arrival, then back to his sister. He closed the door. "How did you get in?"

Shira's gaze met his. "Well, for once, Reid wasn't being dramatic."

All at once, Damien felt like an animal caught in a hunter's trap. He was half-dressed, his hair disheveled and his emotions plain on his face, and his sister's dark eyes took in every inch of it with an acuity he'd never been able to hide from.

Piece by piece, Damien redonned his vest, then his jacket. He slid a hand through his hair to settle it back into place. "What are you doing here, Shira?"

Shira watched it all with a lifted brow. "Does it feel like armor? The clothes. The order. The *control*."

Only his siblings could needle their way beneath his mask so easily. It was because of Shira that he'd learned to be so careful. She always seemed to know everything about him and Loic with a simple glance.

"I have things to do, Shira," he said tautly.

"Yes, of course. Saving the kingdom and all that." She waved a hand as if all his planning, all his work, was hardly worth the words. But it was just like her to shunt the responsibility aside to someone else. She slipped in and out of his life whenever she pleased, lingering just long enough to puncture holes.

"Perhaps I should be more like you, and do nothing instead?"

"You have no idea what I do," Shira replied coolly. "That would require you to be aware of something outside yourself."

His simmering frustration sharpened into a blade. "You've never taken an interest in house business. You even hired someone else to run the verillion fields in your stead. You made a mockery of the Ascension, and after everything I've done for this family, you've left me to carry it all myself."

A wry smile split across her face, and she snapped her book shut. "You say that as if you'd have it any other way. Tell me, little brother, if I asked you right now to share your burden with me, would you?"

No, he wouldn't. Because he didn't trust her. Didn't trust anyone. In the end, everyone lied. Everyone betrayed.

Everyone.

"I didn't think so." Shira's face softened, and she climbed smoothly to her feet. "Arielle is in trouble."

He stilled.

"She got the Heretic out of her body by placing it in a golem. Now it's free and intends to face off against Rezek's in a battle that could destroy Enderlain in another Cataclysm."

She's okay. For a moment, it was the only thought that permeated his mind. Arielle had found a way to free herself of the Heretic, and wherever she was, Shira wasn't immediately concerned about her. Which meant she was safe. But for how long?

After his run-in with Reid, Damien had sent messengers looking for her to no avail. She ought not to be his priority—he shouldn't even *care* after what had happened between them—but his every thought came back to her. What would Arielle think of what he'd accomplished? What would she recommend he do in this situation or that? He missed feeling her beside him. Her soft touch. Missed the way she approached everything with that same quiet contemplation and longed for the sound of her dulcet voice.

What if he couldn't find her because Rezek had done something to her, his last revenge in their perilous game? What if—

He seized hold of the thought, ripping it away. Arielle was not his concern any longer. She'd made that clear to him.

"Rezek's Heretic?" he ground out instead.

"Selvin," Shira said. "He created a chimera body for himself and left Rezek for it."

Did that mean that the chimera attacks, the battle to come, were all Selvin's doing? Was Rezek not even a part of this?

"I'll handle the Heretics," he said tightly. "Arielle doesn't need to get involved."

"She's already involved." Shira tucked her book into her back pocket. "You should know better than anyone that Ari isn't the type to walk away."

He rounded on his sister. "Then I'll find her and stop her myself. She doesn't need to go anywhere near Rezek or Selvin again."

Shira made a small tsking noise. "Is that jealousy, little brother?"

"Rezek is dangerous, Shira. I wouldn't think I'd have to convince you of that."

"Oh, you don't," she assured him. "But I'm not so certain you're any better for her."

"What is that supposed to mean?"

"It means I feel like I'm losing you, Dara." Her voice broke, the rawness in it startling him out of his anger. Shira was staring at him openly, pleadingly, and it made him want to turn away. He'd never seen his sister like that. Not even when their mother died and Shira found him cradling her body. She'd pried his numb fingers loose and held him while he cried.

That kind of sturdiness wasn't supposed to waver.

Shira dropped her head into her hands. "I don't know who you are anymore, and I don't know how to bring you back. But maybe she can, if you'll give her the chance."

"I don't need saving." He hated how much his voice shook, hated even more that he couldn't stop it. Couldn't control it. "Everything I've become I made myself. I single-handedly ended the Eternal War, and it's only the beginning. I can save this kingdom."

"If you don't destroy it first." She looked up at him with tired eyes. "Crushing peaceful rallies, Dara? You're playing right into the rebellion's narrative. How far are you willing to go? How much of yourself will you sacrifice along the way?"

"Whatever I have to." There was no going back now. No other path to take.

Shira stood, closing the distance between them with heavy-footed steps. "And you'll grind yourself into dust to do it, won't you?" she asked, her unflappable calm wearing on his patience. He'd never been able to pick her apart the way he did Loic, so instead he'd pushed her away, another variable he couldn't control. "Have you ever stopped to consider that *you* are the problem here, Dara? That this system is broken, and you are propping it up? The things you've had to do . . . What would father say now, after you've sullied our mother's name?"

"I don't need his approval any longer," Damien bit out, even as the words curled claws beneath his skin. He'd hated implying his mother had been unfaithful, but it'd been the only way to convince people he was the lost prince.

"Good," she said simply, a single word that unraveled worlds. A lifetime of memories. She stopped before him, head tilted in solemn-eyed consideration. "Didn't you ever wonder why Loic was always Father's favorite? It's because of how similar they are. The both of them have only ever been interested in power for its own sake. But you—you're different, Dara. You always have been."

"Then you should know that I can do this." An unexpected desperation edged his voice. "You should be on my side!"

"I'm always on your side," Shira replied, so softly he nearly missed it. "Even when you don't know where that is."

Without warning, she wrapped her arms around him in a viselike hug. He stiffened, struck by the urge to hug her back, to confess every doubt and fear circling inside him and beg her to fix it all, the way she always did. But weakness like that was not a luxury he could afford. That Enderlain could afford.

So when he pulled away from her, locking each scrap of emotion behind an iron wall, his voice was cold as he said, "I know you're working with the rebels. If I see you again, I'll have you arrested."

She curved a hand against his cheek, not even trying to deny it, though it'd only been a hunch. A look he couldn't name crossed through Shira's dark eyes, and she said solemnly, "Lest you forget, you have a brother." She turned for the door. "He's disappeared from Anthir custody."

Then she was gone.

CHAPTER 37

MIKIRA

MIKIRA WOKE TO a yelp of pain.

She lurched upright, vision blurry and knife drawn. The workshop door was open, revealing a man stumbling away from her floating blade. It hovered in the doorway, preventing him from entering, and Mikira was just about to send the second after it when a little black shape came trotting into the room.

"Widget?" She blinked, taking in the snaking tattoos along the man's forearms, the pushed-up sleeves of his long black sweater, his hair like a crow's nest. "Reid?"

"I'd prefer if you didn't stab me today." He scowled, but the look quickly gave way to one of mortification as he took in the two of them tangled in the bedsheets. Mikira winced. This wasn't what it looked like, and yet it was. She wanted to deny it, to explain, but she didn't know the words to describe something she was only just starting to understand herself.

All she knew was the look of hurt buried beneath his embarrassment echoed in her.

Reid turned away as she tumbled out, pulling on her boots and scooping Widget up on her way to the door. Mikira followed him outside, pulling the door mostly closed. Then she just stood there holding the cat. It was early, the morning fog barely beginning to burn off and the scent of factory smoke faint in the air, but she hardly felt the chill.

Reid looked as uncomfortable as she was, standing nearly on the opposite side of the street from her and fidgeting as though he hadn't quite decided whether or not to run.

"I was looking for Ari," he said at last, almost defensively.

Mikira held Widget close. "Us too."

Silence fell again. She felt like a horse stuck at the starting gate with nowhere to run. Desperate to break the mounting tension, she gestured at the space between them. "I'm not going to bite you, you know," she teased.

She expected him to quip something back, but he only stared at her with a quiet, pleading look. "I can't do this, Kira," he said roughly. "I can't play this game."

She flinched. This had never been a game to her. But she was so, so tired of holding on to her resentment. After her reconciliation with Ari and those brief encounters with Reid, the last of her grudge had slipped away, and all that remained was the ease she'd once felt with him. An ease she missed desperately in the wake of all she'd lost.

"I don't want to play games either," she said thickly. "I want—"

She cut off. What did she want? For Reid not to look so wounded; for her heart to make up its mind. For her to understand her own feelings, to not be the broken thing she suspected she was. To say the right thing, for once.

"I want you to stay." The truth came so much easier than a lie, and it softened Reid's edges. She risked a step closer, and then another, and he held his ground until she stood before him. "I know things got messy between us, and I'm sorry for the part I played in that. But I want you in my life, Reid."

She wanted him the same way she wanted Talyana: as a partner, a confidant, a companion. As a friend whose love she could not live without.

"I want that too," Reid said quietly.

Carefully she placed Widget back into his arms. "Then come inside." She led him back into the workshop, where Talyana was finally waking.

"Kira?" she asked sleepily. Then, more intently, "*Haldane?* What in the four hells?"

"I was looking for Ari!" Reid clutched Widget close, glowering at her. Mikira closed the door as he shuffled in, casting Talyana another glare before slumping against the wall.

"Well, we have no idea where she is." Talyana swung her feet to the ground, reaching for her jacket. Mikira barely noticed Reid's answering scowl, her eyes locked on the spot on Talyana's shoulder that she'd noticed last night.

"Tal." She spread her hand across Talyana's shoulder, the jacket half on.

Talyana glanced down at her hand. "What?"

Mikira pressed gently against the mark she'd noticed last night with one finger. "Is this sore?"

"A little bit," Talyana admitted almost grudgingly.

Mikira stared at the mark, the slow shift of pieces in the back of her mind claiming half her attention. Then all at once, they clicked into place and she whispered, "They weren't poisoning you."

"What?" Talyana let the jacket slip from her arm as, behind her, Reid's face went white.

Mikira's gaze snapped up to him. "I'm right, aren't I?"

The question seemed to add ten years to Reid, and he dropped wearily onto the stool by the workbench, his long legs stretched out before him. Widget descended into his lap, where he curled up. Mikira envied the little cat's obliviousness, the way he could sleep undisturbed by the chaos around him. She wanted so badly to do the same. To find a quiet place and sink into it so deeply it was all she knew.

There, she wouldn't have to think about any of this. There, what had seemed like a series of unconnected moments wouldn't have come together into something she couldn't process. Something that changed everything.

Because she knew how Damien had taken the throne.

"Those packets you kept in your workshop," Mikira pressed, remembering the day she'd searched it for evidence that Damien was not the killer she thought. "They were for storing blood, weren't they?"

Reid ran a hand through his wild hair, fingers knotting in the dark strands. "You don't have to ask me this, Kira."

Her nails dug into her palms. Of course he'd say that. Looking away was what Reid did best. But he also protected himself, something he'd been trying to teach her to do too, and that she'd never quite been able to manage.

You make them a shield so they can't make them a weapon.

He'd told her that once when her weakness threatened to overwhelm her. He'd taken the parts of her that were about to break and turned them into steel she could carry into battle. It had gotten her through the balls, through the Illinir, through every painful day of the last few weeks.

But there were some things that could not be turned away from. Some things had to be faced head-on.

Talyana looked questioningly between them as Mikira barreled on. "Talyana and I found a death certificate for the Ranier prince, which means someone wanted everyone to think the prince was dead. So we tried to follow the sigils of the witnesses, which is why we came to you. It wasn't until we received an anonymous tip about a retired royal guard that we caught a break."

Reid didn't have Damien's control. The house lord might not lie, but he bent the truth in ways it should not bend. Reid, for all his faults, didn't play with the truth. He said what he thought, and he showed it on his face—which was why when his expression crumpled at the mention of the royal guard, she knew she was right.

"You sent us that tip," she said. "Why?"

Reid hid his face behind his hand. "I hoped you would stop him."

"From becoming king?"

He peered at her through the slats of his fingers. "He's lost himself,

Mikira, and I don't know how to bring him back. He's pushed everyone away. Me, Shira, Ari, all for the throne."

Mikira thought of her father's hollow-eyed stare. Of the way her mother had withered away in body and soul with each passing day beneath the verillion's grip. What was there to be done for someone set on their own destruction?

You never stop trying, said Lochlyn's voice, long absent from her thoughts. *You bring them back.*

She closed her eyes, wishing not for the first time that her brother had been the one to survive. If Rezek had only taken her, things would be different. Lochlyn would have been there for their sisters, would have known better than to challenge the Kelbras. Lochlyn always had the answer, and now, more than ever, she wished that she had him.

Mikira released a slow breath and opened her eyes to find Reid staring at her, desolate. Lochlyn wasn't here; now she was the one who had to get answers, even if she didn't like what she found.

"Kira," Talyana said softly. "What's happening?"

Mikira took one of Talyana's hands in hers. "To trick the crown, Damien needed royal blood that had yet to bind to the bloodstone. He needed the real Ranier prince's blood."

Talyana's gaze searched hers, her confusion only growing. Mikira swallowed but forced herself onward. "When we were children, Rezek nearly killed you. When your parents found out, they used their connections to put you into officer training." She understood now; all Talyana's parents had wanted was to keep her safe. She was probably never supposed to see combat but hadn't been able to send others into a danger she wouldn't face herself.

"Then the royal guard, the one whose body Reid sent us to, was a friend of your father's." Her eyes flicked to him, but he didn't interrupt, only watched her the way a castaway watched a ship drift slowly out of reach. "And that mark—it matches the one on your arm, Tal. I thought it was strange someone would poison you with a needle in that location, and it's because they *didn't.* The poison was injected in your shoulder. The mark on your arm—"

"Was a blood draw," Talyana finished breathlessly.

Mikira struggled with the words that came next. They knotted in her throat, uncaring that they would change everything.

"The Ranier prince isn't a prince at all," she said. "It's you."

CHAPTER 38

ARIELLE

ARI PRETENDED TO be asleep.

She waited until she heard the sound of the cell slot flicking open before she lunged, seizing the wrist of the rebel delivering her meal. "Where's my sister?"

The rebel shoved a boot against the bars of the cell, using the leverage to pry his wrist free. Her bread roll went tumbling to the ground, but she left gouges of angry red flesh in her wake. The rebel cursed at her, thumping his boot against the bars again before stomping off.

"Answer me!" Ari leapt to her feet. "Tell me if she's okay!"

Only the echoing slam of the door at the end of the hall answered. Ari collapsed against the bars, sinking in on herself until she met cold earth. She had no idea how long it had been since she and Rezek were taken by the rebels, no idea whether her sister lived. She'd slept at some point, the delivery of their meals the only indication of passing time.

The rebel cells were barely more than indents in the cavern walls fitted with metal bars. They'd put her and Rezek across from each other, the faint glow of the enchanted lights barely enough to see by. Their hands were bound, and they'd taken her rings upon arrival, which meant the person who had given the order knew what she could do with them.

Ari had tried telling them that she wasn't with Rezek, that she was a friend of Mikira's, but the rebels hadn't listened. They could have fought, but Rezek had been a mess on the floor, and the rebels had been armed with rifles. So she'd gone with them quietly, hoping that Mikira would hear of her presence and come looking.

She hadn't seen Rivkah since.

Shifting toward the bars, she peered across the narrow hall to where Rezek huddled in the far corner of his cell. It seemed impossible that someone like him had been brought this low, and stranger still that that something resembling pity unfurled inside her for him. Part of her reveled in it, satisfied to see the man who'd had her tortured locked up in a cell of his own. The other remembered the way his voice had cracked when he told her that Selvin left.

"Rezek?" she called. He'd ignored her before, but she hadn't given up. "You have to tell these people what you know."

Someone had to do something about the Heretics, and in the absence of being able to tell Damien, the rebels were their only option. Her bond with Nava had revealed the Heretic had relocated back to the Silverwood Forest, where she'd remained since, clearly waiting for something. But there was no telling when she would seek out Selvin, and Rezek was the only one who knew his Heretic's plans.

Eventually Rezek's rasping response came: "I want to talk to Damien."

Ari leaned back against the bars, desperately trying to stave off the feeling that everything was crumbling around her. Her magic at risk, her relationships frayed, her home and family in danger. She'd come all this way to protect them, and now she'd unleashed a threat bigger than she'd ever been.

Oh, little lion, the ghost of Nava's voice came trickling down to her. *Do not fight this.*

Ari squeezed her eyes shut, trying desperately to block Nava out the way the Heretic had her. She could feel Nava's rage, her pain, even from so far away. They were threaded into the Heretic's very being, into the dreams that still plagued Ari's nights. She saw again Nava's goodbye to her sister, the sight of smoke on the horizon from the impending invasion. Felt her loss, felt her *break*, over and over.

Forcing a deep breath, Ari imagined a door slamming shut between them, and the emotions subsided just as footsteps echoed. She hauled herself upright, another plea already on her lips, and stopped when she saw who it was.

"I should have known," she said to Shira Adair's unimpressed expression.

Shira's lips quirked. "Lucky for you, I have friends in very high places."

Ari was fairly sure that Shira *was* the friend in high places, but she wasn't about to argue with the woman unlocking her cell. Shira *snick*ed her bonds free with a flash of her pocketknife, then studied Rezek in his dark corner. He stared back with one hollow eye, the rest of his face shrouded in shadow.

"Let's talk outside," Shira said.

Ari followed her into a wider corridor with a series of intersecting hallways. Two rebels armed with Sherakin shotguns stood guard outside the cells. One, a thin balding man with a scar along his jaw, stuck out a hand to stop them as they emerged.

"She's not to be moved," he said. "Princess's orders."

Princess? Ari thought. *Eshlin?*

"We're just going to have a chat, Issac," Shira replied airily. "I'll assume responsibility if Eshlin asks."

Issac exchanged nervous glances with the other guard. If the princess truly was the head of the rebels, a revelation that fit right in with the past few days of discoveries, disobeying her was no small feat. For the guards to be torn between her orders and Shira's, the elder Adair had to be of some importance here.

"We'll be just down the hall," Shira added.

Issac nodded reluctantly. "Be quick."

Shira led her onward, picking up the pace once they were out of sight.

She cut down another hall, then darted through one of the doors into a low-ceilinged storage room with a metal table and chairs.

"Rivkah?" Ari blurted the moment the door shut.

"Is fine," Shira assured her, and Ari nearly wilted where she stood. "She's recovering in the medical ward with Vix. I apologize for taking so long to get you out, but I wasn't informed of your arrival until recently. Did you break my inn, or was it whoever now has my Racari?"

"Nava, my Heretic," Ari replied. "I don't know what she wants with it, but—" She stopped, a thought occurring to her then.

"I'm not possessed," Shira said before she could ask. "I never bonded to the Racari, which is why I can't retrieve it now. Do you know what Nava wants with it?"

Ari shook her head. "Rezek doesn't seem to think Selvin has any interest in it, only the third, which belongs to someone in the castle."

"Did he tell you anything else about Selvin's plans?"

"No, but he's obsessed with putting enchanters in control, and if Nava finds him—"

"Their fight could cause another Cataclysm." Shira leaned against the metal table with her arms crossed. She was remarkably calm in the face of the potential disaster Ari had just unfolded before her, but she'd come to realize that this was what Shira Adair did: she put out fires without igniting herself.

"Rezek is loyal to Selvin." Ari hesitated before adding, "But I think he would talk to Damien. I know it sounds absurd, but I think he still cares about him."

In the handful of times she and Rezek had met, Damien had entered almost every conversation. Then there was the way he'd flinched when she mentioned his attempt on Damien's life, the horror with which he'd recounted killing Damien's mother—they weren't the reactions of someone divested.

Something unreadable darted through Shira's eyes, and suddenly Ari became aware of the other unanswered questions. "Why does it feel like you're the only one concerned about this? Mikira was meant to go to the rebels for help. Doesn't the princess know what's happening?"

"She does, but unfortunately her focus is entirely on regaining the throne." At Ari's questioning look, Shira's expression softened. "Ari, are you aware of what's been happening at the castle?"

A feeling of unease crept through her at Shira's tone. She'd been so isolated the last few days, and she'd gone straight from the ruins in the Silverwood to Rezek's to the inn. "No?"

"My brother has convinced everyone that he's the lost Ranier prince and used that lie to win the Royal Ascension." Shira watched her with hawk-eyed acuity as she said, "He'll be crowned the king of Enderlain tonight."

It took a moment for the words to sink in. Shira might as well have said the Harbingers had returned. For Damien to have pulled off a trick of that magnitude . . . What had he *done*?

Her apprehension must have reflected in her face because Shira's expression only grew grimmer. "He's hurt people, Ari. Even I'm not sure how far he's willing to go. And now he's a target for the rebellion, and I don't know if I can stop them from taking him out."

Taking him out.

Ari dropped into one of the metal chairs, barely noticing its iciness. The idea that Damien could have become king without her knowing was too much. It hurt that he'd kept this from her, infuriated her that he'd put himself in this position, and tore her apart that she wasn't there to help him. Because she knew that everything he did, he did to change things, to make them better. He truly thought he could save Enderlain, and he would vilify himself to do it.

But to the rebels, he was the very problem they sought to eradicate, and they wouldn't hesitate to remove him. Would they listen if she told them that Damien wanted to help Enderlain? Would they believe her in the face of whatever he'd done?

Would she believe herself?

She loved him; that hadn't changed, but she knew what he was capable of. Knew what he'd done to reach this point. What they'd all done. In truth, she didn't know anymore which of them were right and which were wrong. Perhaps there wasn't any real difference. Only a matter of perspective, and hers had drifted so far from what she'd known that she didn't know whether to run to him to help him, or to save him from himself.

Shira dropped into the chair beside her. "I think you're the only one that can bring him back. The only one that he might listen to, before it's too late."

"He won't." Her heart clenched, but Damien had worked too hard to get where he was, and he was not in the habit of giving up what he wanted. He sought the power to change things, and she knew the way that kind of strength wriggled beneath your skin.

It made you feel invincible.

Made you consider letting an ancient enchanter with the potential to bring catastrophe roam free, if only you could keep that strength, that safety. Going back to the way you were, to being weak and afraid—it was akin to dying. And Damien had been afraid, she realized now. He'd been scared and broken like her, and they had clung to each other in the dark, done whatever they'd had to in order to escape it.

Shira seemed to sense that Ari didn't just mean Damien. She was there when Ari's darkness had engulfed her and she arrived on Shira's doorstep stained with blood. She'd known the path Ari walked before even she had, because she'd watched her brother walk the same one. They'd gone down it hand in hand.

"You're not the monster you've convinced yourself you are," Shira said softly. "Neither of you are. There is no path you can walk down that does not have a way back."

A way back.

It was the very thing she'd sought by freeing Nava. She wanted to be in control of herself and her magic, to be able to be in Rivkah's presence and feel worthy of it. She didn't want to be afraid of herself any longer.

Issac's voice sounded outside the door, calling for Shira. She tensed, everything about her demeanor shifting. "I need to know whose side you're on in all of this. Will you help him?"

"Always." Ari didn't hesitate.

Relief edged across Shira's face, and she nodded. "Then let's get you out of here."

CHAPTER 39

MIKIRA

MIKIRA EXPECTED TO be overwhelmed by the news that her best friend was a lost princess, but after the last few days, she only felt numb. In contrast, Talyana's hand trembled in hers, her hazel eyes pinned wide.

"That isn't possible," Talyana whispered. "My parents—"

"Your adoptive father was one of the royal guards who helped get you out," Reid said without the slightest amount of tact. "Him and the one that Damien killed."

Mikira shot him a silencing glare, and he threw up his hands in exasperation. "He's right, though," she said gently to Talyana's stricken look. "They're not your birth parents. I'm so sorry."

Talyana stared unseeingly at them both—and then bolted from the workshop.

"Tal!" Mikira shot after her, finding Talyana doubled over in the road and heaving for breath. Mikira placed a comforting hand on her back, but Talyana spooked like a skittish colt. She kept moving, pacing along behind the horses they'd left tied to the hitching post, before collapsing onto a small boulder in the overgrown grass and burying her face in her hands.

Mikira crept closer. "Tal?"

She held up one finger, and Mikira waited, wishing she could do more. It felt like ages before Talyana finally lifted her head, the shock gone in favor of resolve. "Okay," she said. Then again, "Okay. We don't tell anyone."

"Great idea," Reid called from the doorway, Widget on his shoulder. "Except the only person who matters already knows."

Damien.

Why had he let Talyana go after his people drew her blood? In case his plan didn't work and he needed her again? He wasn't cavalier about killing; perhaps he just decided that unless Talyana proved herself a threat, she didn't have to die.

Mikira forced a calming breath. "You're the rightful heir to the throne, Tal. You can disprove Damien's claim." She kept her voice soft, though the street was deserted.

Talyana threw up her hands. "I'm not a princess, Kira! I can't be—*that*."

"Seconded," Reid muttered. Talyana snatched up a stone and flung it at Reid, who leapt out of the way with a yelp and ducked behind the horse.

"Stop it!" Mikira snapped at them. "The last thing I need is the two of you arguing on top of everything. And keep your voices down!"

Talyana ran a frustrated hand through the crown of her hair. "Sorry, I just—" Her words devolved into a cross between a hiss and a scream. Reid peered at her over the back of the horse, clearly swallowing back some remark as Widget clambered onto the horse.

Mikira started pacing, desperate to work out the fervent energy pulsing through her. "You don't have to be queen. You just have to prove your identity so Damien won't be coronated. And if Eshlin brings you in, she'll win the Ascension. Then she can focus on the chimeras instead of the rebellion. After that's handled, she can dismantle the house system and monarchy peacefully instead of with war."

"That," Reid remarked, stepping cautiously out from behind the horse, "is not actually a bad idea."

Talyana considered her out of the corner of her eye, looking one step away from bolting again. Then the tension washed out of her, and she sat back down on the stone. "Fine. We'll try it your way. Let's go back to base."

Mikira let her head drop back, staring up at the clouded sky. "I'll tell Eshlin. Just in case there's any . . . issue. She's been so protective of the throne; what if she saw you as a threat?"

"No way." Talyana shook her head. "You're not doing this on your own, Kira. You have to stop trying to do everything by yourself."

"I'm not—"

"You are!" This time when Talyana rose to her feet, she closed the distance between them, using every inch of her height to stare Mikira down. "This is what you do. You try to carry everything on your shoulders until eventually you break beneath the weight, and then you hate yourself for not being good enough. But no one can do that, Kira! Not alone."

Mikira quivered, every word hitting deeper. For years she'd been the one to carry everything. She'd taken care of her sisters, her father, the ranch. She'd defended them against Rezek, against financial ruin and Damien's threats, and she'd picked herself up time and time again. After her mother, after Lochlyn, after Iri and Atara. She'd known all along that it was eating away at her, that she was slowly cracking apart. But the idea of accepting it, of telling Talyana that she was right, felt like giving up.

It felt like losing, and she couldn't lose anything more.

"I just want you to be safe." She fought to get the words out. "All of you."

Reid snorted derisively, folding his arms as he joined them. "Did it ever occur to you that we want the same thing? I'm not here for the joy of Talyana's company."

Mikira's lips twitched, and even Talyana's iciness melted just a little. She looked at Reid differently right then, as if, just maybe, she didn't want to kill him.

"The leviathan is correct," she said.

Reid blinked, his arms slowly unfolding. "The what?"

"You *are* tall," Mikira offered with a shrug.

Reid's shoulders hunched, and Mikira nearly choked on the laugh that burst from her, so twisted was it with the knot of emotion in her throat. She sobered just as quickly, the need for them to understand propelling her onward. "I care about you both, so much," she said. "Your friendship means everything to me. It might not be what Arielle and Damien have, but—"

"You don't have to explain, Kira," Reid said, softer than she'd ever heard him. Mikira studied the careless set to his shoulders, the cavalier line of his mouth that she would have once thought meant he didn't care. But she knew by now that Reid cared more than anyone.

He averted his gaze as he added, "I feel the same way."

"I hate to agree with Haldane twice, but he's right," Talyana said. "We aren't going anywhere."

Mikira swallowed hard, managing to nod. It wasn't the type of love she'd seen all her life, the kind she'd expected and thought herself damaged for not feeling, but it was just as strong, just as true.

Talyana enveloped her in a hug. She smelled of cloves, of gunpowder and memories long past. Her arms encircled Talyana, and she forgot, if only for a moment, the feeling of the weight of the world on her shoulders.

Then, before he could protest, she seized a handful of Reid's shirt and dragged him into the hug. Talyana grunted in annoyance, and Reid scrambled like a cat thrust into water, but she held on to both of them for one perfect moment.

Then she stepped back.

Reid's face was flushed, and Talyana refused to look at him. She only cleared her throat and said, "Point is, you don't have to do this alone, Kira. You never have to do anything alone ever again."

Mikira shuddered beneath the solace of those words. "Then let's go."

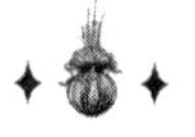

"WHAT ARE YOU two doing here?" Jenest leapt off her chair when they arrived outside the headquarters barrier, Reid clinging to Mikira from behind as her horse slowed alongside Talyana's.

Mikira frowned. "What do you mean?" She knew Eshlin was likely wondering where Mikira had gone, but Jenest looked more concerned than confused. She didn't even comment on the presence of Reid, who was looking about the cavern with obvious distaste.

"Shira just left with the prisoner. She said she got a message from the princess to bring her to the castle." Jenest's expression contorted more with each word. "She was supposed to meet up with you two for transport."

Mikira exchanged looks with Talyana. "What prisoner?"

"Damien's girl. Or I guess she's Rezek's now. I can't keep track."

"Arielle?" Reid asked incredulously.

Jenest snapped her fingers. "That's the one."

By the time Jenest had caught them up on Rezek and Ari's capture, Mikira's head was spinning. "But then why would Shira . . ." She trailed off. "Jenest, where is the princess now?"

Jenest's face grew grim. "At the castle. They're going to assassinate Damien Adair."

CHAPTER 40

MIKIRA

THEIR HORSES ATE up ground at an alarming rate, both enchanted for speed. Jenest had provided them with the route Eshlin and the others took through the underground tunnels, which ran even beneath the castle. Mikira would have expected them to be walled off, but apparently, they'd been kept as escape routes should the castle ever be under siege.

Another thing Eshlin had never divulged.

It wasn't lost on Mikira that Eshlin had made this plan without involving the rest of them. Did she think Shira and Mikira, and by extension Talyana, would choose Damien over her?

They rounded a final bend and reined in their horses outside a stone staircase. Mikira leapt to the ground, heading for the door at the top of the stairs with Reid on her heel.

"What exactly is our plan here, Kira?" Talyana hadn't moved from her horse. "Risk the rebels' success so that you can save a man that you hate and that wants you *and* me dead?"

When she put it that way, it actually did sound absurd. Mikira had sent her horse flying down the tunnel without thinking, but now that she did, her mind kept circling back to Talyana. She was a threat to everything Damien had worked for, the only one who could expose him, and yet he'd left her alive.

Perhaps he'd done it for selfish reasons, but Mikira didn't think so. This was what separated him from Rezek, from the other house leaders. They wielded power for their own gain, but for all his stoicism and secrets, Damien truly cared. Enough that a part of her wished they could have given him a chance.

She didn't know how to explain her complex emotions regarding Damien Adair, so she sought a simpler answer that was just as true. "It's Ari," she replied. "Shira must have gotten her out in hopes that she could convince Damien to abdicate. They might not even know about the attack."

"If anyone can talk him into it, it's Ari," Reid said in a slightly *too* neutral tone. She wondered what exactly had happened between him and Damien. Whatever it was, it hadn't stopped him from riding into danger for his friend.

"And you think she's going to get caught in the cross fire." Talyana sighed.

"Only if the two of you don't hurry up," Reid grumbled. "We may already be too late."

"I never thought I'd see the day that I come running to Damien Adair's aid," Talyana muttered as she dismounted.

Mikira smirked. "How about mine, then?"

"That I can do." Talyana joined them at the top of the stairs. "But do we even know where to look?"

Reid edged toward the door. "The throne room. The mourning period ended yesterday; Damien can be crowned now."

Mikira nodded at the staircase. "Jenest said this should bring us out around the kitchens, but I'm not very familiar with the castle layout."

"I am." Reid shrugged in response to their matching looks of incredulity. "I've been here with Damien, and directions are like patterns. They're easy to remember."

They plunged through the door and up a narrow staircase to a musty storage room full of crates and dusty jars. The door was cracked open, the sound of bubbling stew the only noise in what should have been a bustling kitchen.

Mikira peered through. "Eshlin must have cleared the place out. Let's go."

Their path through the kitchen and up the servants' stairs remained clear. They emerged on the fourth floor, skirted along a narrow back hallway, and then up another staircase.

"This *should* open into the servants' prep room on the other side of the throne room," Reid whispered.

Quietly, Mikira pushed open the door, revealing an empty room and an open archway on the other side. Eshlin's voice trailed in. "Shoot to kill when he enters. We're not taking any chances."

Mikira looked to Talyana. "Are you ready for this?"

There was only one way to get Eshlin to abort her plan, and that was if she knew she could claim the throne by legitimate means. Which meant that Talyana was going to have to tell her the truth about her parentage.

"You don't really have a choice." Reid glowered at them. "If you don't say something, I will."

"Why did we bring him?" Talyana grunted, before forcing a deep breath. "Never mind. Let's go."

They crossed to the throne room doorway, but no sooner had Mikira opened it than she slammed to a halt, her knives nearly tumbling from her fingers as she beheld the scene before her.

The room was littered with bodies.

Prince Darius's throat was cut, a look of disbelief still etched into his face where he sat poised upon the throne. High Lady Dramara had a blade protruding from her chest, sprawled across her back on the stairs, and High Lord Ruthar slumped almost peacefully in his sleep against the far wall.

High Lord Vanadahl was the worst.

His body was riddled with bullet holes where it lay facedown by the door, his shirt stained with so much blood it was nearly crimson from collar to sleeve. Cowering blindfolded in the corner beside it were two officials dressed in royal colors, and a man in the pure white of the Sendian Church Mikira guessed was the high priest here to perform the coronation.

Eshlin surveyed them like a general before her soldiers. "What are you two doing here?"

"You killed them." Talyana retreated a step, the color leaching from her skin. Mikira felt the same nausea spreading through her, Reid observing it all with a cool detachment.

These were not the actions of the benevolent princess they'd dedicated themselves to.

"I saw an opportunity and I took it." A handful of rebels stood at Eshlin's back, some looking vaguely sick. Two loaded their guns while another pair stood watch at the throne room door, listening to the other side. Damien must have been on his way there for the coronation.

"This was always part of the plan," Eshlin said to Mikira's blank-faced stare. "These people are the face of the kingdom's problems. The anchors that keep it stagnant. They would have been dangerous to our progress."

Mikira's roving eyes landed on Darius. "He was your brother."

Something gleamed in the princess's eyes, a seedling of pain fighting to break through the earth. "He was. But he was also a threat, and I can't risk everything we've accomplished for sentimentality."

You've lost it, Mikira wanted to say. The words formed and died on her lips, caught between what her heart told her and what her head knew to be true. Hadn't she known this was coming? There'd been no chance the house heads were just going to turn over their power; nullifying them had always been a part of the plan. This way, they could take control without opposition. No one had to die for their greed.

They died, she thought, and from the look in Eshlin's eye, Mikira didn't think that they would be the last.

I'm tired, Mikira, Eshlin had told her. *Tired of watching my family tear itself apart, tired of playing this endless game. I want it to end.*

Was this what she'd truly meant? An end by any means necessary?

Talyana gathered herself and stepped forward. "There's something we need to tell you—"

Mikira cut across her. "The prisoner Arielle Kadar has escaped."

Reid's gaze snapped to her, but Mikira shook her head just the slightest bit, silently begging him to play along. In that moment, she knew with utter certainty that if Talyana told Eshlin the truth of her identity right now, she would end up just like the rest of the council.

Eshlin scowled. "How?"

"I'm not sure," Mikira lied. "But she's here now, with Damien. I think she intends to talk him into giving up the throne. We should give her a chance."

"I hear voices outside," one of the rebels confirmed. "One is definitely High Lord Adair."

Mikira could practically see the debate playing out across Eshlin's face. The princess wouldn't be able to deny that Damien had done good for this city; there would be people who would see her as a villain if she took his life. But Mikira knew a thing or two about leaving loose ends with Damien Adair.

If they let him live, it might come back to bite them.

"Please," Mikira pressed when the princess's face hardened with resolve. "If we kill him, we're no better than them."

Two of the rebels exchanged uncertain looks; a third was still staring at Royce Vanadahl's mutilated body. Even the one listening at the door, gun at the ready, was regarding Eshlin as if he didn't quite recognize her. It was that look that seemed to change the princess's mind, and it was that look that forced Mikira to recognize the truth.

Something was wrong with Eshlin.

The princess turned her back on them all, facing the entrance. "If he walks through that door, he dies."

CHAPTER 41

DAMIEN

DAMIEN MADE HIS way toward the council chambers for the coronation, flanked by guards. Servants had brought him clothes studded in gemstones and silks finer than he'd ever seen, but he'd opted instead for one of his suits. Black jacket, silver waistcoat, white shirt. Clothes that made him feel like himself.

He still wore his guns, the knowledge that his brother was free of the Anthir cells and roaming the streets having put him on edge. It would be just like him to try to sabotage the coronation. Would he try to team up with Rezek again, their mutual hatred a bond? Rezek had always despised his father as much as he'd craved his approval; he'd probably thank Loic for killing him.

The phantom urge to seek Arielle's or Reid's counsel struck. He had to remind himself that they weren't there, a thought that, this time, did little to assuage the desire. He could no longer deny that he wished they were, now more than ever.

Damien's fingers sought his mother's pocket watch, the memory of the day he'd taken it firm in his mind. Her body had still been warm. Shira had tried to pull him away, and he'd clung to her. She was bigger then. Stronger. She'd dragged him free, and his fingers had curled around the watch's chain. For a moment, it had been the only thing connecting him to his mother—and then the chain had snapped.

He'd gotten it repaired since. Had worn it everywhere he went, keeping a piece of her with him. A piece that served as a reminder of what he intended to do. Her death was the result of a world that played with power like the strings of a harp, a world he wanted to repair. It was the result of Ascensions, and wars between houses and rebels and kingdoms.

The wars between them all.

For so long, Enderlain had lived in a legacy of blood, a legacy he'd been forced to repeat simply for the chance to have a seat at the table. To ensure that what happened to him, his family, never happened again. But this was the decision he'd made. He had placed himself here, made it so that the choices were his.

He could not walk away now.

"State your purpose." The voice of the nearest guard brought him back to the present. He had a hand on the pommel of his sword and had stepped between Damien and someone else.

Damien caught a glimpse of dark curls and said, "Stand down."

"Your Majesty—"

"Take your hand off your sword before I remove it from your arm," Damien snarled. The guard obeyed, stepping aside to reveal an impossibility.

Arielle.

She wore a simple blouse and skirt, like the day he'd met her all those months ago. Her hair was loose, cascading around her shoulders in a wave of dark curls he longed to wrap around his fingers. It took everything in him not to envelop her in his arms there and then, a thought that felt at once like defeat and coming home.

Because for all he'd told himself he didn't need her, for all the fury that had cut through his veins, seeing her here, now—it was like the first breath after a lifetime of drowning.

"Leave us," Damien commanded. The guards split to the ends of the hall, granting them privacy, but he could see only her.

"You're okay," he breathed. "How did you get here?"

"Shira." The simple sound of her voice was nearly more than he could bear.

"Of course." He allowed himself to take a step closer, his fingers seeking the edges of his cuffs to straighten them. "I owe you an apology. I wanted to talk to you sooner, but—"

"You were too busy becoming king." She tilted her head, evaluating him with eyes that had always sheared him to the core. "Was it worth it?"

He was halfway to saying yes before he thought of Shira's look of disappointment. Of the urge he'd had to say something to Reid in the wreckage of the pub, the way he wanted nothing more than to take Arielle in his arms that very moment, and yet didn't move.

He closed his eyes briefly before he replied, "It has to be."

"Because if it's not, then you're no better than the rest of them." Her words weren't cruel, but they cut nonetheless. Through every layer, every lie, to the truth he didn't want to face. From the look of understanding in her dark eyes, she felt it too. They'd gotten here together, built each other up in the face of their darkness.

His eyes slid to the throne room door. The others were probably wondering where he was. They would come looking for him soon; he had to get ahold of himself. But then Arielle slid toward him, and he tracked every inch of space that disappeared between them.

Her voice was gentle as she said, "Do not become the thing you set out to destroy."

He nearly pulled away from her, nearly told her he was nothing like the others. But it was Royce's vanity he wanted to protest against. Niekla's knifelike superiority and Cassian's bending will. Except that wasn't what she meant.

He turned his face away. "What did Shira tell you?"

"The truth—"

He barked a laugh that bordered too close to wild. "Shira never tells the truth. Only a version of it that she can use to sway you."

Arielle's shoulders curved, as if he'd drawn the strength from her bones. "She's your sister," she said simply, and his mind spun with a hundred meanings: *she's just like you, she cares about you, she knows you.*

He knew with utter certainty then why Arielle had come here. Not to join him, but to be a pawn in Shira's game.

Damien brought a hand to her cheek. "I thought you would understand." He brushed his thumb across her lips—and then he turned away.

Arielle seized his wrist, rooting him to the spot. "I understand better than *anyone*." It was the rage in that word that stopped him, in the press of her fingers through his sleeve. He'd never heard her sound like that before.

"I understand that you're clinging to the vestiges of control. That you wear power like armor, cloak yourself in it until nothing is left exposed." She claimed the distance between them, his forearm still trapped in her grip. He let her, until his hand was pinned between their chests, her face inches from his own. Her fury wreathed her, darkening her eyes to depthless pools.

"I understand your dreams," she bit out. "Your pain, your *fear*. I understand the feeling of the world hurtling out of control around you, the way it makes you want to shut yourself down so tightly that nothing ever comes undone, but *you are undone*, Damien."

It startled him, the way she took him apart. As if he had not won thrones and kingdoms, had not outwitted every opponent, every enemy. But that was why he'd fallen in love with her. Because for all his anger, all his rage, all his darkness, he could not scare her away.

She was right: he was undone—*by her*.

Damien twisted his wrist in her grip until their palms were flush together. He held tight to her as he rasped, "I cannot protect anyone if I'm not in control."

"You never will be."

The words stilled him into silence, the truth of them too stark to fully face. He'd fought for this. Played the game and won, the throne his prize. But all that power did nothing to quell the people's anger. All it did was paint a target on his back and drive away those closest to him.

That isn't true, he thought. *I've used this power for good.*

He'd ended the draft tax, and then the war. Once they'd neutralized the threat of the Heretics, he would make sure the heads of houses paid their workers a fair wage. He would introduce new jobs at the Dramara factories, integrate technologies from the north to alleviate their reliance on verillion. Every problem had a solution, and he would find it.

He would repair their broken world one piece at a time, as his mother had always wanted.

He had done too much, *sacrificed* too much, to give up now. He couldn't walk away from this. Not when he was so close.

I don't know who you are anymore, and I don't know how to bring you back.

"I can save this kingdom from itself." He drew back, seeking the words that had carried him through this all. They felt strangely hollow in the face of what he'd lost. In the face of her. "The noble houses, the rebels, they're all dogs that have been fighting over the same scraps for years. Something had to change. *I'm* changing it. Let them make me a monster."

"Only you can do that," she whispered, and he knew she didn't just mean him. "This city is a poison in your veins. Relinquish the throne before it's too late."

"It already is." The things he'd done... He'd severed friendships and clasped hands with his enemies. He'd ruined the lives of people who'd trusted him, turned his back on them when he needed them most, and he'd killed, by his own hands and others.

He needed it all to mean something. *He* needed to mean something.

"Liar." Arielle gripped him tighter. "Shira told me once that you never lie, but she was wrong. You're lying to yourself, Dara. You told yourself everything you've done is to help people, to make Enderlain better, and maybe that was true, once, but now you've built your walls up so high you can't see beyond them."

She pulled him close. "Who are you really trying to protect?"

Damien flinched, the urge to rip away from her surging through him, but she didn't let go. She held him there with the strength of magic, with a gaze that laid him bare. That forced him to look back at the last few weeks and see that the people he'd wanted to protect were gone.

She was right.

He was a wounded creature coiling shell after shell about himself, pushing everyone he cared for further away with every layer. He'd wanted to keep his family safe, to put an end to the violence that had led them to tear each other apart, that had convinced a child to murder his best friend's mother. He'd tried to control every detail, every emotion. He'd cheated the system, bested his rival, and stolen a throne.

All so that he'd never feel that pain again.

But all that power, all that control, had amounted to nothing in the end. It had left him isolated. Paranoid. Desperately clinging to the lie Arielle had stripped bare. But she was his steady eye of the storm, his partner, his truth, and he hated himself for ever having doubted that.

"I know how hard it is to let go after you've come so far. But it is never too late to make another choice. It's the only way to break this cycle of despair." Arielle met his gaze unwaveringly. "I am not afraid of you, Dara."

The strength in that stare, the power—he could happily lose himself to it. Of all the people whose loyalty he'd had the honor of earning, there was nothing like hers, and he knew in that moment, he would do anything not to lose it.

Whatever it took, he would have her look at him like that forever.

"Together," she said, and he could see what it cost her to do so. "We'll let it go together."

Somehow, he knew what she meant. The power, the control—it was what they'd both sought.

The strength to make sure no one ever hurt them again.

He'd spent so much of his life fully trusting no one but himself. He'd forgotten what it was like to let someone in, to tie himself to another. But he remembered now, that strength. How it could envelop you more thickly than any shield, form a blade sharper than any steel.

He was not alone, come whatever may.

"Very well," he said, and thought the words might break him. "I'll abdicate."

The throne room door flew open, and four armed rebels emerged. Shots fired. Damien put himself between the guns and Arielle, but he needn't have bothered—the bullets were well aimed, and only the guards fell.

Eshlin emerged from the group. "Wise choice."

Arielle pulled free of Damien's grip to stand beside him, and he swallowed his relief at seeing her okay. He counted the guns, weighed the odds he could pull his own revolvers quickly enough, and stood very, very still.

"I knew you were involved with the rebellion somehow," he said. "I hadn't imagined you were leading it."

Two others emerged from the chamber: Talyana, who looked vaguely ill, and Mikira, her face deathly pale. Her shoulders sagged with relief when she saw Ari, and she shifted aside as a third figure emerged. Reid looked half-terrified, half-furious, and entirely out of place, but he was there, and for a moment, all Damien could do was stare at him.

The look in Reid's eye told him he understood, but there was something else there too. Something that told him that, forgiveness or not, things had changed between them, as he'd known they would. There were some lines that could not be crossed, and he had thrown himself beyond them.

Only then did he spot what lay beyond them: Prince Darius's unblinking eyes staring back amidst a sea of red.

"You killed them," Arielle breathed.

"And I will do the same to you if you do not cooperate." Eshlin radiated an intensity he'd never seen in the normally meticulous princess. This was not the woman he remembered, who stepped neatly through conversations like an elegant dance. "Tell me who the Ranier prince is."

Damien kept his gaze purposefully away from Talyana, even as the girl went still. "I told you: I'm the prince."

One of the rebels leveled his rifle at Damien's heart. "Give the order, Your Highness, and he's dead."

Arielle slid in front of him. "If you touch him, I'll kill you, and you'll find I don't die easily."

"Don't!" Mikira lunged forward, pushing down the barrel of the nearest gun. "We need them. We can't stop the Heretics without Arielle."

"And Rezek won't talk without Damien," Arielle added quickly.

Damien's eyes snapped to her. "Rezek?"

"Enough!" Eshlin threw up a hand. The rebels watched her with a growing apprehension the princess seemed keenly aware of, and that left Damien certain that, had they been alone, he would have already been dead.

Eshlin's expression resolved into an unnatural calm. "Take them all back to headquarters. I'm going to take back the throne." Her gaze landed on Damien. "You have until I return to change your mind about the prince. If you don't tell me who it is by then, we'll see just how unkillable your girlfriend is."

✦ PART 4 ✦

But stories hold many truths, and many untruths, as is their way.

Stories like this one.

CHAPTER 42

MIKIRA

MIKIRA COULDN'T SHAKE the feeling that she was missing something.

After getting Damien to write an official letter of abdication, signed with his signet ring, Eshlin had stayed behind at the castle to oversee the transfer of power to herself. The rebels who'd gone on the mission with her walked in a quartet around a restrained Damien, much to the dismay of Ari, who watched their every motion like a lion stalking its kill. Reid trailed behind, cursing every time he stepped in mud.

In the absence of direct orders, the other rebels had given way to Talyana's command to keep an eye on Ari, but not to treat her like a prisoner. Mikira was keenly aware that Damien could reveal Talyana's identity at any moment, and she only prayed that he hadn't because he knew what Eshlin might do, and not because he was planning on using it as leverage.

Mikira and Talyana led the way back to headquarters, their horses' hoofbeats echoing heavily throughout the tunnels. They were far enough ahead that the others couldn't hear when Mikira whispered, "I'm worried about Eshlin."

Talyana stiffened but didn't reply. The princess was the one who'd recruited her, recruited them both, and Mikira knew how loyal Talyana was once someone had earned her respect. But the sight of the council's unmoving bodies was etched into Mikira's mind, Prince Darius's most of all.

"She killed her own brother, Tal." Mikira suppressed a shiver.

Talyana's hands twisted in her reins. "I have to believe she had a good reason. The Eshlin I know always has a reason." But Mikira could sense the doubt in her words, the same one simmering inside her.

They turned into the final tunnel that led to the enchanted barrier, falling silent at the two guards keeping watch. The main cavern was busier than Mikira had ever seen it when they entered. Medics tended to the wounded from the ongoing rallies, while new arrivals were split into smaller groups and directed to empty barracks or assigned tasks.

"What are you going to do with him?" Reid was staring at Damien's retinue, which was beginning to draw attention.

Mikira rubbed the side of her face, wishing she could just lie down where she was and sleep. She doubly wished it when Ari approached. "Are you really going to keep him prisoner?" she demanded.

"He can join the other house lords if you'd like," Talyana suggested mildly.

Ari rounded on her, and Mikira stepped smoothly between them. "Enough. We have too many other people to fight to start turning on each other too."

"Like Rezek." Reid buried a hand in Widget's fur. The tiny cat purred quietly, surveying the cavern as if taking in his new kingdom.

"He's a target here," Ari reminded her. "At least let me go with him."

"So you can help him escape?" Talyana scoffed.

"I'll see him safely to his cell," Mikira interjected before Ari could respond, and it was enough to settle the rising panic in her eyes. She regretted the offer the moment she joined the rebel guards surrounding Damien, as the look he gave her was nothing short of calculating.

"Come to gloat?" he asked as they descended down one of the narrow tunnels.

She didn't look at him. "I told Ari I'd make sure you were safe."

He snorted lightly. "There's that soft heart."

"My soft heart is the only reason you're still alive," she retorted. "Which after everything you've done lately is more than you deserve."

"I know."

Mikira jerked to a halt, the guards following suit. She expected to find Damien amused, or with that gleam in his eye that told her he was playing some sort of game, but he only looked tired. Tired and—she caught herself on a laugh, for if she didn't know better, she would have said Damien Adair looked *unsure*.

He was like a bullet without aim, and she hardly knew what to do with him.

"I never meant to betray you, you know," she said as the guards started walking again. "But I don't regret where we ended up. You became just like Rezek."

Damien flinched.

Once, she'd wondered what it took to get under his skin, but she realized now she'd always known. They were the same in one regard at least, the one that had first brought them together. It was Damien's hatred of the Kelbras that had convinced her to work with him, and because she'd believed that he truly wanted to change Enderlain for the better.

Looking at him now, she still believed that, but she also knew what he'd done to achieve that goal. Still, she couldn't entirely fault him. Not without recognizing the ways her newfound fame had changed her too. She'd thought herself important, indispensable, and only ended up trying to do everything herself.

Just like him.

A small, choked laugh built in Mikira's throat, earning a narrow-eyed look from Damien. She shook her head. "It's just—we both wanted the same thing. We should have been on the same side this entire time, but instead, we ended up standing in each other's way."

If the rebellion hadn't made its move, she had no doubt Damien would have found a way to deal with the chimeras himself. He'd sought power not for its own sake, but for the chance to change things, the same as them. Because in the end, that was the rebellion's goal, wasn't it? To take control, so that they might make way for a better future.

Even now, they were not so different. They both just wanted a world where the people they cared about would be safe.

"I . . . regret that," Damien said at last, tilting back his head. "I regret a lot of my choices as of late."

Mikira stared at him, shocked by the words, which were as close to an apology as she'd probably get. Even if he said it outright, she didn't know if she could forgive him. He'd exposed her as a rebel, attacked Talyana, put a bounty on her head . . . He'd tried to make her as afraid of him as she had been of Rezek, and she wasn't sure he could ever make up for that.

But some small part of her wanted to give him the chance to try.

"If you really mean that, then do something about it," Mikira said as they arrived at the cells. The guards unlocked one far from Rezek's at her command, and she left Damien there with her own words haunting her. She'd joined the rebellion because she believed it wasn't too late to change this kingdom; maybe the same was true of them as well.

True of her.

She emerged from the cells to find Ari, Talyana, and Reid clustered together still bickering. Mikira approached them, hoping to broker peace, when Shira's voice cut through their budding argument.

"Oh, good, you're all still alive." She was standing just outside Eshlin's office, exhaustion lining every inch of her. "Get in here."

They obeyed, shutting the office door. It was cramped with the five of them, though less because of space and more because having Talyana, Reid, Ari, *and* Shira all in one room resulted in more tension than a rubber band about to snap.

"I circled back after getting you into the castle," Shira said to Ari's questioning look. "I assume from my brother's presence and the fact that no one is trying to arrest you that things went smoothly?"

"Except Damien is now in chains," Ari replied tersely. "And Eshlin wants to interrogate him for the prince's true identity."

"One step at a time." Shira collapsed onto the edge of Eshlin's desk, folding her arms. "I'll convince Eshlin that the prince's identity isn't the priority now that she has the throne. It's going to take her time to solidify control, but once she's got command of Enderlain's military forces again, we'll need to be prepared to face the Heretics. Assuming that my brother can get Rezek to talk."

At that, Reid actually laughed. "More likely one of them kills the other."

"Which is why I want to be nearby." Ari folded her arms, daring anyone to challenge her. "Rezek is still an enchanter capable of using rare magic."

"Speaking of," Shira interjected, "can you sense what Nava is up to?"

Ari briefly closed her eyes, then nodded. "She's still in the Silverwood waiting for Selvin to make his move."

"In that case, I think everyone could use some time to rest and cool down," Shira said. "It's late. Let's get some sleep and revisit things in the morning."

Mikira balked at that. "What? No. What if we don't have until morning? Nava may be waiting, but we don't know when Selvin will act. Or even what his plan is. We should—"

"You won't be able to do anything about it half-dead on your feet," Shira cut in with a pointed look.

"She's right." Talyana laid a hand on Mikira's shoulder. "I mean this in the most caring way possible, but you look terrible."

Mikira felt terrible, but the idea of waiting until tomorrow to take action tied her stomach in knots. But they were right—she could barely keep her eyes open, the last of her adrenaline fading to a dull buzz. They needed time to prepare to deal with the Heretics; she might as well sleep while she could.

They dispersed, Shira taking Ari and Reid down one corridor while Mikira followed Talyana down another to the room they'd been sharing. Her thoughts grew slower with every step, and it took Talyana three tries to get her attention when they arrived.

The room was small, barely large enough to contain the bed pushed against a wall and a chair tucked into one corner. Mikira collapsed onto the bed, only realizing that Talyana was taking her boots off when the second one slid free.

The sight drew free a memory of falling asleep in Atara's paddock one afternoon. She'd slept straight through dinnertime and woken to the horse tugging free her boots in retribution. The warmth of the memory lasted only long enough for the grief of her loss to break anew, and she forced out a shuddering breath.

Talyana studied her with blatant concern, but a knock sounded before she could say anything. She pulled the door open to find Reid standing there with a bowl of steaming stew, Widget balanced on his shoulder.

He marched inside without so much as a glance at Talyana and proffered the bowl to Mikira. "Eat," he commanded.

"I'm not—" she began.

"You look like a scarecrow," he cut over her.

"Charming as ever, Haldane." Talyana joined them, her arms folded. "But I agree."

Mikira looked between the two of them, willingly standing beside each other in a united front, and sighed. She accepted the stew. It was rich and savory, her stomach coming to life at the taste of it. She hadn't realized how ravenous she was; when was the last time she'd eaten?

Reid deposited himself in the chair, Talyana joining her on the bed while she finished.

"So," Mikira murmured as she swallowed the last of the stew. "Do we call you Your Majesty now?"

Talyana groaned, flopping back onto the bed. "Only if you want to be executed."

"I would rather be," Reid muttered.

"Wish granted." Talyana meant it as a joke, but the moment the words left her lips, a heaviness settled across Mikira's chest. Her breath caught, and Talyana bolted upright, Reid already on his feet. It was the look in their eyes, the one that said whatever it was, whatever Mikira needed, they were there, that finally broke the dam inside her.

A sob choked her, hot tears staining her cheeks, and she buried her face in her hands. Reid sat down on her other side so that he and Talyana bracketed her, a buoy against the dark as she cried. For the things that had changed and the things that had not. For the future that awaited them all, bloodier and more dangerous than the path they'd already fought through.

For Atara, whose absence Mikira felt like a hole in her heart.

She cried until sleep claimed her.

CHAPTER 43

ARIELLE

SHIRA LEFT ARI at her room with a warning to stay put. She'd convinced the guards that Eshlin had requested Ari's presence at the castle, and her return unrestrained meant that she'd been released, but without the princess there to confirm it, Shira couldn't guarantee that her own word would be enough.

Ari waited several minutes after Shira departed before she opened the door and retraced their steps to the main cavern, where people were beginning to disperse for the evening. Flaring her verillion, she cast a concealing enchantment using her diamond ring to hide herself.

She checked the infirmary first.

It wasn't hard to find, as it was the only room lit up off the main cavern. A windowed door revealed rows of sleeping injured rebels. She spotted Rivkah at the far end, and only just resisted the urge to burst inside. Doors opening of their own accord would set off the guards, and Shira had assured her that Rivkah was just fine.

She lingered a moment longer, drinking in the sight of her sister's face, before she forced herself back to the main cavern. There she followed the corridor to the cells, where a guard waited. She tossed a pebble down the hall, catching the guard's attention, and slipped through the door when they went to investigate.

The hallway was long, the cells spaced out, and while she knew Rezek's to be around the corner, she found Damien in the one closest to the front.

They'd left his hands bound, his guns confiscated. He sat with his back against the far wall, his eyes trained on the ceiling as if imagining a game of chess. She took in the faint line of a scar running through his eyebrow, the places where his hair ran a little long, all the little details he hadn't smoothed out.

Like this, she felt as though she were truly seeing him for the first time.

She released her enchantment, and his eyes cut to her, the intensity behind his steel-gray gaze a comfort she'd missed.

"This is getting to be a habit," she teased.

He tilted his head back against the stone, the dim enchanted light illuminating the long column of his throat. "I'm starting to think you prefer me this way."

A smile flitted across her lips. "You're certainly less of a hassle."

He let his head fall forward, his dark hair curling across his eyes. "I am sorry, Arielle. I want you to know that."

"I do." She wanted so badly to say it was okay, to pretend none of this had happened, but she couldn't let go of what had frayed between them. No matter how much she cared about him, the trust between them had cracked, and a simple apology wouldn't be enough.

They both had much to atone for, and it began with the Heretics.

"There is still a war coming," she said quietly. "I think we can help stop it."

Damien scoffed lightly. "I don't think anyone here wants my help."

"I wish that were true." Ari offered a small smile. "Then I wouldn't have to ask you to reconcile with Rezek."

All traces of humor fled Damien at that. She watched him shift ever so slightly, each small movement an attempt to contain the larger sentiment within. In that instant, she wanted nothing more than for him to be furious. To unleash the kind of emotion she'd witnessed the day he learned of her visits with Rezek. To see what burned beneath that cool exterior.

"What does Rezek have to do with any of this?" he bit out.

"He's the only one who knows Selvin's plans beyond his intention to absorb his Racari's power. Without that knowledge, we're at the mercy of when the chimeras strike, and that's assuming Nava doesn't find Selvin first. A battle between them could annihilate us all."

Damien's wrists strained at his bonds. "If your plans rely on Rezek to succeed, you've already lost."

Ari swallowed back the urge to say he might not be the same man that Damien remembered. She knew how poorly that would go over, so she tried a different tactic. "You said you wanted to save this city. This is your chance."

His mouth curved in a wry smile. "Haven't you heard? I'm what this city needs saving from. When this is over, Eshlin will make sure I never get in her way again."

The images from the council room flitted through Ari's mind. The things Eshlin had been willing to do to her own brother, as if their lives were tallies on a board to be erased. Casting a strength enchantment, Ari reached for one of the bars and, with the ease of tearing paper, bent it inward. "To do that, she would have to go through me."

The way he looked at her—the awe, the desire—it was a glimpse of the boy she knew, the one she missed. Their strength was what had drawn them to each other, and for a moment, she wondered if he would still look at her like that if she lost her magic. Her power.

But she knew by now that her abilities were not what made her strong. It was the part of her that realized she was afraid and faced that fear. The part that shoved away her parents' warnings and sought her own knowledge, her own fate. The part that rose furious and reckless from her workshop floor all those weeks ago and didn't stop until she'd reclaimed herself.

That, she would always have.

"You wanted to change things," she said. "But for that to happen, Enderlain has to still be here to change. And if you won't do it for this kingdom, then do it for me."

It was what she should have said from the start, because it was all it took. Damien stood, crossing the distance between them until only bars remained.

"I would burn this city down for you," he said softly. "If you want me to save it, then I'll do that too." His voice sharpened as he added, "But I can't guarantee Rezek will still be in one piece when I'm finished."

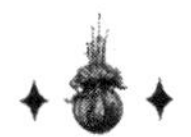

ARI RETURNED TO her assigned room to find Reid leaning against the wall outside her door. She wasn't surprised to see him still awake; the dark shadows beneath his eyes were a constant companion for a reason. Widget, on the other hand, was fast asleep in his arms.

"How is he?" Reid asked.

"Pretending to be okay," she replied. "Just like the rest of us."

"Careful." Reid pushed off the wall. "You'll start to make him sound human."

Her smile came naturally now, a thing that had once felt foreign to her, but it faltered at the uncertain look on Reid's face.

"What is it?" she asked.

"I found the enchanter cell," he replied.

It was good news, and yet it still felt like a blow. If she'd only waited, trusted in Reid, how much of this could have been prevented? She never would have gone to Rezek, never would have given him access to her Racari or pushed Damien away.

He would have found a way, she thought. Selvin wouldn't have let anything stop his ascension to godhood.

He pulled a vial from his pocket. "I was experimenting with a means of destroying the cells to see if I could reverse the chimera transformation, but the magic is too deeply ingrained in their bodies, and I don't suppose you have any use for it anymore either with Nava free."

Ari started to shake her head, then stopped. "Would you be able to check my blood for the cells again?"

He frowned. "Yes, but why?"

"Nava said I'm not really an enchanter, that her presence is what gave me magic and, without her, I'll lose it."

"That doesn't make any sense." Reid scratched the sleeping Widget between the ears. "I can check if you want, but I'm certain that whether your body already had them or they were created as a consequence of Nava's possession, they *are there,* and they're not going anywhere. Not unless you destroy them."

Ari's thoughts spilled in a hundred different directions. If her magic was truly hers, then she didn't have to sacrifice it to stop Nava. She could defeat her, if only she were powerful enough to do so. But their past battles made it clear that Nava was leagues above her, in possession of power she only dreamed of.

"Reid," she said. "You need to make more of that elixir."

CHAPTER 44

DAMIEN

DAMIEN DIDN'T SLEEP.

His mind kept running through scenarios. The ways his conversation with Rezek could go. How to use his knowledge of Talyana to secure his release without putting her at Eshlin's mercy. What to do about the chimera army brewing beneath the city.

Arielle. Arielle. Arielle.

There was no sense of time down in the caverns, so he only knew morning had come when the guards brought him a meager breakfast of toast. He ate it, then they unlocked his cell and escorted him down the hall and around the corner as if he'd just arrived. They shoved him inside another cell before departing.

Damien remained facing the wall, his hands braced against his bonds hard enough to burn the skin raw. He didn't want to turn around, knowing what lay behind him.

"So," came Rezek's cool voice into the silence. "How did playing the hero work out?"

Clenching his teeth, Damien forced himself to face the other cell. Rezek was tucked in a corner, his long legs stretched out before him. Stubble roughened his jaw, his copper hair loose from its bun and sprawling across his shoulders in uncharacteristic disarray.

"Better than playing the pawn," Damien replied. "How did you enjoy being controlled by a half-mad enchanter?"

"I heard you won the Ascension," Rezek returned. "You always were too clever for your own good. Though, by my count, your coronation would have been last night. 'King for a Day' has a nice ring to it."

Damien swallowed back a correction; it hadn't even been that. "At least I didn't single-handedly run my house into the ground. Your father, Kyvin, Gren, your brother—did you know Darius is dead too? Eshlin killed him. Brutally."

Enough so that even Damien had been shaken by the sight, his carefully wrought impression of the princess dismantled in a single moment.

Rezek's eyes gleamed with something bordering on feral. "King or pawn, we're both here now. You and I always were the same."

"Is that what you want, Rezek? For me to admit that I'm just like you?" He held Rezek's gaze, both of them unable to hide from the other. "Will that let you live with yourself for what you've done?"

He wasn't prepared for Rezek's reply when it came, nearly too soft to be heard.

"Yes."

Damien recoiled from the word as if it were a blade. As it was, it cut too neatly through his anger, down to the understanding beneath. Because Damien wanted the same thing. It was why he'd kept pushing for the throne, despite knowing what he might lose along the way. After everything he'd done, all the choices he'd made, he'd wanted them to mean something.

Neither of them wanted to be left alone with the consequences of what they'd done. Neither of them wanted to be responsible. Because if there was no *why*, then all that was left was *them*.

Damien closed his eyes, and in the silence, Rezek's voice was like a lure. "Haven't you ever considered that in your attempts to be the hero of this story, you instead became the villain? At least I know what I am."

"A murderer." Damien tore away from the bars, retreating deeper into his cell. "A traitor."

"A pawn," Rezek replied. "Just as you said."

There was something in his voice. A pain that Damien didn't want to recognize, didn't want to understand. He wanted to tie Rezek up in a neat package and set all memory of him alight. To put an end to this saga while the lines between them were still clearly drawn.

He didn't want to listen when Rezek said, "I didn't kill your mother."

Damien rounded on him, a decade of fury erupting at once. "Loic *saw* you! And I held her while her life bled out in my hands." He seized one of the metal bars, wishing it was Rezek's throat. "I have made every moment of my life about destroying you for that. Don't tell me that you didn't do it!"

"I didn't do it." Rezek twisted his fingers into his hair. "At least, I don't *think* I did. I don't know anymore, Damien! I don't know what was me and what was him. Even when I was in control, I could feel him. His presence was so strong. It permeated every part of me. And when he left—" He choked up, wrapping his arms about himself.

Damien's laugh came out as wretched as it was hollow, an anger unlike any other coating every word. "Did he abandon you, Rezek? Do you feel *betrayed*?" He all but snarled the word, unable to reel himself in. It felt good to give in to this fury, to let it sear him from the inside out. He wished he'd done it sooner. He wished he'd let his rage set the world alight if only so that for one moment, he didn't have to be the one to burn.

Maybe then he wouldn't have had to carry this burden alone. Maybe then Loic would have seen him as a brother, and not the competition he blamed for his own inadequacy. Maybe then his family wouldn't have spiraled apart, he wouldn't have pushed Reid and Arielle away, he wouldn't have sought power at the expense of his soul.

Damien roared, driving his foot into the bars again and again and again until exhaustion overtook everything and he leaned against the cool metal, his loosened curls bracketing the edges of his vision. "You ruined everything," he exhaled, closing his eyes. "You made me into you."

And that was the core of this, wasn't it? He'd sacrificed pieces of himself—his emotions, his identity, his morality, whatever he could to make Enderlain accept him, to be seen as one of them, until he too believed that the ends justified the means, that he could buy safety through strength, through power, but it would never be enough.

After everything he'd done, in order to destroy a monster, he had become one, the villain in another hero's story.

Then do something about it, Mikira's voice prodded. So obvious, so direct. What it must feel like to be that unrestrained—he envied it.

"I never wanted this," Rezek said into the silence. Then, softer, "He made my brother a chimera."

Damien's eyes flashed open. "What?"

Rezek peered up at him through a curtain of messy hair. "People with enchanter blood. Full enchanters, or people like my brother, who have part of the trait, but not enough for magic. They're the only ones that can . . . that can become chimeras."

This was why Rezek had been gathering unlicensed enchanters like Mikira's father. To execute these experiments—and to *become* them.

Rezek's arms curled tighter about his stomach. "My brother was the first. He didn't survive."

And in his place, Rezek became heir of House Kelbra. He got access to power and resources that Selvin needed. And Rezek, a silent prisoner in his own body, could do nothing but watch it unfold. The idea that this entire time the revenge Damien had sought might have been misplaced, that the boy who'd once been his only friend might still be there—

Damien shook his head so hard it ached. This couldn't be the truth. Rezek was a liar. A traitor. He couldn't be trusted. No one could—he was the one who'd taught Damien that. Now he wanted to claim that none of it had been what he'd thought? That everything Damien blamed Rezek for had been Selvin all along?

But when he met Rezek's eyes, saw the fear bright in their depths, logic cut coolly through his thrashing emotions: the Rezek he'd known would never let himself look so weak. Not after a lifetime spent chasing his father's approval, becoming the man, the heir, that Eradas so desperately wanted.

The Rezek he'd known didn't exist at all.

Damien dragged in a deep breath of the cold cavern air. Slowly, he came back to himself, the rage and desperation dispersing like verillion smoke. He wanted nothing more than to disappear with it, to let the silence close over him like a cocoon and lose himself inside it.

But he'd given Arielle his word, and he would keep it.

"Tell me what happened, Rezek."

When Rezek started, he didn't stop for a long time. He told Damien about his father's discovery of his magic, how he'd tried to use it by binding him to the Racari, and then abandoned him when he proved too hard to control. He spoke of the day he killed Damien's mother, then the loss of his brother, and every day after that had felt like living half-asleep, his body never quite his, his mind a place he couldn't trust. How his desires and Selvin's became intertwined, until he could no longer tell them apart.

To this very moment, when he could not tell what was him, and what were the remnants the Heretic left behind.

Damien sank to the floor of his cell and listened, though it ground everything inside him to do so. He hated the way Rezek's story dispersed the blame. How the similarities between them stood out so starkly. Their brothers who always overshadowed them. The fathers whose respect they coveted. The choices that took them further and further from who they thought they were.

"And now?" Damien asked when Rezek tapered off. "What comes next?"

"I don't know." Rezek's voice was raw, his face buried in his hands. "Without Selvin . . . I don't know anything."

"But you know what Selvin plans to do next."

Rezek shuddered, but Damien pressed onward. "I've always had everything you wanted. For all his faults, Loic was still a brother to me. My father named me heir of his own free will. I had the businesses I built up myself. I had Reid, and Arielle, and you . . ."

"Had Selvin," Rezek muttered into his palm.

"Until he abandoned you." Damien knew what Rezek wanted from him, just as he knew that he'd have to give it to him if he had any hope of extracting the information that they needed. But each time he tried to summon the words, they burned to ash in his mouth.

The things Rezek had done had poisoned every part of him. He'd convinced himself that his friends couldn't be trusted, that he didn't need Arielle, didn't need his family. He'd told himself that he didn't have a choice. That trust bred vulnerability, and he could have no weakness, no uncertainties in the face of his ambition.

And now Rezek wanted something worse than trust from him—he wanted forgiveness.

But he could feel his pocket watch ticking away; they were running out of time. That information was the only thing that would get him out of his cell, the only chance they had of stopping Selvin before Enderlain suffered the same fate as Kinahara.

So he forced the words out. "I forgive you, Rezek."

Rezek's head snapped up, his lambent eyes like two pools of light in the darkness. "What?"

He couldn't say it again. He didn't know if he even meant it, only that the words twisted something in his chest, a feeling he couldn't parse.

"It's time for you to start making your own choices," he said instead. "To decide what you want, not what Selvin does." He climbed to his feet. "Tell me what he's planning."

Something changed in Rezek's expression, the last hour of raw revelation giving way to something more familiar: the face he wore each time he and Damien stood off.

Damien only realized it wasn't for him when Rezek said, "He's going to use the underground tunnels to spread the chimeras out across the city, and then unleash them on the fall equinox, when people are out celebrating. He's targeting the rebel headquarters, the rallies, and the celebrations, which means he'll probably strike at sundown, when the streets are busiest."

Was that why the castle had been picking up reports of attacks? Was Selvin testing his new weapons? The solstice would be the perfect time to strike, when people flooded the streets from dawn to dusk in Lyzairin's honor.

"What's the point of all this?" he asked.

Arielle had said that Selvin thought of enchanters as superior, that he wanted to elevate them to what he saw as their rightful status, with him as their god. But he would have expected Selvin to try to take the castle in that case, or to target the royal guard or Anthir, not the people.

"For magic." Rezek stood, his movements slow and jerky. Only then did Damien notice the plates of stale food at the front of his cell, the way his cheekbones pressed against the skin of his face. How long had it been since he'd eaten?

"That's the secret of verillion," he said. "The dirt it grows from is full of magic."

"I know that," Damien replied shortly.

"But do you know how the magic ends up in the ground?" Rezek edged to the front of the cell. "When people die, a piece of them, of magic or their soul or whatever you believe, returns to the earth. *That* is what verillion absorbs when it grows its stalks. *That* is what enchanters burn to produce magic."

Rezek pressed his face into the bars. "And when Selvin kills all those people, he will absorb their power until he is finally strong enough to do what he could not before."

"Consume the magic of his Racari," Damien said with cold understanding. Arielle had caught him up on everything they knew about the situation during her visit last night, but they hadn't known then what was delaying Selvin. Now they did. "But if he couldn't handle the power of the Racari before, how is he going to absorb that *and* the magic released in the battle?"

Rezek was shaking his head before he even finished the question. "You're thinking about it wrong. If Selvin were a vessel with a set volume, you'd be right. If he can't fit a fistful of magic inside himself, he can't fit two. But that's not the case." He sounded impressively lucid for a man letting a set of bars hold him upright, but Damien had a feeling talking through this was the only thing keeping him grounded.

"With each bit of magic an enchanter takes in, the number of cells in their blood that can absorb magic increases, thereby expanding their overall capacity to consume magic," Rezek explained. "Before, Selvin's body wasn't prepared for the level of power from the Racari."

"But once he absorbs the magic from so many deaths, he will be," Damien concluded with a frown. "That's why he's waiting for the solstice. Higher casualty rates."

"That's only one piece." Rezek looked at him from the corner of his eye, as if unable to bear the full weight of his stare. "He wants as many people as possible in one place, the angrier and more violent, the better. The chimeras aren't his only soldiers."

"The rebellion," Damien began. "They're practically a small army. But the princess has the throne; they have nothing left to fight."

Rezek closed his eyes. "They have the chimeras."

And if the rebels entered the streets armed and ready for battle, the Anthir would mobilize against them.

Piece by piece, the truth of what Rezek was saying fitted into place.

Selvin wanted to cause a slaughter, and what better way than with a civil war in the midst of a celebration where half the city was present?

"But how could he have known the rebels would—" He stopped. Who had been the driving force of the rebellion? Who had sought the throne at all costs, putting the Anthir and rebels both under her command?

"The third Heretic," he breathed. "It's possessing Eshlin."

CHAPTER 45

MIKIRA

MIKIRA WOKE IN a cocoon of blankets and wanted nothing more than to stay there forever.

She lingered, letting herself pretend for a moment that her normal life awaited her. That she was back at the ranch with Talyana and Reid, a day's hard work before them and Nelda's cooking come evening. That when night fell, her father would tell them stories like he used to, and Ailene would race her dog through the house, and Reid would pretend to be miserable while Talyana was entranced by the story.

Then she remembered where she was, and what she had to do, and she came back to herself with the suddenness of being bucked off a horse.

By the time she slid carefully out of bed and dressed, all remnants of her daydream had receded, replaced by the beginnings of a plan. Once Damien had the information they needed from Rezek, they would take it to Eshlin, who could organize the troops they needed to face Selvin's army and defeat the Heretic before Nava found him and caused another Cataclysm.

Slipping outside, she followed the hall back to the main cavern, expecting to find it quiet. Eshlin's Ascension to the throne essentially meant their goal had been accomplished. There was no need for a rebel force any longer, as the princess would enact the change they'd all fought for, dismantling the house system and the monarchy and transferring the power to the people.

Yet when she emerged into the main cavern, it was abuzz with activity. Rebels were breaking off into groups, and a flood of people she didn't recognize were entering, their everyday clothes standing out among the rebel reliefs.

Mikira sought Jenest where she was ordering a group of people over to the check-in area. "What are these people doing here?"

"New recruits." Jenest waved another group over. "For the fight against the chimeras."

Mikira recoiled. "They didn't sign up for that. The royal army—"

"Still isn't back from the front lines."

"The Anthir—"

"Aren't soldiers."

"Neither are these people!" Mikira gestured at a group in plain clothes, who were staring about nervously as if regretting their decision. Some had small children clinging to them, ragged-looking stuffed animals clutched in their small hands. Others were old enough that they'd found any clear spot simply to sit down and rest.

Jenest glanced up from her clipboard, something strangely familiar about her gaze that made Mikira's skin prickle. "Well, then," she said without breaking eye contact, "we'll have to hope it doesn't come to a fight."

She stepped away to join another group, leaving Mikira oddly disquieted. There had to be another way to stop the chimeras, but Eshlin had been acting strangely for days, and after what Mikira had witnessed last night with the council, she couldn't help but feel like this was a purposeful choice. But why?

"Mikira!" She turned as Talyana cut toward her from the crowd. "Shira wants to see us with the others. Damien got what we needed."

She returned to the tunnels with Talyana, explaining what Jenest had said. "Something's not right," she concluded as Talyana pushed open a door. "It hasn't been for a while. Eshlin's—"

"Possessed." Damien's cool voice drew her to a halt. They'd entered what looked like a break room, with a large metal table in the center and cabinets along the walls. Ari, Reid, and Damien were sitting at the table, the latter's hands now unbound, and Shira was perched upon the corner, her feet on another chair.

Mikira blinked. "I'm sorry, *what*?"

Ari leaned forward, dark curls spiraling about a tired face. "At the end of the Illinir, I found the third Racari. Rezek said it was gone by the time he returned to the alcove, which was a lie. Its Heretic has been possessing—"

"Eshlin." Mikira slumped into the doorway. This was why the princess had been so furious when Damien took the throne. This was why she'd resorted to such drastic measures as slitting Prince Darius's throat despite the questions it would raise.

Mikira collapsed into the nearest chair, Talyana looking vaguely queasy as she took one of the others.

"I thought someone had to be an enchanter to be possessed," Mikira ventured at last.

"They only need to have the gene to produce the cell." Reid scratched Widget behind the ears as he spoke, the little cat curled up in his lap. Somehow, he'd found himself a cup of tea, and clutched it at chin level as if to hide behind it. "If Eshlin's descended from an enchanter, she could have the cell without the ability to do magic, or simply have hidden her power."

"But *why*?" Talyana's voice broke on the word, and she looked one step away from breaking something else. "What are they planning?"

Shira swung her feet to the ground and faced them all. "That's why we're here. We think the Heretic possessing Eshlin—"

"Rowna."

Mikira leapt to her feet at the voice. In the far corner, hands bound and staring at the ceiling, was Rezek Kelbra. His gaze found Mikira, and though his hair was a mess and his pale skin was caked with dirt, he still managed to smile at her as if she were ten feet below him.

"Enough, Rezek," Damien ordered, and the smile vanished on the spot.

"Absolutely not." Mikira jabbed a finger at him. "I can handle Damien, but not—*that!*"

"It's satisfying to know that you rate me above him." Rezek languidly propped his feet up on an empty chair.

Damien's jaw ticked. "That isn't even close to what she meant."

"Are you two actually competing about who's the worst?" Talyana rested her chin on one fist. "Because I have a thing or two to say about that."

"You have a thing or two to say about everything," Reid muttered, gathering Widget into one arm.

Talyana glowered at him. "And you're the picture of restraint."

Ari looked between them. "I'd have thought the two of you would get along. Isn't all either of you care about Mikira?"

Both of their faces flushed, Mikira's following suit, and then the whole group was speaking at once. Mikira could barely get a word in between Reid and Talyana's arguing, and Damien and Rezek weren't much better, Ari's low voice sliding between theirs.

A high whistle cut through the din, and they turned as one to look at Shira, whose exasperated expression was the most genuine Mikira had ever seen her make. "Look, I know half of you hate each other and the other half are in love with each other, but can we focus on the end of the world now, please?"

Mikira dropped back into her chair, unsure of when she'd even stood. She recognized that Shira was right, and that Rezek was here because he could be useful, but the idea of planning for the survival of their kingdom with his help made her skin crawl.

Shira rose from her perch to open a nearby cabinet. A moment later, she plunked a liquor bottle down in the center of the table.

"Whiskey," Mikira said shortly, looking from her to Damien. "Is this your family's solution for everything?"

"I'll take it." Talyana grabbed the bottle, made a quick face at the Adair label, and popped it open to take a swig.

Reid's eyes narrowed. "At least get a glass."

"We have approximately one hundred bigger problems than that," Talyana returned, pointedly taking a second drink.

Shira retrieved glasses for them all, wresting the whiskey from Talyana to pour a sizeable amount into each one. She even handed one to Rezek, who downed it in half a second.

"Careful," Ari warned, wrapping her hands about her cup. "You don't have any verillion to burn it off this time."

Rezek held out his glass for seconds. "That is entirely the point."

"He'll certainly be easier to deal with that way," Damien muttered, looking as though he wanted nothing more than to join him. Still, he only nursed his drink.

All Mikira could do was stare as Rezek sniped something back that brought a wry smile to Ari's face, and Reid cursed as Talyana attempted to spike his tea, Shira back on her perch and looking all too pleased with herself. The whole scene felt like a dream, or perhaps a nightmare, each piece more incongruent than the next.

She hated Rezek, hadn't forgiven Damien, would do anything to protect Reid, Talyana, and Arielle, and barely knew Shira, except to say that she was very, very glad the eldest Adair was on their side. That said nothing of the others' own entanglements, and yet somehow, the seven of them were meant to work together to stop three ancient enchanters from destroying the world as they knew it?

A familiar feeling needled at her, the same one she'd had standing in Damien's suite with their plans for the Illinir unfurling around them. Like a chain clinking taut. But this time, it didn't feel like being trapped.

This time, Mikira wasn't alone.

Shira let the tumult continue a few moments longer, before seizing on a natural lull. "Now then. I've convinced Eshlin to postpone her hunt for the Ranier prince's identity. She plans to remain at the palace while she consolidates power, and according to Rezek, Selvin won't strike until sundown today, when the streets are at their fullest."

Rezek picked up her explanation. "Rowna is in league with Selvin, who plans to unleash his chimera army on the city to cause as much death and devastation as he can. The more people die, the more magic is released, and the more they can consume and grow in power in preparation for Selvin to absorb his Racari's magic."

Mikira thought of the swelling numbers in the main cavern. "That's why we're still taking new recruits. Eshlin must be planning to station them throughout the city so that they're at the front lines when the chimeras attack."

"And once they start fighting, they'll look like targets to the Anthir," Damien added.

"They'll all be centered in one place," Ari said. "Easy bait."

The thought turned Mikira's stomach. Everything she'd worked for up until now hadn't been to protect anyone. It'd been to fuel a righteous, power-obsessed enchanter who saw people as nothing more than magic sources to wring dry. She took a long draw of her whiskey.

"Damien and I suspect this may be why Rowna orchestrated this rebellion to begin with," Shira said grimly. "She wanted to create a war."

"No." Talyana's face was already flush from the drink, but it darkened more now. "That can't be true. We can't have been doing all this for—for some wannabe god!"

"*We* haven't," Shira said sharply. "Everything we've done, we've done to improve things in Enderlain, and I won't let Rowna waste that. We're going to put a stop to all of this."

"How?" Ari nodded back toward the main cavern. "They're preparing for a war they can't win."

The rattle of chains cut through the room as Rezek adjusted his posture, and they all turned as one to look at him. He did his best to look nonchalant as he suggested, "Kill Selvin, and it will kill the chimeras too."

"They're like golems, aren't they?" Ari asked with a look of growing wonder. In it, Mikira could see how she and Rezek had come to terms. What the two of them had experienced was something no one else could understand, but it still unnerved her. "The truthstones are what made them sentient, and when their creator dies, they die too."

"More or less," Rezek replied. "Their life isn't linked to his magic the way Nava's is to yours. He had to create bloodstone bonds with each of them individually, but the effect holds. Killing one will kill the others."

"So then what's our plan?" Mikira asked.

Damien's chair scraped across the floor as he stood. "We divide and conquer. Since Rezek knows where Selvin will be tonight, he and I will handle that. Arielle and Reid will ensure that Nava doesn't find him before we bring him down." His gaze switched to Mikira. "You and Talyana will take Rowna. If you defeat her, the real Eshlin might call off the rebels and Anthir."

He was the last person that Mikira wanted to take orders from, but he was right that they needed to target all three, lest one side fail.

"While that all sounds good in theory, the last time Ari and I went up against a Heretic, we got our asses handed to us." Her voice thickened at the thought of Atara. "This seems like a good way for us to get ourselves killed."

"That's why I've made the teams the way I have," Damien countered with the air of someone who had very nearly stolen a kingdom. "Selvin won't think Rezek means him any harm, giving us the element of surprise. Nava is partial to Ari and wants her to join her, and Rowna doesn't know that we're aware of her. She'll think you and Talyana are still on her side."

He nodded to Reid, who withdrew a vial of dark liquid from his pocket. "We'll all be armed with an elixir Reid has developed that targets enchanter cells," Damien explained. "We just have to inject them to destroy their magic. Then they'll be vulnerable."

"And we're just supposed to trust you?" Mikira demanded, eyes narrowing on Rezek. "Trust *him*?"

Talyana snorted, spinning her empty glass with one finger. "You'll probably find a way to absorb his power yourself and go after the throne again."

"I'm not an enchanter," Damien said with thinly veiled impatience. That was twice now Mikira had read his emotions on his face, but she supposed even Damien Adair had his limits. Being faced with his mortal enemy, estranged lover, former friends, and meddlesome sister while being asked to risk his life for a kingdom he loved and hated in equal measure might just be it.

Yet it was that flicker of emotion that eased Mikira's doubt, because when Damien looked at her with open honesty, she believed him as he said, "You told me to do something about it. So let me. I'll make sure Rezek doesn't stray."

"I'm not a dog," Rezek muttered.

Reid patted Widget's head. "Debatable."

Rezek's eyes came alight. "Come closer and say that."

"Don't look at him like that," Talyana warned, causing both Reid and Mikira to stare at her as if she'd lost her mind. She glared back at them. "What?"

"Nothing." Mikira repressed a growing smile.

"Hold on." Talyana leaned across the table with a sudden flush of excitement. "If the poison destroys enchanter cells, then why can't Arielle just inject herself, kill her magic, and break the bond keeping Nava alive?"

Ari stiffened, and Reid all but spit his tea back out. "Because it's an unstable cell-destroying poison that I devised all of five seconds ago! For all we know, it'll kill every cell in her body."

Talyana opened her mouth to protest, but Damien cut across her.

"If you suggest it again . . ." He left the threat unfinished, and that alone was more telling than any promised harm. Mikira didn't doubt that he'd put a bullet in every single one of them before he let them risk Ari's life, and she felt the same.

"We're not taking that chance," Mikira said unwaveringly. "Besides, Nava isn't the true problem here. Even if she was off the board, we'd still have to deal with Selvin."

In the silence, they all turned as one to look at Rezek. He lifted one of his chains, letting it fall with a look of disinterest. "It won't work," he said, answering their unspoken question. If they could destroy Nava by taking Ari's magic, then couldn't they take Rezek's to stop Selvin?

If they didn't mind possibly killing him, that was.

"Why not?" Mikira asked, even as she doubted her ability to go through with it.

Rezek lifted the chain and let it drop a second time, then met her gaze. "Because Selvin isn't bonded to *me*," he said bitterly. "Golems are made from clay; chimeras are formed from living enchanters. Selvin's bonded to the enchanter cells of his host, not mine."

Talyana slumped back in her chair. "I say we give it a try, just in case."

"He's telling the truth," Ari said before Rezek's sardonic reply could form. "If Rezek was bonded to him the way I am with Nava, he would be able to sense him. He'd have followed him the moment Selvin left him."

Rezek's cheeks flushed, and Mikira winced at the memory of finding him broken and crumpled on his workshop floor. Ari was right. All Rezek had wanted in that moment was to be reunited with Selvin; he wouldn't have still been there if he'd known he could follow.

"We have to inject them directly." Ari's expression grew earnest. "Which is why I think I should face Nava alone." She looked to Damien. "If she senses anyone else, she won't believe I'm there in good faith."

Mikira half expected Damien to object, but he only met Ari's gaze as if to ask if she were sure. The girl nodded, and that was the end of it.

"In that case, you should go with Talyana and Mikira," Shira said to

Reid. "We can send Eshlin a message saying they've captured the Ranier prince; she'll see you immediately."

"Great." Reid slumped farther in his chair.

Talyana patted his hand. "We won't let her kill you. Probably."

"Tal," Mikira groaned, but her exasperation was half-hearted. Teasing was what Talyana did when she'd accepted someone into her circle, and whether that was because she'd given up on ever kicking Reid out of Mikira's life or because she'd realized they all might not make it back from this venture, that appeared to now include Reid.

Reid scowled at them both, clutching Widget close as he glanced at Shira. "And what will you be doing while we all fight a bunch of impossibly strong undead enchanters that are definitely going to kill us?"

Shira's amusement at their exchange turned grim. "I'll be trying to delay the rebel force. If that fails, I'll lead them into battle and try to keep as many alive as I can." She surveyed the group. "All of you have to succeed, or we die."

CHAPTER 46

ARIELLE

ARI EMERGED FROM the meeting room with a new weight on her shoulders. Though she'd done her best to keep the link between her and Nava quiet the last day, snippets of the Heretic's emotions still reached her. Her determination, her sense of duty.

Her rage.

Ari had meant what she'd said when she suggested she go alone, but there was another reason she wanted to face Nava by herself: she wanted to talk to her, to find another way.

The main cavern was even busier than before by the time they returned. Shira directed Rezek and Damien into Eshlin's office, drawing the curtains to hide them, while Mikira and Talyana stood discussing how to approach Eshlin. They'd left Reid in the meeting room, where he'd begun distilling more of the elixir.

"Ari?"

Ari whirled at Rivkah's voice. She nearly flung herself at her sister, stopping just short when she remembered her injured ribs, and settled for a gentle hug.

Rivkah gave her a tired smile. "Well, that didn't go according to plan."

"Most of your schemes don't." Ari had spent most her life plunging into the fray after Rivkah, ensuring no harm came to her. This was the closest she'd ever come to failing.

Ari squeezed her shoulder as she pulled back. "I'm sorry I wasn't there to protect you."

Rivkah snorted. "I'm sorry I thought it was a good idea to fling myself into the middle of a conflict between warring Heretics." Her gaze shifted to Mikira and Talyana. "Is that the girl you told me about? The redhead?"

"Mikira Rusel," Ari replied. "Come on, I'll introduce you."

The similarities between Mikira and Rivkah only became more pronounced with them side by side. They both had a presence you couldn't ignore, their personalities as loud and bold as their laughs. Rivkah took an immediate interest in Mikira's knives, which she allowed Rivkah to inspect in exchange for a bag of spiced nuts Rivkah had, and Talyana asked her about her travels from Aversheen to Veradell.

As Rivkah finished detailing her work in the local temple archives, Mikira laughed. "You're definitely Ari's sister. Half tenacity, half bookworm."

"Try three-quarters tenacity, one-quarter total pain," Ari countered.

Rivkah stuck her tongue out. "You know you love me."

She did, more than anything, and she was so grateful to have Rivkah back in her life. She only wished it weren't when the city was about to descend into complete chaos.

"No," Rivkah said.

Ari blinked. "I didn't sa—"

"You were about to ask me to leave Veradell." Rivkah folded her arms. "I leave when you leave, end of story."

Ari wanted so badly to convince her otherwise, but she knew when a battle with Rivkah was lost. She enfolded her sister in another hug, looking pointedly at Mikira over her head. "I think she might actually be related to you."

"Kira, stubborn?" Talyana asked with a snort. "Never."

Mikira set her hands on her hips. "I think Rivkah and I should be best friends and ditch you two forever."

Rivkah wriggled out of Ari's hug with a grin. "Seconded."

Ari laughed, and it felt impossibly good. She let it cloak her in the warmth of this moment, in the promise of the future before her. This was the strength she'd sought all her life. This connection, this understanding. She wanted a thousand more just like it, and she could have them, if she let herself.

Promise me you will be fearless, a'huvati.

Her hand closed around her Saba's necklace, the metal warm from her skin as she whispered, "I promise."

ARI LEFT RIVKAH chatting with Mikira and Talyana about the best bakeries in town to check on Damien, who Shira had left alone with Rezek. The woman no doubt had her reasons, probably intending for the two to spend more time together before they partnered in an endeavor that risked their lives, but Ari didn't think it was wise to leave them unsupervised for too long.

"If you don't stop talking, I'm going to shoot you," came Damien's beleaguered voice through the narrow crack in the door.

"I hope your aim has improved since the last time I saw you shoot. Does your hand still shake?" Rezek inquired.

"That was *eight* years ago."

"Was it? How odd. I don't remember time quite the same anymore. Might be the whiskey, or, you know, the possession."

"Rezek? Shut up."

Ari had just resolved to enter and save them from each other when

Mikira jogged over. "Reports have started coming in about chimeras flooding the streets. Selvin is making his move. We have to go."

"Now?" Ari's heart skipped a beat. "But it's too early. Rezek said Selvin wouldn't strike until sundown."

"I said *probably*," came Rezek's lilting voice.

The door swung open, revealing a grim-faced Damien. "Reid's elixir won't be ready yet."

"Then we'll have to delay the Heretics until it is." Mikira grasped her knives, the nervous habit betraying what her solemn face did not. "But we need to be in position to use it the moment it's ready."

Reid had already been herded out into the main cavern by Talyana, several glass syringes of dark liquid in hand. They joined him as he explained, "It has at least half an hour left. Don't inject it before then or it'll be useless."

Shira descended on them with a nervous glance over her shoulder. "You all need to get going, before someone starts asking questions about those two." She glanced pointedly at Rezek and Damien, who wore matching looks of indifference. "There are horses for everyone outside the barrier."

Ari nodded, seeking Rivkah, who hovered at the fringe of the group. She wrapped her in another hug. "Stay safe. I'll be back soon."

Rivkah embraced her in return. "Be careful."

Ari peeled reluctantly free, only to find Reid proffering her two syringes with a look of trepidation. "Are you sure about going alone? I don't even know if this will work. If something happens to you—"

"Damien won't forgive you, I know."

"I won't forgive *myself*." Reid's hand trembled as he lowered it. "Believe it or not, I don't want you to die."

That might have been the closest thing to saying *I care about you* that Reid could manage, and it meant more to Ari than she could put into words. She'd spent so long isolated and afraid that even surrounded by new friends, her mindset had yet to shift accordingly. She wasn't the same girl she'd been when Damien found her, broken and alone. With or without magic, she wasn't helpless, and she never would be again.

Ari squeezed Reid's arm. "I'll be okay. We all will."

He looked reluctant but retreated to join Talyana and Mikira. Ari pocketed one of the syringes, then handed the other to Rivkah. "Eshlin shouldn't return here while we're gone, but if she does, this may be your only defense against her."

Rivkah nodded, and then Ari was joining the others as they swept toward the tunnels. She started for one of the horses, but Damien caught her hand, the intensity behind his gunmetal eyes pinning her to the spot. "Be careful. Please."

"I will." Her lips curved. "Try not to kill Rezek."

She expected some cool response, but Damien's eyes only darkened. Asking him to risk his life for Enderlain was one thing; asking him to do it at Rezek's side was another. In the end, he only squeezed her hand and released it.

Mounting, Ari guided her horse toward the Silverwood, toward Nava and a plan she barely trusted. Her horse trotted onward, oblivious to her distress, and Ari forced her focus elsewhere. She descended into the well of magic inside her, to the strings connecting her to her golems, and felt Nava there among the others. She was moving. Did she know they were coming after her, or had she sensed Selvin's strike had begun?

Ari couldn't let her reach him.

She urged her horse into a gallop as they emerged from the tunnels onto the Traveler's Road. Enchanted for speed, its swift hooves carried them quickly toward the cyrasi trees, the tie between her and Nava drawing tighter. Once near, Ari dismounted, not wanting the horse to draw attention.

Checking the syringe was secure in her pocket, she stepped into the Silverwood.

The ground was littered with shimmering leaves that crunched underfoot, the woods eerily silent. Each step brought the buzz of nervous energy in her stomach higher. This close, she could feel wisps of Nava's emotions:

her determination to stop Selvin, her anger at being thrust into this position again, centuries of pain bottled up over the loss of her home, her family, her friends. Everything gone at Selvin's hands.

Ari took a deep breath, then plunged beneath a low-hanging branch and into a wide clearing. A rustle of leaves preceded Nava entering from the other side. She looked like Ari remembered, dark hair and eyes, and olive skin, but something had changed about her too. Her features had sharpened, somehow become more real, and the power humming down the line from her was unlike anything Ari had ever felt.

Nava made a noise of acknowledgment. "I thought I sensed you nearby. Have you decided to help me after all?"

She asked it so matter-of-factly, as if Ari could only ever agree. Dressed in a simple green blouse and loose beige pants, she was barefoot, with her hair down to her waist and full of twigs and silver leaves. It looked like she'd been living in the woods, doing only the bare minimum to care for her new body.

The fourth Racari was nowhere to be seen.

"I've come to ask you to stop." Ari kept her verillion burning strong. She'd eaten as much as she could stomach before she left, but even her store of power felt miniscule compared to Nava's. "We have Selvin under control. You don't need to get involved."

Nava's head tilted, the motion more birdlike than human. "Whatever you have planned, it won't work. The only one strong enough to defeat Selvin is me."

"That isn't true," Ari countered. "We—"

A thunderous roar reverberated through the woods. A set of luminous golden eyes materialized in the trees, and then another, and another. A creature stepped into sight, its fur the short, bristly brown of a bear. It moved like one, lumbering and powerful, muscle rippling beneath hide that turned to scaled feet.

And then the clearing was full of chimeras.

CHAPTER 47

DAMIEN

IF SOMEONE HAD told Damien a few days ago that the fate of the world depended on him working with Rezek Kelbra, he would have said to let it burn. As it was, riding alongside him without thinking about putting a bullet in his skull was strange enough.

They'd both been provided horses and hooded cloaks, and while Damien had his guns, Rezek had been given a set of gemstones for enchantments and as much verillion as he could consume. Damien felt like they were a small army, and yet from the way Arielle described her short battle with Nava, it still might not be enough to face Selvin.

Their horses' hoofbeats echoed in the long tunnel, throwing the sound back at them so that he almost didn't hear Rezek when he said, "Take a right up here."

They curved into a new tunnel, making their way north toward the Silverwood. According to Rezek, it was home to an abandoned diamond mine that Selvin had made his base of operations, as it had connections to each of the main sections of tunnels throughout the city. Rezek might not have been able to follow Selvin the day he left, but he'd known all along where the Heretic would make his stand tonight.

Their plan was to immobilize Selvin and inject the elixir as quickly as possible. If they got into a drawn-out battle, they wouldn't have a chance.

Since Rezek had the flexibility of using any enchantment, they'd decided he would restrain Selvin, and Damien would wield the syringe, though Rezek had one as well should he see an opportunity.

"Left," Rezek said, leading them down a turn. It'd been this way for the last ten minutes, and though Damien preferred the silence, he could practically feel the words bubbling beneath Rezek's surface.

He'd just resolved to tell him to spit it out when Rezek said, "I know you haven't actually forgiven me."

Damien clenched the reins. They were on their way to face down an ancient godlike enchanter and Rezek wanted to have this conversation now? This was worse than when they'd gotten caught trying to sneak into the Kelbras' new racetrack, and Rezek had told him how furious his father was that they were still friends as they fled the security guards.

As if he couldn't bring himself to speak the truth without a blade hovering at his throat.

Damien nearly pulled his horse up short at the memory. It had been years since he'd thought about that, since he'd thought about any of his good memories with Rezek before his Ascension. He'd locked them away somewhere he couldn't reach, deep enough that it was like they never existed. He didn't want them to, now more than ever.

"Help me kill an all-powerful enchanter and perhaps I will," Damien replied.

The smile he'd come to know so well, the one that sharpened all of Rezek's edges, curled across his lips. "No, you won't. You're not in the business of forgiveness."

And whose fault is that? he thought bitterly.

And yet, wasn't this just another parallel between them? As Rezek asked for his forgiveness, Damien sought the same from so many others: Arielle, Mikira, Reid. There was even a part of him that thought of Loic, that wondered where his brother was now, and if things could ever be as they once were between them.

His mother had often spoken of forgiveness, of the ways in which Kinnism strove to repair broken things: relationships, faith, even oneself. For so long he'd seen her wish as an overwhelming task, the world too shattered to ever mend, but he was starting to realize that repairing the world didn't have to mean fixing everything at once.

Sometimes a world was as big as a single life.

Damien stared at Rezek's back. Could Damien ever forgive him? Could *he* ever be forgiven? Arielle hadn't been his only visitor that night in the cells. Reid had come too, standing outside the bars with Widget at his side.

"You made me feel safe," he'd said, not at all the sardonic remark Damien had expected. Reid was only marginally better than him at expressing real emotions, but in that moment, he'd looked more genuine than Damien had ever seen.

"After my parents died and I had nowhere else to go, you gave me a place to land, and you've looked out for me every day since." Reid stared at his boots as he spoke, his hands thrust deep into his pockets. Damien could just make out the crow tattooed on his forearm that hid the scars underneath. "That was the Damien Adair I knew."

An unfamiliar sense of shame had crept over Damien. For all his fear of disloyalty, all he made of trust, he was the one who had betrayed his friends in the end. He'd burrowed deeper into his own thoughts, turned inward instead of reaching out. So much of this could have been avoided if only he'd *said* something.

Even then he'd wanted nothing more than to let the conversation end, to let actions speak where he could not. He didn't know why it was so difficult for him, but he knew that if he didn't say what he needed to then, there would be no fixing things.

There still might not be.

"I'm sorry, Reid," he'd said. "You were only ever there for me, and I didn't see that when it mattered most."

Reid bent down to scoop up Widget. "That's because you always think you're right."

"I usually am." He'd said it lightly, but Reid only glowered at him, and he sighed. "I suppose I could do with borrowing a little of Mikira's candor now and again."

"One of her is enough," Reid had replied, but this time, he'd smiled.

Damien pulled free of the memory to find Rezek studying him. He said nothing, but there was a look in his eyes that stayed with Damien as he turned away.

It was the look of someone who'd given up.

The image stayed with him as they continued onward, the magnitude of what they raced toward settling about him like a cloak.

"We're getting close," Rezek said after some time.

"Are you going to be able to do this?" Damien didn't trust that Rezek wouldn't see his old possessor and flip right back over to his side. In truth, he'd yet to be convinced Rezek was ever on *theirs*.

"Your concern is touching." A little bit of that familiar mockery returned to Rezek's voice. "But in case you've forgotten, I have ample experience in disappointing father figures."

Damien snorted, only realizing that he was smiling when Rezek grinned at him like a cat that'd stolen another's mouse. He wiped the look off his face, but the feeling still lingered. Once, they'd spent hours lamenting to each other about their fathers' unrealistic expectations, about their fear of failure, and for a moment, Damien could almost picture what their lives would have been had Rezek's father never found that Racari.

It hurt more than he wanted to admit.

Rezek's own smile faded, and he nodded to a turnoff ahead. "There."

As they entered the tunnel, the scrape of claws and the shift of crackling joints echoed. The age-old enchanted lights above them flickered to life as their horses slowed, tossing their heads as the air thickened with the metallic scent of blood.

The first chimera appeared without warning. It took up nearly half the tunnel, its humanoid body enlarged with lupine features. It crouched on the haunches of a wolf, dark gray fur tumbling out from beneath ripped pant cuffs. Its curved back had long, curling spikes protruding from the spine, its face an elongated, bloodstained maw. The remnants of golden hair spilled from its skull, and two impossibly bright blue eyes seared into them.

Damien's horse reared, and it took him several tries to get it back under control. Rezek's sidestepped nervously, huffing clouds of hot breath into the cold air. The chimera growled, and Damien's free hand went for a gun.

"No, wait." Rezek thrust an arm into his chest. "It's here to retrieve us."

Damien holstered his gun as the chimera led them deeper into the tunnels, where the sounds of claws against stone and bestial snarls grew thicker. Groups of chimeras parted to let them through, serpentine creatures with scales along their arms and faces, others with bovine snouts and thickset bodies.

The floor sloped upward to an arch of light, and they emerged into the dried-up base of the mine. It rose on either side of them in a widening conical shape with rungs cut into it. Above, the metallic tips of the Silverwood shone, and the steps of the mine were filled with snarling, howling chimeras.

At the center stood Selvin.

The body he'd crafted for himself was far more elegant than the rest, retaining the majority of its human features. A snow-white mane framed sharp cheekbones and bright gray eyes, fangs spilling out over thin lips that stretched pale when he grinned. White feathers covered his arms, and from the base of his spine flicked a lion's tail.

He'd molded himself after Aslir, already seeing himself as a god.

"Rezek," Selvin rumbled. "I'd hoped you would find your way back to me."

"Is that why you left him to be imprisoned by the rebellion?" Damien asked.

"A rebellion *I* control." Selvin waved a dismissive hand. "He was never in any danger. In fact, I was keeping him safe."

Rezek stared at Selvin in stunned silence, his hands twisted in the reins hard enough to turn the skin raw. The surety he'd displayed only minutes ago was gone, replaced by the look of a disciple before his god.

"Don't listen to him, Rezek," Damien said urgently. "He knows you better than anyone. He'll say exactly the right thing."

"That's right." Selvin's voice turned coaxing. "I know everything about you, boy. I am the only true family you've ever had."

The Heretic held out one white-furred hand, claws curled as if beckoning. "Come. Let us cleanse this world together."

Rezek swayed in his seat, the deep shadows beneath his eyes intensifying his hollow stare. It was the look of a man who'd been parched for far too long and, having come upon a poisoned spring, could no more walk away than cut out his tongue. It was that look of desperation, of gratitude and love and fear all knotted together, that told Damien all he needed.

Rezek had betrayed him again.

CHAPTER 48

MIKIRA

MIKIRA FELT LESS like a girl and more like an amalgamation of edges, each one grating against the next in an ever-growing tempest of anticipation and doubt. She had faith in Ari to do her part, but the idea of sending Damien and Rezek off together strained the limits of her confidence. But if anyone could handle Rezek, it was Damien Adair.

For all this faults, she trusted him not to fail.

The same could not be said of herself. As she, Talyana, and Reid galloped up the King's Road toward the castle and the Heretic who awaited them, she wanted nothing more than to lose the others in the streets.

All Mikira wanted was for them to be safe, but she could not do this alone.

The syringe Reid had given her jutted against her hip bone in her pocket. Injecting it would dissolve the bond between the Heretic and Eshlin's magic, killing one and not the other. For without the enchanter cells, there was nothing for the bond to cling to. She would lose her magic, but she would live—they hoped. Reid had made it clear the elixir was untested, the true impact uncertain.

The question was if she did survive, who would she be?

Had they ever known the true princess, or was Eshlin just as much a threat as the Heretic who controlled her?

"Kira!" The urgency in Reid's voice tore her from her thoughts, and she looked up to find the square ahead blocked by a cluster of bodies. They were all shoving in different directions, trying to escape but trapped by the blue-and-white uniforms of the Anthir.

A voice reached them, propelled by an enchanted loudspeaker. "You are all under arrest for suspicion of rebellion."

Mikira glanced at Talyana, but she shook her head. This protest wasn't one of theirs. In fact, as Mikira slowed her horse to get a better look, she didn't think it was a protest at all. Children clutched solstice ribbons of Lyzairin blue in their hands, their parents holding them close. Vendors cowered behind their booths, performers scrambling off makeshift stages.

"Rowna," Talyana growled. "She's creating targets for the chimeras."

As if in answer, a howl went up through the city, a single note soon joined by a chorus. The crowd started pushing in earnest, the Anthir constables looking about uncertainly. Mikira reined her horse to a halt, Talyana and Reid joining her as they tried to identify which direction the sounds were coming from.

"Everywhere," Mikira breathed as the hum of snarls and hisses blanketed the street. "They're everywhere."

A scream pierced the air, and then the crowd was stampeding, barreling into the Anthir line to escape the square. Guns went off, bullets striking innocent people as at the far side, a handful of chimeras carved their way in. Claws tore into skin, bodies hitting the ground where they were trampled. More chimeras emerged from either side, and Mikira seized her knives, forcing her horse about at a snarl from behind.

A boar-like beast edged toward them on scaled legs, two other lupine creatures at its back. Their maws were wet with blood, their eyes unnaturally luminant.

"Shit," Talyana cursed.

"Stay close, Reid," Mikira warned, and felt his horse's body press up against hers.

Then the nearest chimera lunged.

Mikira's knives leapt from her hands. One pierced the boar chimera through the throat, the other slicing along the ligaments of one of the wolflike beasts. The third took a bullet from Talyana's shotgun between the eyes.

Mikira's knives returned to one hand, and she reeled her horse back toward the crowd with the other. The Anthir's lines had broken as they realized what was happening, and a few of them were desperately trying to keep the chimeras at bay as people ran.

Talyana seized her arm. "We can't get caught up in this fight, Kira. We have to get to the castle."

"We can't just leave them!" Mikira's knives quivered in her hand, waiting for their next command. She sent them flying into the chest of a vulpine chimera moments before its jaws closed around a little boy's neck.

Mikira caught the knives as they returned, seeking her next target.

"We can help them by stopping Rowna," Reid pressed, fighting to keep his horse steady.

"It's the fastest way," Talyana agreed, even as she took down two more chimeras. Her horse danced anxiously beneath her, bumping against Mikira's. The crowd was thickening around them as people realized that this direction had been cleared.

"Tal!" Reid yelled an instant before a catlike beast sank its fangs into her horse's throat. The horse reared, blood gushing down its chest. Talyana tried to get free, but her foot caught in the stirrup. As the horse collapsed, it took Talyana with it, the crowd swarming around her.

"No!" Mikira forced her horse through the crowd until her hooves struck bloodied stone. She spotted Talyana crouched behind her horse's flank, using it as a blockade from the stampede, and her heart settled from her throat. Then Talyana leapt to her feet, aimed, and put a bullet through the chimera's head.

Mikira thrust down a hand, and Talyana seized it, swinging up into the saddle behind her. "We can't fight them all!" she cried.

Mikira knew she was right, but she couldn't bring herself to abandon these people to their fate. Even if she could, there was no way they'd make it through the square until the crowd cleared, and there was an entire line of chimeras at the rear.

Something moved at the far side of the square, and the next moment a group of people emerged, coming *toward* the line of chimeras. Had they tried to escape in a different direction only to run into another attack? No, they definitely saw the line of beasts before them, and they weren't slowing down.

"It's Shira!" Reid called as they neared. Mikira gaped as Shira dove headfirst into the throng, tearing her knives through chimera flesh with the strength of three men. Was she enchanting herself like Ari?

As the last of the crowd cleared the square and Shira's rebel group slaughtered the remaining chimeras, Mikira urged her horse forward. Shira met them halfway, her face and clothes splattered in blood and an emerald ring glinting on one hand.

"I tried to call off the protests, but they're out of my control," she explained, breathless.

"And the rest of our forces?" Talyana surveyed Shira's group.

"Listened when I ordered them to stay put, thankfully," she replied. "Those with me are capable fighters. We'll hold off the chimeras; you three get to the castle." Then she was joining the others as they hurried toward the echoing cries of other attacks.

Only once she was gone did Mikira sheath her blades, Talyana shifting her shotgun into a more comfortable position. "I guess she's not *all* bad," Talyana muttered. "Her or her brother."

"Careful," Reid mocked. "I think you're starting to thaw."

Talyana stiffened. "All I'm saying is I don't completely entirely one hundred percent hate them."

A smile tugged tentatively across Mikira's lips, because in truth, she didn't hate Damien either. Not anymore. She'd been hurt, and upset, and desperate to a degree she never wanted to feel again. But she didn't have any more room in her for hatred. Not when it was consuming her from the inside out, leaving nothing but bitter remains.

"I'm so tired of being angry," Mikira said. "I want to be something else instead."

Talyana's arms encircled her waist, holding her tight. "You can be," she promised. "As soon as we've finished this."

"Let's go." Reid urged his horse onward and they followed, racing along the King's Road. News of the chimeras had spread, people rushing into their homes. Anthir constables jogged through the streets in formation, snarls and howls lighting the air.

The three of them stopped just out of sight of the castle gates, dismounting. Mikira stood guard while Talyana secured Reid's hands behind his back.

"You're enjoying this, aren't you?" he asked as Talyana tied off the rope a little *too* tightly.

Talyana grinned. "Entirely too much."

"The road's clear." Mikira sheathed her knives, grabbing Reid's arm while Talyana took the other. "Remember, we're delivering the Ranier prince to Rowna. She'll want to verify Reid's the real deal, so she'll test his blood against the crown. That's when we strike."

"Preferably before you actually cut me," Reid added.

"So demanding," Talyana jeered, earning a scowl. "Oh, that's perfect. Keep that look on your face and everyone will believe us."

"If you two are done, let's get moving." Mikira started forward, the others following.

Shira had sent word ahead of their arrival, and a pair of guards escorted them in on the princess's order. Or rather, the Heretic controlling the princess, who had to know by now that the city was under siege. Yet the castle security wasn't on alert, and she wondered if anyone here was aware of what had been unleashed in Veradell.

A seriousness Mikira had never seen before descended upon Talyana as they walked. She could only imagine how unmooring it was to learn that the person whose cause you'd dedicated yourself to not only wasn't who you'd thought, but instead was actively trying to destroy the very city you'd put your life at risk to save.

"I'll do it," she suddenly ground out.

Mikira blinked. "What?"

"If Eshlin—if she's not . . ." Talyana swallowed hard. "Who we think. I'll do it. Take . . . you know." She waved a hand at the castle, avoiding the words lest the guards overhear. But Mikira knew what she meant—the throne. If Eshlin wasn't on their side, then Talyana would complete the original Ascension task and become queen.

Reid gave a quiet snort but kept silent in dedication to his part, and Mikira sighed. "Let's hope it doesn't come to that."

She didn't like the idea of Talyana getting wrapped up in Enderlain's politics, not only because it would be like trapping a bird in a cage, but because it was clear to her by now that the throne was a target. The heads of the greater houses, Prince Darius, King Theo, and the Ranier king before him—they were all dead. Eshlin was possessed and Damien deposed.

As far as she was concerned, the throne was cursed.

Muscle by muscle, Talyana readjusted her expression into something more neutral, but it was only when Mikira took her hand that she relaxed the fist it'd become.

The guards led them to the throne room, where the massive doors had been pinned open on either side. Mikira squeezed Talyana's hand, releasing it as they entered.

Eshlin stood at the base of the throne, her resplendent golden dress pooling around her feet and the royal crown threaded into her dark braid. She was talking over a set of papers clutched in Niora's hands. The royal berator's face was flushed, her eyes blinking rapidly at whatever Eshlin was saying.

"Are you sure, Your Majesty?" Niora's voice sounded strained.

"I want the Anthir's number one priority to be rooting out the rebels. Nothing else." Eshlin turned from the berator, who shoved the papers into a case and scurried past them. Eshlin dismissed the guards, and the doors shut behind them with a distinctly hollow thud.

Mikira felt Talyana stiffen beside her. The only reason Eshlin wanted the Anthir focusing on the rebels was so they wouldn't help fight the chimeras, but they couldn't react. It was vital that the princess still thought they were loyal.

"Now, what is so important that you had to see me right away?" Eshlin's gaze flicked suspiciously over Reid. Or was it Rowna's? Ari had explained the possession wasn't a clear-cut thing, that even without the flash of white in their eyes, the Heretic could be in control.

Talyana released a steadying breath, and Mikira spoke to cover the sound. "We've found the real Ranier heir." She shoved Reid forward a step for emphasis, and he scowled back at her.

Eshlin's eyes widened, and her golem snake shifted about her shoulders, its tongue seeking the air. They'd planned for the snake. It was the reason they'd chosen that wording. They *had* found the Ranier heir, but it wasn't Reid.

"*Him?*" Eshlin breathed in delight. "Is that why Adair kept him so close?"

"It would make sense," Talyana replied tightly.

"I'm not who you think I am," Reid snapped with convincing indignation. "Damien's wrong."

"Silence," Eshlin ordered, swiftly approaching. She pulled the crown free, the bloodstone glinting in its center. "We will test his blood."

Mikira withdrew a knife. She would pretend to cut Reid, freeing him of his bonds instead, and Talyana would lunge with her syringe, followed by Mikira. Two syringes, two chances. They had only to—

The throne room door flew open, and a guard stumbled inside. "Your Majesty," he called. "There are reports of—of *creatures* flooding the streets. They're attacking people and—" He cut off when Eshlin raised a hand.

"I have it under control," she said. "Wait outside and do not come back unless I call you."

The guard hesitated, but at a look from the princess he fled back out, closing the doors.

Talyana's hand had fisted in the pocket where she kept the syringe, her entire body trembling with barely repressed fury. Mikira should have known better than to expect this of her. She could barely do it herself, and she'd been practicing at putting on a face for months.

"Did I ever really know you at all?" Talyana bit out.

Eshlin recoiled. "What?"

Mikira lunged, driving the syringe toward Eshlin's chest. The princess's eyes flared a brilliant white. She dodged and lashed out a hand, knocking the syringe from Mikira's grip.

It hit the ground and shattered.

CHAPTER 49

ARIELLE

ARI ENCHANTED HERSELF for strength as the nearest chimera reared back on its hind legs. Another emerged, its body lean and serpentine, its forked tongue tasting the air. One after the other they seeped into the clearing, fangs glistening and claws gouging deep into the earth.

"Get behind me." Nava stepped between her and the advancing chimeras. "They're here for me, not you."

So am I. Ari's heart clenched. Nava truly didn't see her as a threat, not because of the power she possessed, but because of the connection between them. The one that looked at Ari and saw herself.

The chimeras lunged.

Nava met the nearest one halfway, spearing her hand straight into its chest. It came free with a heart clasped in its palm, blood coating her arm to the elbow. Beast and heart hit the ground simultaneously, and she whirled to the next.

Crocodile-like jaws snapped down on Nava's arm, but it was as if she felt no pain. She pried open the beast's mouth, pushing upward with one hand and shoving down on its lower jaw with her trapped arm. Down, down, down, until the jaw snapped.

Ari stood racked with indecision. She could flee into the woods, hide, and let the elixir finish developing. Or she could fight at Nava's side and hope that whatever bond existed between them was strong enough to penetrate a hundred years of hatred. Because as she watched the Heretic fight, felt the power surging through her along their link, she didn't want to silence her.

Nava didn't deserve to die. Not again. She didn't deserve to be stripped of her magic. Not for Enderlain, which had already taken so much from her. Nava may have used her, forced her to do things against her will, but she'd also given her strength when she needed it most. She'd been her only companion in Rezek's cells, her confidant in Damien's and Mikira's absence, a steady wind at her back.

Her fate was tied irrevocably to Ari's, and if there was another way to stop her, a way that didn't mean killing her, Ari wanted to find it.

Ari delved into her own magic, seeking the links she'd been pulling on since she'd left the tunnels, and gave them one command: *Kill.*

The hawk she made for the Illinir came first, swooping down from the sky to rake sharp claws along a chimera's eyes. Then Lady Belda's golem dog was there, crippling another chimera with a bite to the leg.

One by one Ari's golems returned to her, the beasts she'd made in service to a people that would not have her, and she let them free.

By the time the last handful of chimeras fell, magic was thrumming through Ari's body in a heady rush, making her feel stronger than ever before. She fought to catch her breath as she surveyed the clearing, her golems circling at its edge.

Nava grinned, her face flecked with blood and her hands stained crimson. "Look at what we can accomplish together, Arielle. The *power* we possess."

Ari did look, but all she could see were the people those chimeras had once been, and the blood soaking into earth like spilled wine. The scene melded into another that never left her, the sight of her Saba's mutilated body imprinted forever in her mind.

Blood on the walls. Blood on her hands.

A voice softly saying, *Not all monsters look like monsters.*

Perhaps, if this had only been about them, if it were simply her and Nava and the choice between strength and silence, she could have chosen differently. But this was about more than just her. It was about Mikira, and Reid, and Shira, and Damien, and the sister who refused to leave her.

This was not a choice she could make for herself, however much she might want to.

"Please," she begged. "Don't do this."

Nava's lips curled. "It's far too late for that." She held up a hand, brilliant white light gathering in her bloodied palm. "I've spent my time absorbing magic from these trees, strengthening myself for this battle. The things I can do . . . Well, I can see what attracted Selvin to this pursuit. I feel invincible. Like the god he always wanted us to become."

"But you are not a god," Ari said softly. "Or have you forgotten what the Arkala says?"

Nava bared her teeth in a snarl. "Do not quote our people's scripture to me, little lion. I was there when it thrived." She advanced on Ari, and the golems encircling them growled and chittered, but Ari held them at bay.

"You have no idea what it was like watching them strip our culture away piece by piece," Nava seethed. "What it was like having to capitulate to Selvin and his friends. He was an egomaniac, Rowna his loyal dog. They only allowed me to join them to see if I could help accomplish their goal."

"And Morgaren?" Ari asked, desperate for anything to stall the Heretic. The elixir had to be nearly ready, and if she could not convince Nava to listen, it was her only option.

Nava stilled before her. "Morgaren," she echoed softly.

"Where is she now?" Ari spread her arms to the open forest. "You must have taken her Racari for a reason. Is she a part of your revenge?"

"Morgaren's path is her own," Nava replied with careful consideration. "I told you, I took her Racari only to save her from Selvin's machinations. I do this for her, and for all the Kinnish who suffered."

"Then *help* me," Ari pressed. "We can stop Selvin without triggering another Cataclysm."

Nava laughed, dry and harsh. "Selvin's pursuit of power destroyed everything I loved, but it was Enderlain that made it possible. If they had never invaded, none of this would have happened. It is only fitting their kingdom suffer the same fate."

The cruelty of Nava's words shocked Ari. She'd known that the Heretic had spent years simmering in thoughts of revenge, had known that a second Cataclysm was what she'd wanted, but some part of her had thought it a dream fueled by rage alone, that if she could pierce that veil, she could make Nava see sense.

But this went beyond anger, beyond pain. Nava was talking about punishing an entire kingdom for the actions of their ancestors, for Selvin's choices.

Ari scrambled for another argument, anything to keep Nava talking. "And what of all the Kinnish who live here now?"

Nava's jaw shifted. "They made their choice when they came to Enderlain."

"They had nowhere else to go!"

"They had everywhere else to go!" Nava roared. "This was simply the closest place. The most familiar. They ran back into the arms of the people who hated them and let them strip away their identity, their history."

She lifted her head imperiously. "If they want to live as the Enderlish, they can die as them too."

"Please," Ari begged, but she didn't need to hear Nava's answer to know it. She could feel it deep inside.

Whoever Nava had once been, that girl was gone, and there was no bringing her back.

As Nava made to go, Ari charmed herself for speed and darted in front of her. The Heretic veered aside, but the golem dog was there. Nava seized it by the throat, dissolving it back to clay the same way she had Atara, and the power rushed back to Ari.

In a blink, Nava's own speed increased, and Ari barely managed to keep in front of her. She flared her verillion and cast a strength charm, throwing Nava back. The Heretic rolled to the ground and back to her feet, springing at Ari, who stumbled out of the way.

"Listen to yourself!" Ari called. "You're going to kill your own people. For what? Kinahara is gone! This is our home now. *My* home. I won't let you destroy it."

"Foolish girl." Nava advanced undeterred. "You've forgotten where you came from. You all have."

She lunged for Ari.

The hawk swooped down, raking claws across the Heretic's face before darting back into the sky. The wounds healed almost instantly, but in that moment of distraction, a snake struck, venomous fangs sinking into Nava's calf. The Heretic seized it by the neck, turning it to clay. She took one woozy step forward, then straightened, her verillion burning through the toxin.

With a snarl, Nava thrust out a hand, white light enveloping the clearing in a burst of power. Ari shielded her eyes, and when she lowered her hand, the glade was a graveyard of clay. A wave of magic rushed through her as the golems returned to her.

"I thought that you understood," Nava said. "I thought you knew what it was to feel helpless while everything was taken from you. But no matter, little lion—I will show you."

Her hand pooled with white light, and in a desperate move, Ari reached for the bond between them, seeking to tear it apart the same way Nava had to her golems. But one brush of the power told her she could never overwhelm it; Nava was too strong.

The Heretic's eyes flooded white with raw power—and then something slammed into her, knocking her to the ground. A hulking, catlike form hovered over her with a resounding snarl. It was a midnight-black lion, nearly twice the size of a real one, and only the forest-green eyes and flicker of familiar magic told her who it was.

"Widget," she breathed in disbelief.

Had Shira sent him? She'd known that Shira had crafted the golem to protect Damien, but it had always been something of a running joke that she would create something so small for such a purpose. Now Ari understood. Shira had known about the Godstones, had possessed a Racari herself, and had bound a transformation enchantment to the little cat because she did nothing without thinking it through to the very end.

Nava clambered to her feet, barely rattled by the appearance of the beast. "I see our people's art is not as dead as I thought it was." She wiped a line of blood from her lips and lifted one glowing hand.

"No!" On instinct, Ari reached for the bond she had with all golems, but Widget was Shira's, not hers. Yet she found something, an energy source she poured her strength into even as Nava tried to eliminate it. Their magic collided, the link between them coming alight as a vision overwhelmed her.

She stood in a circular courtyard before the royal palace, and this time, Ari understood. She was Nava, peering out at a crowd gathered for Selvin's demonstration. She had no idea what he intended to exhibit, only that it related to the forbidden magic he'd been attempting.

Dressed in all white with his blond hair pulled back into a tail and a circlet of gold above his brow, Selvin already looked the part of a god, his sharp features set in a serene expression. He approached the front of a stage, Rowna and Morgaren remaining at Nava's side.

"Welcome," he boomed, his voice carrying throughout the curved courtyard. "Thank you for joining us. We have invited you here today to witness a spectacle of magic unlike any other."

A chorus of whispers carried through the crowd, and Selvin pulled his Racari from his pocket. Nava expected him to say more, but he only closed his eyes as if in prayer. Slowly, the magic of his spellbook became visible, the white light wafting from the book—and into Selvin.

"What is he doing?" she hissed to Morgaren.

The woman's dark eyes were vacant, lithe figure slumped in resolution. Nava seized hold of her. "Mor, tell me he isn't absorbing that magic."

"He is." Rowna stood with her hands clasped behind her back, broad shoulders set. "He will take his Racari's power and become a new god."

The magic wisped from the Racari faster now, setting Selvin aglow. Nava cursed, debating if she should interfere, when she noticed a familiar face at the front of the crowd. Adah, her sister, watched the procession with wide-eyed fascination.

Then Selvin's magic lashed out.

His face contracted with concentration, but the magic was spurting erratically now, leaping from him and the Racari like an overflowing fountain.

"Stop, Selvin!" Nava darted away from Rowna's outstretched hand. "Stop before you kill us all!"

"I have it under control," Selvin gritted out. The magic was growing more frenzied, the white light sparking like a fire. It'd grown larger, encompassing the Racari in a wide radius.

The crowd was beginning to panic now, some backing away as others took off at a run. The magic grew and grew, Selvin's control failing with every passing moment. Nava reached for the Racari, but he flung her back. Then Rowna and Morgaren were at his side, seizing the book as if to help absorb its magic, but it was like trying to contain the power of the sun.

Nava had to do something. If she could only prevent him from withdrawing any more magic . . . Her hand found the concealed blade at her hip. She didn't stop to think—she leapt to her feet and slammed the knife into Selvin's heart from behind.

The magic erupted.

Nava had one impossibly long moment to realize her mistake. To understand that Selvin had been the only thing keeping the magic contained, and without him—her eyes found her sister's, found her own fear reflected back at her.

And then the magic tore them all apart.

"Impudent girl!" Nava snarled as Ari came free of the vision with a gasp. "How *dare* you. Those memories are mine. That *pain* is mine!"

Ari understood then why Nava could not stop. Why every piece of her hummed with heart-wrenching agony.

She blamed herself for her sister's death.

Her actions had caused the Cataclysm, had destroyed her people's home and left them broken and afraid in a foreign land. That was why she needed revenge so desperately.

For if she forgave Selvin, she was all that remained.

"Please," Ari breathed, her strength waning as she poured the last of it into defending Widget. "This cycle must end."

There was nothing human left in Nava's eyes as she replied, "And so it will."

With a final burst of power, Nava's magic overwhelmed Ari's. Then, just as she felt Widget slipping away from her, Nava cried out. Her hold on Widget's magic released as someone slammed a syringe into her neck from behind.

Ari had one moment of pure, outright terror as she recognized Rivkah, before the clearing exploded in white.

CHAPTER 50

DAMIEN

DAMIEN DROVE HIS heels into his horse's flanks, and it erupted into a gallop. If Rezek was back under Selvin's thrall, he had to end this before it began. He pulled free a gun, and in the split second between when he leveled the barrel at Selvin's head and when he pulled the trigger, one of the chimeras moved. The bullet pierced it between the eyes.

Then something rammed into Damien.

He hit the ground hard, rolling up onto one knee and fighting to catch his breath. The chimera that'd struck him crouched low, its tigerlike body rippling with muscle.

Damien put a bullet in its heart, his mind frantically trying to catch up. He had to get close enough to inject Selvin with the elixir. If he could only—something seized him from behind. He lurched backward onto his feet just as a lupine chimera's claws dug into the earth where he'd been sitting.

For a split second, he thought Rezek had saved him—then a hand curled around his throat, unnatural strength pressing on his windpipe.

"Rezek," he rasped.

Selvin inspected Rezek curiously. "I thought you'd come as his friend."

Rezek snorted derisively, hand tightening on Damien's throat. "I needed a way out of the rebel compound, nothing more. I would never betray you like that."

Only me. Damien had known that he shouldn't trust Rezek, that his words were never more than lies, but there'd been a part of him that had thought maybe . . . *maybe.*

Fool, he thought. *Haven't you learned this lesson already?*

Selvin's gaze darkened on Rezek. "I put you there for a reason."

"And I left for one." Rezek leaned forward, as if desperate to impress his words upon Selvin. "You're in danger. They know about Rowna, and your plans."

Selvin hissed through his teeth. "There is nothing they can do now."

"Maybe not, but Nava can."

The other Heretic's name had a strange effect on Selvin, whose eyes came alight with a manic gleam. "The slaughter has already begun. When I absorb that power, not even Nava will be able to stop me."

It was then that Damien noticed it—the cloak of white light radiating from Selvin's skin. Magic was already flowing into him, the power released from those dying in Veradell. He would grow more powerful with each one. If they had any chance of stopping him, it had to be *now.*

Damien hooked his foot around Rezek's ankle and thrust his head back, feeling Rezek's nose crunch beneath the contact. Rezek released him with a cry of pain, and they toppled to the ground. Damien felt his syringe shatter against his hip, but he was already pulling Rezek's free. He lurched to his feet, gun drawn—and stopped.

This close he could truly see Selvin, and there was something familiar about him. About the broadness of his face and the sharpness of his jaw, and the bitter, bitter gray eyes.

Everything inside Damien was reduced to a single word. "Loic."

A grin just like his brother's split across Selvin's face, and he seized Damien's wrist, ripping the syringe free and crushing it beneath his heel. His grip tightened, and Damien cried out, sinking to his knees.

Selvin released him, running a hand through his white mane. "Your brother made a fine vessel." He dragged his claw-tipped fingers down the side of what had once been Loic's face.

Damien watched, frozen, his mind caught in a dangerous spiral. Their family had enchanter blood. He'd left Loic in jail. Rezek had access to the Anthir cells—he'd been plucking unlicensed enchanters from them for months.

Loic hadn't escaped—he'd been *taken.*

Damien rose steadily to his feet, cradling his injured arm. "Undo it."

"It's quite irreversible, I'm afraid." Selvin flexed his fingers.

He leveled his gun at Selvin's forehead. "Undo it!"

The chimeras surrounding them grew more agitated, but Selvin only laughed. "Are you going to shoot your own brother, *Dara*?" He stepped forward, letting the barrel of the gun press against his forehead. "By all means—shoot."

Damien's hand trembled. His mind told him to pull the trigger, that Loic was gone and he wasn't coming back. But his heart remembered holding his mother's still-warm body, the weight of his father's funeral, and now Loic—he couldn't lose him too.

"Don't touch him!" A hand seized Damien by the collar and thrust him backward. He stumbled and hit the ground. Selvin's hand was outstretched as if to grab him, a motion Damien hadn't even seen him making.

Rezek sneered down at him, every inch the adversary Damien remembered despite his bloodied nose. It was like they were kids again, the day Damien had first seen Rezek in person after his mother's death. Rezek had looked at him like that then too, as if he were nothing.

Not Rezek, his mind surged back. *Selvin.*

Selvin had killed his mother. Selvin had stolen his brother from him. Selvin was the one threatening Enderlain, and Rezek—Rezek was going to help him, because Damien had let his guard down. He'd let himself believe, if only for a moment, that he could forgive the man who'd ruined him.

Rezek turned away from him. "Let me help you," he begged Selvin. "Let me finish this with you." He dropped to his knees before the Heretic, and Selvin's lips curled. This was what he wanted—to be worshiped and adored. To become the god whose power he'd sought for over a century.

Rezek bowed his head nearly to the ground, and Damien knew: Selvin would accept Rezek back into his fold, and his attention would sway back to the boy who'd come to kill him. His chimeras would tear Damien apart, and the army would descend throughout the city until there was nothing left.

It was over.

CHAPTER 51

MIKIRA

MOVE!" MIKIRA SCREAMED at Talyana, but she was too slow. As Mikira's syringe shattered against the marble floor, Eshlin's eyes came alight, revealing the Heretic underneath. She backhanded Talyana hard enough to slam her to the ground. Glass cracked, the contents of the second syringe soaking Talyana's clothes.

Mikira's knives leapt from their sheaths, flying at Rowna. The Heretic dodged with impossible speed, but Mikira barely noticed. She was ten, five, one step away—and dropped to her knees at Talyana's side. Blood trickled from her mouth as Mikira rolled her over. Her fingers sought her throat, desperate to feel the beat of her heart.

Nothing.

"Tal?" Mikira called, shaking her gently. "Tal!"

Talyana drew a sudden, shuddering breath, blood spurting from her lips. Her eyes flared open briefly, and then closed, her breathing settling into something pained but even. It was a miracle Rowna hadn't broken her jaw.

"I've got her." Reid crouched beside them. "Free my hands."

Mikira dug her fingers into the knots, loosening them as a scream of frustration tore through the throne room. One of Mikira's knives had struck Rowna's shoulder. She ripped it free and flung it to the ground, then snatched the handle of the other as it flew by, trying to drag it into her possession. But the blade pulled free and struck for her again, nearly cutting her throat.

"Don't kill her!" Mikira yelled at the knives. They wanted to break the Heretic's bond to the princess's magic, not take her life, but the weapons required her touch to change commands.

Without warning, Talyana lurched upright and hurled a blade at Rowna's stomach. The Heretic plucked it out of the air with her bare hand. She flung it back, and Mikira screamed as the knife pierced flesh. Talyana gaped, a hand at the heart that should have stopped—but it wasn't her the blade had struck.

Reid had thrown himself in front of her.

He stared down at the knife protruding from his shoulder, at the blood tracing the lines of his tattoos in a macabre imitation.

Talyana caught him as he crumpled.

"No." Mikira could barely form the word. Everything in her wanted to fly at Rowna, to cut away at her until every raw part of her went numb, but if there was anything the last few months had taught her, it was how to recognize an opponent she could not defeat alone.

With every ounce of control she could muster, Mikira stepped between the Heretic and her friends, her arms spread wide.

"Stop." Her voice trembled softly. "Please, stop. This wasn't supposed to happen."

Rowna's laugh ricocheted off the high ceilings. "Oh, I'm sure."

"You don't understand." Mikira's knives returned to her hands. She sheathed them but didn't release the handles. "I came here for Talyana."

Bending the truth came so easily, when once, it would have made her sick. She didn't know what to think about that. Even Talyana gaped at her, still dizzy from the Heretic's blow. She clutched Reid in her arms. He was still breathing, his jaw wound tight as his fingers probed at the knife.

The sight of them alive was the only thing that kept Mikira steady.

Rowna's golem snake tasted the air, but Mikira had chosen her words carefully. They weren't the whole truth, but neither were they lies. This wasn't how she'd hoped this would go, and she *was* here for Talyana, as she was for Reid, and her sisters, and all of Enderlain.

Mikira laid out her last card. "The lost heir isn't a prince," she said. "It's Talyana."

Talyana recoiled, looking between her and Rowna apprehensively. She knew as well as Mikira did that the Heretic wouldn't suffer a threat to her rule. If Rowna hadn't intended to kill her before, she would now.

Rowna kicked the crown across the floor to Mikira's feet. "Prove it."

Ever so gently, Mikira brushed a finger against the wound on Talyana's cheek. She held her gaze, then Reid's, before she picked up the crown and pressed her finger to the bloodstone.

It lit up instantly.

Talyana gaped at it, any hope she'd been holding on to that this was all some terrible misunderstanding vanishing in an instant.

Rowna bared a wolfish grin. "So you've proven useful after all, Miss Rusel."

The epithet sent a shudder through her, but memories of Rezek no longer held sway over her. The things he had done to her felt impossibly far away in the presence of what she faced now; all that remained were the lessons she'd learned. About what was really important to her, about how to bend without breaking.

That her love and her emotions were not weaknesses, but the things that let her stand before an ancient enchanter and put on a performance Damien Adair would be proud of.

"Please don't kill her," she pleaded, forcing herself to hold her ground as Rowna stalked forward. She had to trust Talyana and Reid to realize her plan and play their parts. Had to trust herself to see this through.

"The throne doesn't belong to you," Talyana snarled breathlessly. "You've stolen it."

Rowna's laugh echoed as she drew up before them. "All thrones are stolen.

From the people, from other rulers. They are paltry attempts to raise humanity above its station. But king or queen or commoner, you are all nothing in the face of our power. I will be a god, little princess, and you will be dead."

Reid jerked the knife from his shoulder, slashing at Rowna's legs, but the Heretic was faster. She knocked him aside and seized Talyana by the throat, lifting her from the ground. The golem snake hissed, winding down Rowna's arm as Talyana struggled for air.

"Feast," Rowna commanded the snake.

"Strike," Mikira told a knife.

It pierced Rowna from behind, just above the heart. Slowly, she turned to look over her shoulder at Mikira. "You missed."

Mikira tilted her head. "Did I?"

Rowna's eyes flared. The white light radiating from her irises flickered, then dimmed. She released Talyana with a cry and stumbled to her knees, clawing at her own skin as if to carve something free. Her nails tore at her flesh, her scream reverberating through the hall.

"How?" she wailed, her body convulsing.

Reid wiped a line of blood away from his lip, nodding at the spilled elixir. "The knife you threw landed in the spilled elixir. All Mikira had to do was pierce your skin."

"And now it's stripping away all of Eshlin's magic," Talyana said through heavy breaths. "When it's gone, the bond will break, and there will be nothing for you to hold on to."

Mikira caught her knife as it returned. "It's over."

And like a flame burning itself out, the light vanished from the Heretic's eyes, and the princess collapsed to the floor.

CHAPTER 52

ARIELLE

THE FORCE OF the explosion knocked Ari to the ground.

The white light radiating from Nava dispersed quickly, but it took her a few furious blinks to clear her vision of it. She was on the edge of the glade, her aches already fading from the verillion buzzing through her.

A seeping wetness grew along her side, and she pressed a hand to it, expecting blood. But her fingers came away black.

The syringe had broken.

Rolling upright, she sought Rivkah. If her body felt like this pumped full of magic, then her sister—relief swept through her at the sight of Widget, the lion's body curled protectively around Rivkah, whose chest rose and fell in slow breaths.

Ari scrambled back to her feet, dizziness threatening to send her back down again, but she held her ground. Nava panted heavily in the center of the glade. The power of the blast had dislodged Rivkah's syringe, and it lay in the grass at her feet, unbroken.

Nava's gaze followed hers, and she lifted a foot.

Flaring her verillion, Ari lunged, her speed enchantment still intact. She crashed into Nava. They hit the ground, Nava throwing her off with inhuman strength. Ari skidded across the grass, rolled straight to her feet, and lurched for the syringe.

Her fingers barely closed around it before Nava's foot connected with her ribs. The kick sent her spiraling through the air, and she felt her ribs break. She struck earth, gasping for breath, and rolled onto her side to find Nava descending upon her. The Heretic's fingers brushed the collar of her blouse—and then Widget barreled into her.

Nava rolled to her feet, unfazed by the strike of an eight-hundred-pound creature.

Ari's magic reknit her ribs with a painful crack of bone and she sucked down a ragged breath, using Widget to force herself back to her feet.

"Selvin's plan is already taking place. I can feel the magic in the air, feel it becoming a part of me." Nava's dark hair was a wild mess, her skin streaked with dirt and blood. Ari had a feeling she looked much the same, but where her verillion and strength were slowly fading, Nava looked ready to take on an entire army. "You'll never get close enough to me to use that."

"I don't have to." Ari flipped the syringe around and held the needle to her arm.

Nava lurched before she could stop herself, her outstretched fingers curling into a fist.

Ari lifted her head. "You lied to me."

Nava's lips twitched, and then the tension washed out of her with a laugh. Widget let out a low growl, and Ari shifted uneasily. "What's so funny?"

"The idea that you would make yourself powerless." Nava shook her head. "What will you do without your magic, little lion? Go home to the family that doesn't want you?"

Ari flinched, the needle pricking her skin. Nava's eyes tracked the movement. "You forget how well I know you," she said. "I know every dark part of you. You can't let this power go. It *is* you. If you destroy it, you might as well be dead."

Nava spoke straight to the core of her, to the part that even now sought a way to end this that let her keep her power. Her strength. Who would she be without her magic? *What* would she be? The same trembling girl those Kelbra men had pinned to the floor? She might not even get the chance to find out. The elixir could kill her right alongside the Heretic.

"It's not too late to join me," Nava coaxed, stepping toward Ari with her hand outstretched. "I can make you stronger than you've ever been. Show you magic you've never dreamed of. You never have to be afraid again."

She wanted that, more than anything. To be free of her fears, free of her pain. But she understood now that wasn't possible. Those things—they were a part of her. It was that fear that had pushed her to accept Damien's offer. That fear that had bonded her and Mikira. It had opened a door for her that brought her closer to her heritage than she'd ever thought she could be, and nights by the fire with the friends she'd always wanted.

It is fear that creates monsters, came her Saba's voice, surging like a rising river. *Promise me you will never let your fear control you. Promise me you will be fearless, a'huvati.*

All this time, she'd thought her Saba meant she should eradicate fear, rip it from her flesh like roots from soil, and in that time, she'd done exactly what he'd warned her against. But she understood now what he'd meant. He'd never wanted her to destroy anything. He'd wanted her to be brave in the face of fear.

For if she had never been afraid, she could never have been strong.

Nava must have felt her decision through their bond. For the first time, Ari saw true terror in the Heretic's face—and then she leapt for Rivkah. Ari's answering scream cut off as Nava hoisted Rivkah's limp body against her own, a hand on her sister's throat. Rivkah coughed, blinking bleary eyes as she came to.

"Drop the syringe, or she dies," Nava commanded.

Rivkah released a hoarse laugh and spat blood into the dirt. "Wrong move."

Nava took one look at Ari, incandescent with fury, and realized her mistake.

"You shouldn't have touched my sister," Ari said, and plunged the needle into her arm.

Nava screamed as the elixir tore through Ari's veins in lines of fire. She dropped to her knees, half collapsing until she struck warm fur. Distantly, she knew Widget had propped her up, but all she could think about was the agony shearing her apart, that the elixir wasn't just killing her magic—it was killing *her* too.

The burn of verillion in her stomach dispersed, her strength ripped away. She gasped, her fingers curling into Widget's rough fur, and forced herself to look up.

Nava had gone utterly still.

Her face was caught in a tableau of emotions that rang down the dissolving bond between her and Ari. Here was a being that had cradled and nursed its revenge for a century, not yet dead, but never quite alive, only to have that future snatched from it by someone it saw as little more than a child—a child it had, in some way, cared for.

Nava released Rivkah as her dark eyes found Ari's, and slowly, that shock hardened into something sharper. Her lips curled, even as her body disintegrated around her. "Foolish girl," she rasped. "They will never accept you. You will *never* be safe."

Ari swayed unsteadily, a half laugh strangling in her throat. "I know. But I'm making a different choice," she said. "I won't let my fear control me."

Then the cord between them snapped, and Nava's body dissolved into clay. She felt the final echo of Nava's scream, of the unending well of her rage.

Then Ari felt herself

let

go.

CHAPTER 53

DAMIEN

DAMIEN SHIFTED BACKWARD on his good hand, edging space between him and Selvin, who was peering down at Rezek as if transcended. His body wisped spirals of white light, his eyes bright with the luminescence of gold.

"You shall witness our rise, young Adair." The Heretic spread his arms, the chimeras' calls rising up in a chorus of howls and cries that swallowed all sound.

Rezek withdrew something from his pocket, proffering Selvin a leather-bound book wrapped in pearlescent bone. He'd had Selvin's Racari all this time, as if the Heretic had known without a doubt that he would return.

I was keeping you safe.

And now he would absorb the Racari's power and ascend into godhood, Enderlain a playground at his feet.

Selvin's ears twitched, his smile fading. His hand stalled atop Rezek's on the Racari. "What are you muttering?"

When Rezek didn't respond, he lurched forward, seizing his hair and wrenching his head back. Rezek's hand clasped Selvin's wrist, his voice rising. It took Damien a moment to realize what he was hearing, that he recognized not only it, but its significance.

Rezek finished the binding spell.

With a hiss, Selvin flung Rezek away from him. Damien moved on instinct. He put a bullet in the nearest chimera's chest as he leapt to his feet, laying out the second at Selvin's side.

Selvin lunged for him, but Rezek cut between them. "Stop, or Damien kills us both."

Selvin stilled, claws curling inward. "What have you done?"

Rezek held out a hand, revealing a bloodstone clutched in his palm. "I bonded our lives," he said as he backed toward Damien, clutching the Racari. "If I die, you die."

Selvin's chest heaved, his breath coming out in snarls. The chimeras in the upper rungs of the mine echoed his agitation.

It had all been a trick.

Rezek had needed to get close, but Damien had acted before he could, sure that Rezek had betrayed him. He'd snatched him from Selvin's reach twice, prostrated himself in order to gain the Heretic's trust, and now—

"*Rezek*," he breathed.

His once friend looked at him, his blue eyes impossibly bright and alive, and Damien knew what he wanted. Selvin was too powerful for them to fight, his servants too many. Even if Damien shot him, he'd heal just like Arielle did, fueled by his new power.

But Rezek—*Rezek* could die.

Selvin started toward them, and Damien's hand snapped up, pressing the gun against Rezek's brow. Selvin halted, his attention settling fully on Rezek. "You don't want this," he said. "Undo the binding, and you can stand by my side. We can make this kingdom ours together."

Rezek's breath hitched, and Damien's finger curled about the trigger. He couldn't kill Loic when the moment came, and now he had a second chance—if he killed Rezek too.

Not long ago, he would have sold his soul for this opportunity. In a way, he'd done just that. Every choice he'd made the last few months had been to ruin the boy who'd once been his friend. He'd lost himself in revenge, desperate for the power to control every inch of his life, so that nothing like his mother's death could ever happen to him again.

But it had.

Again and again. All that power, all that control—in the end it meant nothing. In the end, all it'd done was turn him into the very people he hated. And now he was standing with a gun pressed against his childhood friend's head, being asked to pull the trigger that would kill him and his brother.

"Rezek," Selvin snarled.

"*Why?*" Damien breathed.

Rezek turned toward him, the barrel of the gun sliding across his brow. "I killed your mother. I made your life a living hell, turned everything and everyone I could against you." His voice was cold and sharp as shattered glass, but the words didn't anger Damien, because this time, he saw right through Rezek. To the fear and the pain underneath, to the truth.

"You wanted me to hate you." Damien's hand trembled. "It was easier that way."

Rezek's gaze turned pleading. "Do it."

"I can't—"

"Then give me the gun and I'll do it myself!"

Selvin roared, and the chimeras on the steps of the mine thundered back. They came streaming down the mountainside, rushing toward them at impossible speeds. Rezek reached into Damien's coat, seizing the other Lonlarra revolver. Selvin moved at the same time, and they both turned, laying down fire.

The white light of pure magic erupted in a shield around Selvin, deflecting the bullets, and the ground began to shake with the stampede of approaching chimeras.

"Do it, Damien!" Rezek's voice broke, and he pulled the trigger again and again until the gun clicked empty. "Please."

I know you haven't actually forgiven me. Rezek's words from earlier came back to him.

Help me kill an all-powerful enchanter and perhaps I will.

That was what he'd said, and now here Rezek was, asking for one final chance at absolution, for a crime Damien didn't know if he blamed him for any longer.

He pressed the gun against Rezek's forehead and told himself to pull the trigger, but he only trembled. Rezek's hand closed around his, his thumb pressing into Damien's trigger finger as he met his gaze and whispered a single word.

"Bang."

Then Rezek pulled the trigger, just as the flood of chimeras struck.

CHAPTER 54

DAMIEN

THERE WAS ONLY darkness.

As Damien came to, the world void of light, pressure all around him, he knew that he had to be dead. That he'd entered the world beyond, where all spirits who passed resided. He wondered if his parents would be there.

Then slowly, bit by bit, he became aware of something sharp pressing into his shin, his ribs, his throat. What had once been total night broke with dim rays of light.

He struggled upward.

Claws tore at his clothes and skin, bodies pressing him down, but he fought until he broke the top layer and dragged in a ragged breath of fresh air. The fading sunlight flooded all around him, illuminating the field of chimera corpses. They had died the moment Selvin did, their bodies continuing their forward momentum and crashing into him, burying him alive.

With his sore wrist, it took him time to pull himself clear of the chimeras and holster his guns. Nearby lay Selvin, his gray eyes open and glazed. Dead, he looked even less like Loic. Whatever had existed of his brother in that monster had been long gone before Damien pulled the trigger, but he still felt the weight of responsibility hanging over his shoulders, the burden of things left unsaid.

If Loic had known the truth of their mother's death, would his brother have forgiven him? Or would he still blame him for bringing Rezek into their lives? Could they have been a family again, or were there some things even blood was not thick enough to weather?

Without thinking, Damien gripped the hem of his shirt and tore it, the rip of fabric the only noise in what had become a tomb. He didn't know the Kinnish blessing he ought to say, so he only held the tattered cloth and stood in silence, until he could bear it no longer.

Then he began to dig.

Carefully he cleared aside chimera corpses until at last, he found Rezek. The verillion in his system had tried to heal the bullet wound, but the side of his head was still a bloody mess.

He felt again the press of Rezek's finger over his, the solid click of the trigger being pulled. He felt the recoil of the gun, saw Rezek's pale face as he spoke.

Bang.

Damien stared at him for a long, long time before he said, "You're right, I don't forgive you." His voice came out strangled. "I don't forgive you for what you did, or for this, and I never will, because—"

You're gone.

Gone, and with him any chance Damien had to forgive him, and he could do nothing but stand there and stare at a body that would never respond again and know that he could do *nothing* to change it. He was powerless, and for that, he hated Rezek. Hated him more than he ever had before.

"You stupid fool," he spat. "You probably think you've won."

As if in answer, one of the chimera bodies shifted, pulled down by the weight of gravity. Damien spotted something sticking out from beneath Rezek's chest, the hard corner of a book barely larger than his palm. He crouched down to pull it free.

Rezek's Racari.

Damien ran a finger along the bloodstone at the center. Like the ones bound to Mikira's knives, the charm was set. To bind the book didn't require an enchanter's magic, only the blood of its new owner. That was all it took to own a piece of a god's power. Perhaps Talyana was right about him after all. Perhaps he couldn't give it up, not completely.

Damien brushed a thumb along a wound on his side, staining it with blood, and pressed it to the stone.

It came alight, and something clicked into place between them.

—don't even need your damn forgiveness. And for the record, you look like you're going to cry.

Damien dropped the book with a start, and the voice went silent. A voice that had sounded suspiciously like—

Did you just hear *me?*

Alive, Damien thought with a relief so incomprehensible, it stunned him. Rezek was *alive.* Alive and—

"No," Damien said aloud. "This is not happening."

I distinctly believe it is, returned Rezek's saccharine voice. *How terrible for you.*

Damien struck out for the edge of the mine, where a staircase had been cut into the stone leading to ground level. He understood what this meant even as his mind railed against it. There was no way he was going to be stuck with Rezek for all eternity.

That isn't going to work, Rezek tsked. *We're both tied to this book. Even if you leave it behind—*

Damien's foot struck the bottom stair, and the Racari materialized in his hands.

—it'll just find you again.

Snarling, Damien threw the book as far as he possibly could across the clearing and rushed up the steps, not stopping until he reached the top. He collapsed onto the first stair, desperately trying to catch his breath, and found the Racari sitting beside his feet.

Try again, Rezek suggested lightly. *I'm sure it will work this time.*

Damien gritted his teeth. "If you try to possess me—"

I can't possess you; you're not an enchanter. Pity, though. That would have been fun.

"No part of this is fun," Damien growled.

Not for you.

Damien seized the Racari. "Arielle will know how to fix this."

If she's still alive, Rezek returned sweetly. *Otherwise, you can have two of us in your head.*

Because, like Rezek, Arielle was bound to a Racari, and if she died while bonded to it—

Damien surged to his feet and into the Silverwood. Arielle had told them she sensed Nava in the woods just north of the Traveler's Road and west of Selvin's base in the mine. Every step was more than his body could bear, exhausted and beat-up as he was.

She's probably dead, said Rezek. *Torn up into tiny little pieces.*

"If you don't shut up—"

You'll what? Kill me? Rezek's laugh echoed through his head, and Damien did everything he could to shut him out as he charged through the wood. He hit the Traveler's Road sooner than he'd expected and debated heading farther along it or plunging back into the wood straightaway. If only he had that damn golem hawk.

Something rustled in the bushes ahead. Damien's uninjured hand went instinctually for a gun that was empty.

A long, misshapen form bounded out from the woods, and for an instant Damien thought it was one of the chimeras clinging to life. Then the creature pinned him with two familiar green eyes, and he realized it wasn't misshapen, but carrying someone across its back. Rivkah was slumped over the lion's neck, one hand pinned to her ribs with a wince, but alive.

Then Arielle broke through the tree line. Her hair was a wild mess, her face covered in slowly healing scratches. Her dark eyes widened when she saw him, and she lurched at him like he was a life preserver in a raging sea.

He caught her as she breathed, "It's over."

CHAPTER 55

MIKIRA

MIKIRA AND TALYANA sat back-to-back at the unconscious Eshlin's side. She'd survived the elixir's effects, but hadn't woken. No news had come from the others yet, and the guards had stayed outside as ordered. The golem snake remained looped about Eshlin's shoulders, snapping at them each time Reid tried to check on her. It only relented when it realized he was trying to tend to her wounds, having bandaged his own using supplies he'd packed in his pockets.

"Do you think the others are okay?" Mikira let her unfocused gaze slide across the stained glass windows. Their enchantments were in need of restoration, the flitting birds and falling leaves moving jerkily across the glass.

"As much as I detest him, I would not want to be Damien Adair's opponent," Talyana replied hoarsely, her throat still raw from Eshlin's attack. "And the only person I'd be more afraid to face down than him is Arielle."

Mikira's lips twitched. "Yeah, she's pretty cool."

Talyana's hand reached back to find hers, and she squeezed it gently. "You're not half so bad yourself. Though if you ever use these newfound skills to lie to *me*, it'll be another matter."

"Says the one who pretended to be an entirely different person to avoid facing me."

"I'm not the youngest to ever win the Illinir. I don't have to have a perfect public face."

Mikira snorted. "No, you're just the princess of Goddess-damned Enderlain."

Talyana tilted her head back against Mikira's. "Oh yeah. That."

A shadow fell over them, and they both looked up to find Reid glowering down at them. "You both sound delirious. Did you hit your heads?"

"Come to think of it, you do kind of look like an overgrown scarecrow right now . . ." Talyana paused. "Oh, wait, no, you always look like that."

Reid scowled, but rather than respond, he dropped into a crouch, dabbed a bit of a clear liquid onto a clean cloth, and pressed it pointedly against one of Talyana's cuts. She cursed, flying upright, and Reid offered her a roll of bandages. "Try not to strangle yourself with it."

Mikira stifled a laugh, feeling every bit as delirious as Reid had said, but cut off as a soft groan sounded. They all turned as Eshlin gingerly sat up. She brought a hand to her head, blinking blearily until her gaze solidified on them. Mikira didn't know what she expected to see in the eyes of the princess she'd never truly met, but it was not annoyance.

"Did you really have to stab me?" she demanded.

"Thankfully I have lots of experience stabbing people," Mikira replied lightly.

"You're welcome," Talyana added.

Reid pointed at Eshlin's arm. "Don't move that."

Eshlin dragged the hand of her uninjured arm through her hair. "Ugh! I feel more hungover than Darius after one of his stupid parties." Comprehension dawned a split second later, and she looked down at her hand as if it'd betrayed her. "Darius. I . . . killed him."

Mikira rolled onto her knees, sitting back on her heels. "Rowna did. You're not responsible for the Heretic's actions."

The princess looked away. "I'm responsible for not stopping her. She took control so quickly, I didn't even realize what was happening. My magic's so weak, I never pursued it."

"How did you even bond with the Racari to begin with?" Reid asked, voicing the same question Mikira had. An enchanter had to bleed on the bloodstone to create the bond.

Eshlin gritted her teeth. "Rezek. I don't know how he got my blood, but he fed it to the stone. Where is that little bastard, anyways?"

"Hopefully helping Damien kill Selvin." Mikira rose wearily to her feet. She offered Eshlin and Talyana each a hand up, which they gratefully took.

"He did." Eshlin dusted off her dress, looking distinctly displeased at its wrinkles, even as she fought to keep steady on her feet. "I felt Selvin's and Nava's energy disappear right before you broke my bond with Rowna."

The relief that hit Mikira was so staggering, her knees almost buckled. What they'd set out to do had felt so impossibly big that she'd never really thought they might actually succeed. She felt Reid at her side and leaned into him, each holding the other up.

"And our friends?" Mikira asked hopefully.

Eshlin shook her head. "That, I can't speak to, I'm afraid. But I can tell you that we have a lot of cleaning up to do. Between the chimeras, the rebels, and this game of pass the throne we've been playing, Veradell will be a mess."

Mikira and Talyana exchanged nervous looks. "And what exactly do you intend to do about that mess?" Talyana asked.

"Precisely what I promised you." Eshlin lifted her chin. "I began the rebellion as myself, and I recruited you as myself. It wasn't until later that Rowna took control. So as soon as I've gotten the carnage cleaned up, I'm making this kingdom the people's problem." A wry smile curled her lips. "Unless, of course, you'd like to be queen?"

Talyana let out a low groan. "I never want to be responsible for anything ever again."

Mikira smiled. "How about a couple of horses?"

"Mm, I suppose I can do that. But only if you're there—and he's not."

Reid scowled. "Who said I would want to be?"

Mikira laughed. "Together, then."

WHILE ESHLIN DEALT with things at the castle, Mikira, Reid, and Talyana had their injuries tended to and returned to headquarters. The main cavern had been converted into a makeshift medical bay, lined with blankets and pallets on the floor hosting rebels and civilians alike wounded in the chimera attack.

Doctors flitted about triaging patients, and among them, Mikira spotted a familiar face applying a bandage with a practiced hand. She elbowed Talyana for her attention, wanting confirmation that she wasn't imagining things.

"You've got to be kidding me," Talyana said as the figure completed their work and then rose, surveying the tumult for their next patient. Instead, their black eyes fell upon Mikira.

Rahzen grinned at them as if they were the best of friends reunited. Dressed in a crimson suit reminiscent of a doctor's, complete with a tie of shimmering gold, the weapons merchant all but fluttered over to them, somehow cutting through the crowd as if it had parted for them.

"The two of you look as though you could use a drink," they said. "Give me a second and I can change cloth—"

"What are you doing here?" Mikira asked wearily.

Rahzen leaned in close as they replied, "Watching, my friend, and waiting. Watching and waiting."

Mikira drew back, unsettled. The merchant only maintained their grin a moment longer before lifting their gaze above her shoulder.

"Shira!" they greeted with genuine delight. "I'm so very glad you're not dead."

"Not for lack of trying," Shira replied as she joined their gathering, attention half on the crowd. Her clothes were flecked with blood, a bruise blossoming along her jaw. "Have my brother and Ari returned?"

"I haven't seen them yet," Mikira replied distantly. Reid poked her in the arm with a quizzical look, and Mikira rubbed her eyes. She felt as though a mild breeze could tip her over; all she wanted was some sleep.

"Kira!" Ari's voice rang through the cavern, and Mikira roused, turning just in time to catch Ari in a hug. She closed her eyes, sinking into the embrace. "I'm so glad you're okay."

"You too," Mikira said thickly, and squeezed her all the harder.

When they separated, Damien and Rivkah had joined them, Widget in the girl's arms. Mikira looked from them, to Ari, to Reid and Talyana and Shira, and grinned so hard it hurt.

They were *alive.*

They were alive, and they'd won. Not just against the Heretics, but against Enderlain itself. The Eternal War was over, the draft had ended, and Eshlin was poised to upend everything. Her family would never again be at the mercy of a noble house. They could come home.

She wasn't a fool; she knew the change in government would take time and work, and it wouldn't fix everything. There would still be problems, still be people who abused power and those who suffered. They hadn't fixed everything, but they'd made a difference, and that was more than she'd once ever thought possible.

Rahzen had slipped away with Ari's arrival, and it was their absence that made Mikira notice another. Her eyes narrowed on Damien. "Where's Rezek?"

He looked away. "Dead."

Mikira didn't know quite how she felt about that. Guilty in her relief, and something starker, but she'd meant what she'd said to Talyana and Reid on their way to the castle.

She didn't want to be angry anymore.

"May his memory be a blessing," Shira said, and though the phrase was softer than anything Rezek deserved, Mikira didn't refute it. Damien, on the other hand, looked annoyed, and he muttered something Mikira couldn't hear but that she swore was meant for someone else.

Then he explained what had happened, pausing only briefly to tell Shira that Loic had been one of Selvin's victims, a pain Mikira could hardly fathom. Losing Lochlyn had been terrible enough; she couldn't imagine how it would have felt to see him transformed, to choose between his life and thousands of others.

Shira absorbed the news as if she'd expected it, but Ari still squeezed her arm, uttering the same phrase Shira had moments before for Rezek. There was a comfort to it, a weight that lent sincerity, and they let the words linger there in the silence.

Then Shira took a deep breath and asked Mikira what had happened with Eshlin. She explained, with interjections from Reid and Talyana, and then Ari described her fight with Nava. She stumbled over her description of injecting herself with the syringe, and Mikira took her hand, knowing what the loss of her magic had cost her as well as she knew that Ari would talk to her about it when she was ready. Ari's fingers tightened on hers, then released, and she took a deep breath to continue.

Her mention of Widget's transformation earned a slight smile from Shira, and then Ari pulled a black book out of her pocket.

"The fourth Racari," she told them. "Nava kept it on her. I guess she meant what she said when she told me she just wanted to keep Morgaren safe. I'd like to find a way . . . a way to free her soul from—" She paused, swaying slightly.

"Ari?" Rivkah stepped forward.

"I'm fine," she said—and then collapsed.

Mikira and Damien caught her at the same time, the Racari tumbling to the ground. Carefully Mikira shifted her weight to Damien, who crouched low in order to lift her into his arms despite his wrapped wrist. Then Reid was there, taking her pulse and gently lifting her eyelids.

"I think she's okay," he said, and Rivkah let out a shuddering breath. "She probably just needs some rest. We should take her back to the manor."

Damien started, looking at Reid as if his words were the answer to a question he'd been too afraid to ask, but he didn't press it. Mikira resisted the urge to demand to come with them. She knew Reid would take care of Ari, and there was so much left to handle here.

"You can take the coach," Shira said. "I'll check in on you later."

Damien nodded, his attention straying to the dropped Racari. "Can you take care of that?"

Shira scooped up the book as Damien turned to follow Reid and Rivkah outside. She tucked the Racari in her pocket, facing Talyana and Mikira.

"I know you're both exhausted," she said. "You should—"

"Stay and help?" Talyana cut in. "Why, you shouldn't have."

Mikira smirked. "We'll do what we can."

They spent the next hour assuring people everything was okay and helping distribute tasks and aid. Most of them would be able to return to their homes in time, but Shira wanted the base to remain operative long enough to ensure an easy transition.

Mikira looked up from a list of supplies she was reviewing, catching sight of Rahzen on the far side of the cavern. They gave a cursory glance about, then ducked into Eshlin's office, where Mikira was fairly sure Shira had locked the Racari.

Frowning, she handed her list to a nearby rebel and darted across the cavern, arriving at the open office door in time to find Rahzen snapping open the locked drawer of Eshlin's desk with the ease of cracking a peanut shell.

"What are you doing?" she demanded.

Rahzen didn't look surprised to see her. They withdrew the spellbook with reverent hands, turning it gently over to reveal the bloodstone on the fore. "Reclaiming my property."

That same uncanny chill Mikira experienced the last time she was alone with Rahzen ran through her, like she'd stumbled across something as unknowable and distant as the stars. Rahzen only watched her, waiting, as if eager to see if Mikira had finally fit together the pieces of some ancient puzzle.

"Who are you?" she breathed.

Rahzen stepped languidly around the desk. A sudden urge to flee struck Mikira, but a primal fear rooted her to the spot. When Rahzen came shoulder to shoulder with her, she stayed very, very still.

"Surely you recognize your friend?" Their voice had changed, softening into something more feminine, more familiar.

Mikira jerked back to find Jenest beside her, eyes bright with mirth. It took her mind a moment to process the transformation, to spiral through how it could be possible, before remembering Ari's explanation about the Godstones. About transformations.

Her eyes dropped to the Racari in Jenest's hands.

Reclaiming my property.

Mikira forced herself to breathe. She had her answer, if not in so many words. It was in Jenest's transformation, in the crimson color of her clothes. In the stitch of wings in Rahzen's past outfits, in the glow of her now-golden eyes.

Still, she forced herself to say it, to give voice to the impossible.

"You're a Harbinger," she rasped. "You're Skylis."

Jenest let loose a resounding laugh, already halfway to the door. She peeled off her suit jacket, revealing a simple tunic underneath. Her shoes she slipped from her feet, tucking them neatly in the corner, her pants taking on a shabbier sheen. The Racari vanished from her hands.

"Me?" she asked, pulling free a jacket from the coat hook by the door. "I'm no one."

"But—*why*?" Mikira blurted, still struggling to understand. "The rebellion, the weapons—you refused to help Shira, and yet you were a part of this already. What did you *want*?"

Jenest slid on the jacket, her transformation complete. "I'm certain I don't know what you mean," she said. "But if I did, I might suggest that interfering was against the rules. Subtle influences, on the other hand, are a gray area."

"You wanted us to stop the Heretics," Mikira realized aloud, a hundred tiny moments coalescing into one. "You told Damien where to find Elidon, but not me, because you didn't want Eshlin to take the throne, and then you armed the rebels to defend against the chimeras. But why did you refuse Shira when she asked?"

"I wasn't certain of her motives," Jenest replied. "But yours—let's just say you're more transparent than a windowpane. Try not to lose that. And, Kira?"

Mikira only stared at her, overwhelmed.

"This is our little secret." Jenest winked at her and then was gone.

CHAPTER 56

DAMIEN

BY THE TIME they got back to the manor, Damien had checked Arielle's pulse what felt like a hundred times. She was so still, so pale, that every time he looked at her, he was sure he'd lost her. After everything she'd done, it was a miracle she was still alive. She'd pushed her body past any normal limit, and without the verillion to heal her—no, he refused to let himself think it.

Reid collapsed into one of the armchairs by the window, having taken Rivkah to her own room to rest and done a more thorough examination on Arielle. Widget clambered up onto his uninjured shoulder, bopping his head against Reid's. Damien remained standing at Arielle's side, watching each breath in and out.

I will do anything, he thought to the gods he'd never prayed to. *Please just let her live.*

His hand encircled hers, clasping it against the warmth of her face, the softness of her cheek. He focused on every tiny detail that formed her, held on to them like a lifeline, and tried not to break apart.

In a moment, he heard the soft snores of Reid falling asleep, until he alone remained awake. Shira visited at some point. She'd taken one look at Arielle and said, "You better not screw that up."

"I know," Damien had replied softly.

"You really don't deserve her."

"I know."

"In fact, when she wakes up—"

"Shira," Damien had growled, exhausted beyond any measure. "I *know.*"

And his sister had looked at him with something that was equal parts pity and deep, unyielding relief, and pulled him into her arms. It had taken a moment for Damien to react. To lift his arms to encircle the one person who had always stood behind him, no matter what he did or why, and to thank her for it, if not in words, then in how tightly he held on.

She was gone by the time Reid awoke, his voice startling Damien out of a near trance where he perched on the edge of the bed. "She'll forgive you."

"I'm not sure I deserve her forgiveness," he said, shifting reluctantly into the other room so they could talk. Reid followed, closing the door to the bedroom all but a crack.

Damien dropped heavily into his armchair, running a hand through his hair before looking squarely at Reid and saying, "Hers or yours."

"What would you do with it?" Reid hovered at the edge of the rug, as if afraid of what might happen were he to slide back into the familiarity of this scene.

It hurt more than Damien wanted to admit. More than he ever wanted to admit, because pain was not something he knew how to handle. That much was clear to him now. He wanted to change that, like he wanted to change so many things, and it started with Arielle and Reid. In finding strength in them, when he could not find it in himself.

"I don't know, to be honest," he said finally, each word harder to speak than the last.

Reid inclined his head. "Come find me when you do." He drifted backward toward the door, his steps slow as if fighting an unseen force. "I'll send someone to get my things. In the meantime, keep an eye on Widget for me, will you?"

Just like that, the knot in Damien's chest released, and he found himself smiling. Truly, smiling. Then Reid was gone, and he was alone.

Slowly, his body still aching from the fight with Selvin, Damien returned to the bedroom. Arielle was still asleep, her breathing steadier than it'd been before.

If you keep staring at her, I'm going to lose it. Rezek's voice erupted in his mind. *Do literally* anything *else.*

Damien released a quiet breath. Not so alone, then. Rezek's voice had come and gone through the entire journey back, his control of his new abilities tenuous at best, granting Damien much-needed bouts of silence.

It was clear to him now that, unlike Nava and Arielle, Rezek possessed only the Racari to which Damien was bound. Rezek couldn't take control of him the way Nava had Ari, but a bond still existed between them, letting through the faintest wisps of Rezek's annoyance.

Damien ignored him, settling onto the edge of the bed carefully so as not to disturb Arielle. It was all he could do. Sit, and wait, and trust that she would come back to him.

So he sat, and he watched, and he made her a silent promise to never leave her side again.

CHAPTER 57

MIKIRA

EVERYTHING ACHED WHEN Mikira woke the next morning.

The previous day came back to her in pieces. The fight with Rowna. Nearly losing Talyana and Reid. Returning to the castle to help Eshlin deal with the worst of the damage, hour after hour, when all she wanted was to collapse into bed and not move for a lifetime.

Skylis.

Some things felt too big to process, like the idea that the mysterious, cheerful weapons dealer she'd met was actually the underground race runner and rebel she'd known for months *and* one of the four Harbingers.

By the time they'd left, the princess had begun working on plans to abolish the house system and establish a new form of government with the royal berator, apparently intent on surviving off an endless supply of tea in place of sleep.

Mikira rolled over to find Talyana half on her pillow, snoring softly. Afternoon light trickled in through her bedroom's high windows. She'd forgotten that they'd returned to the ranch rather than the rebel headquarters. A half-faded memory of her demanding to sleep in her own bed came floating back, alongside Talyana's complaint that it was nearly twice as far away.

Still, she'd come.

Mikira ran one finger along the hand-shaped bruise on Talyana's neck, at once wishing she could make the mark disappear, and thankful for what it represented: that Talyana was alive and well and lying right beside her.

She clambered out of bed slowly, her body complaining as she dressed and went downstairs. The house still felt quiet without her family, who wouldn't be returning for several days, but it no longer felt empty. For once, she relished the silence, knowing that the moment her sisters were back the ranch would be bursting with noise. She owed them so many answers, so many apologies. She knew Ailene in particular would be hurting, as Ari's loss of magic meant that her enchanted dog, Wolf, hadn't survived.

It made her think of Atara.

In the fervor of the last few days, she'd been able to push aside feelings about the horse, but they came rushing back to her now. She hesitated on the final step, hand grasping the banister for support, and let the pain wash over her. Not just for the loss of Atara, but for Iri too. For her mother and Lochlyn and the life she'd thought her family would have.

When she'd gathered herself again, she stepped into the foyer and went to the front door. She'd just grabbed the handle when a knock sounded on the other side, and she pulled it open to find Reid with his hand outstretched.

"That was fast," he said.

"I was already on my way outside." Her eyes dropped to the bag at his feet, where she could just make out the edges of what looked like a pine cone. "Are you going somewhere?"

"I'm getting my own place," he replied. "I have a feeling Damien and Ari won't be sticking around for long, and even if they did, I can hardly stand to be in the same room with them half the time."

A grin tugged at one corner of Mikira's mouth. "Get tired of their silent conversations?"

"How two people can say so much just by staring at each other, I'll never know."

"That's because you talk like there's a prize for most words used."

"And you're as quiet as a Sendian priest," he snapped back.

"Mm, fair point." Mikira stepped past him onto the deck, leading the way to the porch swing. She dropped into it, feeling it sway beneath her weight, and patted the empty space for him to sit.

He joined her, pulling a wrapped bundle out of his jacket that he dumped unceremoniously in her lap. "Here."

She picked it up. "What is it?"

"If you open it, you'll know."

Rolling her eyes, she unfurled the cloth to reveal an irregularly shaped, prismatic stone with letters she couldn't decipher carved into one face. She frowned. "I ask again, what is it?"

"A truthstone," he said. "Atara's, to be exact."

Her head jerked up, but he was staring out across the ranch. The stable hands had let the horses out into the fields already, and they grazed too-long grass she had yet to cut.

"Damien's idea," he explained. "I guess when a golem comes undone, it returns to its original parts, and that includes this stone. So I went to the temple Ari mentioned, and sure enough, Atara's was there."

"Do you think—" she began.

"I honestly don't know," he replied.

Mikira clasped the stone against her heart. If there was even a possibility that Atara was still in there, that they could bring her back, she would take it.

"Thank you," she said, and for a while, they simply sat on the porch in the cool autumn air and let the swing carry them to and fro. Eventually Talyana joined them, wearing only an overlong shirt that went down to her midthighs and pointedly ignoring Reid's mortified look.

She toed Reid's bag. "Moving in?" she asked with a yawn, stretching her arms high above her head before she squeezed onto the swing, halfway atop Mikira.

Reid frowned when she all but put her legs up on him. "Moving out."

"You could, though, if you wanted," Mikira said before she could overthink it. "Move in. You could have Lochlyn's old room." Her throat tightened when she said it, but it felt right.

Reid blinked at her, and for once he didn't say anything, but she had a feeling that he would stay. The silence between them was too comfortable, too right, for him to do anything else, something Mikira didn't think she'd have been capable of recognizing before then.

But she understood now that this was what she'd wanted all along, all she'd ever needed. Not fame and fortune, not her name on a thousand people's lips. Just a handful of friends that mattered to her, and to whom she mattered.

Just someone to sit on the porch and watch the horses with.

CHAPTER 58

ARIELLE

ARIELLE WOKE TO find the bed bathed in morning light.

She felt different. Not in a single way, but in a hundred different ones, starting with the absence of something vital. Her magic was gone. It no longer hummed beneath her skin, no longer filled the hollow space inside her. It was like the day the bracelet had suppressed it, but so, so much worse.

When she'd awoken in that clearing, she'd simply lain there, trying to adjust to that emptiness. She tried telling herself that it'd been worth it to stop Nava. She tried to say that she was lucky to be alive, her body aching in a vibrant reminder. She even tried to convince herself that it would make her safer to be free of Kinnish magic.

Those things were true, but they were not enough.

In time, she turned to look at Damien. He clearly hadn't meant to fall asleep, still dressed in his torn and bloodied clothes. He was only partway on the bed, one leg hooked over the edge, his face only inches away. He always looked so innocent when he slept, even with the blood flecking his olive skin and his Lonlarra revolvers pressed against his ribs.

As though he sensed her even in his sleep, his eyes flicked slowly open, dark lashes against gunmetal gray. For one drawn-out moment, he was not

Damien Adair, once king and head of House Adair; he was just a boy, looking at a girl, as though she were all he needed to see in the world.

Then his gaze sharpened with concern, and he sat up. "What is it? What's wrong?"

The question was all it took to break her. The tears came freely, and the next moment his arms were around her, her face tucked into his chest. He didn't ask her what was wrong again. He knew, like he always knew. So she let him hold her until the tears abated, and the emptiness inside her felt a little fuller.

Then she felt him stiffen, and he hushed, "Enough."

Somehow, she knew that he wasn't talking to her. She pushed herself up, wiping the tears from her eyes, and found him with his hands drawn into fists, a familiar look in his eyes. "Damien?"

His gaze strayed upward, as if listening to something she couldn't hear, and he scowled, the emotion more prevalent than anything she'd seen of him. This was the heat that simmered constantly beneath his skin, the truth of him she'd always sought. His control had come undone, and she wanted to explore what had been hiding underneath.

"Damien," she said again. "What is it?"

"Rezek's soul or magic or whatever is bound to the Racari the same way the Heretics' were," Damien said tightly. Looking almost guilty, he pulled a small black book from his pants pocket. "And I wanted to keep the book. So—"

Her eyes flared wide. "You didn't."

"I didn't know he was in there!"

Ari gaped at him. Then, because she could think of nothing else to do, she laughed. Damien looked as though he couldn't decide whether to be annoyed or to laugh right along with her at the absolute absurdity of it all. In the end, he simply sat there transfixed, as if willing to suffer the indignity if only she'd laugh like that again.

"Do you think it can be undone?" he asked when she'd gotten ahold of herself.

"I honestly don't know," she replied. "Rezek has a lot more experience with bloodstones than I do, and I have a feeling he's not going to be forthcoming."

Damien paused, once more listening to a voice she couldn't hear and could only imagine, and then gritted his teeth.

"What did he say?" she asked.

"Over his dead body."

Ari smirked. "That's an idea, actually. We gave the Heretics bodies, so why not him?"

"Because the only thing worse than having him trapped inside my head is having him running about freely again." Damien ran a hand through his unruly curls. "Shira said that Eshlin is handling cleanup at the mine. I asked her to retrieve his body when she went for . . ."

He trailed off, unable to say his brother's name. Ari squeezed his hand as tightly as she could. He leaned his forehead against hers, and for a moment, she was all that held him upright.

Then he pulled back with a shuddering breath and said, "If you don't shut up, I'll put a bullet in my own head."

"Rezek, be quiet." Ari pushed back the covers. "And I know someone who might be able to help." She slid her feet to the ground, sitting on the edge of the bed with her back toward him. It made it easier to say what she wanted to next. "They're in Aversheen, though, with my family. I . . . was thinking of traveling back there with Rivkah."

Without her magic, without Nava, she wasn't a danger to her family any longer, and it had been so long since she'd seen her home. What had happened there might have been an accident, but until she faced it, faced her fear of it, she didn't know if she could forgive herself the way her sister had.

But that wasn't what scared her most. What truly terrified her was the answer that came to her lips when Damien asked, "What do you need?"

Because she didn't think it was something she could have, and she had never wanted something so deeply. She turned to look at him over her shoulder, kneeling in the bed in utter dishevelment, the most undone she'd ever seen him, and said, "You."

"Then you'll have me," he said gently. "However you want me."

And he kissed her with the sunlight streaming in at his back.

IT WAS ONLY after Ari had bathed, her wet hair soaking through the back of her blouse, that she noticed the teapot. It sat on a table between the two chairs by the window, where Widget lay curled up in a patch of sun. Two notes rested against it. One was from Rivkah, assuring her that she was okay and that she'd returned to the Drowned Crow to retrieve her things.

The other was from Reid. She unfolded it to read three simple words with a growing smile:

Drink it all.

"He's moving out." Damien stood in the doorway to the bathroom, wearing only a pair of trousers and running a towel along his wet curls. "I'm not sure where he's gone."

Ari knew exactly where, and it only made her smile all the more. "Come on," she said. "Let's pack."

It was late afternoon by the time they secured horses from the stables and made their way to the Drowned Crow. Their saddlebags were packed for a journey, their horses enchanted for endurance and to never get lost.

Ari had posted a letter to Mikira on their way out, thanking her for everything she'd done and promising to visit soon. In it, she'd included the paperwork for the Adair horses, facilities, and racetracks, making them Mikira's to do as she saw fit. It had taken less to convince Damien than she'd thought, but she suspected that he was still looking for ways to repair what had been broken.

She'd also sent a message ahead of time to Vix to contact Shira. With Damien leaving, she would need to step up for House Adair, or what would remain of it when Eshlin was finished dismantling what she could of the house system. With the heads of the other houses gone and an Adair on her side, she had only to deal with the lesser houses and the wealthy supported by them.

Shira was waiting for them in the pub, sitting at the bar picking apart one of Vix's soft rolls, which the woman seemed to consume nonstop. Despite everything she had to have been through in the last few days, Shira only looked mildly haggard.

"Running away and leaving me with all the work?" she asked with a glance at their bags.

"As though you'd want it any other way," Damien replied, ignoring how Shira was pointedly evaluating his attire. Rather than his usual three-piece suit, he wore only a long-sleeved shirt, a pair of trousers, and boots, Widget perched on his shoulder, much to his dismay.

"I'll be right back," Ari said. "I figure you and Damien could use some time to talk."

Shira grinned. "There's not enough time in the world for that."

Looking as though he'd rather thrust himself on a spear, Damien reluctantly sat down beside his sister while Ari made her way up the stairs to the rooms above the pub. She found number twelve at the end of the hall and stood outside the door for several moments trying to order her thoughts. Then she knocked. The floorboards on the other side creaked, and the handle turned.

Rivkah barely had the door open before she was in Ari's arms, holding fast with a strength powerful enough to moor her in the flood of emotion that swept through her.

"You're okay," Rivkah murmured.

"I am."

Rivkah pulled her into the room. There was a bed in one corner with a nightstand beside it, a desk wedged beneath the wide window. It overlooked the entrance below, the desk piled with several dishes that gave the impression someone had spent time sitting there.

Waiting.

Ari's heart ached. She should never have let her sister leave that workshop without her. It was only because she'd pushed Rivkah away that she'd felt the need to find the fourth Racari on her own, because of her that Nava had injured her twice over.

Rivkah fiddled nervously with her hair. It was a habit she'd had since she was a child, often causing her curls to frizz and tangle. Ari took her hand and led her to the chair, then began to sort her hair into pieces to be braided.

"Are you coming home with me?" Rivkah blurted, the words coming more easily now that they were occupied.

"I am." She didn't comment at the tension that washed out of her sister. "I want to see our parents, and I want them to meet Damien."

"He's coming too?"

"He is." Ari began to twist the strands into a plait.

Rivkah was silent as Ari finished the last of the braid, tying it off with a ribbon from the desk. She handed Rivkah a small mirror she found lying there, and Rivkah smiled at her reflection. Then she looked at Ari in the glass, standing over her shoulder.

"I'm glad you're coming home," Rivkah said quietly.

Ari wrapped her arms around her from behind. "Me too."

They packed Rivkah's bag and joined the others downstairs. From the look on Damien's face, Shira was in the midst of a lecture, and he all but leapt from his seat at the sight of them.

"Are you ready?" he asked hopefully.

"We are." Ari glanced at Rivkah, who was eyeing Damien with a look fit for a lion that hadn't quite decided whether or not to eat its prey yet.

Damien didn't miss it, but neither did he put her on the spot, only raised one brow at Ari.

Shira stood. "Be safe," she said, and hugged them both.

"We'll see you again soon," Ari said, and Shira barked out a laugh.

"I sure as hell hope not." She waved them out of the pub to where they'd tied up their horses. They'd brought an extra for Rivkah, and she swung up with an ease that bespoke time spent riding. The girl Ari had left behind had been afraid of horses. It struck her, yet another piece of her sister's life that she'd missed, another memory to make up for.

Rivkah was already grilling Damien with questions, from how long exactly he'd been seeing her sister to what he planned to tell their parents when they inevitably asked about his intentions. To his credit, Damien fielded the questions with the ease of someone used to going toe-to-toe with the most politically savvy of opponents, breaking occasionally to threaten Rezek with various degrees of bodily harm if he didn't shut up.

Ari listened to the sound of their voices and felt the emptiness in her fill a little more. They turned their horses toward the Traveler's Road, an adventure far behind them, and a journey stretching out before. A new path, a new opportunity.

Shira's words from long ago about the idea of chet came back to her then, that it simply meant straying from the right path

You can always find your way again, she'd said. *But first, you must find forgiveness.*

Once, Ari hadn't thought that was possible for her. She'd thought of forgiveness as an absolute, given or not, but she understood now that it was a process. It was a culmination of every choice she made, every decision not to stray from the path. She couldn't promise herself she'd be perfect, but she was done trying to be, done judging herself for her past mistakes.

"I forgive you," she whispered to herself, and deep beneath the empty space inside her chest, beneath the emotions slowly knitting that hole shut, she felt something stir.

Something like magic.

ACKNOWLEDGMENTS

THIS WAS A very difficult book for me to write for a lot of reasons, and at times I thought I might never reach the end. Which only makes me all the more grateful for the support of the people who helped me get here.

To my editorial team, Kate Meltzer, Cate Augustin, and Emilia Sowersby, thank you for helping me find the heart of this story, and to do it more or less in 120K words. Thank you to my agent, Carrie Pestritto, for always being the sounding board I need.

I'd be hard-pressed to finish *any* writing without my Guillotines: Tracy Badua, Alyssa Colman, Rae Castor, Koren Enright, Jessica Jones, Brittney Arena, Sam Farkas, and Jennifer Gruenke—you mean the world to me, and I can't wait for everyone to experience your stories.

Joss and Shannon, thank you for always being there to talk writing, life, and pine cones. And most importantly, to remember Mervyn's with. May we all live our best Gilmore Girls era.

Rowan, finish your book.

To Rosiee Thor (for helping me panic cut a few thousand words) and Linsey Miller (for sharing in my publishing meltdowns)—I am SO excited for your amazing new books.

Thank you to the vast and wonderful team across the US and UK sides who helped work on this book and the first: Morgan Rath, Gabriella Salpeter, Samira Iravani, Kathy Wielgosz, Janet Rosenberg, Cheyney Smith, Emma Oulton, Bethan Thomas, and Louisa Sheridan.

All my gratitude to Arielle Vishny for once again helping me make this book more Jewish, and to the incredible audiobook narrators who brought Ari and Mikira to life, Laurel Lefkow and Rebecca Norfolk. Thank you to Billelis for the absolutely gorgeous cover.

Thank you to my street team, and to all the wonderful readers, bloggers, booksellers, librarians, and more who supported this series, and to my family and friends, who still think this is pretty darn cool five years in.

Here's to another five.

VERA
The Silverwood Forest
Barkheath District
Kelbra Manor
Zalaire Manor
Canburrow Square
Dramara Manor
Pendron District
Ashfield Street
Tea Street
The King's Road
The Traveler's Road
Roughsha
Bridge
Rusel Ranch
Kelbra
Dramara
Capital o